G000090776

WE ARE THE BIRDS OF THE COMING STORM

THE FRENCH LIST

WE ARE THE BIRDS OF THE COMING STORM

LOLA LAFON

TRANSLATED BY DAVID AND NICOLE BALL

LONDON NEW YORK CALCUTTA

Seagull Books, 2014

First published in French as *Nous sommes les oiseaux de la tempête qui s'annonce*
by Lola Lafon

© Flammarion SA, Paris, 2011

First published in English translation by Seagull Books

English translation © David Ball and Nicole Ball, 2014

ISBN 978 0 8574 2 189 0

British Library Cataloguing-in-Publication Data
A catalogue record for this book is available from the British Library.

Typeset in Sabon LT Std, Corbel and Helvetica by Seagull Books, Calcutta, India
Printed and bound by Maple Press, York, Pennsylvania, USA

If you must repeat the same movement a great many times, do not give in to boredom, think of yourself as dancing towards your death.

Martha Graham

CONTENTS

PART ONE

DIARY OF YOUR UNLIVED DAYS

37.5°C => 33°C Saturday

Your heart. I watch it slowing down all night long. I stare at the figures and don't understand them.

72. 34. An elf with her eyes half-closed, peacefully encircled in a jungle of perfect wires and screens, a Geek Princess. Your eyelids don't flutter and the tube coming out of your mouth seems perfectly adapted to your anatomy, you don't look as if it's hurting you. You are a flower tightly bound. I look at your small, frozen face. I have never stared at you for so long without your knowing it. As if that could bother you, I straighten up and try to busy myself with something—an urge to be useful, although they have no need for me here.

This is the journal of your sudden death. The few notes I'm trying to take as you remove yourself from your life. This is the diary where I write down for you each and every detail of this present, a present in which you are no more. So I can tell you, one day—some day, of the life I shared with you, while you were unaware of it.

It's past midnight when I'm allowed to go back into the room where you are slowly getting colder, at the rate of 0.5 degrees per hour. Between us and you, there's that nowhere room, an outpost on the border of your state of partial non-life. There, I wash my hands and slip into a sterile smock. When I raise my eyes, my face in the mirror above the sink tells me nothing.

We follow a time schedule here, we need to schedule this time. Leave the waiting room regularly and in that airlock of a room, scrub and wipe hands dried out by the acidic disinfectant soap, slowly enough so time keeps passing, and then get scared of that deliberate slowness and speed up the action. What if something had happened in your room. Go check on you every half hour to be certain.

It is possible that the nurses let me come and go all night because noise will never bother you again. I would like to ask why you don't shut your eyes completely, couldn't they close your eyes so you'd look like you were asleep. The doctors hesitate between several outcomes:

You're going to die. They don't use that word.

You're going to wake up as a vegetable, that's the word the resident uses. At the consonants of the word 'vegetable', the silence of the waiting room bristles with spikes of pain. I don't look at your parents, I lower my eyes at the word and feel my cheeks reddening, hearing them talk this way about your inert body.

He adds that you can also wake up 'simply' paralysed or unable to speak. The range of after-effects, I've lost the thread of what he's saying but I remember that: the range of after-effects.

CALCULATIONS AND DEDUCTIONS

No one can answer the resident who suddenly appears in the waiting room, none of us knows for how long your heart stopped. The doctor who gave you the first cardiac massage in the cafe did not leave his name.

All we have is calculations, deductions. Did he jump towards you. And in the cafe, did the doctor have to push away chairs, which would have slowed him down. A minute and a half. Two and a half, maybe three, your father thinks, diligently trying to answer science as best he can. Three minutes then. The resident twists his mouth sideways and backs out. When he reappears a few moments later, he gives your parents two sheets of paper. I move my chair right up against theirs so we can read together. When the intern mentions the figure 33 in his explanation, your mother doesn't bat an eyelid, she even raises her chin a little in his direction.

The three of us remain in the waiting room. You, you're diving, going down into an artificial, frozen coma, slowly. Your parents' signature gives permission for a machine to put your brain and heart to a full rest at 33 degrees. Your body is in our hands. Sign here. 17 January.

And then, we ask again.
Then, you're going to die, but he doesn't use that word.
Or you'll wake up.

I look at your small face with its half-closed eyes. I watch your heart slowing down all night long. Degree by degree. We take turns at your bedside. Whispering, we check your reverse progress: 'She's down to 34.9.' We're moved, we're pleased with your body, obedient now, which died unexpectedly in the afternoon and has not quite decided to die completely yet. We think of the dumb films you love so much and how you'd really like this script:

'We're going to cryogenize her.'

'Yes, Doctor. The Matrix has encoded all the data that appear in Part B of her brain. The Office can come and interrogate her now! Nothing remains, not a trace.'

The staff drives us out of the unit around 2 a.m. I walk your parents back to their car as if they had come for dinner and I was looking after them, seeing them on their way. We agree to meet in the morning and keep our 'maybes' to ourselves. Some of your friends who came later suggest we go to a cafe, or invite me over to their place to end the night, but I prefer to walk towards the boulevard, alone. I don't know where to go and sleeping seems imprudent, a luxury as absurd as the one I lived in up to now, a world of hearts that never stop at our age.

And since my fine thoughts aren't the only ones I can share with you in these notes, here's one that will make you raise an eyebrow, while I'm walking towards the river, trying to avoid the groups of girls and boys spreading out on this Saturday night and invading the whole pavement to the rhythm of their rising alcohol level—like the bellows of a drunk accordion— the one I miss the most, to have here at my left, is my dog, with her eyes eager for a normal present. I miss a presence that knows nothing of all this, of your stopped heart, of your eyes half-closed, and what if you died tonight.

And I haven't been in the city for so long that it is filled with you and you only. We've walked down all these streets and burst out laughing as we pointed to those postcards with their ridiculously overdone mauve skies, in the bookstore that's open till midnight, and that cinema where the cashier always makes the same joke—no I'm not giving you back your change thank you mademoiselle and we'd give him a nice smile, you have to support that cinema, it only shows old horror films we love—and that huge tree bending along the riverbank beneath a loft with oversized windows and a hundred times over we've pictured its occupants, they're obviously unpleasant, that night bus that takes us from Paris to the station near the Island, everything, everything is yours, with you.

In the waiting room I recite the events of the day to your parents. They listen to me, alert for clues, one of our days among years of days, a regular, nothing Saturday of which only details remain, to be scrutinized over and over.

Our date to go to the pool on the morning of the day that ended your life. I thought you looked pale, your skin almost too thin for your cheekbones. I should have asked you, I didn't ask anything, you were wearing your death that morning. Twice, you come out of the water twice, and sit on the edge of the pool. And I make fun of you, the great athlete. My silly laugh comes back up in my throat like a mistake whose taste is spreading all over, memories spring up suddenly but where from—moments, these last months when your voice seemed a bit flat to me, and your back slumped slowly down to fit your chair, and those phone calls where I hung up too quickly, my curt nonchalance like pulling a nasty face, but since when have you been dying.

'She wanted to measure my time over twenty-five metres,' I foolishly, childishly announce to your mother while we wait. The hand of the giant chronometer on the wall of the pool is blue. No, red. And you announce, 'Thirty seconds, kiddo, and swimming sideways too!' We walked over to your place, did we talk to each other. Already I'm not sure any more. In the staircase, before we got to your door, you paused for a moment, with a sigh. But you often sigh at the next-to-last steps of your five floors.

A ridiculous description, too precise. Why note the way you sat down in your kitchen to have a cup of coffee, why would that have any meaning this particular Saturday. Because it's the last one? Your death at two o'clock—is it processing inside you, or does sitting on your red-and-yellow chair, drying your hair by slowly passing your hand through it, does that moment when I see you against the light have no more meaning than this: we're having coffee in your kitchen and that will never happen again. Your ankles curled round each other, your hand bringing the little red cup to your mouth.

As usual, your afternoon is spent helping children 'with problems' to do their homework (and, as usual too, I think I must have called you the Mother Teresa of the neighbourhood). I agree to take care of Vassili for you, you have an emergency. When I trot out what I'm planning to do with him —take him to an exhibition about Serge Gainsbourg—you comment, 'Alcohol and naked babes, that'll be great, no really, he'll love it, it's original.'

We head for the Métro. That's the last time we say to each other see you soon, I'll call you, on the steps of the Métro, the last look, I always turn round when we say goodbye and every time, you face me, you don't move before I've turned round, a mother at her balcony, you kind of wave to me, your last word.

Your mother doesn't know who Vassili is any more, because with all those names, she's sorry, your mother who hasn't cried since she sat down in the waiting room. Sitting very straight, her tiny shoulders leaning slightly forward, she is a little sprinter through silence.

'The boy on the third floor, remember? The boy from Belarus?'

Couples of thirty-somethings in comfortable scarves and sweatshirts falling loosely over their hips are waiting on queue to get into the show. They're all white, notes Vassili who spends his time counting blacks and whites, I have no idea what he does with his statistics. I make several contradictory decisions aloud, to wait an hour, leave, come back later, the little boy holds my hand, delighted, as if dumbfounded by inconsistency, but serene. I hold his hand firmly to make up for our wandering. Pick up all the programmes in all the lobbies we go in and out of and pretend to know what they say with the concerned look of an adult able to skilfully manufacture a Saturday of coloured words and pictures. A girl hands him the leaflet for the screening of a 3D film about sardines and he gives it to me, relieved to present me with a solution. It's exactly what we need to see this Saturday, I declare peremptorily. I feel bad about the voice I put on to talk to him. Dolphins, whales in 3D, sardines migrating as far as the Kwazulu-Natal coast. We run to the end of the park but I hadn't looked at the programme carefully, the show is already over, the lobby is empty. As so often that afternoon, I live two lives simultaneously— my real life that I perform in the present and then the voice-over for that life which ceaselessly rises up to note what you would like to hear, the details you'll comment on next time we see each other. After over an hour of coming and going between various venues, shows and decisions I don't make or make too late, I notice that Vassili's eyes are squinting to resist the cold. I drag him off to a cafe—

closed—then go back the other way to find another one, and he doesn't point out that we're going round in circles and that we've just come from this street. If I were a mother, you see, I would have zipped up his jacket when we got out of the Métro, I would have known where to take him on a Saturday afternoon and wouldn't joke about the guys who whistle at me when we get out of the Métro at Porte de la Villette.

I feel the need to explain to him that I don't see children too often, I live alone in the country after all. He assents understandingly and talks about you, who know 'all of maths!' Your apparition in the cold of my wandering—me, a ridiculous substitute mother—is like a blanket, arms spread wide, you never criticize my clumsiness, never say I can't believe it, you bump into everything.

These are, I think, the last moments of this Saturday for you.

There is nothing to be deducted from what follows. Of course I didn't become irrational just because you're dying. So I'm going to try not to deform the events, to report them to you simply. This is how it happened. At four o'clock, it suddenly seems indispensable to me to go to the cafe where we go often, by the Canal Saint-Martin. Like a map I might read on a sheet of paper someone handed out. It's about an hour's walk away from where I'm wandering around with Vassili. I don't remember very much about our walk, except that I worry about the cold and my inability to construct a reasonably normal Saturday for him.

I expect from this cafe what we normally expect on a winter afternoon when we've just walked for a long time. That sudden heat in your face, the usual hubbub.

But there is the feeling of a catastrophe about to happen, you see. The lighting in the cafe seems strangely dull to me; the place, exhausted. I don't understand that half-light. And that absolute silence too. Emptiness. No one's sitting there. An oppressive sadness. No, not really sadness. The conclusion of a catastrophe. A bird flying frantically around, knocking into the windowpanes. The thud of its body against the glass, the brutal thump of its hampered wings.

The waitress seems sombre and slow. The waitress with her hollow eyes, very pale, filling our two cups. Her gestures do not have the weight of the end of an afternoon that's been filled with too many comings and goings. Instead, it's as if she were struggling against a strange numbness, as if she had to get out of a clammy nightmare.

Your death is what she has to get out of. Hardly half an hour ago, the waitress saw the firemen and the paramedics take your recumbent body away. Less than an hour ago, you fell from your chair in that cafe, a chair certainly right near the one where I sat down with Vassili.

I'm reconstituting that moment of your life from what they told me later at the hospital.

You pitched forward towards the girl you were sitting with, her homework spread out between your cups. You slid to the floor. Your breathing was extremely rapid. Then you stopped breathing altogether. As in those TV series you like so much, a doctor was sitting not far from you. He didn't leave his name with the firemen but he's the one who gave you a cardiac massage for over forty minutes. That's what the girl who was with you said. This evening, she's sitting on the floor in the corridor of the hospital with her knees bent under her and her face frozen, a statue of sorrow in a white tracksuit. In the waiting room, your parents are not crying.

The electric shocks, the firemen, the paramedics, your body brutalized, turned over, manipulated. Not to have been there crushes me, I would have held out my hands to you so you wouldn't fall to the floor, in that cafe I would have screamed louder, the doctor would have acted faster. Impossible to admit that nothing could have been done, that I was looking at photos of sardines with a child, and shiny, loud pictures of dolphins. And the buses we left along the way to stroll around are biting, throwing up like vital errors of taste. Yes. I would have.

5.30. As we left the cafe, I looked at the time. I thought of calling you, as we do several times a day. Each of our multi-daily conversations ends with 'Talk to you later.' I think it's the first time I give up on it, so as not to interfere with your meeting. And I said this to myself, these exact words: 'Let her live.' I never thought let her live before that afternoon when I finally put down the phone. If I had called I would have fallen into the emptiness of a ringing phone because you were already dead. If I had called, I wouldn't have known, in the emptiness of the ringing, that's it, we're not together here any more.

At 5.30, the ambulance goes into the Emergency Entrance of Hôpital Cochin and what is living in you is the electricity of a machine.

When I bring Vassili back to his parents, it's 6.20, ten minutes ahead of the schedule they gave me, and my 'hello' answering the ring of my cell is noisy, a start-of-the-weekend hello, playful and relieved, too, to be done with the responsibility of a child to entertain. 'I'm calling you about something that's not very pleasant,' that series of bland little words foreshadows and opens onto the present, where your recumbent body is hardly visible.

I don't know what kind of sentence I would find if I were in Lina's shoes. On that January day, she chooses 'I'm calling you about something that's not very pleasant,' then in my silence waiting for that not very pleasant, she pares it down as fast as she can and explains, 'In fact it's not very pleasant at all.'

You fainted, she says, and the girl you were with in the cafe didn't know whom to call, she simply dialled the last number in your cell: Lina. At that moment, I don't yet know that we were, unbelievably, in the same place.

The word 'fainted' is not disturbing. It's almost gentle, a feeling of languor. Its old-fashioned sound tucks it in with rosewood-coloured blankets—you fainted, like those actresses in old films when they didn't say up front 'She's pregnant.' Gene Tierney puts her hand to her brow, closes her eyes and her body sinks down in a slow-motion spiral. Behind her, of course, stands a man. Gene Tierney could not faint without a man at her side.

I just brush the edges of that word 'faint', repeating it several times after Lina, and nothing frightens me for a few seconds, it's all that work, those people who count on you for their papers, their flat, their maths homework and crêpes, and holidays too. You'll go to bed early tonight, that's all, I'll make sure you do (pointing out to you for the hundredth time that a body is something you must look after), I can do it, I can, and I'm overwhelmed with the desire to be with you again, to deal with that faintness.

Heart. Hôpital Cochin. And also 'serious'. Those words Lina forces into the spaces between mine, a struggle, I fill the whole space to stop her from speaking. Then everything turns upside down. Sometimes we read the earth gave way under your feet, that kind of image, you see what I mean. But it's my ankles that don't seem to be at the end of my legs, I walk towards your house where I have to drop off Vassili and he's almost dragging me because in truth I'm not walking any more. Against a tree—there aren't many of them in this street—I stop, looping the words no not Émile not Émile no not Émile not Émile.

With my forehead leaning against that tree, anchored in concrete. In that phone, in Lina's shrunken voice. In nothing, really. Not Émile not Émile.

Later, his mother will tell me on the phone, Vassili will be ecstatic, telling her again and again about his great afternoon full of adventure and the way I navigate the pavement as I sob into the phone not Émile not Émile and he has to take my hand so I can start walking again.

That evening Vassili sent me a worried SMS. And, without punctuation, this word he picked looks as if it were pulled out of a dictionary, separated from its definition: 'Courage'.

Should I write down, in this chronology I'm trying to stick to, how I run through the Métro with my throat so tight that when the train stops for a few moments between two stations, I'm not sure I can manage to breathe in again and that becomes, very concretely, the question—eyes round me are lowered, avoiding me—then the air comes raucously back into my lungs.

Running through a racket of words, prayers mixed with promises and no no not Émile. Pronouncing your whole name, Émilienne, as a question to a nurse looking it up in a computer, both of us have seen so many films with the bad moment when the nurse raises her eyes, gently shakes her head with her finger still on the name crossed out in the list, I'm sorry. But your name at 7 p.m. leads to a place, to an address where you still exist.

Running. Crossing courtyards, passing stretchers, groups of nonchalant doctors in the night made brighter by the cold and all that time, like hands thrown out in front of you to stop something, but to stop what.

Not Émile not Émile not Émile not Émile not Émile.

On the floor of the corridor, a girl is sobbing into her folded arms. Sitting side by side in silence, your parents smile mechanically when I come in, and Lina gets up, hugs me and sits down again. We are in the waiting room of an ICU on a Saturday night. Without you. You seem to have been uprooted, ripped out of the sequence of events. And the script they give me, a storyboard, one freeze-frame after another, of your life at the moment you fall into death, is the first breach in the arrogant fiction of our lives together—that mad certainty. It really is your body that was transported here. But nothing has any meaning, there are so many details piling up, climbing on top of one another, you on the floor, convulsions, the silence of your interrupted breath, those images are words are things are nothing, they accumulate, they're evil and have claws and make your death indisputable.

(Not Émile not Émile not Émile)

33. We're waiting for 33. We're waiting for figures we don't understand. We look at that screen next to you, nothing else explains what's brewing under your skin. When they leave me alone with you, I don't dare speak to you. If I talk to you while knowing that you can't hear me, I'm accepting your death. I'll wait to speak to you until you can answer me.

All that time of your frozen body, there is whispering round you. What if the words happen to upset the process. Each of us has one of your hands. A foot. She doesn't even look bad, observes your mother, standing there and staring at you. Did you see that horrible smock, that pink. When she only likes blue. How come she doesn't really close her eyes. Her feet aren't too cold. Let's ask for a blanket. And what that's number there?

We are already in the life of your stopped heart. This event is no longer an event, nothing but data of your body in this octopus machine room. At no time does anyone speak of the how and why. We are accompanying your present, the present of a body with a stopped heart, of a face with eyes between two worlds. It seems that the imploring whys—screamed out, bewildered—are reserved for the people (families and friends), who slowly leave the ICU demanding answers from death.

Our conversations are little ribbons that hold us together, prevent our thoughts from going off the rails, alone, towards the moment when maybe. From that bed. Towards a stretcher. Covered with a sheet.

In the corridor, a red arrow on a little sign. Follow the arrow. And near the morgue, which is indicated too, a chapel. Tonight I'm domesticating your physical death, your recumbent body with strange eyes is making that possible. But your absence, more immense than your death—that, I can't get used to. Your body we look at without your knowing it, that, I can face, and I can even find it liveable, that real privilege of an end not yet definitive. Let me still have your face to watch. Your hair to arrange on the pillow. Your predicted absence has invaded my lungs all the way up to my eyes, ever since the night before when, for the first time, I couldn't call you. Something is no longer tangible, no longer possible, so reality comes apart, loses its unity. I don't mind having a tiny little life, and besides that's not the way it would be, with both of us in it together. I don't mind a life limited to your continual presence, with no doubt and no fear.

In Apnea on the Eastern Front

As soon as I try to take notes to describe the waiting room for you, the films of Kusturica come into my mind. I don't know most of the people who come in by twos or alone. They say hello to me, they say they've heard about me, 'of course'. Some of them work with you and talk about you, smile at your odd habit of never turning off your cellphone even at night, your compulsion to be there all the time for all the neighbourhood children. I don't want them to discuss you in a soft voice, with a smile showing how moved they are. I also can't stand it when the conversations bury you in voices that are too loud, too lively. I think our silence keeps you warm enough for your life to continue.

The chairs are brought closer together to make room, some people sit down on the floor, between the tangled legs of the chairs. We avoid looking at one another straight in the eye, as if that would add our fears together. We all walk round and round without sharing our circles. We smile at one another. We read. We help one another do advanced sudokus. Our hair touches, concentrated as we are on that reassuring irritation, a 9 we can't put in the right place, the relief of inventing something banal to share in this sequence of enormous events. On the little anonymous table, between old magazines with dried-up pages, some have put bread, biscuits, soda cans and half-empty cups of cold coffee. Sometimes, we conscientiously sweep up the crumbs on the table with the flat of our hand. In one corner, a photocopy machine is covered with a heap of coats—ours—and they keep piling up as people come in. It's like the bedroom of a flat where there's a party, that gloomy antechamber of the place where 'it' is happening.

The nurses shut the door gently every time they take out a dead person on a stretcher. Three times already since last night, the howls and groans of their loved ones reach us. They had come to wait, they can leave now.

A woman has just learnt that her brother is dead. Her sorrow is musical—long cries, horizontal, trembling lines. She repeats the word call. Call, the final *l* rolls out that infinite sound, she never catches her breath, she enters into sorrow as if into apnea.

So we lower our heads over our newspapers and numbers, our bodies wrap themselves in their own heat for protection. Let her be quiet or let us howl louder than she does but get her out of this corridor. We hang on to that moment, the moment when you are nowhere for good, when we don't have to howl, when we can keep waiting, still.

Your Identity, Stolen

At the end of this Sunday, the waiting room begins to look like one of your appointment books with their days filled with crooked arrows, little pieces of paper slipped between the pages, question marks, names underlined and others hastily scrawled down, as if added in the course of the day, always too short for you.

The nurses ask us questions to fill in their information form and we throw out different answers which trample one another. Yes, you work, even if we can't find an exact definition for your frenetic activity, you never stop, always running from one 'child with problems' to another, planning your outings with them, 'ballets narrated'—the word is yours—'for the blind'. And weekends of rock climbing for neglected twelve-year-old girls. The portrait we draw of you hardly resembles you— that series of narratives transforms you into a splendid, dedicated saint. Your poses of a tough fencer, your wisecracks, are not part of these descriptions.

They ask us for your ID. Your handbag is behind our chairs. A sleeping animal, meaningless now, deformed by all your piled-up stuff. And that gesture—opening your handbag and beginning to grope round in it—creates silence. Your absence watches me act.

In your appointment book I see snapshots from photo booths, three of them. I was with you when you went to take them. We had tried the expressions written on the side of the machine. For your ID photos, keep a neutral expression. You didn't pull it off.

Your parents are turned towards the doctor. Very quickly, I slip your photos into my pocket. Now I'm stealing your photos.

Sister Friend Cousin

The nurse tries to set up priorities, to put some order between us as we've been spending our time coming and going in your room for the past forty-eight hours, forgetting to wash our hands properly half the time. I would like to bring a microbe into the motionless air of your buzzing room, something that would tremble and scratch, that would make you open your eyes, make faces, cough, something.

She asks two of your friends to leave, then turns to me. The nurse proposes sister, friend and cousin to me. I hesitate. She frowns and I quickly point to sister. To live through the same moment of the time we'll be alive, my sister my friend. Your parents confirm it, nicely.

The Instructions

Up to then, they packed people in ice. But you are the beneficiary of a protocol that has never been tested on human beings and the release your parents signed makes you the guinea pig of a machine on which a booklet is lying clearly in evidence—the instructions. I skim through it—very simple drawings show how the machine works. These pages look like instructions for all our machines. Several of us break into giggles when a doctor walks into your room and leafs through it attentively, frowning, concentrating on exactly reproducing the requisite gestures. This weekend, the most disturbing things are the ones that tickle us the most.

Technology Kills

The regular sound of those beautiful machines reassures me, you probably can't die, armoured in that protective forest. The nurse leans over your arms. Never deals with your body, only the parts of it connected to cables, which are working at making you still colder.

I move my chair up to you without letting go of your hand.

'You have an iPod?' the nurse asks.

'Music,' she says, 'I really believe in it,' then she shrugs and adds, 'And after all, you never know.'

We finally have something to do. We each compare the songs we have, we argue and our childishness reassures us; it gives an appearance of normality to this Sunday. We gently put a headphone on your right ear, then we have to go behind you and your electric lianas to reach your left ear. We're in class, you are a chemistry problem that's hard to finish, a shop project we must not fail, you are our sick child. We're almost done working round the tubes, machines and monitors when the nurse comes back. She checks, then glances at us and as she walks to the door, warns us in a flat tone, like an instruction manual, 'If you unplug something, she'll die.' And gently shuts the door. We stop for a moment, the iPod in our hands, between fits of laugher and the urge to shake you, to see you as dumbfounded as we are by that sentence. But you don't know. Won't know.

We didn't find the songs you love, the ones that make you stand on my bed when you come to see me and throw yourself into an energetic and incoherent choreographed dance. For once, I regret the absence of Pia Zadora, no one knows that except you. So, in your frozen sleep, you are with Nirvana. Your mother worries about the volume—oh, that worry from another time, a living time, when you had to spare your ears— but your eyes don't blink at all, the only sounds come from the respirator and from our footsteps on the linoleum. I stay by your side and watch for the songs I know bore you, to skip them. The numbers of your heart are not moving. To the pessimistic doctor who appears from time to time, I point out the quiet regularity of your breathing. Indulgently, he agrees. I did not immediately understand the theatre of your lungs— that tube coming out of your mouth links them to your body and without it you couldn't breathe.

Absolutely motionless, while the machines live and belch out their precision, their numbered progression, in fact, you lie recumbent. For how long now that heart, stopped short in the cafe.

SUNDAY, 6 P.M.

I don't know if 33°C is the temperature of death, your body is resting in it and I keep busy, so life round you cannot be interrupted, a long sentence of connected gestures, pull up your blanket, hold your hand, look at your hairless forearms. Your little hands of a Disney princess without bones or veins.

Some people stick in their heads, don't dare come in, I leave them my seat for a few moments and they kiss you on the forehead, whispering.

We never kiss each other hello or goodbye, you and me. We yell 'Hi-i-i-i!' to each other, very loudly. We only kiss on major occasions. Our birthdays, or when other people are present, for example. Kissing hello would take us away from a feeling that hates to be defined. Our hands would have to be intertwined all the time or, I don't know, we'd have to invent an intelligent expandable piece of clothing that would keep our bodies connected. But what we do is call each other. It's ridiculous, how much we call each other. We comment on it ourselves: it's pathological, you say sometimes. We call each other to say that we'll call, we call to find out when we can call, as if we weren't calling each other at that very moment.

KEYWORDS

As if she were talking about astrology, the nurse nods her head
as she repeats to me, 'You have to talk to them. I really believe
in it.' She says 'them'. I imagine her wearing the costume of an
American nurse from the fifties, going from frozen girl to
frozen girl, 'I really believe in it. I really believe in it.' Your
father is concerned that you're not eating, he points to a bag
filled with transparent liquid swaying above your right arm.

'Those are carbohydrates and proteins, of course, not
chocolate!'

Then I start talking about your chocolates, a childish need
to talk about you, to prove that you have a life made of details,
films, breaths and smiles, not just those sterile machines that
are chilling, breathing, forcing your clinical life. I tell the nurse
and your father about your chocolate programmes. The way
you eagerly watch for the Christian holidays at Christmas and
Easter in the supermarkets. Those little balls of gilded paper
scattered all over your room and also one or two deceptively
empty boxes, hypocritically conserved with their cover closed
over unlikely leftover pieces of chocolate. The astrological
nurse quickly takes a little notebook out of her pocket and
writes, like a zealous traffic cop, 'Oh, it's good to know that!
Personal things! When she wakes up, I'll have a keyword to
make her react. Think of other important words you can give
me by tomorrow.' So Chocolat Lanvin is, I'm sorry to say, the
first word of your possible return to life.

What's a keyword, your confused father asks me. I don't know, it's a word that would make her open her eyes. A word that might make her feel like answering something. A word like a home. A password. I don't know. I silently enumerate what I know about you, I think, I raise questions, years, what you confided to me, I reject dozens of words and stories, none of them seem clear enough, beautiful, simple, what a job, choosing the right word, the one that maybe . . .

Later, I find this:

Tuesday, van, the clan of the nuns, the Pelican, case dismissed, questionnaires, Belfast, pass me the Coke, basketball, Harzjaï, psychiatric expertise, Sylvie Guillem, prison, chocolate, calm as a bomb.

Hey, you're calm as a bomb today, girl, you often point out to me when we're having tea sitting on my bunk.

We won't count the Saint-Ambroise station as a keyword.

YOUR BUILDING

is a metaphor for the country since the Election, a biscuit with heavy icing, bitten into on one side and full of lumps with a bitter taste. Not one of the people who live in these dark, luxurious flats says hello to you. The flats are spread out over four floors and the two top floors—maids' rooms—share the cockroaches and the odours from pipes and dinners at any occasion. Every morning, above your place, an American student vacuums his room—ten square metres—and we wonder what he can possibly be vacuuming. At the beginning, when we pass him on the stairs in his white shirt with a jabot and navy blue scarf, you're horrified, sure he's a royalist when he tips his hat (too big for his head) as we pass by. Then you learn he came here for 'Victor Hugo'! And he's studying ancient Greek. His eyes fill with tears at the mention of Thoreau, he walks the pavements of Barbès, filled with wonder, and tries to speak Arabic at the market on Saturday mornings. On Sundays, he leaves with maps of the Fontainebleau forest he found at the flea market, we can see him going up the street leaning on a staff he carved himself. Ever since he learnt of your death and hears me walking in your flat, he squeezes my hand between his when I tell him how you are and offers me his *meilleurs regards*, his 'best looks' as he leaves, although he claims he gives French lessons. It's been a few weeks since you destroyed his illusions. He points to the Sacré-Coeur and you tell him about the revolutionary Commune of 1871. You bombard him with emails and newspaper clippings, every time there's news about Flash-Balls fired point-blank at demonstrators, every mention of 'national identity' is for him. Between your two studio flats lives Harzjaï, who works as a stock boy. When you learn that he just received his deportation notice after working here for ten years, you announce it to me without turning round, motionless, facing the window, '. . . He's the first person like that I know, I mean, not in my work.' On a winter Sunday, such a short time ago, all three of you go for a walk in the Parc de Sceaux and call me to join you. The snow of the park is more beautiful than the wet snow on the Island, which turns into mud. We make plaques of ice crack with the tips of our shoes, almost relieved to get pleasure from it. Each of us in turn comments on the sun, wonderfully stable, wide and normal—it seems to be a remnant from an ancient world, all of us are on the verge of tears. Ravaged by a modern sadness, we smile at one another.

Inserting a Picture

The prime-time telefilm on Channel 1, a melodramatic tearjerker. A sociological horror. You navigate between all your 'cases' with the vigour of a supervisor in a school cafeteria. You hate the expression 'children with problems'. You hate the words 'youth counsellor'. 'Reinsertion' too, as if 'I were going to insert them in the right box, a socio-surgical treatment, yuck'. I bum around, you say when someone asks you what you do. Between the blocks of flats and the bare, stony, little parks of the eighteenth arrondissement, you become a familiar sight, you wander round, have coffee, 'I wait. That's all. For the right time. To say hi, to say hello.' You'll find a high school for the girls who've been expelled from all schools, those girls who steal, bite, scratch or run away. You'll organize trips, look for places, houses where they can stay, and every time, I understand it as a 'house visit', as if you were going to take me on a tour of a model house, I'm preparing their 'house', you say.

And you come back completely exhausted, five days at the seaside, a week in the mountains. Rock climbing, crossing narrow footbridges over precipices, cleaning up beaches—the schedule you set up for the kids who go with you sounds like a Stakhanovite nightmare. You accompany parents to city halls, to administrative courts, they need documents, sometimes fake ones, a place to live, something to eat. You take care of a schizophrenic young man—a chess player, formerly with a ranking, who doesn't dare beat anyone any more, not even you (and at each winning move, he murmurs with embarrassment, I'm sorry, I'm sorry). Once every two weeks, you casually tell me 'I'm going to prison, call you later,' there's always some boy or girl in jail at Fresnes or the Santé to whom you bring clothing, cigarettes, neighbourhood news, or nothing. And for three years, you gave maths lessons to a teenage fence who temporarily entrusted you with kilos of watches or sport shoes he 'found'. Every Saturday, the two of you go to the library to pick out books, which he covers with transparent plastic before returning them. He's arrested one November morning.

Right after Christmas, you get a registered package full of books belonging to the library. Puzzled, you finally manage to reach the prison administration and they're sorry, they didn't think of notifying you. The autopsy will take place the following Monday and, by the way, your protégé Miroslav C. hanged himself.

You know kids who light three firecrackers on the deserted boulevards of August and end their vacation in a juvenile detention centre, families of six crammed into nine square metres—their parents shower you with desserts and good wishes. And then there's the girl you couldn't save this autumn. The one you don't talk about any more. The girl on whom you refused to write a 'report', a narrative telling the life story of the ones you're following and the activities you provide for them.

It's not a story, you keep saying, I can't tell her life like a story. As if you were afraid that as you get into the sordid details, her story would become laughable. She's seventeen. Beaten by the guy who tells all their friends he loves her. Scarred and cut regularly with a knife. When he finds a job that takes him away from her for a few months, you swing into action, now is the time, you say you can put her in touch with organizations that can help. The girl listens to you attentively, I'm not sure Émile, OK, I'll call this number next Monday. Then she disappears from the neighbourhood. You wait. You're fuming with impatience. Only one month left. Two weeks before the guy she continues to call her 'boyfriend' is coming back. Her girlfriends tell you she's home, tired, probably has the flu, they don't know, she doesn't answer the phone any more. When you finally run into her again, she smiles when she sees you're alarmed at how thin she is and points out you're not her mother. Discreetly, F. is escaping from her body, you watch her cutting up everything she eats into tiny pieces, pretexting toothaches. One October afternoon, with only three days left before her 'boyfriend' is to return, you make an appointment with her at the place you met her the first time, in front of the little park near the ring road. Wrapped up in a dark red blanket, she manoeuvres her wheelchair up to you. Radiant. 'See, Émile, I have my own public bike now!' she tells you proudly. She woke up at the beginning of the week unable to walk, paralysed, she says, her eyes wide with astonishment, and she bursts out laughing when you worry that she's not worried. Excused from life at last. At last, this body reduced to nothing.

At last, an exemption from him. She dies two weeks later from a generalized infection. The day of the funeral, I meet you at a cafe at the end of the afternoon. I failed, you tell me, and when I try to comfort you, you interrupt me sharply, failed.

started two years ago, I think. At the beginning, you spoke of a little newspaper for the neighbourhood kids made up of their answers to your questions, and games and jokes. They would sell it and the money they made would pay for a show, or a trip. The questions were nice and banal, 'What kind of profession would you like to have,' 'Tell the last dream you remember.' Most of them were about the neighbourhood, the films they'd like to see in the film club you organize every other week. Little by little you added other questions like 'What don't you dare to do,' 'What do you never say,' 'What would you like to forget,' 'What makes you angry.' One evening when you're walking Vassili back home, he mentions the questionnaire he can't manage to fill out to his mother. Laughing, she gives an answer and you end up sitting with her in her kitchen. And like that for months. You begin questioning the parents of the children you're working with. You transcribe all this very seriously once you're home and tell me, bubbling over with 'the great answers' of your day.

Now you have dozens of neat copies of questionnaires you never gave your colleagues. The newspaper never saw the light of day. These past months, your insistence on keeping on with these questionnaires that weren't going anywhere intrigued me and then actually annoyed me. Sometimes, from the corner of your eye, you seem to arithmetically calculate the interest of all the new people you meet according to how useful they might be. I've got to the point where I know right away if you will ask some of them 'a few questions'. When you're asked why you do this kind of job (for it has become a job by now) you lie and I never give you away. You talk about 'sociological research, a collective volume with some girls on my team'.

Monday between four and six in the morning, like a landing expected at 36°C, your body might wake up. Might, they emphasize. I go back to the waiting room right in the middle of the doctor's sentence

die

vegetable, lost consciousness

or wake up lucid but

While you float up and down at 0.5°C per hour, two people die in the unit, one of them at 33°.

Your friends are young and plentiful. Since the night before, we've been together a lot. We give up seats to one another. We wash our hands in the same room which serves as an airlock before we go in to you, as you're being frozen and resuscitated. We hand one another bags of biscuits without speaking, we thank one another in a whisper. Around nine, a boy in a red sweater and a girl with long, dull hair slide quietly to the floor in the hall outside the waiting room. They cry noiselessly. The others gather outside, I see one of them, the repeated gesture of his hand banging against the hospital wall. The smoke of their cigarettes blends into the haze of exhausted words. Behind the glass door, there is the warm smell of that corridor through which the bodies of the medical staff wind smoothly, circumscribing our fears.

The friends of the dead young man come back to the waiting room, we hold out a coat to them and a bag that was left behind a chair. The fact that we were continuing to wait gives me the impression of a team sport in which you're leading doggedly, frozen, and we're still not eliminated.

34.5°

I don't like the neat way your mother does your hair. When I'm alone with you, I always put your hair back in a more natural manner. I'm afraid of finding you one morning looking angelic, neatly combed, and your hands crossed over your chest—such fear, you have no notion.

Last night's nurse explains to me that when you get back to 'normal temperature', there'll be several of them round you speaking to you very loudly. 'Don't forget my keywords,' she adds as she closes the door. I imagine her leaning over your intubated body screaming Chocolat Lanvin.

But it's Sylvie Guillem who comes immediately to mind.

Nineteen eighty-nine is not the year the Wall fell, I used to tell you when we first met. You'd watch me stretched out on my bed, the ash of your cigarette hanging lightly. No, I'd go on, absolutely not! Nineteen eighty-nine is the defection, the flight of Sylvie Guillem to London, those French morons, with their rules and their hierarchy—they lost her. She had said no. Just think, she was named prima ballerina at the Paris Opera by Rudolf Nureyev when she was nineteen, after being there just one week, can you believe it, first dancer in seven short days, when some ballerinas have to wait for years!

Sylvie Guillem, a keyword, a double keyword and even more than that, a kaleidoscopic word that spreads out like a fan. You pronounce it and like dancers in old musical comedies who disappear one after the other on staircases twinkling with rhinestones, the words contained in the wonderful Mademoiselle Non file by at full speed, glittering.

Just after we met, we had leafed through a huge book of photographs devoted to Sylvie in a bookstore, the book was so heavy we had to sit on the floor and our four knees could hardly keep it open properly. The first chapter began 'Nicknamed Mademoiselle Non' . . . We had smiled at each other and read the list of all the magnificent 'Noes!' that Sylvie Guillem had shouted, to the Paris Opera, to the Royal Ballet, to choreographers, photographers, to the fans who wanted her to sign her worn-out ballet shoes after the show.

You're in love with her, you would conclude after I spent a whole evening showing you the various videos. I protested, saying that I was in love implied it could be different, that you could see her and be indifferent to her. On sites for ballet purists, you sometimes read in the forums that she's not a real ballerina, some people choke over that idea, that naked contortionist should go back to gymnastics. Luckily her name's just Sylvie, there had to be some modest detail about her. One day, in a commuter train, a pale girl with shadowed eyes gets on at Gare de Lyon and sits opposite me, her blue wool ski cap flattening her auburn bangs that blend gently with her delicate eyelashes. She's wearing jogging pants, I think, or maybe I'm making it up. And it's in the window of the train that I see her appear, when Sylvie Guillem is actually right in front of me. Her chin leaning on the palm of one of her hands. Then she gathers her things, pulls up her scarf and gets off the train. Can you believe it, I tell you, all shaken up by it, she was on the train. You nod, perplexed.

During our first year together, I tried to find an exciting programme for your first evening at the Opera Garnier. I had been unable to enjoy ballet as a spectator for a very long time, sometimes I would look only at the feet and notice the velocity of the jumps, at other times I would tense up, terrified at the thought of a girl slipping after the diagonal of the *déboulés*, but those three ballets, among George Balanchine's finest, would almost succeed in distracting me from my fears of dancing. I had the strange feeling that I was about to introduce you to my family and I was also afraid you wouldn't like it;

you'd never been to a dance concert. I tried to explain the way Monsieur B, as the dancers called him, organized space. And those black leotards and skin-coloured tights—a revolution, you have no idea—you would look at me raising an eyebrow as if I were making fun of you, yes it's true, up to then, ballerinas wore white tutus—romantic, as they say. His women too. The ones he had invented, trained and mass-produced, his 'Balanchiniennes', with their eyes that ate up the paleness of their face and those long doe-like thighs. And also his ill-fated love for Susan Farrell, the most beautiful of them all, his despair when she chose to leave the company to get married, since Balanchine forbade his dancers to get married.

It was the evening of a dress rehearsal and the only people invited were the press photographers, the critics and the dancers of the Opera who weren't on the programme that evening. Sitting together, they glumly, severely examined the validity of the *entrechats* of the six dancers, who were their neither-colleagues-nor-friends, and the precision of their pirouettes.

You didn't say a word during the first part of the show. I was watching you, noticing your distrustful look. In the middle of the second ballet, you whispered, 'Do *you* do that?' In *arabesque penchée*, the legs of the prima ballerina formed a vertical line in front of us, her hands resting on the white T-shirt of her partner's shoulders.

As we went out, some dancers I knew said hello and you kept to the side. In the Métro, I wanted to know if you liked the evening, we had hardly talked about the show.

'You all look alike,' you threw out at me, 'Your feet, the way you hold yourself, your neck, it's really unsettling . . .' Then, at the moment of saying goodbye, you confessed, 'I'm not sure I got the story.'

'There is no story, it's . . . forms.'

'OK. Forms . . . So it's forms . . . Anyway, next time, I'll know the Opera, the marble stairs, all that fancy stuff is just a myth, because you and your buddies the dance freaks, you were all dressed like bums. So long, kiddo,' and you walked away, looking awkward in the nice black jacket you must have picked just for the dress rehearsal.

You never tried, it really blew me away. When you didn't like something, you talked about the show with the nastiness of a dance critic. Our evenings at the Opera became our 'other world'. Our pretty tune, our light Christmases—we were escaping from our Tuesdays. Then you came to pick me up after my dance classes. At first, you only saw what we do at the end—the *grands sauts* (the leaps), and the bow to the teacher. As in the first ballet we attended together, you didn't say anything, stupefied by the traditions and the applause of the dancers at the end of their class.

'These guys are so damn *Opera*, aren't they? Come on— the guy gives a class, it's so fucking hard core you mutate into dishcloths, yes you do, just look at yourself! And at the end he thanks you for coming and you all clap . . . Hmmm . . . And you're *paying* that guy . . .!'

And then you wanted to watch a whole class. After several months you had become an authentic ballet mum, as we call those mothers of Opera-ballet kids, stricter than a ballet master with their disapproving looks when their dream child stumbles. You would comment on my adagio, saying, 'The *arabesque* was a little shaky, I'm telling you,' and the leaps, making a face, 'Your left foot hurts or what? It's not stretched out right.' In the street, you'd show me what I should have done, because *you* had really understood the teacher, 'Come on, he told you a hundred times! The movement never stops!' Immobility did not exist in dance— even when it seemed that a body had stopped, in reality, the endless stretching of the fingers was subtly leading to the next movement. 'You almost need air between each disc of your spine,' you would repeat to me gleefully, 'Aaaii-rrr,' joining your arms in a circle over your head to make a stiff, twisted crown.

I gave you the alphabet of dance, that armed religion. You threw yourself into the world of movement with all your being, ecstatic, and then, helplessly, you watched me lose my words and give up.

I have no memory of not knowing how to dance. Or rather, I have no memory of knowing how to talk without the knowledge of that other alphabet—Ballet. First position, second position, fourth. *Arabesque* in *effacé*. My parents used to mention with pride the way in which, like my sister, an instructor had 'spotted' me in the schoolyard of the kindergarten. At that time, the current regime wanted to put together an elite of athletes and artists who would add charm to the Romanian flag. They would be able to go out of the country and travel—unlike the other inhabitants—and represent it abroad.

My sister had been spotted at the age of seven in a park where she had the habit of hanging upside down from the branches of a tree; for me, it was when they saw me undertake a whole series of bizarre little skips on the ledges of low walls barely twelve centimetres wide that I was picked for my first dance class with Madame Niculescu.

That former prima ballerina of the Bucharest Opera Ballet used the living room of her flat to train girls who might, perhaps, get into the Ballet School. The shutters remained permanently closed even during the day, the large rugs were rolled up and put away along the walls. The pianist never said hello to us, she seemed almost artificial, motionless in front of the keys, her Polaroid-red hair pulled back in a bun, with no score in front of her. Sometimes, between two exercises, she would bend down, fumble around in her handbag and take out a cigarette which she would put down in place of the scores that she didn't have. Hey, she's playing songs by Barbara, my mother exclaimed one day when she'd come to sit in on my lesson.

Sometimes the pianist's voice would suddenly rise into the air from the darkest corner of the room, like an unexpected bird.

'And ven-n the alar-r-r-m sounds, if you had to take up ar-r-r-t . . .'[1]

I was the youngest of the group of little girls who'd been 'spotted' that year and Madame Niculescu, in a hurry to stop me from growing, was taking advantage of it to put off the moment when the vertebrae of my back would get awfully stiff. After the other pupils left, she made me lie on my belly in a split at a facial angle as long as possible, with my back tightly stretched between my legs. With her palms flat in the middle of my back, she would push down and keep me that way until there was not even a centimetre of space left between the floor and my belly. She taught me to sleep 'useful'. Lying on my back with my legs tucked up like a frog, every evening I would demand that my sister place a dictionary on each thigh to force my tendons to acquire maximum opening.

When I told you about these very ordinary details of my apprenticeship, you burst into horrified laughter, looking at me with pity. It's true that by way of childhood memories, I spoke to you only of joints, stretched-out knees and facial splits. It's because up to the age of about ten, Ballet for me was a prolongation of physical birth, of coming into the world—a natural state in a sense, something you had to keep up, the way you brush your teeth. It's much later that movement became an intelligible language, one possible way of transmitting sensation.

I was one of the two little girls chosen by Madame Niculescu to be presented for the entrance examination to the

---

1 From 'Göttingen', a famous song by the French singer Barbara: 'Et lorsque sonnera l'alarme / S'il fallait reprendre les armes / Mon cœur verserait une larme . . .'

Ballet School of the Bucharest Opera. My sister had lasted a year there and was reoriented to the theatre after they deemed her too undisciplined for Ballet. The exam seemed easy to me, they'd sewn numbers on our pink leotards, gaunt little racing horses.

That Friday in June when I was waiting for the results, perhaps to steel myself against a possible disappointment if I was rejected, my father asked me if I really wanted to go to that school where, it seemed to him, ballet was a pretext for blind training. You had to become Ballet itself, that geometry of the body, rather than learn to dance, right? I protested, in love with all the gestures they were asking me to reproduce, in love with the sour faces of the teachers I had glimpsed, with the smell of resin sticking to ballet shoes and to the walls of rooms slightly muggy with the sweat of obedient bodies. My acceptance was somewhat debated. Was it right to give this distinction to a child whose father was from a country in Western Europe? But at four o'clock, the jury announced my number, *Doizprezece*,[2] and Madame Niculescu pushed me gently to the centre to thank them with a bow. A man who was very fat shook my hand, congratulating my parents on having chosen to live where true ballet was transmitted, in the Romanian Socialist Republic.

While I was at the Ballet School, I continued to have my Saturday afternoon lessons in her flat. Those weekly ninety minutes were my QED, my notes in the margin. Thanks to her corrections, I knew more than the other girls, and her advice enabled me to have a slight lead. Sometimes she would point her finger at me as if she had just recognized the guilty party at a murder scene—'You're lying? Why are you lying!?'—when I had just finished an adagio, immobilized in fifth position in front of her, my ribs panting under the leotard. Every imprecise movement was 'cheating on beauty' for Madame Niculescu.

---

2 Twelve (a grade good enough to move on to the next level).

Then, in the middle of the eighties, the regime hardened still more. For reasons I do not know, Madame Niculescu fell into disgrace and one morning, my new ballet master roughly commanded me not to mention her any more. Never talk about Gabriela Niculescu again.

The following Saturday, anxious but ready to take my usual lesson, I rang her bell. After a long while, Madame opened the door as if she had fallen asleep in the back of her flat. I was standing in her freezing hallway, my big bag of dance things over my shoulder, the outside light was striking her mouth in a funny way, her lower lip was protruding from her powdered face and trembling, dry and sadly chapped. She greeted me with an embarrassed look as if my visit was not expected, held out her hand to tuck a lock of my hair neatly into my bun and then offered to give me a cup of tea and why not a little crêpe, it so happens her mother had made her some. I had the curious impression that she was talking to people I couldn't see in the room, with that nervous way she had of explaining all our gestures aloud in detail—a nice cup of tea! I even have a bit of Brasov cheese if you like, darling!—she seemed to be obeying and reassuring invisible listeners. As she led me into her kitchen (where, in two years, I had never set foot), she kept informing me in a voice louder than necessary that she would not give me lessons any more. I must not come back, it's over. The hierarchy of our relationship was such that I couldn't talk to her simply and ask the reason why lessons were ending. She was Madame. Doamna Professoara. I reported everything she said to my parents like theorems that defined my body and my presence in the world.

In her kitchen, extremely afraid of this moment of life facing her without a barre or a mirror, I ate a little crêpe with jam served by the pianist Elisabeta. As if she were taken out of the set of an unfinished film, far from her piano, she dragged her feet a little over the tiles, her hands seemed older to me than the previous weeks.

Every one of my gestures took on tremendous importance for me: cutting a little piece of the crêpe without making the jam flow out the sides, spearing it and then bringing the fork to my mouth without bending my head, my back very straight, chewing slowly but not too much to answer madame's questions without making her wait. Not to take the wrong napkin, the one to the left is certainly Elisabeta's. The kitchen contained clock sounds, the one in the living room, and the humming of the refrigerator blended with that hospital sound of an American TV soap—when someone dies in them, the body gives no warning, no blood, no excrement, just a face that slackens and falls back on the pillow, still more beautiful than when it was alive, in the horizontality of an electric sound.

'Madame Niculescu' could perhaps be an interesting keyword.

You'd probably have to make an effort to remember that name, but then, a proper noun—and in a foreign language to boot—strikes the imagination. Perhaps Madame Niculescu might be sketched out in your memory, sporting a particular voice and hairdo. What had intrigued you the most is how her flat became a silent, clandestine dance studio after she was quarantined from the Opera Ballet.

A first non-official lesson took place a short hour after the episode of the crêpe in the kitchen. I was telling her about the variation of the *Nutcracker* they were making me work on at the school, the difficulty of the *sauts de chat, assemblés*, when Madame Niculescu got up suddenly, held out her hands so that I should tear myself away from my crêpe and get up, and then, positioning herself with her back to me, she whispered, 'The top of your bust *effacé*. Like this.' This little trick, shifting the axis of my shoulders slightly slantwise to the audience, would enable me to connect the two leaps in a better way while slightly retracting my hips, which, in this wicked series of moves invented by a choreographer who never could have performed it, were not perfectly placed between the landing of the *saut de chat* and the start of the *assemblé*.

'Ai înţeles? Aşa . . .'[3] Gabriela's feet were stretching the sad fabric of her old slippers, I'd never seen her in them before this Saturday—her feet turned into authoritarian daggers, 'La la-la-a-a-a, la-a-a, lalala, and. And la la-la-a-a-a . . .' and while she was doing the steps, her voice was going hoarse from softly singing Tchaikovsky's measures, hardly touching the notes, so Elisabeta, sitting on her stool, began to softly clap her hands to beat the time. I danced the *Nutcracker* in street clothes in that kitchen, taking care not to bump into anything, a little, precise dance, urgent and hidden. After a few moments, with her finger over her mouth rounded by words she was not pronouncing, Madame Niculescu indicated that I should follow her into the living room where I had spent two years in the company of twelve other little girls. The shutters were open and the rugs neatly in place, but despite all those signs of life, that room seemed more abandoned than ever. The air itself, lukewarm and lazy, seemed to stagnate round the furniture. She closed the shutters and all three of us knelt down to roll up the large rug and lay bare the wooden floor. The mute discretion of her gestures needed no explanation, I suspected that her flat, like ours, must be tapped. What I could not understand was that she no longer had the right to give lessons in her flat.

I've often told you, we never really asked questions about all that, those domestic details—the presence of watchers in our lives, the mikes in the phones and living-room lamps and the members of the Securitate who would break into our flat on Sundays when we left to go picnicking in the woods, and those dinners with guarded exchanges of vague, empty phrases interrupted by fingers pointing to the ceiling as the only explanation for the silence. And then those words, that were only

---

3 'You understand? Like this . . .'

uttered very softly and never at home, like 'passport' and 'Hungary', the country that led to the West.

Our bodies made do with these conditions, moved according to the grotesque, ever-changing rules of the Conducător, and dodged his relentless effort to shrink our lives. Sometimes, though, an event would strike me, when the image was a little out of the ordinary in our daily lives, completely adjusted to the absurd.

My mother would wait till we were outside in the street, of course—none of that would be discussed at home, where we had to keep performing the same dull play every day. Extremely agitated, she would announce to us that one of her best friends had just succeeded in getting out, hidden in the trunk of the car of a cultural attaché from the French embassy, which was searched less frequently at the border. Fascinated, I imagined that tall, blonde young woman transformed into limbs to be folded up as ergonomically as possible in a trunk, her body turned suitcase. And that very evening in my room, I tried, with my sister, to fold myself up in different ways to hold out comfortably for a long time in the boot of a car.

So you played at folding yourself in four, you say to me when I tell you that. I say no, not completely. I played at going unnoticed.

Madame Niculescu kept giving me private lessons every other Saturday through that year, even if she could no longer do it to music. After all, Dance is transmitted visually from one dancer to another. So I imitated her frail arms covered by a beige cardigan. She would raise her eyebrows very high with a scornful look when I botched my double pirouettes, frowned to enjoin me to leap higher and sometimes smiled, nodding her head, when I froze, with my arms in a ring over my head, fifth position, at the end of an exercise, awaiting her verdict. Not a word issued from her mouth. Whispers, when she hummed the adagio from *Giselle* so I shouldn't lose the rhythm, but for the rest, from the warm-up exercises at the barre to the leaps at the end, everything happened in silence. When I would launch into a series of *grands jetés*, Madame Niculescu would motion me to soften my landing. I think I learnt to make very good ultra-silent leaps for reasons that have nothing to do with art—it was all about moving between the orders and the arrests. And so for the pointes, whose sound on the floor was too characteristic to go unnoticed, we would return to the grey linoleum in the kitchen.

The culinary alibi of the Saturday crêpe meant for the mikes of the Securitate was sometimes replaced by a cheese-cake and, in the kitchen, the three of us would talk in strangely loud voices, excited by our great little organization and the mute breaths of our sliding steps that would follow.

34.5° => 36°

There are thirteen of you in this unit. And no one has died in the last sixteen hours.

Nos cœurs que tu connais sont remplis de rayons: 'Our hearts, which you know, are filled with rays of light.'[4] That sentence from Godard's *Introduction to a True History of Cinema and Television* enchants you. And I still have the SMS you sent me on my birthday, a typo or a moment of inattention makes your words sound like a discreet call for help, or a display of love. *Mon cœur que tu connais*, you write, 'My heart, which you know.' Your heart, which I know

Stopped.

---

4 Line from Charles Baudelaire's 'Le Voyage'.

LOOKING BACKWARDS

We rarely talk about how we met. We backed into our friendship and we had to proceed cautiously to return to the joyful trivialities of burgeoning friendships. Our favourite colours and films, the name of our high school, were you ever left by anyone, what kind of yoghurt and coffee, with sugar or not, novels. Brothers, wishes, bedrooms, aversions.

But with us, everything was too serious, those Tuesday Evenings in the big gloomy room, the sound too muffled the first time we met. Besides, we didn't talk to each other. I was sitting opposite you, you were at the end of the table. You were smoking and constantly retying your hair into a bun but one or two braids kept sliding out of your brown barrette.

What I learn first about you are the legal categories of that moment in your life. I learn their date, setting and schedule. I know the comments of the first policemen you go see one September night, you recite them to us, bragging, you're the one with the power in that performance, rejecting the role that *he* assigned to you. That way you have of looking busy, even when you're sitting. Your imitations of the cop who takes your deposition, the awkward phrases of your bewildered father on the phone, it all turns into an ironic, ferocious misadventure when you tell it. Horrified at ourselves for bursting out laughing, we listen to you, delighted to be led through your nightmare. It's your own way of staying alive.

Of all the girls in our group, you're the one *it* happened to not far from home, in your car, and you didn't know the man. I'm the one *it* happened to without a break-in, in a warm room, and *the man* has no police record, as they say—*he* looks honest and pleasant, *he*'s love itself, above suspicion.

I couldn't afford to be sentimental. I needed something very solid—a gang leader, perhaps. Our bodies bonded. We bonded in parallel, against and despite our will. We met on a Tuesday. Forced to listen to each other on Tuesdays. Sentenced to Tuesdays. All the other days of the week, we probably remained alone, dull and cloistered, with dirty images stirring inside us.

As soon as Friday came round, I could see Tuesday coming. Saturday was looming and probably, desperate to get back to what I called life and seeking absent sensations, I would force myself to have fun. The morning of Sunday I would surrender to my defeat, exhausted. I'd have to hold out till Tuesday, that mix of a refuge and a disgusting mirror. Let there be only Tuesdays. But once I was at the bottom of that day, I was filled with anger for needing it so much, so on the Métro platform I would let two, four trains go by, not to belong to that group, not to be part of that meeting which no one round me, but no one, knew about—a secret, shameful appointment.

Because people imagine things. They do. They bring up images, as soon as you tell them. They put together the images that pop into their minds and come to conclusions. You'll say group, victims of . . . no, you don't want to use that word . . . you'll say, trying to talk in a firm, affectless voice, a 'support group', even if it means that people will think soft therapy, soft light and lampshades, women sitting cross-legged on rugs, cups of tea, whining and conversations about men, while you're at it. You'll say—but how will you say it—that you landed there temporarily, it's a shipwreck, one of those eighteenth-century shipwrecks where people often drowned so close to the shore and waved their arms desperately to the people on the bank powerless to save them, watching the bodies slowly being swallowed up.

The two of us start seeing each other outside of all that, of *what happened*, after a few weeks. We have coffee before the meeting, and then afterwards too. We try to take up the story at the middle. We have to start from another beginning, different from the one that brought us together—that's it. We do each other the courtesy of not imagining *what happened* to the other one. We'll never bring up those men who decreed, that year, the end of the first part of our lives. We won't describe *what happened*. We make it a matter of friendship not to bring up the height of the windows we considered, the anxiolytics, sleeping pills, anti-spasmodics advised by doctors and our days spent in a daze, huddled against the radiator. We walk for whole afternoons and you never question my refusal to take certain streets which I still can't manage to walk through for fear of bumping into *him*, the fear stronger than my reason. Our paths are tortuous, our itineraries long and complicated. I don't remember us crying even once in front of the other, nor, of course, together.

One evening of that first year, we're having dinner in a little Indian restaurant in the eighteenth arrondissement. The pink-and-orange lighting darkens our hair. The tablecloth is only white in the middle. Pale, rusty traces of faded stains mark the edges. The others squeezed in next to us—tables with normal conversations—perk up their ears a little because it does seem to them that we're not talking about a love story or some job or other. They scent a nasty business, a secret. I remember being suddenly stupefied by this friendship, this impressive pact. I remember my admiration, hats off as they say—I can only bow to you, that evening I am overcome with my admiration for your courage. There were no more jokes or impersonations, nothing sad either.

When you understood that you couldn't avoid *what was going to happen*, you tried to bargain with him. You're the one who uses that word 'bargain' and I say no, you tried everything, listen, you tried everything. But you can't forgive yourself for not fighting like a manga heroine, you shake your head and in the tawny light of the little restaurant, I can't even move my hand towards you to console you, you're encased in pain like an unbreakable envelope. I'm a coward, still, but never, neither that evening nor any other, do you ask me to confide in you in return.

'In the world according to Bensenhaver, no trivial detail should make less of rape's outrage.'

We dog-eared the page of The World According to Garp, rehabilitated by a novel, a few words. At the moment you understood that it was going to happen, you asked your aggressor to put on a condom. Die but be careful about AIDS. To end the first part of your life, certainly, but get him not to have his skin in your belly, his sperm flowing. With great difficulty, the way you'd confess an unforgiveable act, you were condemning yourself through the verb 'confess'. 'I've got to confess something to you.' That detail—and you stood up in front of me to imitate your concerned lawyer—jeopardized your testimony, that might cost you dear, mademoiselle. Bad victims.

The young, noisy girls in the cafes resemble us. They lean across the table towards one another with a worried look, discuss their exams and burst out laughing. You and I—we spend whole afternoons looking for the right sentences that will classify us as suitable victims, sufficiently traumatized to be credible. You are very knowledgeable about psychiatric-expertise examinations preliminary to trial, you know the difference between 'the "vulnerabletraumatized mush" and the expression "mental health". When you read that in the report, let me tell you, kiddo, you better re-form-u-late your story. Mental means wacko, wacko means liar.'

When we manage to forget our Tuesdays a little, we have to answer the question: 'But how did you two meet?'

Then I count on that histrionic side of yours. With your fingers in your braids to rebalance that soft bun, you put one foot forward, standing like a fencer no taller than a metre fifty-six. Then you make some moves that only I know are a homage to the adagio of the *Corsair*, flinging your arms awkwardly over your head while whirling clumsily, 'Ta ta Ta tatata-a-a-a!'

But the guy keeps at it, wants to play anyhow and answer that burning riddle, while others turn away and find you vulgar with your shirt hanging out of your blue navy sweater like a rag.

Still, we're ashamed, aren't we, since we don't answer, and every time I ask you to volley back the question. So that year, I'm the one who gets on your nerves. We know very well we're ashamed. So what. We're not going to be ashamed of being ashamed too.

BODIES: THE TUESDAY EVENING CORPS

—The one (*three fellow workers in her office after a party*) who will be hospitalized two months later for too many 'fits of rage' tells about her Sunday in a conscientious tone. All those details in which we can guess how she applies herself to that sport called staying alive, making breakfast for the children and apologizing for her screams, just the night before in the living room, that fury, what's left over from the tornado.

—That dark-haired girl (*a friend of the family, it's been going on ever since she was seven*) with a body buried in huge heavy sweaters, who takes a train for a whole hour to get to our Tuesday meetings, went to the cinema with a nice boy yesterday. Their arms close to each other. And his breathing during the film. The same sound as that night, that invasive regularity. Once she got home, she threw up, she explains, embarrassed by her failure.

—For you (*an unknown man who begins by asking you what you're doing out so late alone*), your skit about filing a complaint at the police station remains one of your major hits, with the detective sitting in front of his computer that night to take down the details of your *story* trying a 'So, you're going to make me work overtime, right?'

—The one (*the family doctor*) whom I'll keep calling the whispering spider for a long time because of her inaudible voice that seemed to be trying to get out of her inexistent body, thought last weekend about the many times she cut herself. She has agreed, finally, to talk about it to 'a qualified person'.

—Case dismissed, announces the student (*her ex-fiancé*) who sits opposite me every Tuesday evening. No evidence, she adds, sitting up straight, before she breaks, with her bust pushed forward, and all of us stand up to grab her shoulders and stop her head from banging on the table.

I don't particularly want to claim the status of a victim. Even in the first months that followed, that idea clashed with the idea I had about how the rest of my life should be. It was just impossible that I should be that frightened thing, walled up alive in a daily life that had been crossed out. While every-where, sex was an easy, natural non-event, a choice—the women who proclaimed their magnificent health in all the magazines were outdoing one another to say so. Once in a while, I would read testimonials about what normal women did, how to make sex even better. With their legs slightly spread, the satin of branded panties, finger on a mouth always ready to open, eyes closed expectantly. In reality, they were lying there like corpses, as if dismembered, the better to serve. Their comfortable bodies positioned the best way for

Everything well ordered for

The creams, the beauty care, what had to be done to lose yourself during the marvellous moment that would follow. Open up. Open. Open.

So an animal desire would take hold of me, the urge to escape, to withdraw from words and images, live in the woods, a mountain, on an island perhaps and find consolation for my inadequacy in all that in my excellent dancing body. In the mil-itary hierarchy of ballet corps, the supernatural extensions of Sylvie Guillem and our recurrent bouts of tendinitis, in the fear of injuries and the love for my weakened tendons, those few minutes when my thighs commanded my hips to let go, torn apart on the floor in a split, inhaling the dusty smell of the greyish floor in little cautious breaths. The smell of sweat, camphor and resin of dance studios came to me every morning like a protected piece of land for an animal that has to be calmed down.

To take off my street clothes and put on tights and a leotard, put an elastic band round my waist, place my left hand on the barre. *Pliés* in every position, forward, back arched. Place my right hand on the barre. *Pliés* in every position, forward, back arched. Every day, like vertebrae, the corset of a life. Reproducing a gesture, then modelling my flesh until it becomes that gesture, hunting in the mirror for what separates me from it. Then, muscularly swallowing the very sensation of that gesture and dancing with my back to the mirror, blindly, totally, excellently honed.

I try not to think of the reasons that caused

I try not to launch into long whys. Not to rationalize that act. No 'it happened because'. Not put myself into *his* head, which thought up *the act*.

I think of the awkward bodies of men, poor, uncomplicated and dull, of men who don't have a body, who have only legs to get up from a chair and walk forward, with their sex in the centre of their cumbersome flesh, their dumb, venerated sex. And the unbearable bodies of female dancers, the pleasure they take in themselves, in their electric bodies.

I try not to see things this way, not to think for one moment that for this, I was punished. Ripped out of my skilfully happy body. *He* would remark when I came out of a performance, 'You always have that invincible look after Dance.' I would laugh like a pathetic little girl who wants to please.

I won't go begging for a psychological explanation which would turn that night of *14 September* into a fact, an event. With its for and against. I was defeated. I believed in words, what a funny thing for a dancer who had scorned words since she was four the better to draw words with her foot and put her signature on the moment.

A fearful little animal with her supple skin crushed, turned inside out, held down, who nonetheless pronounces what she still thinks is the magical passport, No.

The police report states naively, 'I said no several times.'

Watch out when you come back home late at night. If you're followed in your stairway, knock on a neighbour's door. Make sure the door is securely locked.

My beginning was the exact opposite of everyone else's. *He* had the keys and greeted the neighbours pleasantly. *He* would fume over a recent article in *Le Monde Diplomatique*. Signed petitions. Wrote me letters where the words were well put together and were certainly a sign of love.

That night, when I come back to the flat I'm sharing with a friend at the time, I mention a violent quarrel. Unable to find a name for what just happened. All I can remember about the following night is objects, static things. A radiator I stay huddled against and my answering machine that goes off regularly, *messages* suggesting we should *talk*. About *all that*.

I still go to my compulsory ballet class, my body as if swallowed up by a delayed-action virus. Some mornings it seems to me that nothing happened, I line up diagonals of *grands jetés*, double pirouettes with balance maintained, maybe I will dissolve that night in Dance. I blindly follow the orders and corrections of the ballet master—and put my body in his hands so that excellence might make me forget. The dysfunction is already on its way and I can't see anything. I strain to perform these movements as if their perfect line would give shape to the heap again, the wreck I was on *14 September*, that limp thing sprawled out, powerless, smothered. I correct myself and tell myself off when I move forward in front of the mirror for the adagio, I don't know what to do with the violence of my repulsion for that form which is me. I cannot face myself any more; maybe I can fool other people, who see pure *arabesques*, a romantic way of holding my arms, but *I* know. This body doesn't belong to me any more, let it be returned, alone, to its filthy night.

From September to January. *He* leaves several letters on the landing of my flat that rationalize why. How. '*You have to understand . . .*' I put these letters away. Some of 'our' friends call me—very few. Their suspicious, sugary 'How are you?' tells me that *he* has started telling *the story*. And love—that detail—turns me into the accomplice of my own end, a guilty, negligent and negligible accomplice. The walls covered with pretty cloth, the flickering candles round the bed, sheets, perhaps even chosen together—this setting weighs on me like a sneer of denial. So I keep quiet, the terrifying carrier of this foul-smelling story, all that negation of love, my memory soiled with flesh.

I go out as little as possible, the street grabs me with fear, *his car, his cologne* on a passer-by. I can only relax in the buses and the Métros *he* doesn't take. One evening on the phone, a stupid mistake, I say to one of our common girlfriends, you know, something bad—terrible—happened—raped, and the moment I pronounce the word I blush but with no tears at all. She lets a moment go by and, in a scolding tone, points out that it's a very serious word I've just used in French. She adds 'in French'.

As people keep politely suggesting silence to me and I obey, Dance leaves my body, declaring it a pariah, contaminated.

In February, I stay out late at night on a bench in a deserted part of the city where *he'll* never go. And the man who sits down next to me because what are you doing all alone could we, I smack my hand on his face I grab his eyes his hair, standing up I smash his head against the edge of the bench.

I don't go to class any more.

One afternoon, my roommate knocks softly at my door and announces *his* visit. *He* is here.

He says you've lost weight it makes you look . . .

He says you OK

Repeats several times you OK

We have to talk

He is dressed up, his shirt is tucked into his trousers.

He says I won't do it again

But

It's because

You're so complicated

You know

You're really unmanageable sometimes you know

He says I'm sorry

He promises I'll come back later

I'll come back

I don't remember if it's on that day my roommate gives me the phone number—one of those 08 numbers—after we'd talked almost all day.

A voice suggests an appointment at noon on a Monday. The woman who greets me is short, busy and has light brown hair, she leans her whole body towards my inaudible sentences. Tells me about Tuesdays, at the Saint-Ambroise station, you think you might go? And one Tuesday evening I meet you, we don't really have any choice.

Describing the process of filing a complaint here, with its different strata, might come off as a plea for comfort, an attempt to be understood. Neither you nor I are trying to be understood. We won't get into a debate. Persuade. Line up arguments. Justifications. Argue. Give 'valid' reasons. Like saying yes it was so serious that. It hurts so much that

The word rape, when speaking of what seems to be a couple, a pair, who even held hands in public, is a disgusting fantasy that I seem to have initiated. I've smeared *a man above*

suspicion and when I pass by, sometimes, faces turn reproach-
ful and severe, really, I'm 'going too far'.

You're sure, they ask, friendly but suspicious.

Isn't there some way you two can work it out, between
civilized people

It can't be that serious, he loves you, you two have to
patch things up

How can you do that to him

He loves you

I really can't see him as a

I hear, Maybe it's a misunderstanding

He's not that type, really

And some of them, thoughtful psychologists, look for
what I did wrong— something must have happened. What did
you say to him, what did you do, for him to end up doing that.

I yield to your fears, that heap of fears mounting so quickly
before me. I set you free. No one wants to know that the
aggressor had the key and would regularly bring flowers. And
let's not say anything about the legal system, its way of settling
this *kind of case*, as the judge opposite me says. Let's not say
anything about the psychiatrist the psychoanalyst the psychologist who ends the session with a little frown, '*Supposing that
all you've said here is true.*'

Let's not say anything let's say nothing about those clever
films that make girls cry out in a weak little voice when they're
flipped over nothing about the porn films that make girls' faces
wince in pain against a pillow nothing about the non-porn
films that have women close their eyes like dead bodies at the
moment men thrust into them nothing no nothing about the
laughter in the audience when a man is sodomized and howls
like a woman nothing about the friends loved ones as they say

who don't want to know it's your private life it's between the two of you it's your own business maybe you made a mistake do you realize how much you're going to hurt him what if he went to prison you realize prison's pretty serious stuff.

Dumbfounded, I look for the words I could say to convince them. I keep looking. I have this rotten mixture in the back of my throat and well brought up as I am I never throw up. Every night, I dream I'm howling with my mouth open, I strain, I try hard to only pretend to yell. As on *the night of 14 September* when, emptied of myself, I watched myself being ripped apart.

When my lawyer looks over his notes that winter and is confronted with the truth, he makes a face, trying in this way to polish up a correct version of *the night*. It's awkward that *my adversary* should have been my 'boyfriend' at the same time, awkward that his name should be in the credits of many films. There are perfect rapes and others not so perfect.

Telling the police, a psychiatrist, reformulating, repeating, answering the same suspicious questions several times. A confrontation with the person who will be called the *adversary* is set up in the office of a judge with a weary face.

He will readily admit it: on the night of *14 September*, I 'didn't seem right', he says in front of his lawyer, and she's embarrassed by this admission. You clearly heard her say no, asks the judge. He darts a sidelong glance to his lawyer, she tenses up and opens her mouth to speak but he's ahead of her.

I didn't really understand didn't hear she didn't say it not very loudly anyway

Maybe she did say no

But not no/no/no.

Then all of them together start counting my noes, evaluate how my voice carried, how clear those repeated no(es) were on that *September* night.

Rare are the moments when you can feel, almost materially, the fragility of the additions of what we call our 'ideas', those layers of beliefs—the bases, they say, of the construction of our psyche, which is the setting for the human envelope, a ready-to-live conceived for this democratic setting. I might even have bragged, occasionally, that I was not one to believe in the legal system.

During those months when the two of us are becoming closer on Tuesday Evenings, I am waiting for the outcome and it looks like I'm moving towards officializing my status as a victim. Then one thing follows another. The choreography is set without me but its fluidity is remarkable. First, the letter announcing that my case has been dismissed for lack of evidence. Since I did not die on *14 September* and *his* defence was that he was madly in love. Dismissed does not mean that the *things* you brought before the court have been dismissed. It indicates the degree of damage that was done. A meticulous examination of the flesh constantly reopened with a cold finger which would conclude that no, definitely not. It is not objectively certain that.

I remember your slender arms round my back on the street at the announcement of this dismissal, I couldn't catch my breath, my body was giving way as if taken by sudden death.

The show of justice ends in a rapid coda on 12 December of that year, when I receive a registered letter. The name of the legal office on the envelope gives me no warning. The letter will be opened in the street. It contains two signed pages. It is a summons to appear in court. The Law has decided to deal with my *case*. There actually will be a trial in May. I am accused of slander and abuse of process. *He* is the plaintiff.

Two pages on handsome thick paper—all it needs is a seal—that heavy ceremonial, those time-tested formulas, the space provided for *his* name, there, and mine, here, specifying what I am 'charged with'. A little official paper, so clean, so blue, with that stamp proud of its centuries of history. And the words they use, the 'plaintiff', the 'accused', this paper is a whole world, a land that guarantees *its citizens* that they can move as freely as they wish, I beg your pardon but there is no doubt whatsoever of that.

My new lawyer is very young. At our first appointment he explains that he has mainly defended aggressors and this is completely to my advantage—he knows their arguments. We need witnesses, he says. We have to find respectable, credible people who would come swear that they never heard me talk in public of the *night of 14 September*, to clear me of the accusation of slander. Look for people who don't know anything, whom I will ask to testify in court that they don't know anything. Of course, to convince them to come, I'll have to tell them what they don't know. It would also be good if the same people could confirm that I am not insane. In addition to the witnesses, a new psychiatric expertise will be necessary to prove my innocence. An expert will observe the degree of veracity in this whole *story*.

Three Tuesdays go by on which I don't go to the Saint-Ambroise station. Suppressed movements go through my body. I slam doors so hard it gives me migraine, the inside of my teeth suddenly flare up to the rhythm of my steps, I run, escape from bars, parties, questions and parks, and the springtime too, I run on the boulevards, I acquire the technique of zigzagging so as not to be slowed down by a red light and go from one pavement to another. The pain of my heart inside my ribs hardly slows me down. I give up words. The sounds in my throat take airless corridors and come out bestial and naked, tears, fits of rage, I wallow in self-pity and shame. I watch my parents exhaust themselves for having failed with me, my friends and family horrified and hurt. And pain is a foul-smelling, awkward ballet, crawl, sob, never will any gesture be ugly enough to root out of me that thing *he* introduced and planted there. Impaled on that ugly night, I leave traces of it everywhere.

When I finally succeed in getting back to the Saint-Ambroise-Tuesdays, I try to adopt your attitude, turn this story into a surrealist gag. The moment I reveal the formidable conclusion of all that, the trial in which I'll be the accused and *he*, *the victim*, the looks the other girls give me seem made of a substance which will become so unbearable a few months later that I'll choose to run away, escape the stupefaction of the others, their embarrassed silence when they don't know what to say to me any more. As for you, you have your feet on the table, you rock back and forth on your chair, a little sheriff with your hair in a swaying bun, that true calligraphy of braids. Then you raise your hand, as if you had to take the floor immediately, as if you were voting for something essential. You are willing to be a witness for me.

We make a date in a cafe that's not too noisy. As I come out of the Métro, I see you before you see me, sitting alone up against the window, one eyebrow raised, ready to fight.

You help me draw up a list of 'reliable and respectable' individuals who could be witnesses in addition to you. Our conversation takes a wonderful turn—we're looking for the kind of people who would know nothing about me and would agree to come and swear so in court, and also declare that no, I'm not that crazy.

You spill your hot chocolate over our list empty of possible names, it flows onto my army pants and when you get up to ask the waiter for a sponge you seem miniaturized in that real life bustling round us. Seated round our table of motionless, silent bodies all those Tuesday Evenings, absent from the reality that was continuing outside, your voice would orchestrate the funerals of the first part of our lives so skilfully that often you seemed tall to me.

'How will you prove I'm not crazy?' I asked you, as we were walking to the Métro, without having found anything conclusive.

'Hey, relax, you're calm as a bomb, give me two minutes!'

So you were my witness that afternoon in court, at the Palais de Justice.

They made us wait from 2 to 4, all of us in the same room. I had to deal with the unexpected proximity of *his* physical envelope (I don't like to say 'body', a word too loaded with warmth, with movement, I can't do it) while being careful not to lose my breath. Let pain and disgust be distilled slowly, smoothly. Sitting next to me, you kept repeating 'Don't look' in a severe voice. I only saw his shoes. Dignified, clean shoes with lovingly nourished leather, shoes that aren't left lying around.

Sitting in the dock, with my lawyer far behind me, to my left. To my right, the one they call *my adversary*.

At the time of the trial, I had been let go by the company I was dancing in after two warnings; I had missed too many rehearsals without any injury as an excuse. You had then suggested that I come dance a few famous solos from the classical ballet repertoire for your 'protégés' so they could see for once in their lives Odile's variation in *Swan Lake*, you said to me. I danced an excerpt from *Les Sylphides* in the concrete yard of a housing project, on the slightly sticky linoleum of a gym in the eighteenth arrondissement and Kitri's[5] variation in the dining hall of a shelter for battered women too, then, for friends of yours, in a squat that was about to be evicted.

The lawyer responsible for convincing the prosecutor of my guilt described me as unstable, and 'dancer', in her mouth, took on all the meaning it had in the nineteenth century. Now really. She was just fired from a company. What does she live on. She's after his money. Professional success. Now really. Look at her. Slightly turned towards her client, she concludes her plea brilliantly, smiling to him. When it was my turn to speak, unfortunately, I was exactly the picture she'd just painted of me. Now really, look at her. The words had a hard time coming out, my hands went up to my eyes to see clearly

---

5 Character in the ballet *Don Quixote*.

through the deluge. I repeated my compliance to the members of the jury, I haven't spoken for a year, I swear. Even on Tuesday Evenings, I never talk about it. Never said his name to anyone, never put my finger on his name on a film poster.

Then the judge called you to the witness stand. You carefully chose your phrases, scrubbed and polished, one by one, precise and dry, you took hold of them the way you grab a book on a shelf. In fact, you looked like a doctor or a fussy archivist. You looked straight in front of you, I remember the theatrical effect of your voice in that room and hearing you speak about me without looking at me, 'she', 'mademoiselle'. You confirmed. I had all the symptoms you yourself had experienced and *you* were a pretty good victim—actually, your aggressor had just been convicted by a court.

'No, I had never pronounced the guilty party's name in public.' The judge corrected you very quickly. 'The plaintiff.' You gave no apologies, shrugging your shoulders. They thanked you.

On your way back to your seat, you turned to me. Your eyes were tracing a line, air you could put your hands on to help you sit very straight again, firmly rooted. Your grey, slightly round eyes with long straight eyelashes. Your T-shirt still sticking out from under your sweater when you went back to sit in the room.

When *he* rose to complain in a dignified way of the fact that because of me, his career didn't look so bright any more, I gave up. I eliminated the sounds of voices and I just let go. What I had to do was simply wait for the day to end and leave. Not struggle. Because really. To say what. In a serious, low voice, *he* invoked love, his sorrow at being betrayed, his 'stupefaction' and his sadness to see me struggling with those perhaps suicidal thoughts that *he* had been suspecting 'for a few months', and at the moment *he* added these words, *he* lowered his voice, focused on what he was confiding to the judge. I turned to my lawyer. I was touched by his shining eyes, in fact, he had no experience, we were the same age, I felt like consoling him. I don't remember the conclusions of the judge, of the prosecutor, all that was totally unimportant. My lawyer picked up his papers nervously, with a shaking hand, and once the verdict was pronounced and I was definitively guilty, he asked to speak again, I must add something, he said, as if he were going to be banished from these halls for ever, 'the harm was already done when they turned my client into the guilty party.'

Once *he* had been officially declared innocent, *he* shook his lawyer's hand, smiling as if after a good tennis game and then turned on his cell, returning to real life, to appointments put off for a few hours at most.

A dark-haired volunteer from our Tuesday Evenings who repeated to us every week that it would be crazy to feel responsible for what had brought us there stammered I'm sorry I'm sorry and I reassured her that guilty and victim were only words. What difference did that make. You pulled me by the arm before I could talk to the dancers who had come to testify in my behalf along with the physical therapist of the company. He was irrelevant there in the Palais de Justice, ripped out of his world of sprains and dramas over tendinitis—I had opened the dustbin of my life to him and I apologized for it. His nose was red, he held my hand, massaging it gently, his mouth slightly open onto nothing, the hint of a silent smile.

Both of us walked towards the river without speaking. I couldn't tell you something like this: nothing would ever be able to fill up or cover what had just ended. And why I was crying that evening was not about being found guilty but about the impossibility of preserving anything from the stains that would spread over everything little by little, and the awareness that I would have to say farewell to so many things: to the coming spring, to Tchaikovsky on Sundays and white chocolate, to small pleasures like speeding down blinking boulevards on a bike in December or your imitations of my bow at the end of the *pas de quatre* in *Swan Lake*—all those things impossible to define. I realized that I could never be light or carefree again. And that, strangely, I was still very young.

Neither of us could ever figure out how to tell other people what happened to us. Our animal fears, you in the dark corners of the city, the deserted streets, the long corridors in the Métro with their blind turns, the parking garages, the parks at twilight. I, with any nice, considerate boy in a closed space, a friendly flat, or any face-to-face situation. Ever since *that night*, I calculated, I manoeuvred, cancelled the invitations made to my walled-in body, I asked you please come with me and you never smiled at that. We accepted each other's every mood because we knew where it was coming from; we saw dozens of films without grabbing each other's hand when a rape scene came up on the screen. We weren't going to commune with each other about it. I never saw you naked and you never saw me naked either. With our T-shirts, our fun sweaters, your scarves and my sweatshirts piled on top of one another, our bodies feel restored; we are almost normal now, superbly adorned. Occasionally, when we had a date together, seeing you walk towards me, very quickly I would wonder what you were like before. Who you were before. I find it unbearable to think of you begging, crying with your body shaking, thinking you're going to die.

The girls we were on Tuesdays, do they seem that far away to you, I ask barely a few weeks ago on a night you're having dinner at my place. You don't answer right away, as if you were attentively examining scars, their condition.

I know you disapprove of my isolation, which is lasting a little too long to your liking, and I also know that when I moved to the Island, some of our friends called it 'an escape'. I supposedly 'ran away' to the Island after my 'disappointment' at the court's decision on my case. The story. The thing. What happened.

THE ISLAND

It's absurd to give the smallest piece of land in the country the pretentious, romantic name 'Island'. Clasped between the river and the stream, from the place I'm in, not one path that could lead to me escapes my attention. You make fun of my penchant for small, closed-in spaces, secret passages, like the one that goes from the rue de Maubeuge to rue de Rochechouart in the ninth arrondissement, so narrow that the people who live in facing buildings could touch their respective fingertips just by sticking out their arms. I like your studio flat with only one window and no hallway. And also, without knowing if this could be put in the same category, your samples of perfume and creams, finishable things.

'You buy everything in small sizes to be sure you can run away with them, is that it?' you joke as you go through my handbag. I'm afraid of the invisible, afraid of what's behind it, of missing a sign, a clue, afraid of not seeing ahead of time.

When someone told you about an old lorry for sale in good condition, you called me, excited to have found a way to get me out of my one-room flat, something that would seem like an adventure. 'Let's take it let's take it! And if you can wait for me, we'll leave in two weeks. I'll read the maps and you drive, don't tell me you can't read a map! Hey, what're you paying for your place . . . three thousand euros?'

I hadn't left my place in two months, or hardly at all. You'd wave evenings at the cinema, your friends, even public forums at me, and now a trip to Romania, why not. I imagined high iron running-boards and driving sitting high over the other cars. In reality, the lorry was a very seventies van, sky blue. You had to go into contortions a little to get in but I knew right away that's where I wanted to stay for the time being. The little space contained a double bed and wooden cupboards in a tiny kitchen corner. I gave up my studio flat without even thinking, we'd see what happens. Leave the city, the fear of crossings where you can never see *the man* who might suddenly appear and, anyway, I hadn't gone anywhere in a long time. I left most of my books with you and at least thirty pairs of worn-out ballet shoes I'd held on to as souvenirs in roles I'd particularly liked. At that moment, I wasn't saying to myself I won't dance any more. I had just sprained my ankle but not too seriously, after a bout of lumbago that had kept me on my back for over two weeks. One thing after another. Movement was leaving me.

As the Election neared, the city was stiffening, bodies seemed to be savouring a certain brutal triumph in advance. We left the city in the spring, ready to drive to Bucharest. We had driven for hardly more than an hour when, as we were looking for a turn-off that would take us to the right road, I saw a police car in the rear-view mirror and, as in the worst TV series, it was signalling me with big, incongruous white headlights in broad daylight. I pulled over, overcome by a fit of nervous laughter, you leant your head towards the guy who was motioning me to lower the window, he must have thought you were crying, you were wiping your eyes.

'You seem . . .' he said to me, with the smug expression of having found the exact description of the offence, 'kind of lost.' I agreed, I had no idea where the turn-off we were looking for was. He then asked me to get out. I held out my passport, he took it with an 'OK, good' and went to his car 'to run a check'. You weren't laughing any more, you were standing to the side, we had been driving really slowly, nothing serious. He came back, asked what we were doing round here and how long I'd been in

France and what I did exactly. I looked him in the eye only intermittently, the way you hold your breath before entering a garbage shed. His two partners had got out of the car and were standing behind us, they exuded a massive contentment with being men, their thighs slightly spread apart, I imagined them tightening their belt buckle every morning, grossly aware of their warm organ. They felt like keeping us, this lasted over an hour, during which we remained careful not to offer them the slightest excuse. One of them joked about your long braids, 'I bet you like reggae,' and the other, when I spoke about dance, breathed out in a knowing tone, 'Oh . . . a dancer.' I was standing as straight as possible to raise a rampart of classical dance in front of the little hormonal sounds he was giving out, you must be very flexible, mademoiselle. Then, the one who was still holding my passport decided they were done and he gave it back to me, reminding me that 'You shouldn't slow down in front of a detention centre, mademoiselle.'

We started out again in silence, nothing serious, but neither of us could get rid of the uneasy feeling of having had to act nice, negotiating and smiling so we could get out of it faster.

About twenty minutes later, the van suddenly went silent, I drove its last few metres one way or another and parked it by the side of the road. A little bridge crossed a river with a name unknown to us. The guy we asked about the nearest garage and also where we were, exactly, seemed really sorry about the garage, it was quite far away, but to our left, the Island was almost uninhabited, we could leave the broken-down van there in the meantime. We were freezing, tired from not having travelled and having already stopped, the heater in the van smelt of liquorice and the simple fact that this guy had uttered the word Island seemed hilarious to us, as if everything in our aborted journey was becoming weirder by the minute.

We pushed the van through trees squeezed onto a very thin strip of land. I had avoided bodies, eyes and words for a long time but now it was love at first sight for the second time in less than a month. First my blue van, broken-down as it was, and then this river once we had passed the tiny, rusted locks, a permanent liquid presence that opened like a stage curtain onto those few little acres of desert with strange, mysterious birds—I knew nothing about birds—we were right next to an ornithological reserve.

That evening, we toasted the coming year. You decreed it a 'year without movement', a way of acknowledging the coming Election. We listened to Cat Power, you always pretend you're falling asleep when I put on Cat Power or Leonard Cohen, but now, sitting on the bed for our first evening in the van with a can of tuna in our hands, it was perfect. The next day, you succeeded in connecting the van to the low-tension electric box of the lock-keeper's house and then I walked you to the nearest train station, hardly five kilometres away.

'You'll need a dog,' you said as you strode briskly along, 'And I'll come next weekend.' Then I saw you were crying, although we'd spent such a sweet evening together and your braids fell out of your bun like a curtain of silence before your eyes, 'And if you get sick of your Island, kiddo, call me, come back. You'll live with me. My exiled little kiddo . . . Oh, shit.'

No one came to the Island except for a few high-school students who went there to smoke joints on a big tree trunk that blocked the road right near the van. During the first months, I'd walk all over the land every day—it didn't take long. I wanted to know when this or that building was built, for how many years the lock had no longer been used by little steamboats carrying logs. I would jot down those details, promising myself to learn the names of the trees and the algae, those regular stripes on the river. In autumn, the late morning sun would rush into the wind, the few leaves still hanging on the trees would swing, nodding their yellow heads, and the tree would become a stand for giant Post-its. The leaves like matte cloths waved round by Chinese acrobats, the silk Post-its of the Peking Opera. I would stay there, I would walk round the branches on the ground, I had nothing to do, all the time in the world. I would leave the tree, too invaded by those dark leaves that contradicted autumn, a sudden invasion of red, rustling butterflies, both beautiful and disturbing.

The crimson brick house that used to be the lock-keeper's has been empty since I've been here. The old paper mill was repainted last year, I heard a theatre company has just bought it. At night, the pale lighting of the soccer field with its bare lawn comes through the trees and mingles with the moon. The players' shouts reach me like wandering moans. Almost every day, I keep going to the spot where the path is lost in the brambles, just to see the water appear on both sides of the trees and feel myself at the prow of this piece of land. Two benches were built there, years ago no doubt, and one of them is lying upside down with all its weight of stone, like a silly animal on its back. Then the tall weeping willow closes it all out—the tree ends the land.

No one here talks to me. The village on the other side of the lock seems to have sent the island along the river. 'She counts the swans,' that's how they describe me. She counts the swans, she goes out to untangle the ferns. They shrug their shoulders, taking care to show how little interest they have in me. It is true that I can't help waiting for the moment when four swans cross one another in lines of two, better than the quadrilles of the Paris Opera and without the sharp sound of ballet shoes on the wooden floor.

I bought reams of paper and notebooks in the only store, a grocery–tobacconist's–post office. When the shopkeeper pointed out to me, like a cop who just found a particularly compromising clue, that no one round here bought as much paper from him, I explained: I do translations, you see, it's very convenient, I can work from a distance. I never ventured, or at least not yet, as far as the garage. I like the van the way it is, an immobile flat open to the sky, and I don't feel the need to go anywhere else.

You make fun of my reclusive life, how slow I am for all practical details, the shopping I put off as long as possible in the week because I'd have to cross the little bridge that separates me from the village and, as you say, 'Come back to the world, the real one!' When you come, you bring things that can't be found round here. 'Hey, kiddo, look—Russian tea! From the city!'

A car passes me, honks, the window's lowered, it goes 'Slu-u-u-t' because of the wind. Guys point at my electric blue leotard, this happened even today. And spy on our Sundays when you join me here, with the songs of Mariana Sadovska through the open window. Some of them still talk about the time when Giselle ended her charge at a pigeon in the moats of the old chateau of the neighbouring village after a gliding flight four metres long. We had walked forward very slowly, terrified of having to face the corpse of a dog, but then we spotted her, crawling to climb up the slope, knocked out, her eyes with stars round her head like in a Tex Avery cartoon, delighted with her astronautical experience.

The nearest thing to Dance in my life here, as you know, was that dog who wasn't called Giselle right away. She would prowl round the van every morning and back off, rolling mad eyes when I held out a little bowl of water to her. As soon as it got a little warmer, she would lie on her back in a position that made her look like a motionless toad, with her ears upside down on the grass, showing their pink inside. Thanks to my efforts, the dog finally answered to the name of Giselle and she stayed with me. You'll see, tomorrow morning, I would say when you came on weekends, I let her out over the flat, bare area there, and sometimes, even though there's no obstacle on the ground, she does *grands jetés*, I swear to God, real *grands jetés*. Perfect. And you really understand the importance of keeping your bust straight when you look at her. Head high, shoulders low! You would give me dubious looks as if I were sleepwalking in a hypnotic trance and you were trying to put me back to bed very quickly, '. . . Perfect *grands jetés* . . . Well! Giselle, come here, please, let's look for Prince Albr-r-r-r-echt outside.'[6]

She very much enjoyed going to what I call the spine of the island, where the rocks in the water pile up to form waterfalls. Jumping into the clumps of trees every day made her so deliriously happy that sometimes I felt like following her. I'd jump along after her, breaking away, then we'd come back to the van, and she would be calm now but I would be frustrated, unhappy to be thinking, still, about that, the sensation of leaping.

We had planned to begin repairs on the van after the New Year, and that's what we were discussing before your sudden death. The insulation is good and I'm never cold here, it's not humid either. But the engine has partly rusted now, we should have replaced it ages ago.

When you brought me the DVD of *Lola Montès* last year, we played the scene where Martine Carol first appears several times—she's blinded by an icy blue light, a livid, caged circus animal, indifferent to the men who queue up to put their hand on her to make sure she has surrendered and is now this degraded creature. What if we turned our van into something like the gypsy caravan Liszt and Lola Montès lived in, you suggested seriously later in the evening. Stretched out on a royal blue velvet sofa with a gilded frame, one arm sweetly tucked under her black hair, wearing a negligée also made of velvet, Lola Montès presents her bare feet for Franz Liszt to kiss. The beauty of Martine Carol's pale skin, made pink and fresh by Technicolor, is completely in her adorable feet, almost devoid of visible bones and tendons. Warm feet, elastic, celluloid flesh. '. . . No one would dream of kissing your feet,' you whispered to me, piercing my ribs with your bony elbow during the film,

---

6 Character in the ballet *Giselle*.

concurring with my own thought, which was shamefully inartistic. So when you set out to decorate and furnish the van with me, since I didn't have feet like Martine-Lola, you did all you could to make sure I too had blue velvet curtains at the windows and light blue cupboards along the walls. The little kitchen corner is covered with your finds: a Russian glass you found for me at the flea market to drink tea in, an old 1975 calendar, photos of beautiful girls with a mocking look in cowboy costume and a road map of the Balkans on which, one evening, I traced the route my family had travelled since the thirties.

When you're not here, my evenings are all alike and it doesn't really bother me. I needed to grow a new skin, close the doors behind me, I don't know—that isolation during the first months after the trial allowed me to breathe. I did an immense amount of reading. I finished all my books very quickly, and in the village, the bookstore sells only magazines. So I reread everything while waiting for you to bring me recent books. Then one evening, I had just put down *Dancing on My Grave*, the memoirs of the prima ballerina Gelsey Kirkland, when I felt the need to see her—to illustrate her words. When I told you about her, you had quite correctly summed her up as 'the antidote to Sylvie Guillem'. The career of Gelsey Kirkland, Balanchine's stubborn dancer, whom he chose when she was sixteen to embody the perfect baby ballerina, at first looks very much like Mademoiselle Non's career. What a marvellous little girl. Those flexible tendons, that obedient back . . . They all gather round Gelsey who executes what is asked of her, and faster, and better still. But now she's wondering. Would like to know why, have it explained to her. What is the meaning of this ballet, should Odile be seen as a swan, or, rather, isn't the bird-woman only the projection, the fantasy of the Prince who wants to enslave her (so think of dancing with your arms down, to show the impossibility of pulling away from the prince's domination). In order to dance, Gelsey wants to understand. So the masters begin to think that Gelsey's words are getting in the way of her body, all those sentences, appeals, her demands. Decidedly, Gelsey doesn't give as much joy as before, she frustrates the pleasure of those who want her to bend in silence. Raised to please, Gelsey does not frankly say no. She swallows the word the wrong way. Her refusals to embody the mute ballerina, to be a passive body, are billed to her one by one. In the last videos I find of her on the Web, she seems to be floating, her face looks haunted and her gestures lack precision. Her huge, staring eyes seem to have been pasted on the mask of a dying little girl with too much make-up, the parody of a broken object. Gelsey swallows only air and cocaine, she reels in starving emptiness and diligently tries to die on stage before turning thirty, amid the general indifference of the company that employs her and the indifference of her famous partner Baryshnikov.

Watching ballet instead of dancing it. I know what you think of that. All those movements made by others. But if you watch so many of them, it means you miss dancing, you argue. I can't explain to you anywhere else but here, by writing it, that my body has become a clumsy, mute envelope. The accumulation of wounds, these last years, is such that I can no longer forget the fear of hurting myself again. And I can no longer manage to mould my legs my buttocks the slit of my sex into tights and a leotard, mimic freedom with open arms, head thrown back, blood beating at the bottom of my belly.

For the moment, Émile, I write to you one day, I want to be forgotten, so I can slowly melt into the future where there are no more memories of *that event*.

So I don't know if dissecting videos of *Coppélia* every night is a step towards dancing again, I don't think so. But in a way you're right, I linger over those images of pirouettes, adagios and *arabesques penchées*, and they comfort me, because even as an ordinary spectator, I can retrieve my mother tongue, my sensory alphabet. Yet it is painful, the suffering of an exiled lover.

'Was she tired, was she depressed, stressed out, did she work out, too much perhaps, does she still smoke, how does she sleep, any recent shock or aggravations?'

We think. You who almost died once, a few years ago, what got into you, to die again suddenly one Saturday afternoon. What are you dying from?

Dying of exhaustion, dying of weariness, dying overcome by that fragile shame that has gripped us for months. Dying to do something different from this life, that's all. Dying for want of something to do, dying the way one hides. We're filled with regrets as if by thick water, invaded, shut in. It's because breathing here is no longer an everyday affair. Disjointed, jumbled up, invisibly dead, we're laid open to all kinds of devastation. In recent days, both of us have been living in suspension, like the others. The sensation of being seated, constantly, whatever you do, even on days when we'd walk briskly from one place to another, feeling forever seated, set down in this country and open to those mechanical arms that can open us up and methodically fill us with what is necessary to keep walking, with our bodies like dolls, like empty bags. And that fatigue you can't escape from, a numbness that starts in the spine, some days you accidentally catch yourself in a chance reflection and then what you see is a body hunched over as if under a rain of blows or silent orders. Immediately, you straighten up, swaggering again.

You often tell me about the emails you get, you're buried in messages all saying URGENT, full of lives to save and support, of figures, their ages are unbelievable, they go down like the temperature of a dying person, one seven-year-old or, these past few days, six months old. This one no longer has exclamation marks. So many messages of protest and indignation to sign, to circulate.

URGENT is an email URGENT is sent from an address that answers to no one. URGENT and IMPORTANT come before URGENT but behind **URGENT** or, better still, **URGENT!!!**

For the past two years now, we've been greeting each other like this: it's horrible/it's terrible/did you hear the latest/arrested yesterday/turned in by a neighbour/the police came into the school!/a kid of seven/a three-week-old baby couldn't possibly sign the deposition!

You turn yourself into the spokesperson weary of ever more serious, more brutal stories. You tell me about those bodies, those Others who are under fire, those girls and boys of the 'projects'. The ones who are mathematically defined by counting the degrees of separation from our correct US: first generation, second generation. You tell me about your friends stunned at having exhausted all possible adjectives. Oh, that game of badminton, that studious exchange of indignations over drinks before dinner, those 'Did you see what HE said?' 'THEY're going to vote that bill through and no one says a thing!' 'I can't believe it, it's incredible, how far will THEY go?' Then the chorus falls away gently and we go our separate ways, with the aftertaste of 'What's been happening to us since the Election' almost gone. We walk briskly to the Métro, troubled not to feel anything already, silently lost in those comfortable nights, of course THEY'll go as far as we let them, you tell me.

On the Island, I stupidly felt protected from the Election, as if I were invisible, as if from this little piece of abandoned land I could no longer belong to anything. I was alone in the van with Giselle, it was the first spring since I was guilty. The following week, I watched those videos of the night of the Election on the Internet, when in every city, dazed bodies were marching together in tight ranks, full of rage. The stubborn steps of fast-moving groups ducking like cats between the volleys of tear gas and the water cannons, those bodies bring tears to my eyes. When I call you, you don't answer, I imagine you running, your blood boiling, your anger like a fever.

When you arrive here the next Friday evening, you throw yourself down on the bunk, you feel you're on vacation on the Island and you close your eyes for a long time, exhausted. Holed up here cosily, we can hear only the sharp sound of the branches pulled by the wind, they rub against the window, you jump at every sound, but foxes don't climb on the roofs of vans to scratch them during the night.

AND WHY NOT PELICAN?

The moment I think of that keyword in the waiting room of the intensive care unit, it seems terrific. A word neither you nor I know much about but got into the habit of dressing with our suppositions.

There's what is said about him in the village, his being banished to the Département. The questions I don't dare ask him when he comes by to see me at the van, every day or almost. There are also the trap-words that brought him to the Island. Words pronounced in public. Which multiplied, as if on a split screen with epileptic subtitles waltzing round under it. Since the Election, we've been dissecting words, forcing them to open up still more, so they can vomit up more meaning, abyss-words of probabilities and assertions: verdicts, imprisonments and probations are brandished against them.

Our first encounter takes place on the days just after I've moved in. I don't hear him walking over the grass and when he knocks at the door, I don't answer, I freeze with my knees bent, motionless in my bed. Giselle looks at me in terror and flattens herself under the passenger seat. He leaves. When I go outside, I find a little piece of paper damp with dew on the windscreen: 'Hello. My lorry's behind the big weeping willow. If you want soup.' And the absence of a question mark after soup gives the impression that he's there with his soup every day, that it's his purpose on the Island. I find myself annoyed at this unexpected presence. I had imagined that on this Island

I would not have to face bodies any more. The next few days, when I go out walking, I carefully avoid the weeping willow and it's the grocer who first asks me if I've already met my 'neighbour'. His curiosity has the rancid, tenacious smell of the avid testimony given in front of TV cameras. 'You'll run into him! He never leaves. Doesn't have the right to . . .' The grocer is certainly waiting for me to ask the right question but, after all, I never leave the Island either. And when I hear steps approaching one morning, I get out of the van and sit on the steps in the sunlight. I reassure Giselle with one hand, she's afraid of any change in her daily routine. He walks slowly towards me, very tall, stepping carefully over the mole holes, which he seems to know by heart, a steaming bowl covered by a white plate in his hand. It's a chestnut velouté, he announces. He stoops down slowly and puts the plate next to me, like in thrillers when the hero puts his gun down in front of a psychopath to mollify him, then backs off a little. When he's further away, he waves to me, a funny gesture, I don't know if he means 'stop don't move', or 'hello'. Or perhaps it's a gesture of helplessness, as if to say what are we doing here.

When I describe the man I call the Pelican over the phone (because almost every day he brings me soups—sometimes extravagant soups—then desserts he presents to me in a cute way, 'a four o'clock snack'), you ask me if he's lived on the Island for a long time and I can't answer because we never really spoke to each other.

'No-o-o . . . Not one word? Oh, I get the picture . . . The ragged old guy with his bouillon under his arms and you waving to him, so you communicate in vegetables.'

One Saturday when you're with me in the van, the Pelican knocks gently on the door. Overexcited, you jump to let him in as if he were a fearful animal that could run away even before you see it. You come back to me with a bowl in your hand, completely disconcerted.

'. . . You could've told me! That's not how I pictured him! Really not. It's the soup thing, I was imagining . . .'

I can't say I wasn't struck by the physical appearance of the Pelican. His skin so pale, almost Victorian, and his hands— big, calm, dried-up hands. The hooded jackets he wears the way other people wear hats.

'But this guy has almost violet eyes, magnificent, it's so surreal, we're looking at a bearded Elizabeth Taylor, armed with a bowl of soup!' you sputter, choking over an oversized piece of bread stuck in your cheek.

Sometimes his face seems to shiver, can skin shiver like water, and that sweetness, I can't manage to describe his gaze because he's hardly set down his dish when already, like a spiral, his body turns away and he gently waves goodbye as he walks away. But you succeeded in engaging him in a real conversation one day. I think he showed you the text that got him this forced banishment, this petty regional exile. Sitting pensively on a step of the van with your arms crossed over your body, 'Hey, you know what he's accused of? Probable future subversive activity. It's not what he wrote, you see, it's what is "perhaps" contained in the words, interpretations . . .'

In the nineties, the Pelican belonged to a group of students 'conspiring against the security of the State', he smiles when he uses the official expression in front of you. A few of them were arrested, he among them, accused of having blown up a dozen places used by fascist groupuscules in different cities. The Pelican got out of jail at the beginning of last year. A reporter contacted him for an interview. To the question of whether he was sorry for what he did, the use of arms and explosives, the Pelican very cautiously replied that he did not have the right to express himself publicly on this topic and mentioned creative writing workshops he gave to young children based on a few lines by Maria Soudaïeva, which he recited to the reporter:

'A hundred, no, one thousand attempts to blow up the moon!'

'She-wolf children of the vain wake behind the ship, do not speak: strike!'

'She-wolf children under the flame, strike!'

The day after the interview appeared, he was summoned before the probation judge and banished to this Département, while waiting to hear if he would be incarcerated again for reading this poem, an act which constituted 'disturbing the peace and advocating armed struggle'.

True, neither of us had really paid attention to the measure that was passed right after the Election. They even made posters of it: 'PREVENT WHAT HAS ALREADY HAPPENED!' 'KNOW BEFORE KNOWING!' To be alert to the immediate future of these phrases, to dig into the content of the books, posters and films posted on the Internet and dissect them in order to grasp their supposedly hidden meanings and then arrest in a way they call preventive the people who might one day 'conspire against the security of the State'. The Pelican is the first person we meet who's been declared a probable guilty party in a future imagined for him.

And because of all that, his eyes, his soups, the waves of his hand and his poems, the Pelican is one of the best keywords I've found for you.

MONDAY

These last two days rise in front of my face when I wake up around six, I've hardly slept, lying fully dressed on your bed. I spent the evening at your place, looking for papers the hospital wants from us. On that Monday morning in January, I'm waiting for you, you're back at 36°. I imagine your body, stiff, harangued, unfolded, palpated and the very loud voice of the nurse commanding you to recognize unconnected words. I think: Sleeping Beauty, mango jam and 6381B, the entry code of your building. Would they have been better keywords. When my cell finally rings, between my hello and your mother's first word all possible phrases slip in, with their different combinations of death, of desolation, your body abandoned in ice throughout the night.

At least, your mother repeats. At least alive. But alive how, alive to what extent, the bets, the calculations, the little arrangements with what is bearable we can come up with. In case you can't speak any more. Or get up. So we picture ourselves surrounding you with sheets of paper and notebooks, catching signs, watching your expressions carefully. What if you don't recognize me.

But you thawed out wonderfully. Now you've just succeeded in being slowly born and they're pleased at how prompt you are to answer questions, she's opened her eyes and she can hear sounds, she's moving her arms well, her legs answer to stimuli, she knows it's winter and her name too.

No dead person is going through the door when I run into the ICU, only distraught couples with their foreheads glued to the window, and children they let play in the corridor, gently pushed away by the new Monday morning nurses. Your mother walks up to me, holds out her arms as if to a bride: I am your betrothed.

'She smiled at me!'

It seems like I'm about to go on stage, it must be those repeated mechanical gestures, that ritual we have to perform before we get to you, drying our hands with skin now rough from cleanliness in that airlock we go through before entering the silence of the re-animated, punctuated with regular electric breaths.

Your eyes are closed, at last. Cautiously, I sit at the edge of the bed. You wake up, look at me, but your gaze is no longer yours, as if cleansed of yourself, without fatigue. Is it all right to say hello to someone who is no longer dead, at last. That silence lasts a few moments, I don't dare move. Then I try, 'Hey, kiddo?'

And you softly breathe out, 'Hey . . . bitch.'

I don't know what to say to you, what could we say to each other, so I enumerate the people who're here and who've been waiting for you since Saturday. At each name, you open your eyes wide, 'Really?' You are sweet and lost. I talk to you about your 'great heart' and you smile. We hold hands. Lina sticks her head through the door, she strokes your forehead, you go back to sleep. When the word 'fainting spell' pops up, you emerge from your vague smiles, very surprised, frightened at not remembering your life. So as not to pronounce the words death and sudden, I turn that weekend into a whole adventure, beginning with our last meeting, but you have no memory of the pool on Saturday. 'Did we go there recently?' you ask, and then you go back to sleep.

The person we're watching over now is just sick, she's no longer that body with strange, half-closed eyes. Sitting by your side, we don't dare check the warmth of your feet. At your every gesture, at every sentence you utter, we glance quickly at the screens, those figures again, alert for signs of an accident, and what if your heart could no longer support your life. Around six, you wake up and look round you, visibly troubled by the setting. With a slightly dulled voice, damaged by the intubation of the night before, you seem to be looking for an image, a word, a lost association, then you observe, like the beginning of a diagnosis:

'I can't remember my flat any more, what's it like?'

Your surprise first, then your fear, are palpable—that quest for a setting you might be familiar with. You doze off. When you come back, you declare, as if reassured to be able to put a name on an image at least, 'You love her? Sylvie Guillem? Right?'

TUESDAY

A tear is rolling that has nothing to do with your face, quite calm this morning. I don't know what's making you cry. You take my hand, embarrassed; you don't know what's wrong with you; that tear falls from your eyes, punctuating your words. I move back so as not to get in your way with all those wires but you move your fingers forward over the sheet, you don't want us to let go. I missed you, I say, yes, even for three days, but you don't know you were absent for three days. And I can't tell you how violently I missed you—the prospect of your death. That unusual sentimentality makes you smile, you murmur 'I missed you, too, girl' and I know you don't know what you're saying, not completely. Then very quickly you start crying again, you stammer, 'I'm going to stop, I'll take hold of myself.' Nevertheless, you observe that it's me again who's making you cry. To help you, I suggest, 'Think of Mademoiselle Non,' but you're too exhausted to answer with the adequate gesture, you just suggest it with your wrist.

In a light tone, I tell you about those days you didn't live. Oh really, wow, you say, at the story of your death. I was in the same cafe as you, can you imagine, the same one. I'd like you to marvel at the fact that even in your sudden death I was at your side, inexplicably. But you are actually shattered by my cheap esotericism, I never saw you cry so much. You beg me to tell you the truth. You know you're going to die. Of cancer. You sit up on your pillows with difficulty, repeating, 'I'm going to die, right?'

I leave your room for a few moments, terribly upset by your fear and all that courage you're trying to summon in view of the hypothetical revelation of coming death. In the hallway, I run into the people who accompany you through streets and battered lives, they're waiting their turn to kiss you. I tell them. One of them answers me pensively, 'Tell her: of course you don't have cancer, it's just your heart that stops now and then out of the blue, you died two days ago, nothing to worry about.' I burst out laughing in front of the lift which opens onto a stretcher.

A nurse comes into your room with the newspaper you asked her for. She opens it in front of you, her finger on the photo of a triumphant man, 'Do you recognize him?' You smile at us, happy to please, 'Yes. And I totally trust him, he's great.' Back in the waiting room, I relate this, surprised at your sudden interest in American politics. One of your friends with whom you went through several anti-G8 summits remarks, 'OK, she's turned into a Democratic dope but at least she's not a racist. Think of it that way.'

As the afternoon wears on, you start mixing everything up, you have memory lapses but you also make things up. You have a hard time articulating, words seem a little mushy and bump round in your mouth. You come up with a wave of memories, you tell them to me, looking first pensive, then enthusiastic. You have memories of being a dancer and they're mine.

WEDNESDAY

I count: we've known each other for close to five years now. Sitting up straight and comfortably on your pillows, your braids tied in a pretty ponytail, you agree, trustingly. I freeze, I just made a mistake, perhaps a setback in your recovery, by bringing up our meeting. The circumstances are too heavy, an anchor that could capsize your hospital bed with the trial and those Tuesday Evenings, those girls like a sad blanket, a patchwork of all the possible forms of rape. A panel of snuffed-out bodies.

Because you're so new now in that horrible pinkish smock. When I leave the hospital I'd like them to keep you, enveloped in the smell of linoleum, radiators and meal-trays. At the thought of you back in life, in the streets of life, of dropping you out there with your sudden deaths lurking in your body, I feel overwhelmed with fatigue, a fatigue heavy with all those years piled up on us.

Those last days in the waiting room, like at a wedding, everyone recalled the way they met you, what they did with you. Some of them work with you. Other faces I haven't seen for two years, since I've been living on the Island. I can feel their embarrassment. Their fear of the words that might come out of my mouth—found guilty by the court—they tense up a little, prepare themselves to put on a suitable expression to what I might say about how we met. In a support group for girls. No. For victims of. No.

You get used to other people's fear, to their shame perspiring from their backs when they shrink imperceptibly inside their chairs. You can understand their implicit request not to just drop that anywhere, it seems sometimes that what I do not say is as embarrassing as a disease whose symptoms are too genital to be pronounced in public.

Thursday

When I get out of the lift, you welcome me with pirouettes. A tiny spiral in this long corridor, your pale satin pyjamas make you look like a Shirley MacLaine of the fifties in braids. Your electrodes are capsizing, you make the gesture of throwing a three-pointer into an imaginary basket as you walk back into your room, four days ago you were dead, three days ago you were frozen. I try not to repeat that constantly, not share with you that sensation of a fragile miracle, of threatening horror. But you are bursting with being alive, you talk more than ever, you love anyone who waves to you, you love Barack Obama and the *Basketball Magazine* I brought you, you love the sister of a friend who just called you, you ask for her address, you'll send a letter to tell her how much you love her, you admire my old Doc Martens you've known for years, you're stunned—you repeat that several times—by how handsome the doctors are in this unit. You make wordplays that aren't like you, childish and simple. You erect a joyful construction before me, mischievous barricades. I listen to you without daring to venture a question, any idea that might spoil all that. I can't tell what you still know of your life. We don't speak of what brought you to this room. We don't speak of what lies behind your windows, you don't ask me. I would like this moment to last, would like to join in, sleep with you in this crazy mood. I don't want anyone to bring you newspapers today, not one of us should come to you scratched up by the Outside. You are my absurd child.

You skip around on your bed, disconnected from most of your electric surveillance devices. In forty-eight hours, the doctors will be performing tests on you to understand what happened, how you could have died for four minutes. You are now part of those they call the 'lucky 0.5 per cent, survivors of sudden death'.

Your lively gestures weigh me down, I feel clumsy, hampered by the very recent memory of our daily fits of anger, of the weary despair of living in this aggressive country I now bear alone. For a few moments, a mean feeling gives me the urge to make lists of what you probably forgot. Then you cross your legs in your pyjamas, which are too big for you, someone knocks at the door, other friends come in, bring you sweets, books. They take up so much space with their relief that in the midst of them, at the end of the afternoon, you seem all at once small, frightened and lost. They force noise and life on you, when you yourself are coming back to us only intermittently.

When I leave you, my sadness is a puddle inside me I'm ashamed of, it's ridiculous to be so heavily slow when everyone is rejoicing round you. In reality, never since I have known you have you seemed so light. Never have I seen your face de-preoccupied. What can I tell you about your life or ours. When I reach the end of the escalator in the corridor of the Châtelet station around 7 p.m., I'm crying.

Friday

You call very early this morning and, without even saying hello, your first sentence—almost as if you were waking up at the moment you say these words—is:

'What am I doing here? Why am I here?'

I'm about to give a flippant answer to what I take for one of your jokes, when, from the anguish I can feel in your breath as you wait for my answer, I understand that you really don't know what you're doing in that hospital. So, as if to a child eager to hear the same story over and over, I tell you again, I look for the best way of skirting round death. And when I reach that huge piece of luck—the doctor present in the cafe at the moment you collapse, that magical fragility of your sur-vival—at the other end of the line, you are crying.

It's Friday.

In the afternoon, Lina brought you a very beautiful notebook, you thanked her, the three of us stayed together for a little while. Then she left and you slept. When you woke up, you looked at the notebook and said to me softly, 'Oh, it's so pretty . . . Is it yours?' You had no memory of Lina's visit.

Do you want me to bring you a book? Maybe the blue sweater I gave you at Christmas? We'll go to the Cinémath-èque as soon as you're better, I'll bring you the programme tomorrow. Those different topics of conversation, figurines I move round under your nose, perfumes, and what about that, mademoiselle, does that tell you something? You're not really sure what sweater I'm talking about but the Cinémathèque makes you smile. At least our delightful, cruel afternoons have stayed in your memory. Those occasional moments of hilarity when we sit down in the theatre and observe the regulars. Their insular customs, those bits of conversation we catch as we pass by, '. . . the 1934 version, of course!' and their trousers crumpled like pyjamas, grey from going from one film to another, and their hair plastered down and rumpled up at the back of their skulls, in keeping with the shape of the chair. And the screenings—Minelli, Mankiewicz, all those films we loved there, from which we emerged dazed with dreams, almost aching with beauty.

Friday Night

I write down the messages on your answering machine. That weekend, stunned silences and confused phrases, one after the other, interrupted by a mechanical 'Sun-day, at, noon'. Since your thaw, emotional voices hesitate to express their relief fully—but what message do you leave for a girl who finally isn't dead, and how. I sleep in your bed, eat on your plates and you, you remember my memories.

When you were dead, I said to myself, Émile, we've been pulling each other up to the level of life for all these years. And there's no and. No sequel to this remarkable feat.

That evening I couldn't stand being here alone any more and I went to the Cinémathèque.

I spoke to the girl both of us baptized the Little Girl at the End of the Lane. She's the one who approached me in the lobby after the screening, surprised to see me alone (as you can see, we're not the only ones who observe the people in the theatre . . .). When she introduced herself, her first name seemed invented to me, a pseudonym, so much does the nickname you gave her seem to fit her better.

She seemed extremely affected by the news that you were in hospital. Some people I talk to about it all are touched too, of course, but most of the time, I feel the words 'sudden death' and the general medical incomprehension about your 'attack' leads them to a sudden fear of the same thing happening to them, it's not really about you in your hospital bed.

She suggested we go for coffee, come on, let's sit down somewhere, we can't just split like that. We weren't really wrong when we imagined her literally living in the Cinémathèque—she comes here every day and sees at least two films, often three.

I don't remember if you had chosen 'Little Girl' because of the way she wore her hair, very long with short little bangs cut just above the eyebrows, her woollen tights (poor little orphan girl, do you remember her so-serious grey tights) or because of her red duffel coat, the same you had when you were a child. You observed, horrified, 'Did you see that? Her sleeves only go up to her elbows, maybe she hasn't taken it off since sixth grade . . .'

You're also the one who added to 'Little Girl', 'She's at the end of the lane, all right, the kid's at the end of the end in my opinion.' When she got a cup of coffee from the coffee machine before the show, we could see her hands shaking. And also that way she had of walking slightly tilted, slightly fearful, as if she were trying to avoid a gigantic slap. We noticed her in the autumn, we'd see her at whatever time the show we were going to was scheduled. She was always alone, and however nervous and distrustful she seemed even before she went into the theatre, as soon as she took her seat, she seemed to take it over as if it were made for her. She would pull out a notebook, a pen, we were sure she was a film student or even perhaps a director. An actress.

One evening, she turned round to us just before the film, 'Am I in the way?' concerned that she was too tall. She wore her hair high on her head in a kind of weird ponytail that added inches to her height, she undid the rubber band, 'There.' I had pointed out her feet to you—admirable. Smooth and pale in their little Spartan sandals of brown leather. The kind of feet that make me doubt I'm a woman. Women have smooth feet, soft and pale, or golden and brown. But the feet of a pirouette-worker, those rough feet of a worker bee determined to make them squeak over a floor whitened with rosin, those feet are sexless, and they're mine.

What a beautiful face. I felt embarrassed at my pleasure in detailing it.

Yesterday in the cafe, she talks non-stop. And then the waiter comes over, he gives us our change and she asks me if I ever had the impression that when you make change, all those people who give change back to us or we give change to are sensory stops, safeguards to put off suicides.

I answer no, not really, I'm not sure I get it. Obviously, she says, but not at all nastily. Because you don't know what normal life is, the horror of normal life, real life. Days. Like an apathetic notebook! Line after line crossed out, lists of things to do, to accomplish, so as not to lie down in whiteness—it's too vast. The little bullets of daily life whistling around our ears . . . And those choices! Those never-changing ceremonies . . . Work? Or . . . work? The kind that when you're paid for it answers the question: What about you, what do *you* do? Or, the wonderful, gracious career of a wife—'Darling, what are we doing this weekend'—oh, my career is a complete mess! I wasn't very good at handling the es-sen-tials! So, can't you see, she continues, the checkout girl at the supermarket? The tremendous importance of her hand?? On some days, touching the palm of the checkout girl with the tips of my fingers when I pay her is an emotional event! Something sweet. And often, you see, I feel like saying to her, just a second, Miss, leave me your unknown hand because life . . . hurts me and in fact it hurts you, too. Oh, and besides I'll lend you this book, it's a collection of little hurts . . . So, when I noticed that, I wondered if continuing to pay cash was, I don't know, a form of wisdom, the humility of submitting to my life, or if it was just pathetic to try to seek her palm with coins. And some of them know that very well, they wear gloves now! No more skin, no more contact! The checkout girls at the supermarket must be killed! OK. No, of course not. Be replaced by machines then! So things can become clear. No palm to be touched. Nothing. Facing what isn't there. Facing emptiness, to . . .

She seemed to be looking for the best possible word, a dried flower forgotten in a notebook, but which word. She made a vague gesture—wait a minute, I'll find it—then she gulped down her hot chocolate like a little girl out of breath. The Little Girl, you were right, is really at the end of the road.

When we left the cafe, she dug into her pocket and brought out a small rectangular piece of paper, the instructions for a prescription drug. These instructions—and she seemed almost emotional as she said it—never leave her. This thing may already—she repeated 'may' as if it wasn't completely sure yet—have saved her life.

SATURDAY

The doctor in charge of your unit speaks of consulting a shrink now that you are defrosted. He suggests a name, someone who officiates on the floor below, a specialist in 'dealing with the shock of sudden death syndrome in close friends and relatives'.

During the process of pressing charges, both of us had to undergo an evaluation by a psychiatrist designated to detect in our words the veracity of 'the story'. It was pretty much like a police interrogation, always seeing your sentences as moves in a game, advancing them one by one and staying alert for the question that would follow. Yours had a habit of squinting his eyes and asking in a low voice, 'But . . . in your childhood, was there nothing . . . similar?' as if what you were telling him were not sufficient to explain your 'post-traumatic' state.

As for me, I was aware that my case was 'difficult', as my lawyer would say, and at my first session, I apologized for it: 'It's sort of unusual . . . I know the aggressor.' He seemed delighted with my 'unusual', picking on it very quickly.

'. . . Why do you think it's "unusual", as you put it?' He heard 'unusual' as: 'You're not going to believe me but.' Or else 'unusual' as in: 'Wait, here's a story that isn't like the poor little complaints you're used to hearing all day long, mine is better.' There too, a probable diagnosis of megalomaniac mythomania. The overheated room blocked the sounds of the street outside with its muffled carpets, their thickness worn by words, by all that whining which had circulated in this room only interrupted by a report to fill out. At each session, I would examine the tips of my hair, cross and uncross my ankles while taking care to breathe rather softly, the time for both of us to be rid of my presence. I was there to try to persuade. In reality, those sessions confirmed my feeling that it would have been better if I had died—my case would have become clearer and credible at last.

Women who are merely raped do not arouse empathy. Since I've been living on the Island, I've seen more films than during the whole first part of my life. The best rape victims die, bleed, their head swings from right to left under the punches of a man with clenched jaws, they struggle with heart-rending screams for a few moments, then succumb like saints and regain their purity in extremis by gracefully leaving life. If there's no death, they have to be able to prove they've been tortured. Let them be disfigured. Burnt. But one simple penetration more or less in a sex made to be opened. What's that.

The report of the psychiatric expert concluded that I did present most of the symptoms of rape victims, each of them carefully graded on a scale from one to five. But no conclusion should be drawn from that. It seemed to him that I lacked confidence in myself, on the whole. Perhaps I was made psychologically vulnerable by my 'life choices' and my situation as an exile. He ended the session with these words: 'In short, it is difficult for me to reach a conclusion in this case.'

SATURDAY NIGHT

(When I began to take these notes, it seemed to me that as long as I kept writing you, you wouldn't die. My descriptions of what was happening to you without your being conscious manufactured a 'later' for you. If the encounter with the Little Girl is present in what should only have been the 'Diary of Your Unlived Days', it's because for the moment, I can't explain the following events to you in any other way than chronologically. This page was written on the evening of that same Saturday.)

I ran to shut myself up in the Cinémathèque. The Little Girl at the End of the Lane was there, in a navy blue dress (you'd find it perfect with her duffel coat, sleeves again too short), she complained of the onset of (these are her words) a 'happy migraine', an allusion to the four screenings in her day, Alain Tanner's *Messidor* being her last one.

'A psychiatrist specializing in close friends and relatives?' she asks me after the film, laughing almost hilariously when I tell her.

'I thought they all were! Specialists in parents, family, husband . . . The fulfilment of family love!'

Her own close relatives sentenced her to see a shrink and the one she calls her 'boyfriend' accompanies her to make sure she doesn't miss a session. What followed was a kind of monologue on psychiatrists and other 'guardians of the norm', you would have loved it.

'. . . Those guys wait for THE word, they dig into every-thing, they comb your silences attentively, you never know what there is to pick up in all that, a few dirty little mouldy secrets, childhood lice . . . Do you have to be . . . cured of everything?'

Then suddenly, she declares, 'Whereas I think it's since the Election that.'

'. . . That what?'

'I've been like that since the Election. Generic rage. Let's look into it . . . Hypnotized! I spend my time now watching out for what They do, what They say, what laws They pass. It's as if I were, I don't know, feeding on their shit, but fed any-way. I wait while hating myself for waiting. Well, no. It's more like: dumbfounded. I spend my time waiting for things to get even worse, with my mouth wide open to them. I've turned into a horrible . . . sewer!'

I think of our pact again—the pact we made together—to stop commenting on what's happening in this country, our refusal to passionately hate the Elected, that belching body of a belligerent puppet. That impression of being at the centre of a little whirlpool, churning regularly, all of us facing one another as we splash round, raising our hands to heaven, oh how horrible it is. That phoney theatricalized paralysis makes both of us feel like throwing up. So I liked the fact that she blamed the Election for her distress. That shows class.

I'm including the pages she left me when we arrived in front of your place.

Preamble to a Theory of Instructions (or of the Checkout Girl?)

'They tell me I have to do . . . Things. Apparently I don't seem to do anything, ever since I stopped working, that is, I . . . What do you do in life what are we doing tonight but it's . . . Real life, it's not mine, it doesn't . . . Sustain . . . my . . . my body any more . . . Well I . . .'

The doctor raised his head, waiting for the rest.

'. . . I think it's since the Election. It's. It's the triumph of the and-what-about-you-what-do-you-do, you see? Ah, he does things he . . . sorts out bodies! And I, I . . . look . . .'

'We can sum this up by saying that you can't . . . function any more?'

He didn't feel like biting at the Election but he was worried about my possible idleness.

'You need to do something, mademoiselle, you must become productive again, productive of your own life!'

I smiled, I was waiting for him to put his hand in front of his mouth, apologizing, what a joke, you saw the words we use, it's incredible, really, you see how we have to be vigilant, we are crushed, mademoiselle, crushed by the words we use. But he just finished writing out the prescription with a busy air, satisfied to find something for me to do, even if it was just to swallow. Then he explained that the tranquilizer he was adding would reduce the side effects of the first prescribed medication and would help me sleep. I crossed my legs under the chair.

'You need to talk too. To put all that into words. I'm giving you the address of a colleague, he's very good, very human.'

Recently, I've begun to see hidden alarms in words. I can almost physically feel my body being swallowed by words. Or no, maybe not, maybe it's just the opposite—words swallow me, so to speak. His 'very human', for instance, that label he put on the psychiatrist, well, that word gave me a little moment of stolen joy. Very human.

I came out of there with a prescription for a medication accompanied by a 'You don't have a choice any more now, you've got to take it.'

This medication is authorized in member states of the EURO-PEAN ECONOMIC AREA under the following names.

Symptoms such as agitation or difficulties in remaining seated or standing calmly.

Consult your physician immediately.

You may sometimes not notice the above-mentioned symptoms and consequently you may find it useful to ask a friend or relative to help you observe possible signs of change in your behaviour.

The first time I read these instructions, I tried to reason with myself, you should never read instructions, you know that, they would tell me when I mentioned it. Never look at descriptions of illnesses on the Internet either.

Come on. Cut the crap. Take them. Take them. Come on. Even the fact that I call people to talk to them at length about the instructions seemed to have become a symptom. I was hoping to find allies, hoping someone would wake up, that really was the point. In their patient silence, I could feel them wanting me to get over it, to stop worrying myself, maybe I was talking too loudly, all that racket about nothing. The instructions seemed to them what they were—instructions for taking a prescription drug. And that's all.

Every morning when I woke up, I tried to go over to their side. I had 'to do something'.

Come on, you can't stay like that. Why suffer. If you had a toothache you'd take something well your head's the same thing.

I would take the Instructions out of that great clean little box. Read again. The words of the Instructions were good, implacable words. They were pointing to me with a steady finger, they had chosen me as something to fix. They would know how. Every morning, my mother asked me if I had started. Every evening, my boyfriend asked me if I had finally started, really now. I would say no, I didn't. I'm still waiting a little. But what on earth are you waiting for, take them. Come on. Take them.

'I SEEK FAR MORE THAN I FIND, BUT I SOUGHT OUT PEOPLE WHO DID FIND.' (Sylvie Guillem)

But how do you live at night, every night, all alone in your van, asks the Little Girl at the End of the Lane. I felt like telling the exact truth, getting rid of it. At night, I go looking for new dance videos, searching the Web like you rummage through furniture, you can sometimes dig up a piece of an evening at the Opera or at the New York City Ballet you haven't tasted yet.

I always put on a headset for the sound. Can you imagine how absurd it is, I'm on an island where no one lives, in a van, in the middle of a forest. And I put on a headset. The first measures of the coda from *Don Quixote* ring out, the image is a little shaky, Baryshnikov holds out his hand, an invitation directed to the back of the stage, it's certainly the Marinsky theatre, you can clearly see the stage slanting in a way specific to Russian theatres. That slant is supposedly what makes Russian dancers seem so light, in suspension above the others.

Gelsey springs up rather than appears. You don't see her coming out on stage, she leaves that to those who take one step at a time. Gelsey doesn't know how to walk, she uses the ground, she cajoles the floor with her toes of satin and steel, implores it with the tip of her feet and then a stroke of her wrist closes the conversation, *déboulé déboulé, grande fourth.*

Oh, you dance? asks the Little Girl and I say, I did. I was a dancer.

At the moment, I'm looking for the 1977 *Nutcracker.*

To you, I have never really described the extent and the frequency of my Nostalgia Nights. I remain vague, talk to you about films. I'm afraid that if I mention those videos, you'll take advantage of it to go into your 'when are you going to start dancing again' number. For the moment, I sit back and watch.

In the videos, you can't hear the dancers panting, no picture follows the sweat that changes the colour of the leotards. Along the ribs first, right under the arms, and then, very quickly a thin line surrounds the breasts like a liquid bathing suit and finally covers them completely. The little drops in the delicate, light hair of the temples go round the ear and wind down the neck. On their backs, now, the stain spreads out and progresses down the vertebrae, stopped by the curve of the buttocks.

Dancing is not an occupation one gives up easily. Dance sticks to your body, you struggle to learn to hold yourself like normal people who don't dance and sag slightly, to go back to being a body again that can't do anything with itself. The rectilinear back must relearn to adopt the banal, soft curve of the backs of chairs, the feet that used to follow the exaggerated opening of the hips go back in parallel the way one falls back into line, one morning you stop tying up your hair in a bun pulled as tight as possible and, like a jewel you don't wear any more, your neck ends up abandoning that beautiful arrogance, that neck you used to feel alive all the way up to your hair, a sum of intelligent little bones.

I taught you to spot dancers in the street and you taught me what gives away French cops in plain clothes.

Sunday

Do you feel better, did you sleep well and did the doctor come by? Your 'yes' falls in the middle of my sentences, a frightened sparrow. Then, like a postscript without which a text would be incomplete, you inquire, 'But . . . what am I doing here?'

'You had a fainting spell last Saturday.'

'Really? A fainting spell?'

'They haven't found anything wrong with you for the moment. Your heart . . .'

You cut me off. '. . . which, I know, is filled with rays of light. *History of Cinema* . . . can you bring it to me?'

When I get there in the afternoon, you're surrounded by three people I don't know. You introduce them proudly, 'My boss came to see me, can you believe it,' but the woman you point to looks at you as if you just told a good joke, 'Oh no, I'm not your boss unfortunately,' she explodes, she's laughing too much and you smile, slightly embarrassed. The nurse corrects her, 'Your boss just left.'

You're eager to go back to being the girl we're waiting for you to be, you anticipate the fears of each of your visitors, you get up and throw yourself into something that looks vaguely like an *entrechat*. You're so merry now I'm afraid you'll start crying all of a sudden, like children who need rest. You announce—a queen who must not be contradicted—that you're beginning to remember things, no one asks what. The doctor draws me into the hall, we should work on your memory, the specialist suggests reading a newspaper article every day with you and seeing what you remember of it the next day. When I come back to your room, your friends have left.

Half out of your bed, you look as if you just put pink blush on your cheeks, you point at the young nurse writing down figures in a big notebook in front of you.

'She doesn't believe me! You tell her it's true . . . You remember when it was so cold, that Bulgarian family, the . . . the Valienkovs, who used to live in that horrible hotel for sixty euros a night, plus as a bonus you get cockroaches, mould and . . . what's the word . . . salmonella, no, it's . . . OK, a health hazard. So of course I opened the door of the empty flat in my parents' building with a crowbar! Yes! Right, kiddo? But her . . .' you point to me, 'With her arms of overcooked spaghetti, they're not . . . but her feet, hey, that's serious stuff! I'm telling you, she gave it a kick, she's Princess Hulk, that one!'

The nurse smiles at me, amused. Everything you say is rigorously correct, every detail true.

'And the super-famous writer, a pseudo-philosopher who lives upstairs, oh, he was there all right, I'm so-o-o liberal of course, I'm no racist but you're not going to, I hope, what are we going to do with *these people*, in his hideous pyjamas and on top of it he tried to take the material out of my hands! He was making annoying little noises, you remember, whine whine . . . OK you, back to bed! The flat was empty and now it's full, it's beautiful, it's Christmas. With a dancer's foot and a crow's bar.'

The nurse made a little reassuring wave in my direction as she went quietly out of the room. I sit down next to you without taking your hand, you're not so sick today. If this story from over five years ago is still with you, with all the details you gave of it, what remains from our Tuesdays.

Your words are labelled in a haphazard way. Some have lost their content and no longer mean anything to you, others, on the contrary, haven't moved, you get them out of your head joyfully, like that epic story told to the nurse uncensored. My boots seem new to you every morning and the story of your sudden death has no weight, it's nothing you can hold on to. I came up with a lightened version that seems to satisfy both of us. You were in the cafe, you lost consciousness, the doctor who was there in the cafe—I won't say kept you alive—reanimated you while waiting for the firemen, who brought you to the hospital. No coma nor frozen body in my summary.

You remember the dog, Giselle, who is trying for ever to sleep on a cushion too small for her, curled up like a snail, how she gets sad when a paw goes over the cushion because then she must recognize that her fantasized state of childhood has failed.

You talk about the Island, a lot, and about the van too but without mentioning that it no longer works. You rave about the colour of the Pelican's eyes as if we had just left him. About Sweden, where we met a few of your friends two summers ago, about the boat you take to go to an island hardly larger than mine today, Ingmarsö, so perfectly clean that when you take walks there, it's a little frightening and you can look for cigarette butts all along the path without finding a single one. About Mademoiselle Non and Gelsey Kirkland, 'so skinny', you make a face when you bring her up. About my first dance classes taken in silence and even the crêpes of Elisabeta the pianist, you can retrace everything. You're surprised that I've forgotten an evening of ballet that enchanted you at the Opera, years ago. You ask me if the programme of the Cinémathèque is good, you can't wait to go back there when you're better. Maybe, you say to me, yes, maybe I can see who that is but I don't have the feeling you remember the Little Girl at the End of the Lane.

When I mention your questionnaires, you stop me with a tired wave of the hand, let's talk about something else. Yes, you remember that weekend at the seaside with Bintou, the ten-year-old girl who lives in the building across the street from you. And all those bad pictures we took of her and us, she's almost absent from them, drowned and blurry. Because everything is set for white, you observe bitterly. You remember that lady on the beach who strokes her braided hair in wonderment and asks her where she's from. And Bintou who answers patiently 'from Paris, eighteenth arrondissement' three times in a row even when the woman bursts out laughing and constantly reformulates her question oh she's so adorable but where are you *really* from.

Puzzled, you tell me about that employee in a social surveillance agency who, one day when you're desperately trying to explain why your papers are late, keeps repeating to you, 'I'm taking note of your call. But your call will not. Stop. The process.'

WE ARE
THE BIRDS
OF THE
COMING
STORM
105

You ask if I couldn't bring you a chocolate cake 'since it's the only thing you know how to make, kiddo', you haven't forgotten. You say yes, what a question, I remember those kids very well—Anthony, Carina, Foulé—you're quiet for a moment and you pull your sheet up almost to your eyes, I don't know if it's because you're thinking of Miroslav who they found hanged in his cell, but that's all you say.

You ask me if I'm still afraid. Luckily, I wait for the end of your sentence before answering. The fear you're talking about, it's your own fear when you'd come to sleep with me in the van at the very beginning and you imagined us surrounded by animals and sly villagers. You're taking your fears for mine.

'Do you remember . . .' and right away I'm sorry I haven't weighed that phrase, that worried probe we subject you to so relentlessly.

'What?'

'The translation for the Afghan women, you know, the evening we went . . .' I don't know why I pick that as a test, maybe because it was hardly two weeks ago and we had come out of there carefree and chatty.

That evening, some of your girlfriends are welcoming two young Afghan women, members of RAWA, an underground organization of women in their country. Paris is a stop in their tour of Europe. They want to talk in English so as not to be at the mercy of the official interpreter of the embassy who has followed them everywhere ever since they arrived, they don't trust her. You asked me to translate. When I get there, the organizer shows me to a little room where they're resting. I was told about one 'Gena'. The young woman in a navy blue sweater and jeans who holds out her hand to me introduces herself as 'Sonah'. Later, they explain to me that since the Taliban are after her, she has to change her name all the time. Her smile seems strangely mechanical, a polite punctuation to hide her uneasiness under a polished veneer. She asks about her safety, are we ready to face a possible intervention by supporters of the Afghan regime. Wants to know who I am. Why I'm translating. For whom. I stammer that I'm no one, I often translate for money and here, as a favour for a friend, I point to you in the audience.

Gena/Sonah never lowers her head to look at her notes.

At times, my words get mixed up, I have to correct myself, while you—this image of you is so sweet it's like a little picture in a locket—you stare at me with that mixture of anxiety and pride, leaning forward, your face a little red, and your smile of encouragement gives me the impression of being in kindergarten on a stage in the end-of-the-year show.

Genah/Sonah holds a glass of water decorated with a manga figurine, her fingers nervously tracing the outline of a little armed siren while she says forcefully that the Afghans would rather die in a civil war than live with more than forty-one occupying countries on their land. '*Say that again, please*,' turning to me imperiously. I repeat in French. She would rather die.

After the discussion, when she thanks me, you and I are twelve years old, we want to write to her, bond with all that courage, go with her to Kabul, be extraordinary, but the hand she holds out pushes me away from her and her magnificent life—we leave with an anonymous e-mail address: 'Write that it's for Sonah, they'll know it's me.'

You have a very good memory of the Afghan woman in jeans forced to live in Pakistan to stay alive, who teaches little girls to read in the silence of clandestine flats, and you didn't forget either that when we left the hall, our excitement at having met her turned into sobered-up silence in the Métro. All that bravery, her pretty hands tense round her mustard glass during her recitation of figures and dead women. But us, what were *we* doing there?

WE ARE
THE BIRDS
OF THE
COMING
STORM
107

Today, we're not really sure what you're doing in that hospital, your only illness is having died a week ago for no reason and, in the morning, to no longer have much memory of what was said to you the day before. It seems to me that you don't miss what you no longer know. As if you had deliberately taken it out of your memory.

So I don't tell you that Pina Bausch and Merce Cunningham just died, now there's the year with no more movement for you, I don't tell you about the pages written by the Little Girl at the End of the Lane, who carries round Instructions for Anti-Depressants in her pocket and never takes them; the way you have of greeting me in the morning, smiling, so adolescent it's almost unsettling, it's a banner you wave in front of us all: No thanks, no.

It's snowing when I walk up the avenue. We grow old in fits and starts, perhaps, like that, as a small accomplice to censored keywords. I'm doing you the friendly honour of being a lousy TV programme, a sequined piece of entertainment, I don't say anything, don't persist. I don't lacerate your world, which you are rebuilding as a touching, glorious amusement park.

Year-Without-Movement-Métro-Saint-Ambroise-Trial-Election. I walk faster to feel the back of my thighs lengthen at the moment my heel hits the pavement. Outside, do you know that with night coming, it's hard to distinguish the expressions on the faces of the people walking quickly so they can finally—and they use this verb—'plop down' at home, aware of that burden, a body heavy with nothing, empty of damages swallowed like so much accepted abuse. The streetlights turn them into sad heaps, attentive not to brush against one another. In the Métro they slump down with their arms wrapped round their heads, protecting themselves from punches they do not return.

When I get out of the Métro, a message has appeared on my phone: 'How about you, kiddo? Your keywords?'

MONDAY

I tidied up inside the van this morning and every single thing I found on the floor or in my drawer takes me back to you. A few questionnaires. A poster in A4 format of *The Children's Hour* with the black-and-white faces of Shirley MacLaine and Audrey Hepburn, both of them uneasy and sharp, mice with tilted faces. And an old leaflet announcing the lecture of an English 'rape specialist'. We were eager to hear her, I was doing the translation and the newspapers spoke of a 'new way of looking at sexual violence'.

It is possible to avoid rape. The aggressor will choose for a victim a woman who, he thinks, will not defend herself. An aggressor can feel that. There are women who are rapeable and women who are not.

I pronounced those reassuring words. Instructions so as not to be among those little feverish bodies. In the audience, the girls were taking notes, studiously. I continued to translate even when you got up and left the room. When I could finally meet you outside, you were waiting for me, your back against a car and your arms crossed accusingly.

'Come on! Let's go back in.'

No, that's enough, Émile, we're leaving, it's OK, but you insisted, come on, let's ask her what she means by all that crap.

You looked me up and down. Then, quickly, you walked inside where the woman, the one who classified our bodies, was standing. Of course, I was expecting it, you got up on the stage. I just hoped you weren't going to point to me, wouldn't

WE ARE
THE BIRDS
OF THE
COMING
STORM

109

denounce me to the others. Almost calmly, you took a piece of paper out of your pocket, a note probably written outside. You then asked people to listen to you. The young Englishwoman turned to me, looking in my eyes for an explanation, a mocking wink in your direction, that little young woman is so funny, she's going to give us a speech, declaim something perhaps?

But your text made my heart—more uneven than at the end of a diagonal of *assemblés jetés*—go flying, your pale hands I know so well were transmitting their trembling to the paper they were holding but you were gripping the floor with all your weight. Not one of your sentences began with 'and yet' (as in: it happened to me and yet I was unrapeable). You simply enumerated our cases, the Tuesday Evening girls. Like an elegy. Your voice turned into the sound of sea spray, ocean swell, we saw you higher than we were, at the prow of a ship, calling into the wind. To my first name you added 'dancer / stands so straight' and that last point was a response to the specialist in anti-rape locks who had pointed to (bad!) 'that propensity women have to send the wrong signal, to stand slightly hunched over, unassertive, not sure of themselves on the street'. A few people in the room applauded, the others continued to turn their backs on you, showing their allegiance to that discovery—a new body on the market, unrapeable, which neither you nor I, nor the spider girl, nor any of the Tuesday Evening girls had thought of putting on.

When you came off the stage, a little group was sniggering quietly, with a look of pity for your clumsy body and that T-shirt hanging half out of your sweater, it gave you cute green coat-tails. Once we were out on the street, you gratified me with what you imagine to be an *entrechat* and the tip of your nose was pink when you wiped off your cheeks. We went to celebrate in my favourite vegetarian restaurant—'Come on, we won't eat anything that has a so-o-u-l,' you make fun of me when we're alone but you refuse to touch a chicken drumstick in public, 'Because it bugs me when they bug you.'

THE LITTLE GIRL AT THE END OF THE LANE

She was fired from her job for gross misconduct. She raises her eyes to heaven when she pronounces gr-r-oh-ss. Has no desire to specify what she did before, since that's just it, it was before and she doesn't do it any more. She says, 'I have no memories.'

When someone speaks to her, a waiter in a cafe, a home-less guy on an underground bench or I, she nods very quickly, greedy for bits of phrases to nibble on, 'Hmm.'

She steals. Everything at her place is stolen, everything, she smiles proudly and, with a big gesture, opens wide her red coat like an exhibitionist. Inside, she has sewn pockets to put her acquisitions away discreetly. She talks about practice, it's a matter of breath and a sport. Stealing so as not to be afraid, she says, not for the things themselves. She smiles and traces little circles in the grass with her hand when she describes her boyfriend's horrified look at her Theory of the Checkout Girl, 'as if he had to face a mistake, an embarrassing, stinking mis-take . . . stinking, yes, that's it, my words stink!'

I read the texts she holds out to me, some are recent and concern me, others not at all, she writes, accumulates, surren-ders to words so as not to be knocked over by them.

WE ARE
THE BIRDS
OF THE
COMING
STORM

111

Two days ago in this department store, a woman calls me by a first name that's not mine, though it sounds like it. When I don't react, she apologizes, she no longer remembers my exact name but does remember me. Very well. And with precise images, even.

She mentions two dinners in Paris where we supposedly met, common friends. Then, very quickly—and at that moment people shove us and come between us, impolitely reaching an arm across to grab a sweater or a skirt as if they were casually entering a bathroom—she confides to me that it's a good thing we ran into each other. Because something upsetting is happening to her, she'll have to go into treatment. She adds, 'But it's not really schizophrenia. No . . . Loneliness is eating away at me.'

Maybe she uses the words 'is weighing on me'. Extremely ill at ease, under the pretext that my cell is vibrating in my pocket, I leave the store. She screams my name on the pavement, where the stupid crowd is going from one shop window to another, magnetized. I am cowardly enough to keep the phone glued to my ear as if it could keep the ideas stored away inside my head from emptying out. She comes closer. Right next to me. She smiles sweetly at me, apologizing, 'You weren't really going to leave without saying goodbye, were you? I'm sorry . . . I can hear myself when I talk to you. That . . . haemorrhage of words scares me, too. I am so. Lonely.' She repeats this word pensively, without apparent pain, as if she were assessing the extent of the damages to a devastated house.

I relentlessly take note of this kind of rough spot in my day. Examining my fear. First the fear of the troubling superiority of that woman's brain since she has managed to put a name to my face, whereas even today, no image of her (and in what circumstances?) comes back to me. Then the other fear, a pathetic one—the fear of being 'with' her, of recognizing, in what she tells me, my own solitude, my own symptoms, only more advanced, stripped bare.

Something to compare to another event for the Theory of the Checkout Girl.

What do I think of this text, the Little Girl asks, and the reddish light of the cafe where we're the only customers transforms the hair escaping from her braid into a seventies halo.

She has arranged her braid in a Russian crown round her head, some sort of distinction. She stares at me and then, suddenly, draws closer, scraping her chair over the floor, my thigh is between hers. Apologizing in advance for her cold hands, she raises my hair. She smells of warm violets.

'Hey . . . You look a little—no, a lot—like Voltairine de Cleyre.'

I burst out laughing for the first time in a week. Voltairine. That name would really make you laugh. Why not Voltairette.

She lets go of my ponytail, embarrassed, 'What? People tell you that all the time, is that it? Yes, but I'm behind in everything . . . Six months ago, I didn't even know who she was . . .'

That evening I learn of the existence of a Voltairine de Cleyre, born in 1866, an American feminist anarchist. The Little Girl promises to bring me her lectures and poems one of these days, 'It'll blow you away,' she assures me.

So I'm going to call you Voltairine, if that's OK with you, Voltairine. Sorry to bury you under all these loose pages, as they used to say in high school. I found these pages last night and I'd like you to have them before we see each other again. Don't think you have to read everything, skip whatever bores you, it's just because of what I wrote about the two of you that I'm leaving you these words. Who knows.

WE ARE
THE BIRDS
OF THE
COMING
STORM
113

SO TOTALLY, FIERCELY HIGH SCHOOL

Serious side effects: suicide attempts; hostile, oppositional and angry behaviour.

The M&M's broke my heart, I kept repeating this phrase to myself on my way home, it made me laugh but I wiped my nose and eyes with my free hand, it was past one in the morning. When I opened the door, he moved back slightly on the couch to have a better overview of my person or perhaps because this body from which everything is flowing little by little (tears/blood/humours/ life) is slightly repulsive to him.

'But where are you coming from? And why do you look like that? Were you crying? Outside?'

Crying outside was a sure symptom of decline, I was crying outside and it rained every day, it was August and I had finally just been fired for gross misconduct and could put off looking for a job until at least autumn, in reality, I had nothing to do all day long, except escape from the chemical injunctions of my family, come on take them take them. I didn't bring up the Cinémathèque much any more to people who were worried about my non-schedule. To confess that I was spending all my afternoons there was certainly a thing that could have figured in the Instructions.

'The Cinémathèque? That must be a little . . . austere for you at this time, don't you think? Why don't you go watch a film at a regular cinema instead?' he had said to me when he saw the programme for the month of August posted on the fridge, schedules underlined, reassuring, at least two films I wanted to see every day.

The Ghost and Mrs. Muir, Summer with Monika, The Spirit of the Hive, Badlands, The Hired Hand, The Hussy, The Apartment, Cria Cuervos, Messidor, The Effect of Gamma Rays on Man-in-the-Moon Marigolds, Some Came Running.

The lawn all round the Cinémathèque was dry, wild, sparse and undefined. That was fine with me. The theatre, full of urban defectors in apnea, like me. Before they sat down, they would look for a seat like dogs turning on their old blanket and crumpling it with their paw to make it more familiar. Then, once they had settled down, they'd put away the book they were reading in their bags, check several times that their cell was turned off, reread the programme they already seemed to know like a prayer or a recipe. Young women, couples with the same grey, crumpled trousers; pale, with thick, dry, tousled hair. The air conditioning in the theatre spared me, allowed me to think of nothing. I didn't know anyone and we didn't say hello to each other. So many people in the audience came there alone that no one noticed me. I hoped that they, on the other hand, didn't realize I was observing them. They would all take a lot of notes before and after the screening.

But those girls stood out a little, they made me think of film-lovers happy to be there for the summer who would go back to the big theatres as soon as the fall blockbusters were advertised. Once, they sat down just behind me and the knees of the tall blonde with very long hair were pushing gently against my shoulder blades, an intermittent massage.

That evening, the evening of the M&Ms, the shorter one began by spilling her drink (drinks were only allowed in the lobby) before the film. A whole commotion ensued, with Kleenex asked of neighbours, giggles and anxious looks towards us, that caste with severe authority. And then the tall blonde made a meticulous selection in her M&Ms. She sorted them out, methodically swallowing the red, yellow and brown ones. When she only had green ones left, she gave them to her friend who thanked her with a calm smile. That gesture emptied me out, rejected me into my nothingness filled with the palms of indifferent checkout girls. Someone. Who would protect my absurd manias. Who would not be anxiously watching out for them, brandishing the box of antidepressants at the slightest suspicion.

After the screening, I got back on my bike. Everything was going off the rails, even the road, my tears, disciplined at first, right cheek, left cheek, were totally out of control. I was holding the bike with one hand, trying to move forward anyway but the wheels were bumping into my calves. Finally I sat down on the kerb with the bike lying next to me. Crying at home had become dangerous—all it took for him to brandish the box of the Instructions was bright eyes. See? Come on . . . Take them!

My tears didn't sort anything out really, they just carried away heaps of pieces of me, all tangled up and useless. Such pain. It's not just that I longed for an elbow touching mine on the armrest of the Cinémathèque, no, after all, if that was the only thing wrong, I did have the elbow of the man I still called my boyfriend,

WE ARE
THE BIRDS
OF THE
COMING
STORM

115

despite my screams of the past few weeks, the Chinese teapot thrown on the floor and sometimes insults too. What left me sitting on a pavement that night was the way the elbows of those two girls were arranged. Naturally, without pushing each other, almost ergonomically. I saw them sharing the armrest in a way that signalled braided love, so well intertwined that it didn't even look like love—that love just goes forward simply, almost stiff in its nakedness.

When I imagined how they met, I thought everything had surely begun in high school. I could see them painting together perhaps, I don't know why, on the other hand, I couldn't imagine them pushing baby carriages side by side. There was something so totally, fiercely high school in their way of coming here at all hours of the day or night with their plastic bag full of soda cans and M&Ms.

Sometimes, it's only about films, the ones we both go see after I leave the hospital:

The colours of Technicolor send me into psychotropic states! The purple of the curtains and that lilac in the corner of the room echoing Lauren Bacall's bluish gloves. And the walnut brown of her thick hair, probably waved and lustred. They make you think of a musical movement, an adorable animal. I don't remember that Douglas Sirk film where diamond drops rain down next to the names during the opening credits but often I find I can bear the world (and what it sells off, dilapidates and spits out) only because of Douglas Sirk and his diamond-shaped tears carefully wrapped in squares of purple velvet. And I would like to say to you, 'What's funny is that, on the one hand, I don't feel so good and, on the other, I feel just great.'

And you will conclude, 'That's because you're going a little crazy.' (*Messidor*, Alain Tanner.)

PS. I'm enclosing this little note cinephilically yours (I don't have any more envelopes and I want to give it to you right away) in a piece of paper you can read later, too (nothing is wasted!) if you wish.

The 'envelope' of the note is in fact printed on both sides:

It's the Election, I repeat without convincing them. I should specify. It's their faces putting on an air of consternation during dinners the way you grab a poverty-stricken child in front of a camera, that way they have of thinking like academic economists, those sententious phrases: 'The situation of this country is . . .', 'The main danger is China' or 'It is obvious that Islam is a major threat.' The Election is their symptom and I, I'm really sick. Take them.

Even more than that man, the elected President, it's that ballet of afflictions that makes me sick. Their 'with what's happening to us now'. Oh, that choice of delicate words, as delicate as an illness, a dangerous, cruel typhoon that's supposedly devastating the country. A letter that supposedly reached us by mistake. Everything that's taking place now is not *happening* to us, we've known it, we've seen it being built up for years. *What's happening to us, what's hitting us.* Those words are therapy, group consolation they exchange to persuade themselves that they have, like valiant doctors in TV soaps, 'tried everything' but unfortunately.

One night, after I'd left an intelligently cynical dinner of young people, I was sitting on the pavement (again!) first making fun of their exchanges, oh those serious voices, those conventional worries *how far will it go pretty soon we won't be in a democracy you know*, but soon the relief of my laughter was exhausted and I began to moan aloud out of pain and helplessness, a ridiculous urban mourner. My boyfriend was trying to pull me up—the pavement was cold, I was going to get my clothes wet, you're really scary you know, and then I pushed him so hard he staggered in the road, 'OK, that's enough, you're a complete mess, you've got to take them. You're just impossible.'

WE ARE
THE BIRDS
OF THE
COMING
STORM

117

PS.

The other night as I was walking up my street, a pigeon was lying on its back in front of the Greek grocery. Half dead, it was mechanically moving a claw, in slow spasms. People would walk by with their arms full of groceries (enough to fill their bodies for the weekend!) and that recumbent bird, belly up, preparing to die, was the only noisy, living thing in the street. First I cursed my sentimentalism, hey, some animal is dying, so what. I kept walking, barely a few steps. Then I told myself that this dying body had to be picked up. Now I'm walking back, and then—but only a few moments had gone by—as if I had made up the whole thing—it was gone, cleaned off the pavement, not a trace of blood. It is out of the question to die these days, flat on your back, while the others busily come and go and come and go.

It is sometimes said that events accelerate. Not this time. With her, from the very beginning, everything has seemed precipitous to me, quick. We talk in one of the lobbies of the Cinémathèque, then in a cafe, then I read pages and pages that come out like news reports, then she comes for the first time to visit me on the Island.

Her red duffel coat covers a flared black-and-white chequered woollen skirt, and her little short-sleeved sweater is so worn that in some places the cloth isn't really black any more. Only her shoes seemed to have anticipated the outing, good, solid clodhoppers. She touches everything in the van, a child at Christmastime, points at the little blue sky you made for me, the absurd crocheted doily with a circled A embroidered on it particularly enchants her. We remain seated on the bed for a good while, talking. The skin of her pale arms is dry, she touches it constantly, as if she hopes to soften it. Her nails are so bitten down that her fingertips are reddened from it; her very blue eyes seem to wash off on my peripheral vision, the rest of the van matches their colour. As I look at her face completely free of make-up, a genuine skin, with texture, a tiny red pimple on her cheek seems important and almost beautiful to me. I can already hear you deciding that I'm 'in love'.

I show her around, you know the itinerary. First the official reception path that trails through the forest narrowing the more weeping willows you pass and leading to the tip of the Island. Then, in transversal mode, you walk by the empty paper mill and the rusted miniature lock on the river. We walk

WE ARE
THE BIRDS
OF THE
COMING
STORM

119

along the riverbank, pushing away the branches with our hands, no more path traced out there. Without Giselle, the walk is not as spirited, still lovely, but too silent probably. Sometimes the leaning trees frighten me a little. Giselle used to go through the thickets, coming out of them with thorns stuck in her ears, a little breathless martyr, I thought she was in front of me but she'd already had the time to go back and forth twice and would come charging out of the river, skinny and trembling, overjoyed to find me again after those long minutes of separation.

'Are those meringue flowers?' asks the Little Girl, pointing to those fragile things trembling in the light. I know nothing about botany, but my ignorance after almost two years here seems hard to confess. I nod. Then she plants herself in front of me and puts her hands on my shoulders, for a moment I think she's going to draw me into a downy round dance in the sunlight.

'But meringue flowers don't exist, Voltairine! I'll have to drown you in the river, you can't be trusted! Come, Léopoldine, be brave.'

Later, in the van, she asks, 'If I sing you something, can you dance to it?' I say, 'I don't dance any more,' like announcing that the store is empty.

She takes off her hiking boots caked with mud and stretches out on my bed, her tangled hair forming commas on her shoulders.

'I won't ask you "the reason why", they're phoney words, "the reason why". You rarely give up something important for a "reason", for something, right? So . . . For whom do you no longer dance? Or for when, too, that's it, for when . . .'

I swept away all that without answering, dodging the question with 'I'll write you a letter.'

She breathes out, lightly. 'Nothing. Nothing and nothing. Nothing, Voltairine says, nothing,' she smiles. Then adds, humming the air from *Sleeping Beauty*, 'Sleep, sleep . . . until her time to wake has come.'

I offer an explanation, raising my foot towards her, 'Sprain. Right, three years ago, then left. Too much looseness in the joints. Lumbago, of course. Chronic tendinitis in the left groin,' I pointed to my thigh. 'Muscle strains don't count, they're too routine.'

The Little Girl stared at me from under her fringes, 'Oh . . . OK, I see . . . Crippled and mute . . . A real Brontë Sisters heroine . . . Watch out. An ugly cousin resents you, your beauty torments her. One night, she will throw you out of the window of your room and you won't be able to cry for help, the governess is in cahoots with her.'

We made ourselves slices of bread with powdered chocolate, I don't have anything else that's very festive in the van these days. Half choking, she tells me in a voice dried up by the bread-and-cocoa mixture, 'Hmm . . . So—three films a day minimum, as you already know.'

I didn't have the time to point out her obsession with the hands of checkout girls too, odder to me than her voracious appetite for fairy tales, when she interrupted me to add to the clinical description of her case, 'And when film-makers die, oh . . . You have no idea how sick it makes me feel. Sometimes I'm afraid there won't be enough watchable films!' Then suddenly straightening up, she says, 'Unless I change my style soon . . . And stop watching films.'

From her bag (an old, scraped leather bag, a schoolgirl's briefcase or a doctor's bag from the fifties), she roots out a red notebook with its spirals all twisted. Turns the pages until she comes upon this one, which she reads to me, interrupting herself, glancing at me after every sentence as if she expected me to grade her.

WE ARE
THE BIRDS
OF THE
COMING
STORM

121

Vomit out what they're stuffing me with, their blueprint for life. Love department. Work department. Leisure department. When I question them, they enjoin me to consult a physician. They put me under Instructions. They talk constantly to me of 'life'. I recognize nothing that can sustain my body in their definition of 'life'. I conclude from this that I am not living in life.

I am beginning to realize that I am exiled from my sex. A voluntary exile. In armed struggle, in resistance. Against the woman I should have been. The real life I should have led, a life of round, clear fingernails, fully equipped kitchens, stretched-out bellies ready to be emptied, sexes just moist enough, ready to be spread apart, of wooden spoons carefully drying in the dish rack, hair smoothed with silicone. Of clever laughs and charming looks. Overbooked early weekdays—it's so stressful, I'm running round all the time. Concern for your breath and panty bottoms how to keep your underwear absolutely WHITE. Vocal cords tamed down since adolescence, shouts and jumps in volume corrected one by one, how vulgar! You're like a bulldozer, you're so . . . brusque, they tell me. Exiled from that desire (impaled in us) to be bought, which goes so well with being hurt about not being bought (he didn't call me back!!!).

'I don't want to join the herd, I don't want to lose myself, I don't want to forget myself, I don't want to be their doormat. I love myself as the girl I am. I want to be a grave jutting out over the sea. An ebony virgin is watching inside me. I want to be honest with her,' writes Violette Leduc.

I'm so afraid, Voltairine, that they'll take me back, that they'll snatch away my desire to wiggle out of my biological destiny . . .

You want me to keep going or are you scared now, asks the Little Girl at the End of the Lane, her cheeks all pink, as if she had just caught a bit of fresh air and health. No no no, she says as she avoids the mole-holes, I-do-not-want-to! Join the herd. I want . . . To tra-vel light, hey, that's a good epitaph too,

'*Consult your physician immediately . . .*' that's what you think, right? And I love you so much, Voltairine . . .' And right away: 'Oh! I must I must I must tell you about the Haymarket, Voltairine de Cleyre and the Haymarket.'

It's already dark when we go through the little village stuck to the Island, the show is at 7 p.m., and she's sorry but that film—she doesn't want to miss it. On the way to the station, she says nothing. Our steps make a clock-like rhythmic score, intermingled rhythms: tum/ta/tum/ta/tum/ta (*posé-pas-de-bourrée-assemblé-allegro*).

I don't know if you remember the purple-and-orange lighting in front of the Cinémathèque, those carnival Japanese lanterns, a calm, little path before the white, aggressive light of the city streetlamps. We were, the Little Girl and I, in those provisional gleams, and from the end of the park a slow, sombre music reached us—descending, cavernous notes played by an orchestra of fake synthetic violins. When we drew nearer, intrigued, we saw that the merry-go-round, the one that never works, was turning. Four or five children were sitting on pink pigs, a horse or a rigid deer. Adding to that morbid music was a kind of rhythmic framework composed of the clicking and squeaking of the gears in the merry-go-round's machinery. The children were intimidated and didn't move, their faces serious without being sad, little anxious vampires. We remained standing there for a good while, smiling reassuringly at the children. They looked at us as if they couldn't see us, enchanted by their mechanical night.

Then we followed the river for a long time in the night, the same river that goes through the Island. We took the big wooden footbridge that leads to the thirteenth arrondissement. Then, above the water, the Little Girl leant down towards the empty space, so far that I wondered for a moment if I should intervene. When I got near her, she was quietly repeating these two lines from the film we had just seen:

WE ARE
THE BIRDS
OF THE
COMING
STORM

123

'Oh . . . how close happiness is . . . Oh how far off happiness is . . .'

At the moment we parted, she hugged me, furtive and embarrassed to leave me yet another text. She closes her hand over mine, holding the two A4 sheets of paper.

The greatest adventures of women are lived between four walls—home, gym, offices, department stores or in that body always tightened and firmed up by diets.

'Home' . . . those walls, those little bits of decoration like so many failed attempts to escape. The graveyard of desires. The photo of me on my sixteenth birthday, surrounded by my best friends. We had hitch-hiked to the Pyrenees to go climbing. I'm afraid I'll talk about that week again one day in a voice laden with longing and melancholy. We'd talk loudly on the street, a line of four, our bodies bumping into one another, but we didn't want to retreat on the pavement. Our vows never to become those girls who swallowed everything, the most popular girls with the boys in the class.

The night before last, with the door locked, the weight of that reasonably reinforced door—all that seemed to me pitifully sad. That door was closed to what. Those locks protecting what. Then movement surged up in me like an orgasm on the way. I could feel how shut in that flat was and the numbing heat like a dirty, deleterious fate and the locks sheltering two stupid bodies and their satisfied happiness to be going to bed 'early this evening to be in shape tomorrow'. To have dinner face to face. To chew things for a long time as if it were an activity, I try not to dwell on the mouth sounds, the sounds of a loutish body.

I tried to turn all that into a dialogue. What about you, don't you feel that urge to escape from.

He kept repeating: what, escape from what, and the more his words were repeated, the more the mouth that repeated them

seemed to me an automaton out of whack: fromwhatfromwhat-
fromwhattellmefromwhatfromwhat.

All that ended with 'Come on, now, take them.'

They all make improvements to their houses, all of them. Sometimes, I wonder what they're preparing for, the arrival of what
messiah. And now the whole country's madly into it, repainting,
remodelling bedrooms, kitchens, an obsession with nooks and
other nests and burrows. They enjoy acting as if they had to make
everything with their own hands. Invent, imagine the best way of
being tightly held and cosy. Like old infants wriggling round
because they're warmer.

Soon they'll go from my-home to our-home, that 'our' they
use like a visiting card.

Our-home right down to the viscera. The intestinal passion of
that 'our-home'. A passion they put into it, inside, cooking slowly,
coddled for hours at a time, the passion for origins. National
origin. But what region does this dish come from. Proud, emotional memories of their regions like so many little intestinal flags.
I'm from Burgundy, but post-central Burgundy, actually, it's not
the same thing. And the attention they give to everything 'going
down' well, the public announcement of the activities of their
belly—for me, onions don't go down so well, I can't digest 'em.
And now you're the guest of honour of flatulence, as you will be
later of their procreative attempts, when with a little serious and
silly smile, they announce to you that they're 'going to start a
baby'. Kidnapping you, throwing you into their unknown, moist
bed, making you a witness of their attempt at human production.
And you'll have to comment on their new 'project' the way their
trip to India was commented on the previous summer, tell it in
detail again, re-evaluate it taking account of the disappointments,
'still nothing' (and in those cases, the woman will give a preoccu-
pied sigh and her partner in this project will lower his head, guilty
of that still nothing).

Their efficient productive-love, a highway of conscientiously manufactured babies, whereas love produces nothing but sparks (unforgettable, sometimes . . .).

Oh, Voltairine, please, let's not be from here. No 'our-home' between us. Instant wandering for all women! And let's get to work on a Declaration of Un-descendants! We would affirm our not wanting to descend from anything or anyone. We would rejoice at being the children of words, of ideas that keep you warm, ideas we invent. We would read Guyotat: 'The reduction of affect to the little human zone that is the family, and worse still, afterward, to the couple, is something terrifying to me. One should be able to live with all of humanity.'

You may sometimes not notice the above-mentioned symptoms and consequently you may find it useful to ask a friend or relative to help you observe possible signs of change in your behaviour.

WE ARE
THE BIRDS
OF THE
COMING
STORM

127

TUESDAY

At the beginning of this dream, I'm in a dance studio. A barre
runs along the walls facing the mirrors. I stretch out on the
floor to warm up and it's so real, so incredibly precise, I can
feel that pain in the groin I know so well, my stiffened tendon
when I open my legs in a facial split.

When the teacher comes in (he doesn't remind me of anyone I know), he announces that today we'll dance to a 'wonderful' piece of music, he ceaselessly repeats it's wonderful, it's
wonderful. He begins to show the steps. I raise my hand like
at school to tell him there's no music, he's wrong. You appear
next to me, you seem very concentrated on your movements
but you're parodying them with weird little faces. You indicate
that I should be quiet with a strange, pantomimed, exaggerated gesture. The silence in which we are dancing turns little
by little into a soundtrack with music of a somewhat metallic
nature, horrible, grinding sounds, a tangle of asthmatic
breaths. I keep trying to make myself heard by both you and
the teacher. To point out that it isn't the 'wonderful' piece he'd
announced but you ignore me, I can only see one side of your
face now, you refuse to turn your face to me and suddenly I
see that you're dancing with your eyes half-closed, as they
were when you were in a coma ten days ago. Instead of feeling
sorrow, I feel rising anger, a terrible hatred at your ignorance.
The way you both have of supporting each other's blindness.
So I grab a teapot and throw it on the floor with both hands.
You open your eyes and say, 'What are you doing there?' You

don't say, 'What are you doing here?'—no. 'Here' turns it into a different question from yours, an ordinary one. I fall on my knees, silent sobs take over my whole body, stifling me.

When I woke up, I tried to see each of you as you really are—the Little Girl, with her anger, breaking things in public, which she explains as a sign of her inability to get her boyfriend and her family to listen to her. You, perhaps, with the silent request I can perceive in your present good mood, not to talk to you of anything that is not 'wonderful'.

When I told you my dream over the phone this morning, you laughed and then you added, 'You know, don't you? . . . What I'm doing here. You know and you don't dare to tell me. That's why you're trying to make me laugh with your dreams, right.'

When I get to the hospital, they're checking the visitors' IDs. A queue has formed, we wait, like at the airport. A woman asks for explanations, it's only a hospital, why are they checking. And in the weary bodies surrounding me there is that perceptible shrinking, that stiffness in their muscles—too short, not used to movement—I can feel all those bodies added together retracting under their coats, as far as possible from the woman who just broke the charm of diligent obedience, that woman who demands to know what we're doing here, showing our ID to the cops in front of a hospital.

But you are fine. Your heart is perfect. There is no medical explanation for your sudden death. But we can't just leave you like that, adds the doctor who's going over the tests. Science imagines a hypothetical future in which there is only a very small chance that your heart will stop again, one day, for no reason. That future will have to be taken into account and your heart lined up with a permanent monitor. This doctor (you continue to find him incredibly handsome every morning) uses the words of an utterly unabashed inspector: surveillance, watcher, sounding the alarm. They're going to put in a defibrillator.

'Did you tell her?'

'Not yet, the decision has just been made. It's a very small procedure. But unfortunately, afterwards, certain things will be out of bounds for her. Dance, at her level, for example, with the danger of falls or shocks to the device, that will no longer be possible.'

At her level, I repeat, without fully understanding what he's talking about. Then he talks to me gravely about the end of your career as a professional dancer. I don't correct him, I don't say no, that's not her, it's me.

I don't ask him the other question either, to find out when my answers to your 'What am I doing here' will lodge in your memory instead of disappearing, as if they were still not the ones you were expecting.

You have dozed off. Your braids form a star with supple, gilded branches round your head. Books, DVDs, chocolates (but not the ones you love) all round you. I put on your table a little poem-text that the Little Girl gave me for you.

A sweater studded with black stars
My tea strainer
The pleasure of doing nothing
A good quarter of my life
Lost, lost

To lose and then count over
What might possibly remain
More or less than the day before
Than the year before
Lost, lost

The desire to return
To where you didn't know
Yet what you know
That lightness of steps
Lost, lost

At the crossroads of the lost
Not to keep going
And while they're not looking
Let go of the assisted steering

Of a career plan
Absent this morning
And start suddenly

Thinking of violets, of side roads, tiny little pebbles, storms under
the night, the streets of Bucharest, of losing oneself further on

And remain hidden
While waiting for
That horde to pass by
Which will never admit
It is lost, lost

'Will you read it to me?' Gentle and blurry with sleep, you
look at the words on the paper.

WE ARE
THE BIRDS
OF THE
COMING
STORM

131

    I try hard to respect the rhythm of the phrases but the end
of each stanza is a little problematic, I whisper those 'lost, lost',
trying to soften the repetition, still that fear of hurting you, in
each 'lost', I wouldn't like you to hear 'clueless amnesiac poor
girl'. You sit up a little on your pillows, tie your hair in a bun
and cross your arms, looking at me from underneath.

    '. . . At the crossroads of the lost, wow. At the End of the
End of the Road . . . And the streets of Bucharest, specially
dedicated to you? A text-appeal, obviously.'

'What are you talking about? She expressly wanted me to give it to you, I shouldn't even have read it to you.'

'That's exactly what I mean, it's a father/mother kind of appeal, I'm your parent and you have to get permission . . . to . . . fu . . .'

I rush at you to gag you with my hand, you're capable of launching into a rap or standing up on your bed. Nothing holds you back now, no intravenous drip hanging from your arm, just a few electrodes on your chest. And you feel so much better that, like on the phone this morning, you'd like me to tell you—and for once your question makes sense—what you're *still* doing here.

PART TWO

It is time to move from nausea to vomiting.
Mujeres Creando

We're sitting in this cafe, squeezed against a couple of dry thirty-somethings in suede moccasins, the young woman has braided feathers into her hair, a child with a trendy, mediaeval name is sitting between the two of them.

I grab a newspaper lying round on the table and before I have time to read the headline, the Little Girl tears it out of my hands so hard the page is ripped. She bursts out laughing, glances furtively behind her towards the bar to make sure no one saw her and I stay there, a little scrap of page in my hand. She puts the newspaper back on the table in a pile, smoothing it out with that pale hand of a young bride she has, and gets up to pay.

I can only see bits of the headline upside down: 'FALLING BIRD . . .' and already she's pulling me into the street by the sleeve of my sweater. I don't mind hearing her checkout girl theories and her Instructions but her ripping the paper out of my hands worries me. Then she walks towards me, a few halting steps, and gently holds me against her a little, I'm sorry, Voltairine, she whispers in my ear. Three police cars high on speed and car chases drive by and drown out her words while she's explaining.

It's because I'm trying to follow a new programme I based on Lautréamont.

'And Lautréamont said not to read newspapers any more?'

WE ARE
THE BIRDS
OF THE
COMING
STORM

135

'. . . Wait. Voltairine . . . There's an epidemic of . . . sudden death, a . . . very discreet epidemic. It's war in a temperate climate, now—when I say that people laugh in my face, you don't know what you're talking about, war, what war! We have to. Watch out for the signs of contagion, see. Point to them— THERE. Expose the crap that doesn't seem like crap . . .'

She's breathing like a child walking with a very small flashlight in her hand in the darkness of a forest with no opening. I don't know what she's talking about. But I do know what she's talking about. Because I don't want to know what she's talking about and I don't want her to keep talking.

'They say nothing's happening, they complain about that, oh look how dead the country's been since the Election! But it's not true! There's fighting behind the lines, plotting! And the newspapers leave all those actions in a heap, a heap of disorders that don't make sense, inconsistent, incomprehensible moods! Vain gesticulations! But it's exactly the opposite. And what do they talk to us about? Falls! Renunciations. Ah, the great sad tale of those who tried but were caught . . . That's not news, that's suggestions, velvet slogans. Twist your slightly fractured brain until . . . Since the Election, you can look as much as you like, cerebral escape, even a brief one, is impossible! I mean, it's more like they're selling escape to us as being unthinkable and out of date, yes, fighting is something from another century, I heard that, can you imagine. They don't tell you about those escapees who've been on the run for a long time, or the happy unemployed, and those girls not traumatized by their abortion but relieved. They'll never be mentioned! But they do tell you, oh man, do they tell you, the terrible story of the cut nerves! They distil it out for us every day, Voltairine . . . So, about Lautréamont, wait a second . . . I kind of forgot the beginning but it goes more or less like this: ". . . unhappiness is described to inspire pity and terror. I will describe happiness to inspire their opposites . . ." As long as my friends don't die, I won't speak of death. There. I'm putting Lautréamont into practice.'

The Little Girl pulls on those too-short sleeves of her coat one after the other, she talks and talks while trying to keep up with me on the pavement, I speed up, a need to be alone a little, without texts to read, keywords to look for, words to understand, phrases to avoid.

It's strange, we're right next to the river and I raise my eyes to the sky because it seems to me I can hear seagulls. She grabs my arm, repeats my name—the name she's given me. Voltairine, wait up, Voltairine. I don't want us to talk only about dead birds she screams. She steps back, slapped by the sound of her own voice shot back in her face by the wind, she walks towards the river and suddenly squats down, holding out her hand to some greyish, skinny ducks. The Little Girl at the End of the Lane sways from side to side, she ceaselessly repeats we're not going to make it we're not going to make it, like a disease, a terrible diagnosis, a certainty that has just landed on earth.

I walked up to her and sat down with my legs dangling towards the ducks and the floating beer cans. The slate blue sleeping bags of the people sleeping under the bridge hardly shivered at our shouts.

She recited the front-page headline of the paper she'd ripped out in the bar. She didn't use the words I want to protect you, but, carefully, picked up a lock of my hair that had escaped from my blue barrette and her fingers touched the skin of my cheek. And I'm the one who was at the end of the road.

WE ARE
THE BIRDS
OF THE
COMING
STORM

137

'An Employee of France Télécom Throws Herself out of the Window. The woman's co-worker, who was in the office, says, "I saw something falling out of the window and I said to myself, Hey. Hey, a bird's falling."'

We're not going to count the birds one by one. Point to them. Hey, another one's falling. We're not going to comment. Gaping, watching, waiting for the falling birds. 'Cría cuervos y te sacarán los ojos.' Feed the crows and they'll rip your eyes out. It's a Spanish proverb. Let's stop feeding the sugary crows they serve us, they stuff our bodies with them.

The other day, I wanted to tell you about Voltairine de Cleyre and the Haymarket but I'm not a schoolteacher and I'm worthless without my notes. I read the way I choose films and that thing, I won't lie to you, I found it completely by chance—the biography of Voltairine de Cleyre was mentioned in a newspaper article months ago. It was among the books found in the flat of that girl who was arrested for possession of explosives (I don't know if you followed that empty, crazy story, no evidence except for a few books, weed-killer in the boot of a car and a few appearances in post-Election demonstrations!). I'm into reading suspect books since recent films have a hard time being suspect.

What I wanted to share with you is only a little sentence I found looking through a story full of false suspects—hanged. Yes. (I'm summing up to get to that sentence I found, you understand.)

1 May 1886. A general strike breaks out in several American cities. The strikers oppose the mechanization of labour, the exploitation of children and demand an eight-hour workday. Three hundred and forty thousand workers demonstrate in Chicago, joined by students and even laundrywomen. On 3 May, August Spies, a young bookseller and editor of the *Arbeiter-Zeitung*, the

Workers Daily, addresses the crowd. At the end of the demonstration, strike-breakers attack, rocks fly and the police fire real bullets. They kill six strikers and wound hundreds of others. Horrified, Spies rushes to write a 'Revenge Leaflet' (published in the newspaper *Alarm*), he calls for a peaceful gathering the next day on Haymarket Square. Thousands of workers, women and children, and even the mayor of Chicago, Carter Harrison, come to listen to Albert Parsons, an activist who also writes in the *Alarm*, and Samuel Fielden and August Spies, who have all been deeply involved in this movement for months. It begins to rain. People disperse. A police regiment (under the command of Captain Bondfield) suddenly appears, encircles the remaining demonstrators and declares the gathering illegal. Fielden hardly has time to finish his speech when the police charge. And no one knows where it's thrown from but there is a terrible explosion, a bomb explodes. The police fire on the crowd. In a few minutes, seven policemen are dead and dozens of demonstrators (during the trial, the possibility that the police shot one another—since they were the only ones who were armed—is hardly mentioned . . .)

The very next day, the cops carry out a search, arrest and interrogate hundreds of people suspected of being linked to the 'ringleaders'. This is the beginning of a veritable hysteria, a witch hunt for anarchists, even Voltairine de Cleyre is fooled and denounces the 'anarchist bomb-throwers' (but she soon realizes people were being manipulated).

The *Chicago Tribune* of 6 May 1886 calls for the 'deportation to Europe and the extermination of the ungrateful hyenas, Slavic wolves and wild beasts—particularly the bloodthirsty Bohemian tigresses' . . . Meetings are attacked, newspapers that sympathize with them are placed under surveillance. August Spies, George Engel, Adolph Fischer, Louis Lingg, Michael Schwab, Oscar Neebe and Samuel Fielden are arrested and declared guilty of murder. Some of them were not even at the demonstration. Spies and Parsons left very early.

21 June 1886. In Cook County criminal court, the trial is the trial of anarchism. On the first day, Parsons, who had gone into hiding in Wisconsin, enters the courtroom and calmly sits in the dock near his friends. The prosecution (according to the judge's own words . . .) is not based on their actual participation in the acts and acknowledges that the bomb-thrower is probably not in the courtroom. But, says the district attorney to the jury, 'The question you must answer is essentially this: Did these men encourage, advise and support the bomb-throwers with their writings and speeches?' (I read a lot of texts from this time and anarchists often referred to dynamite in their writings, but mostly as a symbol, I think.)

19 August. They are sentenced to death except for Oscar Neebe (not in Chicago on the day of the meeting), sentenced nonetheless to fifteen years in prison . . . Two others, Schwab and Fielden, are sentenced to life.

Louis Lingg commits suicide in prison on 10 November, not giving the State the right to take his life. August Spies, George Engel, Adolph Fischer and Albert Parsons are hanged on Friday, 11 November 1887, a day called Black Friday ever since. Those who witnessed the execution said that not one of them had his neck broken and their death by strangulation was slow and horrible.

Two hundred and fifty thousand people stand silently along the way to the cemetery and over twenty thousand people march behind their coffins, singing the Marseillaise.

No one ever learnt who threw the bomb. What is certain is that none of the accused could have done it. Who cares, you might say, but in 1893, after an investigation, the governor of Illinois, John P. Altgeld, pardoned the survivors and condemned the 'murderous bias' of the trial procedure.

Today in Paris, on May First, resigned crowds march along the customary route from République to Nation. The words they chant are merely pretences of threats and combats. We will. Never-retreat. We will. Never-retreat. Sobs of rage choke me when I run into these gatherings circumscribed by policemen and garbage trucks following them slowly, picking up and erasing the traces of a disorder that has not occurred.

I found a photo of the Waldheim Cemetery in Chicago. A monument, a very solid stone stele, holds them all there, historic characters made inoffensive by forgetfulness. And these words, engraved, the last words of August Spies, pronounced through the sheet covering his face at the moment the trapdoor opened beneath him:

'The time will come when our silence will be more powerful than the voices you strangle today.'

My silence is weak and lonely, Voltairine, it is just a banal non-voice that nearly smothered me once. So, with the help of what I've read and seen these past months, I try to feed that silence so it may at least turn into a hard mass, something resistant. It's them or us, Voltairine.

Forgive me for yesterday's birds.

PS

The poem Voltairine de Cleyre wrote for the martyr August Spies ('The Hurricane') begins with this sentence (that he said to the judge, I think, during the trial):

'We are the birds of the coming storm.'

WE ARE
THE BIRDS
OF THE
COMING
STORM

141

Where does it start. How does the story I'm telling you begin. The simple fact that one thing leads to another—what we choose to do or not—is that a logic in itself. Is the 'Diary of Your Unlived Days' a logical succession of events.

Am I right to choose your prevented death as a starting point. Why that death rather than the other one, which sentenced us to Tuesday Evenings. Why date your first unlived day to the moment when the medical profession records your sudden death and not years before, with me in my dead van on the empty Island and you putting your questionnaires away in drawers one after the other.

What am I doing here what am I doing here, you've asked me since you woke up, your agitated insistence never satisfied with my answers, tirelessly seeking a reason, a cause. So once again I tell you the story of your heart stopping and your rapid provisional death, that tale even doctors have a hard time believing. And maybe it's only a banal case of post-traumatic shock and your memory truly erases my story every morning.

But it's your words that give me the starting point, words full of fear and anguish, vague words which, finally, put a closing note on our deaths.

What am I doing here

What am I doing

What do we do here now?

A discomfort in the back of the throat, an irritation of the skin, a late, stray bullet. You were about to fall asleep and there it is again, the question comes back to you, floating. What are we doing what are we doing here, doing nothing with these words, like with all the others that go through us, that muck of agitated questions reduced to almost nothing, so much does the comfort of our deaths thicken the air we think we breathe. But then one evening the mechanism stalls and, like an irritable lover cross at having been put aside, the words freeze without any more discussion. Demanding to be noticed.

What was done with them. What I did not do. What am I doing here, Émile.

WE ARE
THE BIRDS
OF THE
COMING
STORM

143

We decide to do it. It's almost a joke at first, an idea thrown out by one of us (which one, I don't know any more).

We collect:

—Sheets of A4 paper

—Several markers of different sizes

—Cut-out sheets: folded in two to make them more solid

—Wire

—Paste and buckets, brushes. Rolls of oilcloth. Do not forget anything

—The map of Paris

We spend the afternoon:

Writing in letters that are big enough, legible. Darkening the inside of the letters with markers on the oilcloth banners. Carefully calculating the space between each letter to be sure to reach the end of the sentence.

Choosing the busiest streets. The bridges too, bridges which are most used and least watched.

What about the bridges over the beltway, she says to me, squatting over three metres of sheets sewn together, a marker in her hand. 'Because there, you don't even have to raise your head, you can see everything! And the traffic . . .'

Do we expect answers to our question. Or is asking it what matters. And if we want answers, we need to leave an address. What address? Who are we?

Up to then, I lived without any kind of punctuation, the way we all do. A life of one day leading inevitably to another. If there's no period, no breathing or even parentheses, you repeat indefinitely, you babble away under oxygen. The only thing that progresses more than I do, in a way, is my notebooks, these pages which I sometimes distribute to people and have so often gained me only alarmed, dismayed looks in return. Not to mention my psychiatrist who read them stoically but he's paid to remain impassive in all circumstances, you must be the first person who read my Theory of the Checkout Girl—extremely neglected these days—and didn't call me disturbing/demented/ take-them take-them, you know the tune.

There are two of us. Our ridiculous lack of numbers is nothing new, it's just that I had never undertaken anything so great with someone else. Tonight will be a period that will enable us to move to another sentence. A new paragraph. Tomorrow, for the first time, I will punctuate my life.

I propose that we have a meeting to be sure of our itinerary. I can skip the 7 p.m. screening and be on the Island by 5 p.m.

Yes, what we do that night doesn't accomplish anything. Will not change anything. All we will have done is put down words in the city. Eyes will go over them for a very brief moment, wondering what they are. There will be a pause. A question breathed lightly in a carefully ordered space of answers constantly following one another, the unhinged mechanical flow of a soliloquy that never catches its breath, leaving room for nothing.

On the night of 28 January, there were only two of us, with our map in our hands, concentrated, dealing with all kinds of unexpected, silly details—feeling the sticky mixture in the paste bucket slowly seeping through a tiny hole in the plastic bag and spattering our knees at every step. Not finding an answer to the questions from passers-by: 'What are you doing, there?' Nor to the mockery of the people who stopped in front of us as we squatted clumsily in front of the shop windows and walls, waiting for the sentence 'WHAT ARE' to be completed. Being congratulated and not coming up with an answer. Having to go back the way we came, hiding the bucket and posters as discreetly as possible when there were cop cars patrolling round our objectives. And then. Holding hands to go still faster down the rue de la Folie-Méricourt, laughing at the paste cracks deforming the skin of our hands and imagining these cracks invading our whole bodies, how would we explain this strange illness which had struck only the two of us.

Buying something to drink in a little grocery and testing the coolness of the cans against our cheeks to make our crimson faces a little paler. Going back to our map after every street we covered to cross off the preceding line, go on go on cross it out, we're making progress, we really are.

The night of 28 January, there were only two of us but we thought the results were admirable. Five Paris arrondissements in which we had spotted the most naked walls and the most visible intersections. The windows of the big department stores, a few banks despite their cameras. A bridge over the Canal Saint-Martin and another crossing the Seine. We only crossed that one very early in the morning. Our bodies leaning far over the water, trying, with our clumsy, frozen hands, to tie the wires we had pushed through the plastic of the tablecloth-banner onto the architecture of the footbridge. Three young American tourists, all bundled up as if on an expedition, asked permission to take our picture for their blog. We pulled our scarves up to our eyes, the Little Girl concealed my hair by hiding it in my bomber jacket. I put my head on her shoulder while they were taking the photo, in it she's pointing to the banner that is swinging a little too much for anyone to imagine it's going to stay up there very long, hanging over the river.

WHAT ARE WE DOING HERE

WHAT AM I DOING HERE

WHAT DO WE DO HERE NOW?

WE ARE
THE BIRDS
OF THE
COMING
STORM
147

There's this text she gives me the day after our WHAT ARE WE DOING HERE night:

AFTER ALL / REALLY

In the end, perhaps it was mostly a matter of words. The Election's main goal was to reuse words, to present them again, all freshened up, to a new public. Vermin. Invasion. Clean, honest citizens. They. Thugocracy. Zero Tolerance.

From their national questions, they hung a piece of intestine dangling from the belly of a corpse, and the piece is coming out, coming out quite nicely. And the whole country is eager to answer, they can't wait to give their opinion! Stinking of dried shit, the clean, honest citizens pour out what's left of them onto the Web in free and open forums, technology deodorizes all right. The words, Voltairine, are screen-polished. A constant, lukewarm purr, emptied of their electricity.

But the bodies, I can see the bodies, Voltairine, our weary, anxious bodies, trembling and tough at the same time. In the supermarkets, their skilfulness, that strange knowledge we've acquired in manoeuvring our body-carts with enough precision so they never collide. Our bodies have become the stupefied, incredulous spectators of our moral submission. All the way to that *after all*.

At what moment, Voltairine, do people slip into the *after all?*

Oh, I will grab you, squeeze you, rub you, yell into your ears, wrench you from the grip of that insidious *after all*. For *after all, really*, is the terminal phase of our condition.

I witnessed its progressive triumph all last year, even at ordinary gatherings of friends. That evening, the park of a nearby city where political refugees had been living for months has just been evacuated by the police under the eyes of the media. We all watched that not-to-be-missed film. Dragged along the ground like shapeless bags, hit with electric clubs when a disorderly movement slows down the convoy.

We begin the exercise. Half-heartedly comment on what happened. Once 'terrible' and 'inhuman' have gone round the table, our indignation moans, sputters, protests that it is not asleep yet. Then one guy, with a body I imagine cool and stiff, concludes the evening with an 'It's horrible,' and, after a few seconds' thought, adds, 'Really . . .' In that vertigo of petty, cowardly comments piled up like a heap of smelly secrets, 'after all, really' propels these refugees to the first rank of shameful acts, but barely. The prize for the best indignation.

Then they bring up a demonstration in a nearby city that didn't go as expected, didn't politely clean up the traces of its passage, and methodically broke the windows of banks and real-estate agencies, finally lighting a big fire in front of a detention centre where the people we'd just talked about are locked up.

I express my admiration. That meticulous choreography between two pavements! Here arms are raised to throw stones, there legs accelerate, bodies duck and anticipate, alert, trained. Round the table, they listen to me with an indulgent smile, the skin of their faces taut with excellent health. Their bad mood grimaces behind their smile. Bad mood from feeling themselves brought down to the weight of comfortable flesh trained to watch, to hold forth. And then what. They break windows. That doesn't accomplish anything, right. All it does is bring insurance companies more business. Ha.

A good number of the peaceful demonstrators got arrested too, says a girl. Some of them got time in prison. Then, like old adolescents protesting half-heartedly about an unfair parental punishment, 'after all' makes a splendid comeback. The adorable

WE ARE
THE BIRDS
OF THE
COMING
STORM

149

little round of *after all, really* and *democracy*. Freedom of expression! (after all after all). If you can't demonstrate any more (really). An imperceptible relief slips into the wordy indignation. The social order ended a movement we don't belong to. So we can come on stage armed with indignation—after all. Then. Empty silence. Then. A hand reaches for the bottle of wine. Anyone for cheese?

Your body and mine are part of the mass. Our white, quiet lives never set off motion sensors. What are we doing with them? What will we do with our uncontrolled bodies (for now, for now . . .),

So after reading these texts, I'm the one who can't sleep. Her chaotic words invade me, like the annoying sound of a sewing machine swarming round me, highlighting my doubts; they are extricating themselves from the order I've been perfecting for years and overflowing it. All those well-intentioned *after alls* that pushed me out of the city, out of the streets that *he* can still walk through, *after all he's not a rapist, do you realize what you're saying there, really.*

And mine: life on the Island isn't so bad, *after all.*

Why I give the Little Girl at the End of the Lane this text at that moment, I'm not sure. It's probably because that's the way she presents herself to the world, out of breath and stripped of everything, raw, new, mad and so very alive that, next to her, you feel small and shrivelled up, half-asleep. You can't just stay there watching her go by, the Little Girl has initiated the movement, everything circulates, the blood, the *reallys* and the *after alls*, the sweet smell of violets and the what are we doing here.

I give her these two pages, which I am reproducing here.

(This text was requested by my lawyer after our first appointment, I am not changing a single word, including what was crossed out.)

Dear Mr. . . .,

I met my adversary almost two years ago in a professional set-
ting. I was a dancer in the N Ballet Company and I was look-
ing for original music for a pas de deux *to present at the*
competition (in a ballet company, the competition is the way
to be 'promoted', to go from coryphée, for example, to soloist
in the corps de ballet.)

I had heard of his work as a composer for films and songs.
Our relationship was at first professional, then turned more
personal.

(at this spot, the story stops, it's a first draft. The text continues in longhand in the form of sketchy notes)

We had a falling-out in the month of July and during that
quarrel he

He

Following that

In September, I had made up my mind to leave. I am aware
that all this is not very good for my case, hard to explain and
I should have left as soon as   . But I was hoping

(a whole paragraph crossed out)

I know you need an exact sequence of events but I don't
remember the beginning of the evening of 14 September any
more. We had a date at his place, as we often did. I didn't want
to get angry.

WE ARE
THE BIRDS
OF THE
COMING
STORM
151

I didn

The atmosphere was very tense but I didn't want to get angry. I think I wanted everything to go well. Sorry, I don't recall the beginning of the evening

He

As I told you at our first appointment, I did say no (several times). Afterwards, when I realized that he that it didn't then I couldn't (physically) pronounce words any more he got scared when he saw me (that was afterwards)

When I picked up my clothes, I remember,

Here, a few empty lines and the text that follows seems to be written hurriedly, some words are hard to read even for me, perhaps I was thinking of reformulating them later.

I say it again in a voice   I say again no stop you're hurting me. I say it. When I say it and he's not stopping I'm still acting like a human being

my face against the pillow I'm crying (turned sideways so I know he sees me.) He

it hurts.

At this point there's a big blank of silence in my head I know everything explodes I know that I It's happened. He comes with a cry of joy. I'm crying. I'm mute I can't manage to pronounce   Nothing. He gets scared bawls me out, he

Extremely upset I get up (I don't want—to be dressed— not naked it's he shoves me against the wall grabs me by the shoulders shakes me

He picked up his things   But (I think) he wasn't completely undressed   I'll drive you home he says. ~~The way you load smelly meat dirty laundry.~~

(in the car, he drives very fast) I repeat I told you no his eyes on the road he answers so you should have said it twice.

I was immediately sorry I'd left all that with the Little Girl. I said to myself it's over and done with, may those days be swallowed in oblivion, especially those evenings, riveted to the weird flood of rage of the one we called the Little Girl at the End of the Lane as soon as we saw her. I was embarrassed at embarrassing her. I waited for her call for two whole days. And when she finally did call, she didn't say anything special, just asked if I'd be in the van the next day at the end of the afternoon.

WE ARE
THE BIRDS
OF THE
COMING
STORM

153

I was watching the moon slumping over a line of poplars, it was so wide that night. The Pelican was the one I spotted first through the window of the van. I pulled a big sweater over my nightgown and I put my feet (in socks) on the running board. The Pelican was followed by the Little Girl.

'I got lost . . .' she said, the cold breeze moving through her hair, wispy in the night. The Pelican turned down a cup of tea, he walked off slowly and raised a hand towards us when he was far away.

There is absolutely no talk about big things. We don't discuss anything. The Little Girl stares at me, standing straight like a tennis player who has no intention of sweating for very long on the court and I begin to love her.

That night she talks as if we were conspiring, with her lukewarm cup of tea pressed against her cheek and her knees squeezed against her chest, her whole body seems huddled up, in waiting. To simply cross out and undo the silence, to stop it. Act so he knows that I know. So he can never forget that we know. Let it get out of that room, out of that bed. So that you and him should no longer be left face to face, she says. I'm going to unmarry you from the nightmare, from that piece of garbage, she offers.

I listen to her telling me her plan in detail. She asks me for the address and the entry code, maybe with a little luck, it's still the same, what does the street look like, do people walk by there at night. The memory of that narrow street where I haven't been since *14 September* blocks my throat. Going to the slaughterhouse.

Late into the night, we watch this film while eating a peach pound cake, a present from the Pelican. Sylvie Guillem is backstage in the flies before the show begins. Filmed in profile, she sits leaning forward, slightly stooped, a bony boxer, and her fear surrounds her like an electric garment. Mademoiselle Non exhales, her pale shoulders rising, almost framing her face. We can hear the muffled sounds of instruments tuning up in front of the stage. Dancers of the corps de ballet are hurrying, all clothed in the same short, white tutu, the one from *Swan Lake*, Act II. They go by and the tulle whispers in front of the camera, they stretch out, grab one leg and flatten it against their chests, exchange a few phrases while checking their chignons with a quick hand. Mademoiselle Non seems to be storing something that could provoke a nuclear accident, a seismic shock. Then, suddenly standing, she moves forward to the side of the stage, taking off her greyish wool leg-warmers, slides her warm-up jacket to the floor and a dresser hastens to pick it up. She shakes her head jerkily, tests the solidity of her headgear, a fake diadem planted on her lacquered chignon. An agitated stage manager walks in front of her and motions to her, we hear fragments of what he says to her in a low voice, 'Three to go . . . soon.'

Then the marvellous Mademoiselle Non stands up on her points, she spreads out her arms, in one straight line, they race past her bust, turning her into a long, terrifying cross, a prophetic idol angrily drawn in one line. Sylvie Guillem glides above the stage manager, spinning.

She comments on the images in a voiceover. First there's a little agitated laugh, then in a rapid voice, she adds, '. . . You dance to escape the legality of normal, ordinary gestures . . . It's movement against death, isn't it? But movement, in the body, I mean, where does it start—and when? In reality, the movement started long ago and I'm following it, emphasizing it . . .'

Later, the Little Girl lies down at my side in my bed, which is a bit too small.

I'll go tomorrow, during the night, she decides, and then goes to sleep right away, turning her back to me.

She checks the last details of the address, feels the pockets of her red coat filled with cans of spray paint. You would give her your children to babysit and your plants to water on the spot, you would even entrust her with a whole building, the Little Girl at the End of the Lane is so fuzzy with sweetness that night. All slimness and floating hair.

And while I walk her from the train station to the Métro that will take her to that street where I no longer go, I feel a blanket of stiffness leaving me, a breath of air not quite perceptible yet. We leave each other without saying anything special.

And I run to the train, to the village, to the forest on the Island, the swishing of the river a graceful accompaniment, and as I'm running and crying, I have to catch my breath in hoarse gulps, and I still run to the van and when I finally stop, I sit on the front seat for the last darkness of the last night. Those last hours before she finally punctuates the time, a time I stretched out so much.

There are more people on that street than in your memories and I couldn't write the sentence we had planned. I hope you will find the one that came into my mind acceptable.

My heart is ravaged, Voltairine. My heart is ravaged, Voltairine. And still. While I was writing the date on that wall, I was sweating, fear no doubt, I don't know, from being close to the body of that guy who was certainly asleep. Everything that happens too late has the taste of those tears. But at least it has been written

WE ARE
THE BIRDS
OF THE
COMING
STORM
157

somewhere for a few moments. As an epitaph, I wouldn't mind: 'Had her soul slashed up from time to time and she hung it on the line as if it could be dried out in the sun.'

Around four last night, she stopped in front of number 56 of a street in the historic centre of Paris. Took out two cans of black spray paint. On the door of the massive building, inscribed in big bristling letters

14 SEPTEMBER

Twice.

Then, with my little map in her hand, took the paved street on the left and easily found that quiet little courtyard protecting a music studio in which there is also a bedroom nook. On the windowpane that looks out on the courtyard, inscribed in spray paint

14 SEPTEMBER NO JUSTICE NO PEACE

The next day, the sun finds its place between each of these moments—birds struck by the surrounding sweetness make a stop on the river, the Little Girl stretches in front of the van in a sweater and black woollen tights, the shortened shadow of the Pelican moves slowly towards us with a plate covered by another in his hand. It's a strangely precocious spring, all that light makes you feel like whirling round and running stupidly, skipping in place until you can feel your hamstring muscles, and at the same time that sudden sweetness of the air intimidates the body and makes you aware of its numbness.

It's past noon, we've eaten all the Pelican's gingersnaps when my cell rings. Your little voice informs me that you may have surgery in a few days. Come see me before I'm no longer completely me, biologically speaking, you say, worried. I write down your room number, they moved you into another unit. Then, a few seconds after I hang up, my cell rings again.

Behind the words, I can make out cars, street noise. I imagine *the hand* holding that phone and the *steps*, rapid, irritated. His exact words are: '*I had a hard time getting your number. Are you hiding?*'

Then: '*I'm calling because something strange happened last night.*'

'*Someone . . . Spray-painted a date on the door of my building and also on the studio door . . . The same date.*'

The breath breathes in breathes out breathes in breathes out regularly, a raging clock.

WE ARE
THE BIRDS
OF THE
COMING
STORM
159

I won't volunteer the first words, let *him* tell me *himself,* explain to me what that date is.

'*Someone spray-painted a date. Do you understand?*'

In the emptiness of my silence, *he* can't say the night when

Can't ask about the night when, you remember.

Can't find the word—the night when. But when what.

'*It's the date of the worst thing I ever did in my life.*'

Now he's whining, both serious and moved at himself, all that courage it took him to confess—a guilty child, proud nonetheless to have found all that fine honesty in himself. Did he choose the words when he woke up. The night of the worst. Really, yes, really, that night, *the worst in his life.* Does the memory of that pleasure, the sexual cry of the pleasure of the kill, *of a goal attained,* does all that come back to him as he's groaning out his confession as if he had done something dumb.

'. . . *When I saw that, the graffiti . . . I got scared . . . I was scared for you, that . . . I was scared that something . . . serious happened to you. I thought . . .*'

Something serious.

'. . . *Maybe you had . . .*'

'*That something might've happened. You . . .*

It's not that I'm not listening any more but at that moment the words are all connected together as if on a graph. So I know *he* knows what he did. *He* has always known. Even *at the moment when.* Even right at *the moment* when *he. He knows.* That one might very well, after a night like that, even two years later,

'. . . *might've jumped out the window.*'

He hollowed me out, a hole of silence. I think of my back folded, manoeuvred, laid out in the best way that night, ready to be used. I think that at one point I encouraged myself to endure it—come on go ahead what's the difference tonight—

do it like you paste stickers on paper in school, die, croak wide open as best you can. And the awareness that *what is happening* is an execution, not a sexual act.

Silent at my side, probably understanding nothing, the Little Girl and the Pelican watch me get up, then sit down again. I laugh, I burst out into that telephone, no doubt about it, I could bite flesh, dig my fingers into his eyes, bang his teeth against stone, against a pavement, I'm alive. The Pelican gets up a lot less slowly than usual, does not hold out his arms to me, he catches me as if a storm were going to break, a big stone dropping from the sky, his heart in his chest making a wall for mine. The telephone is still on my ear.

The tone of *his voice* is perfectly composed.

'*Did you talk again?*'

Not did you talk *about it* again, but: Did you talk again.

At no time does *he* get off track. No threats. No violence. No shouts. To be so sure of one's place that one only needs to *recommend, to suggest calmly.*

'. . . *Anyway, this has to stop. You hear me. This has to stop.*'

I hung up. Everything was all knocked to the ground in a heap, an incredible mess. Everything I had tried to believe and make myself believe. That maybe *he* didn't know what *he* had done that night. Maybe. I had seen *things* in a certain way and I was too insanely sensitive. Maybe I really was guilty of having slandered *him*.

With two spray-painted phrases, the Little Girl at the End of The Lane had uncovered the words and exposed the war.

The Pelican walked away to wash the plates with the hose in front of the van. What are you going to do, she asks me. If

WE ARE
THE BIRDS
OF THE
COMING
STORM

161

you'd rather we shut up, we will, just tell me, come on, tell me, what should we answer. I suggest we wait. A little. She slumps over and I want to move closer to her but with her outstretched hand, she pushes me away, closes her eyes for a few seconds, then straightens up.

'Hey,' she says, looking at me. 'Look. Another one. Another bird falling. Because, Voltairine, *he was waiting for a phone call*. A call, one of these days, which would inform him that gee, you fell from the effects of *14 September*.'

In the afternoon, I'm the one who asked the Little Girl if she could go back to that street and write the same words that very night. Again.

He did not deem it worthwhile to call me back in the face of such disobedience.

And those few letters, probably clumsily written in black paint on a door in the night—I will never see them, for they were erased as quickly as possible (oh to imagine *his* quick, furtive gestures, sluicing it down so the neighbours won't remember that unfortunate *14 September*.)

But those words, N O J U S T I C E N O P E A C E, are an army to me, bodies and bodies of letters that are attached to one another and form a living wall, breath, blow air between my naked body and shame, and then a way to go on at last.

The next day, I decide to put an end to this narrative and go to the hospital with the intention of giving Émile this 'Diary of Her Unlived Days' that I kept for the two weeks preceding her operation. Surrounded by sweets, fruit and magazines, Émile is sitting on her bed, her braids like the cords of a doll's house curtain round her mouse-like face. The nurse and the doctors greet me, here's your 'sister', and no one corrects them. They speak of going back to Dance very cautiously after the operation and then seeing what level Émile will be able to reach and no one corrects them either.

We look at each other, smiling at all those optimistic phrases—the hardest is behind you, you'll be as good as new, you'll see—with which families and friends think it useful to encumber hospital rooms. Then an uncle, or a cousin perhaps, turns to Émile and wonders at my daily presence at her side, 'But how did you two meet?' Émile answers nonchalantly that she has absolutely no idea any more.

'How about you?' she asks me, '. . . it's been so long now . . .'

I don't correct her. And there are so many friends in her room that afternoon that I keep the notebook with me.

All those years, we pulled each other by the hand. We shared the experience of a dead life. We watched for each other's fears, leaving one of our bodies behind would have made the whole chain of our lifeless nights crash with a terrible racket. And perhaps we ended up fusing into each other and adding up our fears to form that heavy magma of tangled terrors.

Protecting ourselves, locking ourselves up on Islands, in vans with no engine, filling out hundreds of questionnaires, wondering all the time what we're doing out there and shoving the answers away in a drawer because we don't know what to do with them. Decreeing the beginning of the year without movement—this one. Raising our glasses to the year without movement. Which never existed.

BARELY FORTY-THREE HOURS

She's waiting for me at the corner of the boulevard and the hospital, she wants to go home and change. The flat does not look like the place of a girl whose anger deserves a whole list of chemical Instructions. Nothing's lying round on the floor, there are more DVDs than books in the shelves and a few photos tacked over the desk. The Little Girl, very young, surrounded by three other raggedy-looking, laughing girls, then her again, with her head leaning on the shoulder of a young man looking into the camera with a satisfied air. A small, slightly damaged poster, probably bought in a museum and when I linger over it, she observes, 'I have to talk to you about that.' I don't have the time to see the picture in detail, two boys with vague eyes as if infused with psychotropic drugs, lying on a sort of drifting raft, she drags me into the bedroom, come here, come and see. We sit down on the bed and she tries to pick up the books, a good dozen of them on the floor, her texts are stored in cardboard boxes with a few sheets of paper sticking out of them. Sitting on the nightstand, a bric-a-brac of wooden sticks, some of them painted purple, a naive little piece of art and a dried tree leaf of faded red. Tacked onto the wall above the pillow, two pages ripped out of a notebook. On one:

to laugh at those old lying loves and strike those lying couples with shame

And on the other, a single word written in the margin:

PATIENT:

After the colon, the space on the page is empty. Her laugh seems slightly embarrassed for the first time since I've known her when she explains the meaning of that paper. It's because she can't tack everything to the wall. She apologizes for perhaps seeming paranoid, you're going to tell me, come on, take them for God's sake, she adds before I could even think that.

She pulls one of her notebooks from her handbag, 'I always have this one with me,' in which she shows me the same page, 'PATIENT', followed by its etymology.

Adj. **1.** 1st half 12th century 'patiently bearing others' faults' (*Oxford Psalter*, 85, 14, ed. F. Michel 123); **2.** 2nd half 14th century 'suffering adversities and contrarieties without murmur' (*Brun de la Montaigne*, ed. P. Meyer, 3126); **3.** 1370–72 t. didact. 'who is subjected to something' (Nicole Oresme, *Ethics*, V, 23 ed. A. D. Menut, 327); *ca.* 1380 subst. use (J. Lefevre, *The Old Lady*, 196 in T.-L.). **B.** Noun. **1.** 14th century. 'sick' (Brun de Long-Bore, *Surgery*, Salis ms., folio 102d in Gdf. *Compl.*); **2.** 1617 'person sentenced to torture' (A. d'Aubigné, *Adventures of Baron de Faeneste*, I, 12, ed. Réaume and de Causade, II, 419.) From Lat. *patiens* 'one who bears, endures', adjectival pres. part. of *patior*, 'to suffer, to bear, to endure'.

II. – *Noun* and *adj.*

A. One who is subjected to something, who is the object of an action.

1. *PHILO*. [By oppos. to the agent] The person or thing who is subjected to something, who is passive.

2. *LING*. [By oppos. to the agent] The person or thing who is subjected to the action (the *process*).

B. *Arch.* or *Lit.*

1. Tortured.

2. *By ext.*

a) Person who is subjected to a punishment, who faces a painful ordeal.

b) Sick person; one who undergoes or will undergo a medical examination or a surgical operation.

'Not bad, don't you think? The kind of word you like to rummage around in, even trepan.'

Then she puts her arm on my shoulder and with one finger points to the two postcards tacked above those two ripped-out pages. A young woman wearing her hair up is not looking at the camera, she's staring at someone we don't see, perhaps in a corner of the picture.

'She looks like she's asking a question and . . . Man . . .! She won't give up before she gets an answer . . .' I whisper, without really knowing why.

The Little Girl at the End of the Lane smiles at me, she seems proud of my conclusions, 'That's Voltairine de Cleyre!'

The other photo, more classic, shows her with her head slightly bent, serious, a cameo round her neck and a little bouquet of flowers in her hand, violets I think.

'And this too, here, read it, I cut it out of the newspaper.'

OPEN PRISON

A concept of pedagogy and therapy through work in an open prison has been developed in Witzwil (Switzerland). Each prisoner needs about a month to know what he has to do and how to do it. Why not escape when you can? Because it's useless. In 2009, all the escapees (twenty-seven) were recaptured. Some of them came back on their own, others were found at home (they had given their address to the prison administration). In Witzwil, bars

WE ARE
THE BIRDS
OF THE
COMING
STORM

167

are replaced by a social contract. Knowing each prisoner, his needs, his potential and his problems is pivotal for security.

On his visit, the minister declared, 'This system is transposable to France: soon, we'll have a prison adapted to each personality, we'll have the traditional prison but also a regime of quasi-freedom where constraint is exclusively moral.'

She smoothes down the article, thoughtfully, 'The supermarket of punishment. Quasi-freedom   . . .' and right away her eyes are full of tears, she fans herself very rapidly with one hand as if to dissuade the tears from piling up.

The Little Girl at the End of the Lane was a salesgirl in a clothing store, then a waitress in bars and not just any bars, she tells me, oh no, the worst, the ones where firm, young white bodies get together, they're in—she gets up and throws her arms to the sky like a circus rider when she says this—'Business events! Communication!' She worked for a telecom company a year ago. And in a foreign-exchange office, her last job. She tells me, adding that she wasn't complaining about that job, just taking note of a few facts, that's all: the advice given to 'Job 1' employees not to mix with the 'Job 2' in the company cafeteria.

Forbidden to go to the bathroom without asking the 'boss', who is adamant about being called 'boss' in English, forbidden to keep a cup of tea on your desk—you're not in your kitchen—and that compulsory training session in 'Civic Denunciation' where employees receive a circular from the prefecture with a free phone number in bold letters at which they can leave 'securely and anonymously!' the identity of foreign customers who seem 'suspicious'. She asks if dancers have a CV, too. Tells me she's thinking of drafting her girl CV, femininity is a job, after all. Or are you sentenced to it, what do you think?

Let's write our banal, exemplary CV, Voltairine, she suggests, her energy completely restored. She recites at top speed with her eyes closed, 'So . . . Encouraged to be docile very early on, praised for her gentleness, her gift for listening, her patience and her pretty feet. Anorexic, of course, from the age of twelve to about nineteen, what else . . . Doesn't scar well. Allergic and sceptical. Declared socially fit to be penetrated, she soon gets weary of mucous rubbings and stuffs words and images in there until it all begins to overflow dangerously and her loved ones—oh those words those words—advise her to do something.'

'Want to go to a party tonight?' she suggests without any connection to her previous sentence.

The red dress she hands me doesn't fit, the sleeves are too long, 'You are a tall Little Girl,' I remark. She takes a hairbrush, sits down behind me and brushes my hair, concentrating on undoing the knots. We don't talk of the legal complaint that will certainly fall on my head, we don't speak of that night we spent without sleeping. The Little Girl grazes the edge of my ear with her mouth, 'Voltairine, tonight we're going to tear up our ridiculous carnivals. Then we'll deal with our scars.'

In the living room, over the poster of the two drugged young men, a yellow Post-it is a reminder, like a little list of things to do, not to forget:

'Question Instructions / Spread questions

Who cuts nerves?'

WE ARE
THE BIRDS
OF THE
COMING
STORM

169

At that party, the voices form a sonorous pile, a ball of wool made of the lonely little desperations of everyday life, but no one sheds a tear over anything, oh you're the serious type, no kidding around over here, right, a girl says to me when I turn down a drink. The Little Girl at the End of the Lane is wearing knee-high Argyle socks over black woollen tights, she's sitting at my side. The pattern stops where the wool of the tights becomes thinner, she's holding her hands clasped under her thighs, I would like this winter to last for ever, because of her tights.

The girls bend their heads whenever a boy speaks to them. Wave their hands when they talk, fingers slightly spread out as if their nail polish were never dry. Carry food to their mouths with a sullen look and when they dance, only their pelvis moves. The girls at this party use their gender as an ID, a sum of carefully chosen details. I've lived alone on the Island for so long that this accumulation of skins filled with knowledge, a whole programme, gives me the impression of being an escapee from femininity, something all round me, a place where I would never go, like a pool in winter. The Little Girl glances at me with she-wolf eyes, she's funny, standing there a little hunched over, she looks, in this light, like a young Charlotte Rampling.

She doesn't seem to know a lot of people, I even wonder if she hasn't landed here by pure chance.

'How did you meet?' a young man asks us.

The Little Girl gives him a quick, frowning look before answering in a serious voice, 'You jerk.' Then she whispers to me, 'Jeanne Moreau, in *Eva*. You saw it, I hope.'

A girl asks who's going to participate in the No-President Day planned for the following week and hands shoot up quickly. A reminder of the rules: you're not allowed to mention the president for twenty-four hours, it's true, we're sick of him, something must be done, where will it all end if we don't do anything. Good, prudent children behind the locked door of their cosy rooms, flashlight in hand, who would jump at the slightest noise their secret activity produces.

'How about going to check if the banner is still up there?' I ask her wearily.

The coats are piled up in one of the bedrooms. The Little NO JUSTICE NO PEACE picks one up, shakes it slightly, I'm about to tell her it's not hers but she smiles at me and does it again with another one, then a jacket, and then with another coat. In hardly ten minutes, there's a bunch of keys on the bed. She shuffles them like a pack of cards and holds one out to me: 'Go ahead!'

'What?'

'Put it in-to what-e-ver-coat-you-want!' she hums in the voice of the Sugarplum Fairy, as she starts sticking a car key into a beige coat.

'Let's go, Mademoiselle Voltairine!'

While we're walking to the bridge where we hung the WHAT ARE WE DOING HERE banner, she wants to know if I still feel like a foreigner here and I can't find an answer. We're both sleepy, that's probably why we're laughing so much, it shakes us up in jolts, we're laughing because we're cold, because we're stepping on each other's feet to make room for a group of cops who're taking up the whole width of the pavement, we laugh from laughing too.

We're near the banner, it's still there all right, a little torn in the middle, the oilcloth caught in the sharp wind. What was she thinking when she spray-painted the door the previous night? Was she afraid of being caught?

'I was afraid someone might ask me what I was doing there. I was actually very disappointed, Voltairine.'

'By what?'

'Because I was scared. I've read so much, seen so many films . . . I thought that was a kind of training. But just writing two sentences, I was scared. I have to work on myself, in resistance . . .'

'I can show you, if you like . . .'

'What?'

Now we're on the bridge, I put my left hand on the guardrail and, with my legs open in first position and my back absolutely straight, I show her how to do a *plié* very slowly, in resistance.

We have nowhere to go, not to her place anyway and the Island is out of reach, no more trains. So we keep walking. I tell her about Émile, about that terror of losing her, so invasive that it hasn't yet been replaced by the relief that she's here, finally, alive. And I add, even if that thought makes me a bit ashamed, that it won't be enough for both of us to be breathing normally, to content ourselves with just that mechanical function. We move from the stopped heart to the Saint-Ambroise Tuesday evenings. So I do tell her how I met Émile.

I would like to know: Why did you do that for me. To tell you the truth, Voltairine, she says to me as the cold makes her walk faster, it's that or forgetting, on the other side of what I did, there's only emptiness, nothing. There's you, hidden on your Island, while the one you call your adversary is disgustingly enjoying every street in the city. All I did was write down a date and the two of you are the only ones who know its smell. I didn't write rape/rapist on the wall. I only scratched a little piece of silence. That's what I'm doing here. In just forty-eight hours, the fear has shifted. He knows that someone knows, he doesn't know how many of us know. His movements, his comings and goings, will be more furtive, anxious. He's certainly going to file a complaint against you again, even if I'm sure he knows you're not the one who wrote those words.

Her breathing is almost noisy, whistling, she stops for a few moments and shakes her head when I want to put my hand on her shoulder, no. Unmask the war, Voltairine. Expose all its hidden wires, all those circuits carefully covered by normality, before suddenly our hearts stop beating.

A few buses go by, exuberant in the emptiness of the boulevards. Suddenly the Little Girl bursts out laughing, 'Sorry. I'm thinking about the keys. We've just created a little mess ... The Great Night of the Keys!'

I would love to deviate from this chronological account, I would love to be able to wander off a bit so I can tell how, since that NO JUSTICE NO PEACE, I feel almost stupid with lightness, like at the end of convalescence. I would love to draw lines between the different possibilities which came up that night, the streets we chose to take. To tie up those little bursts of random choices with a tight ribbon. And what if we hadn't taken rue du Chemin-Vert. What if we hadn't heard those voices, would the Night of the Keys have been no more than that—a thrilling *pas de deux*.

Public gardens are closed in Paris at night, so when we walk by that little park surrounded by huge, dried-up trees and hear conversations in the night, we head for it. It's too dark but we can still make out a group of twenty-odd people.

'A conspiracy!'

Delighted, her face pushing up against the fence, the Little Girl picks up her skirt and tries to insert the tip of her boot into a tiny space in the wrought iron. We climb over it pretty easily and walk over the grass towards the little group which turns to us when they hear us coming. We say hello and, very matter-of-factly, the Little Girl sits down in their circle, making a little room for me next to her. As we don't say anything, they may think we're late and don't ask who we are. They make up a disparate assembly. Pale whispering girls with blurry eyes, blowing into each other's hands to warm up, two young women with their hair covered by scarves silently taking notes, nervous boys all bundled up in thick, black mufflers, some of them with their faces hidden by a hood or a tuque. A girl with big shadows under her eyes frequently turns round towards the end of the park as if she were afraid. And then there are the ones grouped together, a group within the group, their bodies poorly covered by dull clothes, in coats that don't seem to belong to them, too big, or, on the contrary, wearing trousers that reveal a thin band of skin marked by the elastic of their socks. One of them is looking for a tuque, he lost his own in the shelter, he says. His slightly wavy hair strains to cover his skull, and his fingertips, when he offers me a plastic cup of hot tea, are so callused they seem made of cardboard. Several of them have missing teeth. It's not a gathering of people our age who come to drink in a park in the middle of the night, they don't all look like students. I cannot read their grave, mysterious faces at all. The Little Girl passes me a little note: 'Paranoids preparing for summer camp or a sleeper cell of spaced-out conspirators?' She leans towards me and whispers, fascinated, 'But what are they doing here, Voltairine? Oh! Did you see out there, at the end of the park? An old bandstand!'

They're talking about some imminent departure but where to, no one knows, no destination is mentioned except for a vague 'pre-arranged spot', their precautions are intriguing. One boy seems to know more and he's the one they ask, 'Will we stay a long time?' 'Do we need sweaters? Will it be colder than here or less cold?' 'What are the risks?' 'OK then, what should we bring?'

'The minimum, really . . . We're not going to haul around huge Hollywood trunks! So, underwear and a toothbrush!' We laugh along with the others, especially because we don't understand a thing and we're very sleepy. The cold is tightly hugging this February night, accelerating the laughs, sharpening the voices, the air is excited with riddles and enigmas.

When we part, one of the girls advises us to make sure we're on time at the Bercy station the next day. We haven't seen a film for over forty-eight hours.

We ought to sleep, we should pause, put a full stop here. And, like a bad, lazy habit, for a brief moment, I suddenly have the urge to retreat and continue that life in which I am not living, all that torpor stretching slowly from night to day. Too many people, too many streets, questions, too much Little Girl at the End of the Lane messing up my keys. My Achilles tendons, suddenly abnormally short, are stretched at every step. We have hot chocolate, then I take the first train back to the Island and she'll rest for a few hours at her place, we talk of calling each other later, without too many details or decisions.

Alone between two weeping willows, the van seems to me old, almost a memory. I pick up a few pieces of clothing and put them away in my bag, the fear of sleeping alone in there, a bad film kind of fear, a background shadow, everywhere.

I'm warning you this has to stop.

Just before falling asleep, I watch a documentary about Sylvie Guillem's *Raymonda*[7] for a few minutes. Every eight measures, like an incongruous slap in that gilded red set, Mademoiselle Non claps once, then crosses the screen diagonally, *piqué tour attitude assemblé soubresaut*. And I don't know if it's the fatigue of these last few hours. Or if I really have no choice. But I'm not going to stay here like a good girl and wait for an official piece of paper on which *his* name will

WE ARE
THE BIRDS
OF THE
COMING
STORM

175

---

7 A ballet by Marius Petipa in three acts.

be preceded by the words *the plaintiff*. But the sound of Sylvie Guillem's palms clapping against each other once—that imperious crack of a whip—rails at me, injects itself into me, surprising and fresh. And I am still seated but I can no longer pretend I don't know what I've been doing here, and for way too long.

In the morning, I go over to the Pelican's. He's already outside, a long body busily picking up the cans and stones the village kids throw at his van when they come to the Island to get drunk on Saturday nights. We drink spiced tea with his pistachio cake, sitting silently facing each other in his minibus, which is roomier than mine. You can hardly see his mouth in the middle of his beard, and that makes his eyes even clearer, vertiginously lively. At that moment I don't think that I'm leaving all this behind, no, like every day, I'm going to the hospital. And then I'll meet the Little Girl who has become my cloak, my brass knuckles and also a sweet home, all of this mixed in with her theories, her texts and her Voltairines. And her legs, that instant of naked skin that I imagine between her knee-high Argyle socks and her black tights.

So we say practically nothing to each other. What could we possibly say to begin?

I would have liked to tell the Pelican that it really would be good if we could find some kind of beginning somewhere. Because, what were the two of us doing here for months, aside from counting falling birds and Endings we feared but still expected, sitting next to our stationary vans.

Surrounded by machines again, Émile is alone in her room for a change.

'How do you feel?'

'I'm OK. I'm trying not to think I'm going to swallow a computer tomorrow morning . . .'

'You're having second thoughts?'

'. . . If everyone's reassured by my swallowing a nanotechnological cop . . .'

'But . . . Aren't you scared your heart might stop again? This way, you'll have nothing to worry about.'

'. . . I have no memory of my death. You're the one who were scared, I mean all of you. Me, I simply died in the cafe. Hey, what an incredible commercial by the way, just think . . . At the MK2 cafe, the coffee kills! I woke up here, you all looked like naive, cheery Christians. You talked to me as if I were a retard, no no, you're fine, you just die unexpectedly once in a while that's all, and I've been hassled ever since with newspaper articles to learn!'

Émile talks of her heart the way she talked about the end of the first part of her life, when she made us laugh to death on those Tuesday evenings near the Saint-Ambroise Métro, and she sits up in her bed to perfect her imitations of her dying moments.

She insisted that I shouldn't come back to the hospital, no kiddo, I'll come to the Island next week, I'm getting out in four

WE ARE
THE BIRDS
OF THE
COMING
STORM

177

days. She asked me what I'd been doing recently, I brought up the Cinémathèque and the Little Girl too. Then she held her cheek out to me in an exaggerated way, her pretty braids tilting like a dismal pendulum. 'Come give me a little kiss, since I've been deceased, everyone kisses me, come on . . .! You Romanian bitch.'

I gave her the finger and closed the door. I did not mention the graffiti.

When we meet again, the Little Girl and I, hardly forty-eight hours after NO PEACE, we don't speak right away about the group in the park and their appointment at the station. But the programme of the Cinémathèque doesn't interest us either. In my bag, I have a change of clothes and a toothbrush, my passport and an old Opera programme given to me by the Pelican.

The sky is drawn in a straight line, slate-coloured and static, and I would love it if it snowed, we're still waiting for it to snow here. We're facing each other in a cafe, intimidated by these last few days so full of fun, there's this polite distance like the day after love. She's drinking a hot chocolate, her foot shaking under the table is jolting the saucer under my cup. The arrest of a female student is being commented on TV: '. . . thanks to the presence of mind of the suspect's neighbours. Again, if you have the SLIGHTEST DOUBT, here's that special daily anti-terrorist vigilance number to call.'

At that moment, we're no longer just sitting next to each other on the cold plastic cushions of that greyish burgundy banquette. We are linked together by acts. I am more guilty than ever and if up to now that judgement kept me sitting, almost knocked out, now, too many restrained movements are loading my blood with the desire to fight, again. Two years. Spent dissecting, in a foggy state, Gelsey's pirouettes and translating other people's words. Honestly, that whole time fills me with shame.

WE ARE
THE BIRDS
OF THE
COMING
STORM

179

'Give me your hand,' she orders. She moves hers forward on the table, checks that our elbows are lined up right, her hands are freezing. She wants to arm wrestle, hasn't done it since junior high. The waiter goes by and turns round to us. She smells of warm violets when her arm throws mine down with a totally illegal shoulder butt, her breath grazing my cheek with a laugh. My heart choking, as if tangled in words I can no longer say, her smell entering my body, a little, steady, tenacious wave, a refrain.

When the waiter comes back with the bill—we've spent over four hours in this cafe—and he hands her the change, very ceremoniously she motions him to give it to Mademoiselle, pointing to me. The young man's fingers graze my palm. She gets up, lively and elated, I know she's thinking of her Theory of the Checkout Girl and of those avid, lonely palms, a category to which she no longer belongs.

No point looking, there's nothing to be found, no future. We're no longer who we were two weeks ago when we met, there's no place to go, nothing to continue. Empty and on the alert. And it seems that between the moment the Little Girl came back from her NO JUSTICE NO PEACE night and the moment we'll have a toast with total strangers in a practically empty night train, time has not been punctuated by sleep or night. Or it's the opposite, and all there is now is moon, stars and cool wind.

Why not just go check it out, they're kind of nice. It's true, people who meet at night in a nineteenth-century park in which there are three Turkish hazelnut trees, a Chinese golden rain tree and an Osage orange tree—golden rain tree, she says, I like that. Yes, let's take a look at the station, see if they're really leaving.

Scattered over the platform, they don't regroup, as if they didn't want to look like they were together. As soon as she sees us, the girl with the big shadows under her eyes comes to meet us, asks if we have ID. At that moment, I don't really intend to get on a train for who knows where. But there is a sense of pleasant excitement. Something like preparations for a party, and that feverishness with which you attend to the details of a table or the choice of lights in a room where there will be dancing later on. What about the tickets? I ask the boy who seems in charge, who has the tickets? His mouth is hidden behind his muffler and the words he pronounces float hazily in the air, defying the city, the night, and the soldiers in camouflage on every platform with a machine gun in their hands.

I think of the long khaki coat of Romanian militiamen in winter. Of their tense, sullen faces as if the Bucharest cold and their obligation to watch the streets and the people—that allegiance to the regime—was really getting to them. The next day, they might have been schoolmasters or grocers. Whereas here in France, every face since the Election seems to me full of a desire to participate, a real urge to join in that national effort which is carefully sorting out bodies. With that permanent attention to tickets properly punched in stations, under-grounds, the security guards at the entrance to bars, shops and supermarkets, their relentless search through bags and those surveys that count the cheaters, the fraudulently unemployed supposedly hidden among 'us'.

Some time before her sudden death, Émile calls me one day, she's coming out of a museum where she took some neighbourhood boys. The woman at the ticket window demands that one of the youths produce written proof of 'low-income status' for his reduced price ticket. He goes through his pockets for a while, then presents an official document but from over three months ago. The ticket lady inspects it for a long time then hands it back to him, shaking her head. 'No, that doesn't prove anything.' Émile intervenes lightly, after all, it's a museum, art, 'Let him in . . .' while the other one repeats, 'I'm just doing my job, that's all, my job.'

Standing on the platform with her back to me, the Little Girl is making a phone call. Almost defiantly, because up to now, I haven't been very bold, I walk up to the step of the train, I didn't pay attention to the announcements and I really don't know where it's headed. It's almost 10 p.m. and now someone's pushing me, shoving me to get in too. The people from the park are super-excited. Pleased with myself, I motion to the Little Girl to move it, she puts her hand in front of her mouth, she's probably giggling like mad, she joins me in a hurry. At the moment we leave the station, they all start shouting with joy, hug, run from one compartment to another, 'We did it, we did it!' The Little Girl doesn't move out of the corridor, her forehead pressed against the window like Giselle when she travelled, with her nose glued to the motion of the trees whizzing by.

I may never relive anything as fluid as that night. It's quite possible. So I call up the smell of a night train, too cold. I call up those faces I know nothing about, not their first names, nor what they're doing there. And then those conversations. I start one with a girl, a guy comes over, we are becoming a trio, discussing things without ever having spoken to one another, I turn round and my glance meets the fox eyes of the boy with hazy words, he holds me in his arms, we toast, I let the night reinvent me. We run, dislocated by the jolts, two cars out of the five we go through seem to be empty rooms in a dark, freezing house. We move that night with the rapidity of silent-film actors, we keep coming and going. Go find Ivan, someone tells me. But who is Ivan. He's the tall guy in a blue sweater, you'll see, he must be over there. Now we're out looking for the blue sweater, we slam every door, yell between the cars, our bodies tense with pleasure in that noise of machines and wind, bracing ourselves against the fear of being torn away from life, this one, so beautiful at last. We run, we bump into one another, we apologize, we smile at one another, you OK, and you, what compartment are you sleeping in, the train is a big suite where nothing has been planned for us and we want to embrace every part of it, sit in every seat. Then a girl proposes, 'Let's have a toast!' and we head for the bar in a clumsy little line.

We know our destination now, yet it makes no difference. We look at each other, the Little Girl and I, happy at this third night together, but no idea what we're supposed to do in that city. The conductors are furious; they pick up our IDs and, in the corner they use as an office, write out forty-two fines by hand. At 2 a.m., we successfully cross a border, they don't make us get out, and the Little Girl slaps my hand like an American basketball player, the train starts up again and makes me fall clumsily forward into her arms.

Neither she nor I are concerned about what the group is getting ready to do. We're going ahead without premeditation. NO JUSTICE NO PEACE and even the Night of the Keys are small steps, bubbles, we go from one to the other, thrilled by our success. What we started seventy-two hours ago must not

WE ARE
THE BIRDS
OF THE
COMING
STORM
183

stop here, there's no way we'll go home at this point. When I close my eyes for a few moments, the conversations in the compartment don't prevent me from sleeping, I'm floating in the pleasure of this aimless moment, I would love to have no destination, I'd like the train to just go, keep moving forward, the time for me to recover from having done nothing all these years. And where I'm coming from, I have no name for it while I run, escaping into the dark corridors of a night train, bumping into the windows at every turn.

Around three in the morning, the train stops for a long time in the strange silence of a snowed-in station, another stop for customs, most of us have dozed off, there are only the quick steps of the conductors explaining to the customs officers the story of this group with no tickets. A few people step down onto the platform, stretch, make little movements with their arms to warm up, smoke, and—I think the first one comes from a young conductor—a snowball hits Ivan. The Little Girl jumps up from her seat, 'What's happening? Are we there?' On the platform there's a snowball fight under the orange lamp posts of a little mountain station. I hardly have the time to put on my jacket, she's already in the corridor, limping as she puts on her shoes in a hurry, shouting, 'Let's make two teams! Let's make two teams! People on the Godard team, with me!' A bartender, laughing so much he can hardly breathe, runs behind the cars like a terrorist in an American TV series to catch us, he drops his cap on the tracks, too bad, the train's going to start again, we help him get back on board, he says the drinks are on him. The Little Girl leans out of the window into the freezing air and declaims, 'The whi-i-i-i-i-te terror of your prisons will invade your unreason . . . In your black n-i-i-i-i-ghts, stagnate ther-r-r-e, you had Fritz Zorn and Alain Tanner-r-r-r-r!!' She is wildly applauded. Towards 4 a.m., some are drunk, talking loudly and a little too much and grabbing on to me whenever the train pitches, the bar has been pillaged, my feet and hair are soaked from a mix of sparkling wine and water the bartenders greeted us with a little while ago, a welcoming dousing in response to the snowball fight. You guys know where we're going, we ask, trying to take advantage of the intoxicated state of some of the people. I kind of catch a plan to enter a symbolic place. The Little Girl and I are impressed and enchanted by their mistrust, not only of us, but of one another—and that organization, that meticulous preparation, the phone number of a lawyer they give to everyone along with advice on what to do in case of arrest.

During a last stop, we unite with the waitresses to take potshots at the train on the other side of the tracks. Lucie, the girl with the big shadows under her eyes, hops round waving a white T-shirt for us to spare her. Then the air regains its breath in the dawn, a beautiful silence descends restfully on us, sleep till eight o'clock. I wake up freezing and strangely, I'm in great shape, I've slept on Ivan's shoulder. The Little Girl isn't there, I find her in deep conversation with the bartender. He's leaning towards her, smiling at what she's telling him.

Ivan and Lucie round us up, they have each received several phone calls. The atmosphere has changed. They did not take over this train just to have snowball fights. When we enter the station of that European capital, we all pile into the corridor, ready to get off, and I don't ask myself what I'm doing here, I've left nothing behind except for Émile of whom I think with a new sense of lightness. And the voice announcing a ten-minute stop is an exciting detail, one more adventurous stop that I'll tell her about soon.

On the platform, a young couple is waiting for us, they motion us to hurry, quick, get out.

Ivan hands me my passport, the conductor had given it back to him along with the fine. He promises that we won't pay it.

When you don't know a city, the first steps you make in it remain in your memory as incoherent vignettes, a puzzle.

WE ARE
THE BIRDS
OF THE
COMING
STORM
185

Massive stone statues of horses, raised fists and churches. Steps, a slightly chipped chalky landscape, and trees, poplars I think. Rows of palm trees, too, and vendors of T-shirts and flags. 'White Power' caps. And that arrangement of shop windows, the identical bland smell of all European downtowns with, as a mirror image, the jerky little steps of women studiously trying to copy the plastic bodies in those same windows.

During the next few days, the press devotes a whole page to that 'operation meticulously prepared from Paris, probably made possible thanks to the complicity of people who knew the functioning of the Villa and what events were planned there'.

But those military-sounding terms are very far from the extravagant atmosphere of our arrival that morning. The place the press calls the Villa has been, since the Election, the vacation home of the wife of the Elected, and the meeting place for the regime's thinkers, its most zealous friends.

When we got to the wall surrounding the huge estate, Ivan walked ahead for a few metres, examining the details of the stones with a map in his hand. Then he froze, asked for help and, without even hiding from the passers-by, climbed over the wall. A few minutes later, he whistled to us and passed us a big, greyish wooden ladder. I remember the astonished eyes of the taxi driver and the bus driver who were stopped at the red light. One after the other, most of us very clumsily, we put our feet on the ladder to get into the estate. Some of us were pitching to and fro, crying out softly. And that sensation of being in an animated cartoon when we all began to run single file and in silence into the rectilinear pathways of the Villa, between the Italian stone pines and the statues of lions. From time to time, a burst of giggles would come from the bushes like the crackle of a fire, and then the others, as they kept walking towards the Villa, would turn round in a chorus of shhh major.

WE ARE
THE BIRDS
OF THE
COMING
STORM

187

We opened a very heavy wooden door with these words engraved in stone on it: 'To Napoleon, the grateful arts.' Ivan and the others expected to encounter some resistance, people in the salons, something. But the room with huge ceilings in which we found ourselves was totally empty, a smell of stale tobacco and dust put a stifling veil over the morning light. We stopped there. The party was over. Empty champagne bottles in an impressive format, glasses turned over, sometimes stripped of their stem, and everywhere dirty plates smeared with dried pink streaks, precious little china Frisbees. In this day-after-the-party decor, we seemed too young and too dirty, shabbily dressed, clumsy with fatigue. Out of place. These signs of opulence, the nonchalance of the broken dishes and the scattered food drew a border between the group from the train and those people who had been celebrating who knows what in this palace. We felt the leaders of the group at a loss because they hadn't met anyone to whom they could explain our improvised trip and the meaning of our presence (which I still didn't know) . . .

The people I had noticed the first night in the park because they seemed to be permanently freezing—all bundled up in disparate clothes and most of them missing a few teeth—sat down on the big couch. Maybe not exactly a couch, a museum piece rather, as the material covering it was embroidered with faded hunting scenes. They sat in a strange way, crossing their legs as if they were facing a very elegant interlocutor. One of them looked distressed and constantly stroked the green velvet of the armrests. I smiled at him, we hadn't spoken to each other much in the train, he'd been asleep during our snowball fights. The sun was making his eyes teary, he was nodding as if to say I'm going to stop, I'll get a hold of myself.

We found a kitchen that was also in a state of total devastation. We opened every cupboard, every drawer, took out cups, coffee, maybe there was bread somewhere, we had the appetites of a band of lost children. In the bathrooms, decorated with little armchairs of adorably faded dark-red velvet, at the foot of huge mirrors with the patina of age, very delicate beige or black tights, all torn, lay rolled up into a ball on the floor.

There was talk of writing a communiqué for the news agencies to explain our presence. Neither the Little Girl nor I intervened, we just listened to their discussions. I fell asleep for a few moments, rocked by their voices and that sun, a warm line through the windows. I have never felt so safe, so at peace, as during those few hours on the priceless rugs of the Villa.

Towards noon, three appalled French officials arrived, and in a falsely hearty tone tried to find out who we were. The Little Girl and I answered their questions good-humouredly, no, we had no idea what we were doing there and knew no one. They went round our laughter, oh come on, that can't be, really, and we repeated, cheerfully and absolutely honest, yes it's true, we really don't know what we're doing here. Neither the Little Girl nor I had understood that they were members of French Intelligence urgently dispatched to try to see who this disparate group was and what they were up to, as they had entered this palace so easily, without really breaking in. They took notes, one even furtively pulled out his phone to take pictures of a few of us (Ivan among others). His phone was thrown out of the window with enthusiasm.

A woman in a grey suit, a Villa official, was running from one room to another, livid, her cell in her hand, I heard her deferentially pronounce the name of the minister of culture while, in the smoky salon, the group was discussing every sentence of a communiqué in progress.

Then, like rumpled young monarchs with swollen eyes and queasy stomachs, the partiers of the Villa finally came downstairs. Famous actors, journalists, I also recognized two writers and one minister, the court of the Elected had spent the night at the Villa after a party whose leftovers we had just found. They were facing us. We scrutinized one another. Ivan began to speak. You could feel that he was moved, tired too, from having thought about this moment for months, I imagine. He was a little like someone out of a poem, Ivan, he suggested we 'enter the universe like a dance, uninvited'. Lucie read the communiqué aloud. I don't remember the exact phrases, but I really liked the way they defined themselves: 'the contaminants'. The choice of the Villa was perfectly clear in the text. To enter where entering seems impossible. Provoke the unexpected. Invade and fill a space reserved for Others with the unexpected. Dynamite the great discreet Triage, that indisputable *Us* as opposed to *Them*. The people of the Villa bent their heads towards us as if to better understand the functioning of rare animals, never daring to speak to those among us whose bodies revealed poor food and neglect. I could see them looking for clues, the shape of the sweatshirt, the vocabulary, the age too, all those details that would make one of us an acceptable interlocutor of their rank. What were we doing there, trying to speak to them. Their voices resembled the voices that announce train delays, an assemblage of words indifferent to movement, repeated no matter what.

'Of course that's very interesting really interesting but after all you can't force yourselves in like that this is a special privileged place how lucky we are in France after all we're still in a country that respects culture art after all right you can't you can't just turn up like that but it's interesting interesting yes barely surviving yes but it's normal yes normal that there should be places like this privileged and what are you doing here it's pointless it's violent really really invading a place you have no business here what are you doing here but it's interesting of course after all yes. But us. We have nothing to do with it. But. Can't do anything about it. That's the way it is.'

I could see Ivan, Lucie and the others whose names I hadn't retained, crumbling, the features of their faces getting blurry. From a little salon next door, the conversations of guests who had not wished to 'take a stand' reached me, they were waiting for 'all this to be over with'.

'They didn't break anything? / and how about you, is your novel going well? / are you invited Tuesday? / OK, this is a little too much, they're all very nice but I have a splitting headache / what they're saying isn't so dumb mind you / but.'

By the middle of the afternoon, we finally found something to eat, a few brioches and some dried-up leftovers from the previous evening. The way the day was progressing made no sense, with no hours and no rest, nothing but little intervals of sleep anywhere in the Villa, alternately curled up on rugs or couches. I remember the suddenly splendid paths of the grounds, the walks we took in them. We would stop before those statues, dumbfounded and clumsy, two peasant girls invited into the world of the nobility.

Then, like little girls happy to invent something to do on a no-school day, the Little Girl and I spent the afternoon sitting on the ground trying to make nail scissors cut some thick sheets we'd found in one of the second-floor bedrooms to make a banner. Squatting opposite each other, we exchanged smiles, both of us looking terrible, and remembered our 'what are we doing here' perhaps still hanging over the river.

We had to climb over the big main balcony to hang this one up. The woman in the grey suit was trying to negotiate and have the banner signalling the 'incident' to the outside removed while Ivan took advantage of being perched on the balcony to yell his answers to the reporters interviewing him down below. TV crews were questioning the group of passers-by who were trying to understand the banner. The words, pathetic no doubt, had been traced with a marker that was too dry to blacken the last letters properly:

WE ARE
THE BIRDS
OF THE
COMING
STORM
191

'THE COURAGE OF BIRDS SINGING IN THE FREEZING WIND.'

The more time passed, the more unknown faces appeared among us, trying to strike up a conversation. One of them asked me where I got my 'slight charming foreign accent'. I don't know why I began to think of Émile who prided herself on always detecting plainclothes cops. And of the Tuesday Evening group where we used to burrow, like furtive animals. To look for presentable words, acceptable to the judges, words that would in fact be useless. Ivan called us over, the situation was becoming tense, we were being invaded by plainclothes men, did we agree, as we had planned, to demand that the director open the Villa the next day to the people of the city to organize discussions?

And by the way, what are your names, you two, Ivan asked me. Voltairine. And she, I added is the . . . Little Girl at the Edge, no, at the End of the Lane. She nodded, adding, 'Actually, we . . . are the little girls at the end of the road, it's a . . . collective.' Stressing the We.

As soon as he left, she asked me, 'Did you see it? I didn't' and I learnt that *The Little Girl at the End of the Lane* was a film from the seventies with Jodie Foster. We promised ourselves to watch it as soon as possible.

I was relieved when night finally fell, every sign of the time spent in this place a small victory. The partiers of the Villa had gone back upstairs to their rooms, annoyed and indifferent, just one of them stayed on to talk with us in the salon. The director of the Villa, who had come back precipitously from an official event in Paris, received Ivan and Lucie. He agreed to open the Villa the next morning in the name of 'freedom of expression'.

Then, little by little, a strange cold crept into those huge rooms, one by one, and we realized that the heating had just been cut. They wanted to make the night difficult for us. We settled in on cushions for a few hours of sleep, Lucie gave out survival blankets.

Late in the night, the Little Girl, lying on her back with her arms folded under the back of her neck, whispered to me something that sounded like a motion she alone had just voted for: 'We have to think of a theory of the ladder, Voltairine.' Then, in the face of my perplexed silence, she went on, 'All those films where the police is omnipotent, you know . . . Their scientific intelligence! And to foil them, you have to be super-trained or . . . an IT expert, decipher codes, all that stuff. And . . . We entered the Villa with only a wooden ladder . . .'

She got up from her sleeping bag. In her panties, she tiptoed over the sleepers and, glued to the window, admired the stone lions of the garden under the moon. In her notebook, I saw:

Look for wooden ladders everywhere!! Also: make a list of End of the Road symptoms.

She motioned to me to get up and follow her. Behind the salon, we found a little emergency exit that led to a blue room in a state of neglect. The somewhat damaged, rough floor, a dull beige, gave out different sounds at every step. I enjoyed testing their variety, stepping from one slat onto another. Truly, I danced.

The belly—a palpitating shield—responds to the vertebrae, the foot at the end of the ankles is an arrow that is perfectly aware of what it's doing there. In slow motion almost, an attempt, a reunion, I crossed the room in a diagonal of *déboulés* ending in a double pirouette in front of a mirror with a dirty gilt frame. She applauded, whispering enthusiastically, 'Bravo bravo,' the tip of her nose red from cold. Shivering, we went back into the large salon where everyone was still asleep. In my sleep, the rustling of our aluminium survival blankets blended into a sound of seaside and wind. Very early in the morning, our bundled-up, motionless bodies on the floor resembled great golden sweet wrappers, a gigantic New Year celebration.

And I didn't hear anything, I must have fallen asleep just before they arrived. Cops in balaclavas and black gloves, a special unit no doubt, are suddenly there, screaming, the French plainclothes men, extremely nervous, stand far back while they're kicking us. Terrorized and numbed with sleep and cold, some remain sitting in their blankets, dazed. Between the noise of boots on the stairs and their irruption in the salon accompanied by the director and the Villa official, still paler in her grey suit, it all goes too quickly for us to get up and gather our things. I recognize the guy from the day before who, in a friendly voice, had explained to the Little Girl that he understood the idea behind this expedition—to show we're not surrounded yet, spread the possibilities of actions. I think they even talked about Deleuze together. This morning, he's wearing an orange armband and his eyes catch, snap up a piece of warm meat when a girl gets dressed in front of him.

We regroup in the centre of the room, most of us in our underwear, our hair dull and tangled, Ivan yells, 'Hold on to each other's arms, it'll be OK.' The Little Girl is behind me, I can't see her but I hear the sharp sound of someone spitting and the whole group is shaken when two cops rush her. The director is wiping off the saliva flowing down his cheek and the moment he calls her a slut, just before the second spit that hits him in the eye this time, the disgust deforming his voice, the voice of an intellectual in charge of a splendidly cultural place, is surely due to his mistaken assessment—the Little Girl is not, on this day, at the End of the Lane.

We slowly walk down the steps of a very narrow service stairway, they want to get us out of the Villa discreetly, far from the cameras waiting in front of the main entrance, I concentrate on our feet, afraid that one of us will fall and drag down all the others, I'm afraid and the masked bodies surrounding us are all holding gas guns in their hands with their fingers on the nozzles, at the ready, a boy keeps repeating that if they fire gas in here, we're screwed, screwed. Outside, the TVs get the idea and go round the place. They hold mikes out to us but we can't hear anything, their questions are drowned out by the orders of the cops who push us into a big bus, hitting people in the back with clubs if they don't move fast enough.

Unlike Ivan, I don't feel betrayed by the phoney promise of the director of the Villa to let us go free. In the evening edition of *Le Monde*, he'll describe the group as a band of students and artists, but also, he will add, 'among them, some people visibly homeless'. His 'visibly' examines, with the experienced eye of a man from the Ministry of Art and Culture, the bodies with missing teeth, dull skin, bellies swollen from cheap liquor, that 'visibly' which clacks like a file quickly shut, 'visibly' setting the Others apart from an Us with supple hair and lively voices whom he imagines to be artists.

WE ARE
THE BIRDS
OF THE
COMING
STORM

195

The central police station doesn't have enough seats or benches for us. The captain gives our papers a lengthy inspection, one by one. When it's my turn, he goes from my passport to my breasts, strides up and down my body like a possible path open to him. I can't understand what he's saying but the laugh his sentence sets off in his colleague is a clear subtitle. He leans with interest over his computer screen. I don't know how to say 'Is there a problem?' This is taking too long. He hands my passport to a colleague, she's half-heartedly chewing on her gum, the flesh of her pink arms squeezed into the tight short sleeves of a navy blue blouse makes me think of a leg with a sick calf. She orders me to get up and follow her. As I go back into the big room where the other people in the group are held, sitting on the floor or on benches, waiting to be checked, some of them, upset at seeing me taken away elsewhere, curse the policewoman in English. As for the Little Girl, she goes into the captain's office after me.

She interrogates me for what feels like an hour. I'm very thirsty. She wants to know what I'm doing in France. What I'm really doing, she means. What network, my 'dance', topless? she asks, with a nasty smile, her English as shapeless as the discoloured chewing gum that appears between her teeth. My court conviction, which she can certainly read in detail on her screen, doesn't help, she stares at me, delighted at the godsend of having fallen upon a case like this. Frowns as if the smell of my life story, something in it, were invading her, disgusting her.

Since when have I been connected to this group. Who is the leader. Were you ever involved in violent actions of this kind in other countries of the European Union. Then she changes her mind the way you change TV channels, bends her head, articulating words plasticized with saliva. Do you know that holding someone against his will is tried in superior criminal court. Terrorism Category 3. I smile, I wait for her to do the same, holding whom, what Class 3.

She takes no notes during my story, as if she were waiting for me to give her a better version. When I confirm that I have nothing to add, she emits a sound between a sneeze and a clearing of the throat, nerves no doubt, gets up and her chair scrapes the tile floor. She takes me back to the others. The Little Girl is still with the captain. 'You OK, little girl at the end of whatever? Listen, we're not signing anything, all right?' Ivan takes advantage of a trip to the bathroom to make a discreet phone call to a lawyer in Paris.

Later in the evening, we squeeze over to make room for two young Romanian women. They are anxiously waiting to find out if they'll be sent back to Bucharest, where they know no one, they never lived there. In a low voice, we reminisce about different neighbourhoods of the city, I draw them a rough map of the downtown area. My emotion is so strong I'm embarrassed, I laugh a few times, so they're not alarmed at the tears in my eyes, they are so totally from the West while I, I've always just pretended to be.

Some people in the group are sleeping on the floor, exhausted. We ask for something to drink, a boy has to take his asthma medication, he'll get nothing, we'll get nothing, neither to eat nor to drink. I feel a certain sense of relief at this. They are not courteous, we are their enemies.

Being guilty of nothing when everything leaves scratches on you makes innocence heavy and hard to bear. And that innocence is akin to the fearful precautions, those reasonable decisions you make every day to stay in the same position,

WE ARE
THE BIRDS
OF THE
COMING
STORM
197

not to budge from wherever you in fact find yourself rather comfortable.

Before the trial, my experiences with the police were mostly connected to my country of origin. Its rules, what is left unsaid. The sneaky skills you needed to never have to deal with the Securitate. Be clever, discreet and silent. On Sunday mornings, Romanian television used to show old episodes of *Bewitched* and I could glimpse that magical world about which I knew nothing except that—an American flat of the fifties, straight avenues and the outmoded hairdo of a house-wife conscientiously trying to be dumb and funny.

Life in the West seemed to me like a kind of gift bag in which there would be a passport, a kitchen full of appliances and conversations far from the microphones hidden in our telephones and lamps, the whole thing slightly scented with a fresh smell, soluble lilac perhaps, never the smell of grilled pork sausages which invaded the Bucharest summers. I thought that by passing from one border to another, one would acquire that transparent, sanitized life, easy living with-out complications, plots, uniforms and letters of denunciation.

During my first years in Paris, I was delighted to let myself be swallowed up, under the spell of the Monoprix super-markets, popular programmes on Saturday night TV and the young pupils of the School of Ballet. I copy their blasé non-chalance, their sweatshirts carefully ripped with scissors. The children of the West are afraid of nothing and I adore their aversions. Their eyes are filled with tranquil knowledge, they capitalize the word Rights, they know that their problems, if they have any, will not last. In two months, I have nearly lost my foreign accent. When I'm asked where I'm from, I say Canada, Austria, places I know so little they seem unverifiable.

At family gatherings, I watch those familiar foreigners, fearful silhouettes dressed in their reasonable, discreet clothes, and I hate them. I despise their meticulous lives. Their constant effort to get good grades from the French, that terrible energy they put into not being at fault, but for what. Their eyes cast down in the Métro as soon as they might be noticed. I hate my parents' advice, their smiles which freeze on their lips when I talk Romanian too loudly in public. Just be careful, they tell me. Be nice. You have to be nice here. Swallow it down, swallow. Often, friends of my parents would congratulate me on being blonde, it's true you don't look Romanian. And it seems to me they're praising me on my smell, less strong than expected, that's something to be thankful for. Make yourself pleasant, supple, white and modern. We, the Others—since I'm part of them too—even if when I got here I copied you, we strive to disappear, brought up as we are to be discreet. Noiselessly, we melt into the background, we bend, fold ourselves acrobatically into the trunks of cars. '*Girls from the East are more understanding,*' says *the man who will become my adversary* to his amused friends during a dinner, '. . . *better than with a whore, you can do anything and it's free.*'

'I'm kidding,' *he* adds.

Until that trial that identifies me as guilty, I operate perfectly. I smooth myself out, lie down and sell myself to this country which is constantly orating, proudly exhibiting its flares of social anger very rapidly extinguished, as evidence of its left-wing magnanimity. Its Rights for all, its SOS to racism.

I'm very careful and it works, while year after year, I see the French getting bolder. They turn round on the street to look at women who cover their hair, smug—it sure gets you to see that here *in our country*—on TV, second-rate young singers, all excited at being interviewed, talk about the smell of the Romanians in the Métro to an approving audience, often people beg me to have a sense of humour, come on, and I smile at them, stick to them and their healthy breath and teeth. I have no enemies, I've been told they all died with Ceauşescu. The mere idea of enemy is an image out of a bad

WE ARE
THE BIRDS
OF THE
COMING
STORM

199

TV series, a dark, bearded kind of guy looking for a suitcase full of money. Modern girls have no enemies.

Then I meet Émile and the other rejects, the girls hiding out inside the Tuesday Evenings, pushed by a thrust of the pelvis into the great Democracy of Rape, that disgust at an identity reduced to spread legs.

We've been in police custody for close to fifteen hours. The captain takes the trouble to speak in English so we can all understand when, coming across one passport, he deciphers a name he thinks is Jewish, 'Ah! One of Hitler's pals,' he pretends to pinch his nose in a childish gesture, before a body dressed in frumpy, dull trousers, he says, 'God, you stink,' to girls in T-shirts, he trumpets 'I'll drill your ass,' and to the ones whose hair is covered by a scarf he hums, 'Bin Laden Bin Laden.' Next to him—a perfect number of complementary duettists—the lady cop. She raises her eyes to heaven and stays heavily seated.

Then they make us go into a room where a policeman is sitting in front of piled-up documents. And another one, with a camera. The first one grabs our hand, stains our fingers with ink, then points to a little blank space on the sheet of paper: 'Sign here.' One by one we answer, 'I won't sign anything.' The guy doesn't even seem to hear us, he just motions us to walk forward in front of the wall. We follow each other. The Little Girl is soaping her blackened fingers in the sink, I prepare myself to be photographed. Just at the moment the flash goes off, she turns to me and shakes her soaking hands in my direction. In the photo registering me in the Europol file, I'm bursting with laughter, delighted.

We come out of there starving, with dry throats and bleary, sunken eyes. Morning is hitting the pavement of the police station, shrill horns mixing with the colour of the ochre houses, laundry swaying on the balconies and the women's thighs are as pale as the plastic flowers on billboards. A bus

WE ARE
THE BIRDS
OF THE
COMING
STORM

201

chartered by the police and the French Embassy will take us back to Paris, it's leaving at the end of the day.

We take a walk together until it's time to take the bus, our clothes are dirty, our hair too, and in the little bathroom mirror of the cafe where at last we have a cup of tea, I have the impression of seeing myself again, of recognizing something in my face red from lack of rest and excitement, a path I may have already taken. It's the mood of an escapee, of time pushed away somewhere else, later, further on. The Little Girl picks up the slices of bread from an enormous three-decker sandwich, removes bits of tomato and two completely flattened shrimps that she grabs and throws into an ashtray.

'We've been so successful, Voltairine, since we've stopped going to the cinema . . . Well, let's not brag too much though, we only have a record, they're not after us . . .'

She got an additional fine ('resisting arrest and contempt of a person in authority by means of gesture, word or look'). We talk about Émile, whom I miss, talk about the way she protects me, how attentive she's been for years, about the way she forgives my various paralyses, the cosy warmth of her love. I feel like going back. But I don't know where to go back and to what. At the same time, the Little Girl is looking at her skirt, all rumpled, and without raising her head, she says, 'We can't just pick up from where . . . Can we?'

Later, it's almost time to take the bus, she shakes her head forcefully and bursts out laughing. 'You know, the people who mutter, "What won't they think of next" . . . It may be a cry of despair. A terrible realization. What won't they think of next! But what will become of us if we don't think of things to invent next? There's such a lack . . . I don't know who said it, a society that abolishes all adventure makes the abolition of that society the only possible adventure . . .'

She waits a little, with angry eyebrows, then, like a child who hasn't eaten anything since the previous day, she suddenly moves near me and throws her arms round my waist with her hair resting on my shoulder.

'I love it I love that you never tell me: be simple . . .'

The bus is almost clean for the first few hours of the trip. Ivan is standing at the centre, holding on to the seats and I don't listen to any of his heartfelt phrases, it seems to be about planning what to do next, no point worrying, our trial will probably take place in the spring but the accusation of conspiracy with attempt to hold someone against his will can't stand up, we did no damage to property and forced no one to stay with us. Ivan still seems to think there's some connection between what people do and what they can be accused of doing.

The driver agrees to stop every hour, we smoke cigarettes on desolate parking areas with their tired lamp posts. We nibble on chocolate bars, sweets, biscuits soft with humidity crumbling into the depths of our seats.

She's sleeping, with her face against the fogged-up window. When we cross the French border, I wake up the Little Girl. Paris is approaching, a grimacing mouth, dirty, gaping with emptiness and dangerous turns, blackened with neighbourhoods where it is no longer possible to go, like a video game, some itineraries are flashing, suddenly forbidden. To go back there would be to apologize, I tell her, don't you think? If we go back now, contrite, dirty and ragged. No? Don't you think so?

She adds pompously, yawning, 'And with a Europol file, if you please.' Reassured, I fall asleep, for hardly an hour. My body has subsisted on the minimum I've given it ever since we left, grabbing a bit of sleep on a train, the water of a coffee and slices of limp tomatoes pulled out of a sandwich.

When I wake up, she holds this out to me:

WE ARE
THE BIRDS
OF THE
COMING
STORM

203

Be simple. Couldn't you be simple. Couldn't you be clearer.

Let us be clear! An army of simple bodies, proud to know the password for this Kingdom of the MRI. That transparency.

Be soluble. Summarizable. Scrape off the rough surfaces the way you burn weeds. Put yourself in categories, departments. Love work sex family leisure. Work *on* yourself and make yourself your greatest work! Sum yourself up in a short, pleasant sentence so they can go through you rapidly, without stumbling on what is hard to grasp.

In the Kingdom of the MRI, bythinellas will triumph. Our lovely bythinella lives.

PS. *Bythinella navacellensis* is that tiny snail the size of a grain of rice that lives in underground water. It doesn't have eyes any more, they disappeared since they were of no use to it. You can see its brain and intestines right through it. The scientists who discovered it did not classify it as an endangered species but as a vulnerable species because of its transparency. It wouldn't take much to make it disappear.

She folds her long legs on the seat, sitting cross-legged, she just got an idea! I have to trust her, Jumièges! she suggests. (I have no idea what this is.) Or the sea! I mean the ocean, not ordinary water, only volcanic water. Her hair, tied up tight, seems darker that way. I sent several SMS to Émile without saying too much about our trip, for the first time I'm not giving her details. I ask the Little Girl if she told her fiancé about her departure, isn't she afraid he'll call the police. We don't know anything about each other, we never talked about high school, university, boyfriends, parents or home. Nothing but stories, film daydreams whose images tremble from the emotion of time. Perhaps because of all that—the Cinémathèque, the graffiti and the banners of our beautiful 'what are we doing here' night—we're detached from time as it flows by. We have no future, we have all the time in the world.

Some people may have thought we had organized and planned everything. In reality, that's absolutely not true. There's that moment when things 'take a dramatic turn', as human interest stories put it (and besides, exactly when does that happen? When she decides to overcome my fear during the night of the graffiti? Or when we get off the bus before reaching Paris?), we have no clue about what we're actually doing. Besides, we're not doing anything. Just clumsy attempts, we're completely at the mercy of chance. And it's that swaggering ignorance that I cherish today.

Our slightly ridiculous arrest and the outrageousness of having a Europol file on us for 'occupation, hostage-taking and terrorist associations' has freed us from fear. For me, already convicted, entrenched in my silences and the Island, being accused now of a tangible fact, even an aberrant one, is somehow soothing. I can say I'm guilty of having entered that place, I can say I'm guilty of having climbed a wooden ladder, but I couldn't say I'm guilty of the night of *14 September*. The Little Girl at the End of the Lane also seems almost re-energized by that ruling, as if all those months she had been diluting herself in the loneliness of having to touch the palms of checkout girls and threatening Instructions. She was looking for guilty parties and she's found enemies—that's even better.

Uprooted from nothing and instantly threatened, our hotchpotch of desires, those faltering attempts at a possible life—we're beginning to hold them tightly against us, little packages impossible to relinquish. And it's either that or conforming to their injunctions right away. That or grabbing at the chance of not having to dread punishment any more, since it has already been done. They made the choice for us. We've gained the time lost in fear.

WE ARE
THE BIRDS
OF THE
COMING
STORM

205

Close to 5 a.m. on that February morning, we think the last cigarette stop is the right one, the one that, judging from the map, seems closest to that Jumièges where the Little Girl absolutely wants to go.

The bus drives away, the windows white with frost animated by the farewells of those who're already up, waving friendly hands.

'It's like going on vacation,' she's hopping up and down. Happiness is infusing her blood. At certain times, you can almost see that electric happiness breaking her skin, a joy so senseless that it makes her laugh, the embarrassment of that gratuitous pleasure bubbles up in her voice and overflows. The pleasure of being together, just the two of us. Of being outside. With nothing, nothing more than the nothing of this morning, when we're about to go wherever it's good to be, just to see.

Every time we come out of a shelter, it starts to rain, you'd think spring was coming if the rain weren't icy. After two stops, one under a useless poplar and the other in a deserted, stinking cafe, our third attempt is showered on again. The Little Girl raises her hands to heaven, she laughs with her mouth wide open, her skirt is sticking to the inside of her thighs and her eyelashes make little umbrellas on her eyes, false eyelashes of rain gleaming with diluted mascara. A car reels towards us and stops right where we are. There are three of them and they're actually going through Jumièges. We're squeezed against this guy of twenty-something. It's not sure he's doing it on purpose, he's probably not even aware of his thighs widely spread on the seat, his jeans touching my closed legs. It's also not sure that their laughs and those innuendoes are anything but a leftover from last night's drinking spree. But my fear creeps up like nausea, this car, we shouldn't have, they're three of them, we're two. Anger at being afraid of all those trifles, that permanent counting, my practical assessments as a girl. Weary disgust at feeling the fear of a weak animal with its back arched before danger. On the seat, I move a bit nearer to the Little Girl who's making conversation with the driver, she hasn't noticed anything, isn't looking at me. And what are we doing here, all alone, he says, and they exchange little signs in the rear-view mirror. Then she cuts in. Suddenly decides it's over, 'OK, that's it. Stop there, at that stop sign right ahead of you.'

'But Jumièges is still far from here . . .'

WE ARE
THE BIRDS
OF THE
COMING
STORM

207

And all that's nothing, we can't blame them for their vulgarity, for the confidence in that spreading of open thighs, for their breath too close, those furtive glances at my mouth every time they ask me a question, there's not much room on the back seat after all.

But my fear, the tense voice of the Little Girl just allowed it to sweep through me, I'm bristling with it. They start laughing as if I'd just made a great joke, imitating something shrill, my trembling voice when I say, 'We want to get out we want to get out.' Disguising their voices in a parody of a little terrorized girl we want to get out we want to get out. I don't see her searching round in her bag. The Little girl opens the door with one hand, the rain slants into the car, the guy turns round screaming she's crazy, that's dangerous, in the other hand she's holding an open fountain pen and I don't understand a thing, the guy sitting in the passenger seat who hasn't said anything until now, we only heard his laugh, turns to her, tries to close the door with one hand and then screams and puts his hand on his neck. The ink makes a bad scribble out of the cut, a rough draft purplish with blood.

'Do you think he's going to press charges,' she says, under the rain of course, in the middle of the little road. And without waiting for my answer, hiccupping with laughter, 'You think . . . we're . . . we're . . . going to . . . have . . . a ri-al, a tri-al?!'

She grabs my hands, drags me into an ultra-fast concentric round, our movement whips up the drops of water and sends them waltzing all over.

Rule number one, Voltairine, the Little Girl tells me where we're finally in Jumièges having breakfast, 'Avoid the Christian trap of obligatory feminine redemption. Not become saints, if you see what I mean. Right? In films, the girls who take a trip alone always end up killing a guy or a cop in a weird way and die at the end of the film. That way, everyone's happy. They tried to go off alone but . . . oh, the wo-r-r-rld is dan-ger-ous. You have to pay for getting out, ladies. So, rule number one: let's not pay, OK. A fountain pen, yes, but more than that . . .' she concludes, undoing her hair without dropping the crois- sant in her mouth, '. . . isha job.'

WE ARE
THE BIRDS
OF THE
COMING
STORM

209

'I DECREE THAT THE FORCE AND POWER
OF THEIR BODIES MUST BE WEAKENED,
SINCE THEY HAVE DARED
TO USE THEM AGAINST THE KING, THEIR FATHER.'

When we enter the grounds of the Abbey, she reels off dates and names, very quickly, as she often does, 'The *in tam arduo negotio* of the abbot who hesitated to convict Joan of Arc. True, he didn't hesitate very long. Corinne de Tygier. Don't ask me who that is. But she built the cloister. To be named Corinne is already quite something when you build a cloister . . . Oh! Here it is! The yew tree! Planted in the sixteenth century. Let's touch the yew, Voltairine! . . . In 996, the peasant revolt in Normandy, it took place round here, I think. No, 997. I just love to say that: nine hundred and ninety-seven nine hundred and ninety-seven! They wanted free use of the rivers and forests, they had established some kind of parliament together, to live according to their own laws. Oh! Touch it . . . Come on, touch the bark! Come back here right away, Voltairine, you're not made of sugar, it's only rain!'

We go into the museum and even before she can point it out to me, I recognize the painting—it's the one she tacked up in her flat. She leans towards me, whispers, still very quickly, her words mixing with those of the guide who has just stopped in front of that same painting.

Calm—horror—Simone de Beauvoir—the surrealists—aquatic coffin—painting—apparently normal—rip out the nerves and tendons.

A raft on a river. A raft made up to be a bedroom. On it, two boys are lying, young wild faces of rock stars at rest, propped up lazily on thick pillows. The hand of the one to the left is dangling over the water. Their calves are wrapped in several layers of cloth, white like bandages, held together by thin leather straps. An embroidered blanket has been placed on their bodies, almost a shroud. At the front of the raft, a reliquary, like a little mystic prow, decorated with roses and topped with a candle with a flickering flame. We are alone in the room before the painting by Evariste-Vital Luminais, *The Enervated Boys of Jumièges*.

In a book next to the painting, we read:

This painting is based on a well-known legend. Painted in 1880, it shows the two sons of Bathilde and Clovis II, who entrusted his power to the elder when he left on a pilgrimage to the Holy Land around 660. The son then fought with his mother and plotted against his parents with his younger brother. When Clovis returned to France, he had to contend with an army led by his two sons. After they were defeated, the king decided to execute them, but Bathilde suggested a type of torture (which lasted at least until Charles Martel) that consisted in burning or ripping out the nerves and tendons of the calves, depriving the victims of their mobility. Thus, the characters are not enervated, they have been enervated. Transformed into apathetic, docile bodies, suffering terribly, Bathilde's two sons became extremely religious. Not knowing what monastery to send them to, their parents left them to drift aimlessly down the Seine on their raft, which ended up in Jumièges. There, Saint Philibert, the founder of the abbey, recognized them and made them monks. Legend has it that they are buried in the tomb of the Abbey of Jumièges. But the story is historically false. In fact, Clovis never went on a

WE ARE
THE BIRDS
OF THE
COMING
STORM

211

pilgrimage to the Holy Land and died too young to see his
power contested by his sons; neither of them—as each of them
reigned in turn—was ever a monk, 'enervated' in Jumièges.

The Little Girl turns towards me, speechless. Her silence is a subtitle. That terrible but apparently normal calm of their bodies. It's not immediately clear that the relaxed appearance of those bodies is the relaxation of death. Oh, but how peaceful, what a relief not to have those nerves any more, to be made powerless by our Fathers . . . With nerves slashed, drifting is all that's left, the breeze is gentle, nothing to be done but let things go on.

That's the poisoned story they tell us and we ask for it tirelessly again and again, our favourite, the poisonous story we recognize even before they feed us the ending, the legend indispensable to our sleep. The one we believe in with the will to keep believing it, and in all its forms. It's the restful legend of the impossible escape and its consequences, a legend at once so sweet and sad that we've been chewing on it since childhood. Watch out. You're going to hurt yourself. Oh, a falling bird, don't look. The story of the threat that awaits girls who venture out to places where they'd been told never to go, the story of girls who pry open doors and nights, climb over walls, walk through forests, streets and parking lots. The story of every Thelma and Louise who drink at the wonderful speed of their journeys, immediately apprehended, always caught. And who then, to defend themselves, kill as if by mistake. And they can keep running all they want, they're now as clumsy as animals deprived of their daily outing, with no solution but their deaths, a definitive surrender. That's what happens to women who escape.

Today I can't say the painting was the starting point for all that or just some kind of catalyst. Any more than dancing round at top speed while holding hands in the winter rain of Normandy or seeing blood mixing with ink and getting a lift from it. Any more than the Instructions, those contemporary Enervatings kept in one's pockets like so many warnings and crumpled with a trembling hand, so we won't forget what lies in wait if we yield.

Starting points don't exist, Voltairine. Or else they do, and they're all over, constantly, passing discreetly by. (The instant is what comes and goes, what returns and thus allows us to *get hold of* what had been forgotten.)

We'll only need an instant to ignore those legends, those litanies of the terminally Enervated, and then, in the end, not to know what we're doing any more, so we can do it at last.

WE ARE
THE BIRDS
OF THE
COMING
STORM

213

She's standing there on the doorstep without moving, her ankles pallid under the yellowish beige of her tights. Each of her responses is punctuated by a bizarre exhalation followed by a tense silence, like a fit of rage that never explodes. She runs a little guest house outside the village and when we knock, she doesn't answer, but one hand picks up a corner of the curtain in the window. No more rooms, she shakes her head, puffing, pointing to the cars parked in the garden, nice cars. Check out the new town, there's a place that might take you in, she adds, and her eyes sweep over us, a beacon scanning our dirty details, skirt, hair and nails.

There aren't even two kilometres between the paved streets where proud signs signal a church dating back to the eleventh century and the new town. Shreds of blue and white posters remain from the Election, you can still read 'WE WILL SURPRISE YOU!' and also 'WELLNESS PLAN: MENTAL HEALTH FOR ALL!' There, on the main square, the directions give us a Giant Champion supermarket and a home with a poetic name of flowers, I can't remember if it's Mimosa House.

It's a mistake. We think this is where we can find a room for the night. We go to the reception desk. On the brown Plexiglas table, brochures present the Home that the new town's social services have set up. It takes in 'isolated senior citizens of very limited means as well as struggling young workers'. Nowhere does it say anything about renting a room for the night, besides there are no prices posted, just little photos, some slightly blurred, with colours running into one another. The senior citizens at the cooking workshop. The seniors at the creative writing workshop. Our young workers and seniors at the photography workshop.

A young woman suddenly appears in the hall and sits down behind the Plexiglas, 'Hello, I'm sorry, I didn't hear you come in. We've been expecting you! OK, some are a little anxious, you'll see, as soon as we change activity teams, it gets complicated! And since you're a little late too . . . Third floor!'

We thank her and walk to the lift without talking to each other. Ever since the Little Girl has been at my side, parks rustle with the sound of chaotic trips, words turn into actions, dates are extricated from my belly and doors open. We never stop appropriating space without ever paying the price.

'Well . . . ?' she says, delighted.

'. . . I don't know . . . A sleep workshop for the night wouldn't be so bad . . .'

The greenish neon of the lift amplifies the dulled colour of our shapeless hair and our crumpled, stained clothing. In the course of three floors, rubber bands are tied round hair and attempts are made to smooth out the wrinkles in skirts. In the dark corridor with its flat smell of worn, synthetic hotel carpeting, the Little Girl stops me with one hand, fumbles round in her bag and pushes me against the wall. She gets to work. She draws me a carmine mouth and pinches both my cheeks very hard. She wants a handkerchief and I don't have one, so she presents her palm for me to kiss, I can't understand why she wants me to kiss her hand but she sighs and presses the palm of her hand very hard against my lips. 'It was too red!' she whispers, attenuating the print of my mouth on her hand, all coloured now.

There are fifteen or so of them, sitting round several tables placed end to end, a big beige rectangle, and they greet us

WE ARE
THE BIRDS
OF THE
COMING
STORM

215

politely. Suddenly the door opens again on a breathless woman with very short hair dyed orange, a knitted blue sweater coordinated with absolutely everything she's wearing—from her turquoise earrings to her navy blue glasses to her socks, which peep out from the bottom of her sky blue slacks.

'My apologies! I was looking for you, they told me you went upstairs. Ah,' she has a hard time catching her breath and goes to sit down, patting one or two heads on the way, 'Here's our group of seniors! May I introduce you . . . ?' She holds out her hand to us.

'So . . . The . . . collective of little girls in banishment, sorry, at the end of the lane, and our president, Mademoiselle Voltairine,' says the Little Girl charmingly.

It's a misunderstanding but not a joke. We stay in that room for almost three hours. Those bodies grouped in categories appropriate to their degree of wear speak all at once, it unfurls and piles up, we learn that there's a question of another workshop during the week, 'A life workshop! Yes, exactly! It'll be a life workshop!' adds the orange-and-blue lady. A writer will come and take down their words, 'your life sto-ry!' to make a real novel out of it. Immediately, some of them protest, their lives will be stolen! And they turn to us distrustfully. What are we going to do with them? Then, at the last minute, I remember Émile's questionnaires, the ones she never used to finish.

I ask to consult with my colleague, who is giggling. Everything has made us laugh for the past eighty hours or so, the word colleague too. We step out into the hallway for a few minutes. The Little Girl is sceptical, some of them look so sad, she even wonders if we shouldn't . . .

'What? No, come on, we're not going to leave just like that, not giving our workshop would be a lousy thing to do.'

It's probably not a creative writing workshop. It's certainly not group therapy either. In fact, I don't really know what to call our improvised session. The Little Girl takes down their answers at top speed, she doesn't stop, fills pages with abbreviations, I notice arrows in front of first names. Sometimes she raises her hand to ask for a sentence to be repeated, so nothing would be wasted of that afternoon at the Home of the new town. We never made a novel out of their lives. If I'm attaching the Little Girl at the End of the Lane's pages here rather than talking about them, it's because it seems to me that she was able to grasp what poured out that day, the sunny spells of their exhausted bodies.

People over 65:
The usual recommended first dose is 5 mg a day.

Tell me, I say stupidly to get things going, as if as soon as people have white hair they are required to rummage through their drawers in front of others, tell me what you used to dream about when you were twelve.

'My sister and I had planned to kill our father. I was twelve, I talked about it to everyone in the village, the neighbours knew what was going on in our house all right. We had hidden the axe behind the kitchen door, see. But we screwed up, I mean, we didn't do it right. So we ran away with our mum during the night and we spent a few days hidden in the woods. Right near a zoo! We could hear the lions at night . . . Couldn't you organize an outing to the zoo?' the little girl with white hair in a pastel sweater asks avidly. 'I'd really love to see a lion in the daytime . . .'

Odette nods (energetically, as if to confirm a decision to go on vacation.) 'Gotta kill,' with her arms crossed in front of her orange juice.

The axe of the little girl with white hair in a pastel sweater hidden behind a door.

WE ARE
THE BIRDS
OF THE
COMING
STORM

217

Consult your doctor immediately if you have thoughts.

His words come out through some of his remaining teeth. No, nothing, he repeats, I have nothing to tell you, so I feel as if he won't let me check his ID. It's over sixty years now, you understand. He wipes away tears with a dry hand without hiding them. Says nothing. Breathes in.

Like animals . . . The women round here, when I was growing up back there in the country . . . You know what we used to call them? Marne animals . . . And the other guys would laugh, right . . . Marne animals.

It is thus very important to follow exactly. Not to stop.

Her long, grey hair makes a braid of cluttered clouds. Every day they ask her to cut her hair. Come on now! You can't keep hair like that at your age. But she grabs her braid with both hands the way you throw yourself onto a raft, in the loneliness of a life at sea. Dina laughs broadly, still at sea. Her laugh chops all her sentences as if to keep us at bay.

'I'm here . . . Why already . . . To . . . To watch the flowers grow (laugh). It's better for the others outside, right. Seems I was too angry . . . Twelve years old? Never was twelve. Wasn't twelve ever, mmmmno! (laugh)'

The woman in charge of the home becomes agitated, glances at us in a panic, her voice comes out of her like the siren of a blue ambulance, you know, anger, that's life after all, you do know that don't you Dina, that's life!

'Oh yeah?' Dina suddenly turns her whole body towards the agitated ambulance. 'I'm alive? Me?. . . First I heard!!' And gripping her braid in her left hand, she bursts out laughing.

And when the real activity leaders call at the end of the afternoon to apologize for not having come that day, we have nothing to explain because no one gives a hoot. Odette leans towards us with the tone she used in recommending axe murder in certain situations, 'We were afraid we'd have to tell secrets, things that only belong to us, see. But actually, we didn't. We shared some good words together. It's been nice,' and she ceremoniously shakes Voltairine's hand, then mine.

WE ARE
THE BIRDS
OF THE
COMING
STORM
219

Lying on the little bed in the room of the real workshop leaders. The cream-coloured bed lamp turned to the ceiling. We can make out the voice with orange hair screaming in the halls from afar: 'COCKTAIL TIME! . . . DRINKS! COCKTAILS AND CRACKIES!'

Sleep is looming, the sweet smell of perfume.

I want to play Cat Power for her, but the Little Girl takes out a Dolly Parton CD for me, just once, just *I will always love you*, you'll see Voltairine, you'll never make fun of her hairdo again.

I agree. Lying on her back on the bed, she put her hands over her closed eyes, her breasts come to the edge of the blue-grey T-shirt, its neck is slightly damaged. In the silent room, I slip her old CD into the player. After the first chorus, she opens her eyes, sits up, her elbows balanced on the soft mattress and, with the gesture of a mafiosa, orders me to do it. Dance!

I have to roll the rug up into a corner of the little room, watch out for the table and slip between the chair and the bed. My foot in second position *développé* brushes against the lamp. The song lasts three minutes and four seconds. At the last note of the slide guitar, the Little Girl charges to the player and puts the song on again. I avoid *arabesques*, there's not enough room, my pirouettes are braked by the carpeting, and then, it must be the slide guitar, my hands begin to trace my hips and I stare at the Girl, like in the choreography of a

Texan bar. Then she comes and stands behind me, I don't stop dancing and she puts her arms on the circle my arms form above my head. How do you do it, to make it so pretty, she asks in my ear. You have to imagine, I whisper, a drop of water flowing down your arm, if you raise your elbow too much, it's lost. I'm out of breath. Three minutes four seconds. Again. And again. The material of her dress is slightly rough. The Little Girl takes me by the hands so I'm facing her. Then. The palm of her hand presses the hollow of my back towards her belly. Her fingers go through my hair, taking a pin out of my bun, then another.

'. . . I am Frank . . . Sinatra . . . It's that film . . . some came running, you know,' she whispers in my ear and ruffles my hair, for a long time. Her knee splits me between the legs, I am melting.

When she sleeps, it seems to me that her face is watching crumpled Instructions, wooden ladders and checkout girls on the run. I think of axes hidden behind kitchen doors . . . mangy, sick lions in zoos in the night.

WE ARE
THE BIRDS
OF THE
COMING
STORM

221

When I wake up, she's kneeling on the floor in her panties and a sweater with a piece of Scotch tape between her teeth. Round her, pages of her spiral notebook placed end to end make a fan of the same question in the room.

'WHO CUT THEIR NERVES?

FLUSH OUT THE BARBARIAN KINGS

WHO CUT THE NERVES AND BROKE THE BONES OF THOSE CHILDREN OF THE BARBARIAN KINGS?

WHO CUT YOUR NERVES AND BROKE YOUR BONES? The Little Girls at the End of the Lane.'

'Let's buy beautiful plastic tablecloths! With flowers on them! We're in the country, Voltairine, we have to adapt.'

Cutting up the plastic, framing it with thick Scotch tape, putting wire in the holes and going over the letters with a marker, a very black one. We buy a hiker's backpack to put the banners in, their size is more modest than our mega 'WHAT ARE WE DOING HERE?'

I wonder how long all this is going to last. Could this still last, drifting, idling, I have charley horses in the back of my thighs and our hair smells of the same outrageously flowery soap we used to wash it this morning. Because we're constantly together, one next to the other, I can't tell her what can only be written. So words desert me, and anyway they would have formed a banal little heap of—I never felt that before sometimes it seems that it pierces me if you only knew I'm set on fire by you oh to lay you down under my hands.

We give two more workshops. All we have to do is throw out a question and it's bedlam, the room goes wild. They have everything to tell us, one on top of the other. Their lives pounce on us but not invasively. The Little Girl and I come out of those afternoons as if taken over by speed, launched into motion again.

I can't remember the exact number of days we spent in the new town. Everything is thrown in there, floating images that don't follow one another chronologically. The rows of yellowish buildings, that 'Passage of the Breach of Dreams' we walk through to get to the supermarket and those boulevards that never stop, only the large concrete space scribbled with dirty papers and bird droppings near a blinking chemist's allows us to get our bearings, to meet. The women with covered hair avoid my eyes, since the Election they are condemned by law. Then that morning when I slip on a puddle of yoghurt and sprawl out in the supermarket, two veiled girls rush over to me, pick me up, insist on taking me to a cafe and cleaning my skirt, they're worried about the huge bruise on my knee. Next, one of them invites The Little Girl and me to tea at her house. She reads us her poems, we applaud and stay till dark when she talks about what she calls the 'strategies' each of us uses. We all have our ways of being left alone, of not being bothered too much, you obey an order too, don't think you don't, the poetess of the new town says to me, look at yourself . . . And it's not because the suggestion is more 'in' that it's not an order! For me, it's the headscarf. To each her own personal

WE ARE
THE BIRDS
OF THE
COMING
STORM

223

piece of cloth that will help her be left in peace. Men often choose the material that women wear, don't they . . .

What gives its rhythm to our stay at the Home is the ceremony of 6.30 p.m.—the distribution of medication. First you can hear heels clicking in the hall, then the residents gather round the activity leader with orange hair and greying temples. The way she walks makes her too-short dress with black flounces waltz round her solidly pinked legs. Out of breath, she collapses on a chair for a few seconds, then stands up and yells with her hands on her hips, 'COCKTAILS!' One by one they file by a big plastic box, each compartment containing different pills. Sometimes she seems to cheerfully plunge her fingers in it at random, 'COCKTAILS FOR EVERYONE!'

One Sunday, there's an outing with Odette, Monique and Dina to a huge dam four kilometres away. They drop their bikes noisily on the little road, pounding their thighs and laughing themselves to tears when we announce that we forgot our picnic in our room, yes, the hard-boiled eggs too. We all scream when the concrete of the huge bridge shakes over the wild waters of the dam.

And that park where we meet the boy we'll call 2007. Sitting on a bench, alone, because it's holiday time, he's been listening to us indiscreetly for a while (I'm telling the Little Girl about a piquant episode of a 'no' out of all the 'noes' of the wonderful Mademoiselle Non.) Maybe we offer him a biscuit, I no longer remember, but we get acquainted (he's heard about the new activity leaders at the Home) and very soon he tells us about the death of his brother, knocked over on a scooter by a police car last autumn. Over there, in 2007. He points to the square in front of the park. In a flat voice, he repeats, 'I can't forget 2007.' Then, in the tone of a TV psychologist, '. . . But if I let it get to me, my whole life will be turned up-side-down, I won't be able to live my childhood normally.' He's been observing his childhood, concerned about that possession of his which is escaping him in torn-up bits. We leave the park, the Little Girl all upset—'Should we kiss him or find him a weapon, Voltairine, console him or consolidate him, it's unbearable, you know, they're . . . too little.'

We witness an inspection from social services at the Home. The Little girl takes these notes:

The inspector talks about individuals who are 'very sick' and didn't come down from their room, the only ones who have 'an excuse'. She adds, 'Of course people have the right to get better! But if you don't come down we are obliged to apply sanctions for absenteeism.' She detaches the syllables from one another, peels them like dry fruits. Her 'OK?' at the end of her sentences sounds to my ear like a grunt, she's like a regretful but methodical butcher whose grunts help him crack bodies. She constantly repeats, 'I think it's normal to verify your income and punish fraud, OK? That's our job. We are all part of a structure that has its rules.'

On one of the last days we spend in the new town, we go with *2007* to an 'afternoon of well-being' for 'children with problems', the terms Émile hates. The psychologist suggests a game, she articulates so exaggeratedly I think she's going to start sobbing, so much do the words cut into her voice.

'We'll begin by the letter *p*. Tell me what comes into your mind, O-K? You have two mi-nutes! Go!'

The little boy of the park goes, 'Pow. Passer-by. Papa. Psychotherapy. Pharmacy. Prison.'

(Very long silence.)

'Purgatory,' he says. And

'Pull out?'

'The two mi-nutes are o-ver, thank you! Martina, *l*, el-l.'

WE ARE
THE BIRDS
OF THE
COMING
STORM
225

For the past two days, the only person I've spoken to on the phone is her mother, but one morning I finally get Émile, the operation went well, not even twenty minutes, can you believe it, she's amazed. She would like to take a training course, anything, but stop working in the neighbourhood. Can't wait to go to the cinema. Asks me where I am now, I talk of a long weekend in the country, omitting the train and the Villa. You know, I say to Émile, it's the first time since your . . . accident that you haven't asked me what you're doing there, what happened to you. In a soft voice, still a little tired, she goes oh really, then, as if in a hurry to move to something else, asks me if I'll be back this weekend, couldn't we see each other at the van. And I have a video for you, kiddo, Svetlana Zakharova in *Les Mirages*!

When I hang up, I hitch up the bottom of my slacks, take off my shoes and lean on the table in the little bedroom of the home cluttered with the Little Girl's papers, along with Scotch tape and enormous markers. The first *plié* in first position puts my lost thoughts, vague ideas and sunken vertebrae in place again. Then *dégagés* in all positions and I move to *ronds de jambe*. My grounded leg, trembling and fearful, scares the hell out of me, I didn't realize I could hardly stand, panting and hanging on to the barre.

We decide to leave by train one Saturday morning. The Little Girl has two tickets for a special evening at the Cinémathèque, a gift she picked out for me before we left, we can't possibly miss that. We promise each other not to hang around in the capital and to leave again quickly; I would gladly give up that screening but she gets upset and implores, it's a big surprise, I'm going to love it, she's sure of it!

We give our last workshop. All participants have written a letter to the person of their choice. Dina's letter is the only one addressed to us. I ask her, as I do the others, if I can read it aloud. She agrees, twisting her grey braid with both hands. Her letter speaks of boats and birds. Birds you thought would fly by again later in the day. Birds you follow with your eyes as long as possible, leaning out into space the better to see them fly away. Birds you imitate, with your arms spread wide. Crushed birds. Old birds too. Birds tired of the sky whose claws get stuck in swamps. And the cries of birds going round in your head, you keep silent about their screeching or you'll be knocked out with more neuroleptics. I stop. Apologize. Because as I read her letter, I can see her, all tiny with her braid, going back to her room after the workshop and waiting every evening for the COCKTAIL while we move on, enchanted with our experience, one among many.

I start reading again. But I can't speak French any more. 'Dina, you has moves me very much, sorry.' Everyone turns to Dina who twists her mouth hard to one side, severely, with her arms crossed on her chest while her eyes are racing towards tears. She pushes the chair away roughly, the threat of feeling grief is making her furious. I stop reading. Someone has to get a handkerchief for her. People get busy pulling a curtain over Dina's birds. The Little Girl at the End of the Lane—a big flower trembling in her navy blue dress patched under the armpits—stands up and hugs her, Dina hangs on to her arm for a moment, now both of them are standing as if facing something that I can't see, a monster hidden there in the flames. Then Dina bursts out laughing as she blows her nose and the others shrink back, frightened. At the end of this last workshop, they offer us a glass of cider and biscuits, preciously taken out of a sewing box. The little girl with white hair and a pastel sweater holds out a package under the eyes of the others who wait for me to open it. I unfold a handbag, black and shiny, entirely knitted out of thin magnetic tapes from audio cassettes. 'Musical bag, you see? All my old tapes, I don't have anything to listen to them with any more, so . . .' As I kiss her to thank her, she puts her hands on my hair, 'When you come back we'll go to the zoo, OK?' and I don't want to start crying again, so I speak too loudly without promising anything, while stroking the cutting edges of the musical handbag. A few of us take the lift. At the floor where Dina has her room, I transform myself into a weather announcer, all sugary and affable, my words shiny with lies, and I say, 'See you soon, Dina.' She stops for a moment before she gets out, asking me with the voice of an eagle, 'Really? Oh? Really? Soon?' Then she backs out into the hall and bangs into the wall, in tears again. Grief goes through her body like a suppressed storm. Here in the Home, her file says Dina is very cultured, she has probably read a lot of books, all kinds of books. They picked Dina up in the street two years ago. She was calculating square roots aloud, her hair all caked with dirt, her skirt soiled with shit, she grabbed her hair with both hands when the hairdresser of the Home tried to cut it—it would be much more appropriate, Dina, at your age.

What were we to do. Not go back to the Home, not begin something. Not get mixed up in something that wasn't asking to be our business. Not cross the path of the Old Little Girl who no longer had a road—and who signs her letter like this: 'Little Girls at the End of the Road, you say. I just hope you're not lying and you really go all the way to the End.' I spoke too much, so I'll let Emily Dickinson close: 'I hope you love birds, too. It is economical. It saves going to Heaven.'

On the train to Paris, we cut out the article in the local press about our nocturnal collage, with a photo to back it up. Sitting opposite us, a young couple gives off the same smell of amber and lemon, a mix of banal scents. The lips of the girl are little pieces of dead fish incongruous in that landscape of uniformly dull beige skin. He looks well fed, brutally satisfied with everything—with his train-company meal, with the way his body occupies its place on the seat, with the Election, which he presents to his companion as 'Something new, perhaps! . . . Let's be open-minded!' they swam with dolphins in the Bahamas two weeks ago, last year it was Indonesia.

'What about you, what do you do? You're a mum too?'

Using my penknife, the Little Girl at the End of the Lane cuts out a slice of pear and nibbles on it, her eyes are shiny, acid, her smile shoots out these words scornfully, 'Excuse me? What's that?'

Then, curtly, 'Voltairine is on holiday, you see. She died suddenly three weeks ago. She has reborn, um, is reborned. Sorry, rebornated. But ordinarily, we're in . . . business events.'

And it's because of me, or at least because of my advice, that later, the Little Girl finally uses her phone to tell her boyfriend she's coming back. She says almost nothing, hardly a yes OK from time to time, then she holds the phone out to me, glumly—he wants to tell you something. In a rather gentle, tired voice, he introduces himself and apologizes for having insisted on talking to me, it's not that he doesn't trust her but, after all, it's more reassuring to think she's not alone. Where are you, I didn't get that, we were cut off. And the topic seems to interest him tremendously, his words pour out, as if he didn't have enough people to speak to these past few days. The hideous embarrassment of hearing him undress her in front of me. His hands protected by gloves, he peels the Little Girl at the End of the Lane—*the cognitive markers of that pathology— the doctor is absolutely positive—you must have noticed—she doesn't know how to take care of herself—moments of crisis— what do we do now, what do we do.* He says it's not nothing, you understand, she suffers from a symptom of oppositional disorder after all, twice he repeats it, enjoying those words he learnt recently, perhaps—oppositional disorder.

How about you, how do you find her? Answer with yes or no if you're afraid she'll understand we're talking about her. Violent? Agitated? Have you noticed times when she's incoherent? Moments of exaltation?

The Little Girl taps me gently on the shoulder and points to what she's just written on the window of the train with her marker, SILENCE EXILE CUNNING, then, in very small letters, she recopies from her spiral notebook open on her lap:

PS. it's because all of us are strange birds, stranger still behind our faces and voices, that we don't wish people to know it or we don't know it ourselves.

I hang up right away, I would like, I whisper to her, to root out of your body those who scrutinize it, Instruction it. She says, I would like to root out of your body, but I don't let her finish her sentence, people round us in the compartment are stiffening, we're smeared with tears, the heating system with the iron taste of this journey is reddening our cheeks, her tongue goes over the hollow of my lips again and again like a consolation.

SYMPTOM OF OPPOSITIONAL DISORDER: being in opposition to one's surroundings.

Note: To know-it-alls who see the future like a beautiful wave, I'll say it again, There was no starting point. Nothing, neither that call nor reading the newspaper I borrowed on the train listing the preventive arrests taking place in the context of the new law. And, in particular, that of a man placed under house arrest about whom the prefect is happy to say that he gave himself up 'without violence'—the Pelican.

PARIS

The two of us are walking like conspirators on that big boulevard that leads to the hospital. Europol and Dina's letter are like a wave of joyful energy pushing me on, or it's from being in 'business events' with her, taking that little walk together along the Road to the End. During the trip we continue a game we had started at the Home, complete the sentence A LIFE . . .

To: Wander / Do nothing with / Read in the morning / Run (with no one behind!) / Get over growing up? The life of an escaped tree (from all forests).

I would like to go to the van, I miss it a little and I'm sick of washing alternatively the only two pieces of clothing I had thought to bring along the week before. The official letter, which has certainly arrived, is holding me back now. As if the little blue paper from the court was going to bind me and lay me down, as inexorably as a sedative, and put an end to all this.

The same lobby as three weeks ago, that mentholated heat, those muffled sounds and the medical personnel passing one another, moving skilfully down the highway of the corridors. The door of the room is half open. The nurse greets me with a 'Ah, here comes the little sister!' Émile's bed is empty. Her parents kiss me, find me pale. Émile has just gone down to the floor below, the doctors are testing the nano-computer placed under her skin between her chest muscles, which will watch her cardiac wanderings from now on. The Little Girl's concern creates silence all round her when she wants to know if Émile will still manage to die one day, with this new infallible heart.

When she comes back into the room with little attentive steps, a big, white T-shirt over her navy blue pyjama trousers, I take Émile in my arms at last, and the idea of her sudden death rises in my throat, a violent flash of heat and sweat. Today, the last day she's spending in the hospital, I officially introduce the Little Girl at the End of the Lane to her, the Little Girl stretches out her silhouette, even thinner than usual, so as not to make any noise. And it seems to me that I'm mending time, constructing a stairway linking the past to now, an escalator with the lively body of the Little Girl and all those sleepless kilometres both of us covered in less than a week. I introduce the Little Girl to her the way you'd say to a mother who came to get us at the end of summer camp, look, look, Émile, how I did the right thing, watch me burn the broken-down van and the immobile Island.

The three of us spend the end of the afternoon in that room. And if we don't tell everything to Émile that day, it's only through lack of time and concern for priorities. You can't say in a few sentences, look how we're undoing the darkness and the silence, look at your year without movement—which was mine too—look at it rolled up in a ball on the ground, like an old coat you can't stand any more after wearing it for years.

Émile gets out of the hospital the next day. That first night in her flat, every one of her sighs wakes me up.

Despite my doubts—shouldn't she rest—the next day, we meet the Little Girl at the End of the Lane in the lobby of the Cinémathèque as if nothing had existed since September when we noticed that her hands shook and her coat sleeves were too short. I know right away that I never should have let her go home again, out of our electric waltz. She seems to have swallowed angles, she's as pale as the roaming air. I ask her if she's all right and in a low voice, she begs me, Voltairine, we can't go back I can't go back to where I left off. Then she hands me my ticket, the one she thought of getting for me before we left—my surprise. It's a documentary never seen before about Mademoiselle Non followed by a discussion with the man who wrote one of her most famous solos for her—William Forsythe, my favourite choreographer.

The wonderful Mademoiselle Non drains the screen while she stretches and arms her body with tendons and muscles. The Little Girl takes notes. During the whole screening. During the discussion too, she never stops writing. From time to time, Émile glances at me with an embarrassed look; what bothers her, I suppose, is what she thinks of that girl, and the jokes she no longer dares to make, at the End of the Road. I watch one, then the other, as if I didn't know where to go any more.

'What interests me,' Forsythe is explaining, 'is the archaeology of movement, not the movement itself. Deconstructing, destabilizing, that's what I work on, the moments when limits

WE ARE
THE BIRDS
OF THE
COMING
STORM

233

are being transgressed, when a fall is imminent. When I improvise with the dancers, I try to maintain a state of vibration, a moment of trembling. Can what gives birth to movement be represented?'

He keeps quiet for a moment, then leans forward a little and murmurs into the mike, as if making a note to himself, 'But what if movement didn't emanate from the centre of the body? What if there were more than one centre? And the origin of a movement were a whole line or a whole plane and not just a point?'

When we leave, Émile feels slightly dizzy and we go quickly into a nearby cafe.

How all that begins. Perhaps the Little Girl has noted, first, the moment in the documentary when Mademoiselle Non explains that dancers economize their bodies, try not to make other gestures than the ones used in dance. I confirm this and talk about my childhood where horseback riding, skiing, running and roller skating were forbidden. So as not to build muscles adverse to dance, not thwart the formidable construction under way—manufacturing weightlessness. I tell them of the constant fear of falling, of steep pavements, irregular steps, of not playing hide-and-seek with the other children, especially in parks because of the holes treacherously dissimulated in the lawn. I make both of them laugh when I confess that even today, I go down stairs like a grandmother with stiff legs, so strongly has the fear of falling been instilled in me (dancers call that falling for nothing, in contrast to falling after a quadruple pirouette, for example, an expected occurrence).

Then the Little Girl organizes the notes she took during the film, reads them over very quickly, goes from one page to another, apologizes, after all she was writing in the dark, not easy to see where you are. She draws her chair closer, the three of us huddled together now around the tiny cafe table. This is something I knew, she says, but now it's wonderful, I finally understood what I already knew. 'The thing about the ropes

. . . That ballet at the beginning of the film, right?' she says. Before I had time to come out with an extremely worried 'You remember,' Émile herself tells the Little Girl about that ballet, which we both saw.

She tries to describe the dancers—it was painful to watch them, falling, landing heavily from their jumps. With their torsos twisted back and their heads rigidly thrust into their shoulders, they didn't seem to be able to open up. As if they were held back by invisible ropes. Then 'At a certain point, the music stopped. It's soothing at first but very soon you felt anxious because all you could hear was their feet and their breathing—groans almost. Horrible . . .'

Their heels were hitting the ground clumsily, punctuating their gasps of people dying, submitting to something but you couldn't understand to what. And we, in the audience, felt a growing desire not to see that—we felt anger, the need to be offered something else, something loose, supple. At the end of the performance, half of the audience began booing violently, as if the spectacle of painful, hobbled movements was unbearable, was a slap, a mirror, whereas we had come to eat freedom and air. In the programme we were given after the performance (usually they give it to you before), a text by Forsythe explained that during the three months of rehearsal he had bound each of his dancers in ropes that limited and even hampered their movements. Then, a few days before the premiere, he had them take off the ropes and asked them to dance the same thing. We had just witnessed their memories of ropes.

'Bound, hobbled, enervated bodies,' she repeats, and the Little Girl seems to be calculating ideas, as if everything were multiplying in her mind, yielding equations, quick results that intoxicate and terrify her at the same time.

'You see, Voltairine,' she says to me, her cheeks flushed with heat, 'we always come back to that, always the same question, always, how to root the barbarian kings out of oneself, and those ropes we swallow and swallow and keep swallowing.

WE ARE
THE BIRDS
OF THE
COMING
STORM

235

We have to . . . Be so watchful . . . And! We have to explain it to Émile! While you were Sleeping Beauty, Émile, we started an excellent theory of birds!'

A brief space of silence in the cafe. Tweet tweet tweet goes a girl's voice. And the little group sitting at the table next to us explodes in laughter.

Hurt. The pain those laughs inflict on her. They might as well have traced the path of the blood along her terribly thin forearms with a box-cutter. Or shaken her like an empty doll, pummelled her so hard she swayed. It would be less cutting than the whinnying sniggers of those onlookers.

She moves towards them and it's not the owner who calls the police but one of the guys in the group. I see him discreetly picking up his cell while a waiter grabs the Little Girl, puts an arm round her neck to make her drop the broken glass she's squeezing like a jagged lamp-bulb edged with blood.

We leave the cafe under a rain of insults, Émile and I each holding one of her hands to make her walk faster. I go hopping through the gutter. We have no reason to take all those turns, all I think about is putting some distance between us and what just happened. When we finally arrive at Émile's place, I go back down right away to buy a toothbrush and panties. When I get back, Émile opens the door and whispers, 'She fell asleep. I think she was very tired . . .' and I love her for using no other words than those.

For the first time since her sudden death, we sit in her kitchen facing each other round the half-table, never completely wiped clean of the grains of sugar poured into coffee. She cocks her head as she watches me, her hands of a Disney princess without bones or tendons round her cup.

I would like to be sure we both agree. I want to talk about it, talk with Émile about it, about that moment when the Little Girl walks over to the group. Tweet tweet tweet goes the girl laughing into the sleeve of her beaded sweatshirt, probably

Japanese. 'What're you laughing at?' inquires the Little Girl. And the girl doesn't face her, no, she nervously squeezes her spandex knees together, her body has the scrawniness of an abandoned object, already.

'Birds? Is that it? Tweet tweet tweet. It's not the right story to tell in a cafe? That cracks you up? What department are birds in . . . Oh, of course! Birds are always in the leisure-and-poetry section! You know, I'm afraid you . . . That all you have under your skin is sections, departments . . . That's right, nothing else . . .' and the Little Girl is right next to the other one who's laughing nervously and keeps repeating, 'OK, OK! Come on, relax!' while her boyfriend repeats, 'Hey, take it easy there, it's OK,' extending an unsteady arm towards the Little Girl.

'You're so . . .' she says, looking them up and down, '. . . pathetic. The way you . . . Obey orders that . . .' she grabs the girl's iPhone, it falls, 'No one ever gave you . . .' 'Who?. . .' and the Little Girl starts walking round the table while she goes on, 'Cut . . . Your . . . Nerves . . . Who . . . Cut . . . Your . . . Nerves.' She accelerates and starts capering lightly round the group, 'Who . . . Cut . . .'

And I would like us to be on the same page, Émile and I— nothing is more absolutely true than what she's chanting in front of those people sitting there with their heads down over their glasses, they're so afraid of that tall girl in a red coat hopping round their table with her tense face belying her light steps. And the Little Girl turns, she's turning faster and faster until she changes sentences and direction, as if moved by the signal of an invisible ballet master. 'What . . . Are . . . You . . . Filled . . . With. What . . . Are . . . You . . . Filled . . . With. Ask yourself what what what you are filled with what you are filled filled filled with.' And then yes. There is that glass she breaks on their table, and pandemonium, the howls of the girl threatened by the Little Girl—but honestly, she didn't even touch her, I can testify to that and, after all, it's her own blood on the glass, let's not make a big deal out of it.

WE ARE
THE BIRDS
OF THE
COMING
STORM
237

'Why are you crying?' Émile, brand new and worried, asks as she drags her chair next to me. I don't want to get into that discussion Émile and I never even had, not ever, the one the Little Girl has just begun without knowing it. What did we fill ourselves with. With what story. The story we tell ourselves as best we can until—the heart fails, the ankles get twisted, until the spine stiffens and then the story has to be filled up faster and faster over and over, you have to put flowers on it like a grave filled with what we will no longer be, put flowers on it, ruin your grave with pictures, with videos watched over and over every night, with Instructions and prescriptions in order to keep on believing in that story without birds or storms. Keep telling yourself you're at peace and die from it, die from being at peace.

I would like to say to Émile, thank you for everything, thank you for the Island and the van, thank you but I don't want to sleep, thank you but what are you filled with, questions must not stay locked away in drawers, but who cut your nerves.

In the middle of the night, her voice wakes me up, Voltairine Voltairine come here. It's still dark out, I step over Émile, who's asleep, and I open the door of the tiny room where the Little Girl sleeps. She's rolled up in the blanket as if we were camping, sitting cross-legged on the mattress. She smiles to me, whispering, 'You know where there's paper here? I don't have any left, my notebook's full.'

I find her a stack of paper covered with dust, she rips out the last page of her notebook and holds it out to me.

I will be unsalvageable

Withdrawn attitude, antisocial behavior, mutism: 2 mg.
You don't know what you're saying they tell me when I say what I know. What *are* you talking about, they tell me with no question mark at the end of the sentence, an injunction, not a question.

You need to talk to 'someone' about that, they advise with a worried look, when the words of a bird that might very well fall are beyond their comprehension. That 'someone' is a function-being, more efficient than a human being, summoned to the bed-side of birds who don't know what they're saying any more. Come on, talk talk, so we can get a clearer picture, exhale those sick words and quickly please, we have rows of bodies like yours filled with a mush of words all entangled, all glued together. That 'someone' helps you heave out odourless vomit, helps you find

WE ARE
THE BIRDS
OF THE
COMING
STORM
239

how to start up again, get back into rhythm—anything to get the body going again, functioning again.

But that's just it, I don't want to be repaired. Preserved. Patched up so I can keep going. I would hate to have them plug up what I'm desperately trying to undo, to unsew.

You see, I'm working at being unsalvageable, unredeemable. As fleeting, irretrievable and fragile as a moment in time. To become impossible to grip, I will have to enter into silence the way one goes into resistance. And to their every question, answer: I don't know, I wonder, I'm seeking. I raise and put down questions. I create doubts.

We don't know what we are in the process of creating, Voltairine, we know we're 'in the process of' something. But what beautiful silence. We know we desire more and more, we have more and more desires, we know it's utterly necessary for both of us to be together for absolutely no reason, under no heading. And so, since we are together, we look for what we could do together. When we have found it, we will also have the list of what we have to undo. We'll rewrite that list tirelessly. We will scrub our skins, track down what we might have swallowed by mistake, things so naturally encrusted in Us that we no longer perceive them as artificial limbs that force us to walk straight. Because, as you know, we have to start moving to feel the stiffness of our gait. What is left to destroy must be found in our mouths too, since our words are riddled with artificial devices.

Just think that one says about oneself, and before witnesses, 'I'm going to get a hold of myself.'

Just think that one affirms proudly, I'm reasonable—an admission which really means I will let You make me see reason.

PS. I must tell you about August Spies, one of the men who was convicted after the Haymarket Massacre.

Back in bed next to Émile, I listen attentively to the rhythm of her breathing. From the room next door, I hear nibblings, a tiny spade seems to be digging, revealing what might be hidden. At times, the pencil leaves the paper. Then starts again. I can hear the thought of the Little Girl at the End of the Lane accelerating. I hear her putting down periods, what she's questioning and what is beyond all doubt.

I can't get back to sleep, so I test my ankles under the sheet. Point. Flex. Point. Outward, flex, inward. It is imperative to leave again and find a place that is not part of this present. I search my mind, I enumerate places, possibilities. France is a deadly country of penned-in, timid places and swampy informers. Rancid. They elected Inspectors. And while I dread the blue papers that would send me back to court, I'm even more afraid of saying, wait, I'll do it myself, I'll *get a hold of myself.* Afraid of forgetting the theory of the wooden ladder—so joyful—afraid of ending up looking only for pretty country retreats where one can feel comfortable, for burrows or nests to build, afraid of carefully lining them with blankets and making sure to put in only indirect, soothing lighting. Afraid of finally settling down in the oasis, in the lull, and forgetting we were just passing through before leaving again. Of ending up concerned only about preserving one's own body—a pretty, fresh plant to arrange, care for and feed. Being content with *approximately* and *almost.* And no longer knowing how a storm begins nor even what a storm is. Fearing, even cursing it, making fun of it as soon as you sense it's coming, repeating all the while—nastily, nervously—'That won't make any difference,' and catching yourself wishing there were no more storms because you've got used to days like these, *finally.*

'We're in an epidemic of discreet sudden deaths, Voltairine,' the Little Girl told me not so long ago. And I don't understand anything she says, I think they're the same slightly whimsical sentences of a tall girl with bags under her eyes, oddly wearing dresses with sleeves too short for her. Whereas she is taking

WE ARE
THE BIRDS
OF THE
COMING
STORM
241

note of what takes place before our eyes, of what is happening right here in front of us.

I stretch out my foot under the sheet and I can feel the cramp mounting in it like an orgasm. Brace yourself with all your muscles. Not dance with the memory of ropes. Not dance without remembering that you may very well be dancing with the memory of ropes.

Then, probably, I fall asleep and Émile's the one who shakes me in the morning. 'Come see . . . you've got to see this . . .' She half opens the door of the room.

Sleeping on her back with her arms stretched out on either side of her and her head turned sideways, concealed from the light of day, the Little Girl at the End of the Lane is clearly defined, surrounded by dozens of sheets of scribbled paper. Surrounding her body, they seem to give her broken wings.

We settle down cautiously in the kitchen. Émile offers to go to the Island instead of me to see if I have mail, pick up some clothing and say hello to the Pelican.

'But didn't you hear? He was arrested.'

'Really? When? But that makes no sense, they're not going to keep him just because he recited the wrong poem, everything will be OK . . .'

The Pelican on the Island. Who stayed there to wait for them. With his tall, calm silhouette. His way of walking backwards towards the forest, the little wave of his hand. His chestnut soups.

And it's not even nine yet, I begin a normal sentence, subject verb and immediately that sentence tires me out, I drop it, since we've come back to Paris, there's no time left or it's the opposite and we're still wallowing in all those years spent arguing, evaluating and commenting, and that time makes me scream that it's not time which makes no sense, it's what is / happening / right now /

Émile turns livid and urges me to calm down, she talks loudly as if already she can't stand me any more, come on stop it you're crazy stop but exactly what did you do last week stop it.

And I've never done that before, I've never even understood how someone could do it, I grab a little teapot I gave to Émile as a present the first year we met one Tuesday Evening and I throw it against the tile floor of the kitchen, Émile Émile,

WE ARE
THE BIRDS
OF THE
COMING
STORM
243

you need a full stop here, there's no going on, on and on, stop being Sleeping Beauty!

The Pelican's soups are breaking my heart, I say, laughing a little to apologize for crying. Émile folds her naked feet under her and sits there without saying anything while I sweep away what's left of my ridiculous gesture, all our gestures are too loud and absurd when you become estranged from the thoughts of others.

The Little Girl comes into the kitchen, bewildered, and her long white thighs are the legs—I can't help noticing the way muscles are used—of a slender frog.

'What's happening? Who shouted?'

'I broke Émile's teapot. I . . . I'll be right back.'

I leave them, extracting myself from too many explanations and anyway the air will do me good, I'd like to buy a new teapot, the same one.

How best to describe the atmosphere of the city since the Election. Has it changed the air. The famous charm of the old stones of Paris under the humid light. The fact of running into various uniforms at every street corner, like so many possible examples of order and arrest—here, typical French policemen in blue, there, soldiers in camouflage uniforms, in the Métro, private militias right out of American TV series. Their faces never tired.

I stop for a moment in a cafe, the TV's on, reflected in the rectangular mirror. The president is belching out his endless pleasure at forcefully thrusting out 'thugocracy / *enragés* / not going to poison our lives / police-record pedigrees'. Now, more than his continual speeches in the media, I see the slimy seepage of his words slipping into our bodies so much that it becomes part of our nature.

Paris is now swarming with a satisfied clientele, old customers, the Little Girl says to me one day as we're coming out of Losey's *Monsieur Klein*.

ALL HELL'S GOING TO BREAK LOOSE

A blasé clientele, used to arbitrary arrest, to ID checks. Who wanted the Election of a great Inspector (a man who can act!) and self-inspects on a daily basis. A busy clientele, skilled and modern, who knows how to worm its way in everywhere and never lingers too long in places where petty crimes are committed daily.

But these days, a slight shudder is going through the city centre, the secret hope that something may become dangerous,

WE ARE
THE BIRDS
OF THE
COMING
STORM

245

historic perhaps. So, like children boasting to their friends about the fire truck they're going to get for Christmas, you can hear them: all hell's going to break loose, it can't go on like this, that's for sure. And they repeat this diagnosis, all hell's going to break loose, as if they were talking about a meteorological phenomenon which concerns no one in particular, knowing that the event will take place elsewhere, on the outskirts of Paris where they never go, where those Others live, the ones they pity and fear. They predict the spot of the first flashpoints, far from the centre. But from far off, it will be perfectly visible. And in a low voice, confidentially, they worry about the unreliable pyrotechnicians. Those Others who will make all hell break loose, those Others they'd like to love if they weren't uncontrollable Others, *unmanageable (for really what on earth do they want? They don't even know themselves.*) Then they resume the conversation that had been hardly interrupted: And how about you, what's up?

Someone lowered the sound in the cafe and the TV is broadcasting silent flames. A fire is ravaging a new building that looks like a beige Lego prison; in front of it, an announcer with stiff, light hair opens and closes her shining mouth. The text files by at the bottom of the screen: 'FROM TONIGHT CURFEW WILL BE ENFORCED IN ACCORDANCE WITH THE DECLARATION OF A STATE OF EMERGENCY.'

The three of us spend that day together sitting round the new teapot full of chai, I could kick myself for that quarrel.

The curfew. We don't know what to do about it. Then Émile gets a phone call. She repeats incredulously, 'No! Oh no . . .' Some of her friends were arrested in their flats by a special intervention brigade very early this morning. No one knows what they're accused of. Finally, we find this on the Internet: they were spotted during the demonstrations on Election Night, kept under surveillance for weeks, a search of their flats led the investigators to find books and 'suspicious material', large quantities of weed-killer and confectioner's sugar. They are suspected of 'terrorist acts aiming to undermine the security of the State'. We look at each other, our plates on our knees, our forks in the air. We shrug, then we repeat the words terrorism-State-confectioner-sugar like a complicated puzzle. And it's Émile who's the first to explode in the shrill laugh of a little bird invited into a game whose rules have suddenly been turned into laws.

'Wow . . . I think . . . Me, too! I have lots of . . . sugar in my cupboard . . . I'm . . . a State terrorist . . . In addition to being dead not so long ago . . . The script's getting complicated!' she spits into her cup, bubbles of tea are dancing inside her sinuses.

'We've got to be up to it,' the Little Girl confirms while she takes a few blank sheets of paper from the table and begins to draw columns, frowning. Later, she combs through the Internet like a treasure-hunter and is thrilled by that business

WE ARE
THE BIRDS
OF THE
COMING
STORM

247

of the fire whose first images I saw on TV. A huge fire has been burning for over twelve hours at a detention centre for foreigners, a few detainees are still standing on the roof, they're waving sheets with words written on them. Apparently the cameraman hasn't been authorized to shoot the whole sentence, the only thing we can see clearly is a WHO, followed by a   ?

On the radio, a journalist is talking about another fire, this one right in the middle of Paris, where all the government buildings are located. 'An unknown group has claimed responsibility for the act, a group saying it has in fact nothing to claim but the fire.'

The Little Girl at the End of the Lane raises both her hands to her mouth, breathes in as suddenly as if she were about to dive, 'Claiming nothing! But that's . . . Brilliant! Leave out the question, let the fire be the question, Voltairine! Because . . . wait, I'm writing it down . . . Come to think of it, the moment you claim something, you . . . close the question, you limit it, right? You say, I'm doing this and I want to get that. And if I get it, I'll stop, I'll calm down! But there! No stopping! Fire opens the page to everything! Let's go out. Let's go see. Come on let's go! Voltairine!'

The curfew doesn't worry us. We have the feeling (the aware-ness?) of being nothing. Harmless, no distinctive signs, no importance, so invisible and barely awake, confined as we were to our islands and flats for years. Convinced, without even admitting it, that a curfew is a man's business, a business for the main characters.

I don't remember our exact itinerary that night, all that remains is the smell of those hours, the mark they left. And if I had to make a ballet out of it, I would opt for a series of small diagonal leaps, feet well stretched, cutting sharply, *glissade glissade petit jeté assemblé.*

The Little Girl goes through the streets at top speed, like a dog told to go fetch. Holds her arms out to me for a silent waltz in the darkness of twisting blind alleys, there's no one outside and it's exciting to have the city in this state, as empty as Paris in mid-August, it's Assumption Day multiplied by Christmas. And in the euphoria of a race that ends with the three of us seated on the pavement weeping with laughter, with a theatrical gesture, I grab a bunch of old newspapers in a dustbin and I set it on fire (not easily and not completely, with a lighter). I'm holding this little bouquet burning quickly in my hand when Émile asks, hey, what's today's date what's today's date, I think it's the seventeenth, one month since I've been dead! she observes proudly. The Little Girl jumps towards the dustbin and takes out other newspapers that she lights with mine. We stand there, with our paper mini-torches—happy birthday Émile—and before it burns my fingers, without thinking, I throw my ashy bouquet down under a police car parked in

WE ARE
THE BIRDS
OF THE
COMING
STORM

249

front of me. We stay there for a few minutes, the flame doesn't seem to take and we run away, overjoyed.

Let's say it's a therapeutic act, I explain to the Little Girl who's totally stunned, once we're back in the flat. And Émile's silence encourages me to tell the story of that February afternoon when I filed a complaint at police headquarters on the rue Louis Blanc.

WAS THERE A BREAK-IN?

They come in and out of this office constantly, some cops hang around the time for me to finish my sentence, maybe to hear how *he*

I force myself, for the four hours of the deposition, to say the unsayable, I force myself to go through with my story the way you try to finish what's on your plate, the way you spread your legs to lessen the pain, a pale little Romanian girl wearing the clothes she carefully chose that morning to 'look serious', sitting up straight on the chair of an institution in the country of the rights of man. I articulate the details of *the act*, precisely, eager to do well, how many times I said no. In the tone of someone who declares a theft to an insurance agent, and yet I assure you the windows were all locked, monsieur.

DETAILS

Like the hair of the officer who takes my deposition, for example, waved and lacquered, he's probably been collecting Johnny Hallyday concert tickets since the sixties. All those details, the photos tacked over the officer's chair. Pink thighs spread, shiny lips and manicured fingers. The fingers with pearly nails of the girl who spreads her lips in the photos match the dyed iridescent hair of the cop perfectly. I imagine the man who took the pictures—a little more, go on, spread. The cop calls *the acts* what I have to describe in detail in front of those gaping girls with dead eyes.

DRESS REHEARSAL

It took me a few Tuesday Evenings to perfect my deposition. Several of us polished up the best possible version of *that night*.

When I came out of the police station on rue Louis Blanc, Émile was waiting for me. We walked to my dance class, I was relieved, I felt everything was in order. We held each other by the arm, damaged little machines, useless but absurdly lively still.

(The Little Girl is silent, she shakes her head and brings her hand up to her neck a few times the way you readjust your necklace to centre it exactly, except that she she's not wearing a necklace.

So I go on with my story.)

THE ACT

And now what?

Now, mademoiselle, your adversary is going to give his deposition as well. It is your word against *his*. But you can be confident. Given the details you gave me about *the act*, the odds are on your side!

Thank you, I answer the lawyer, you know, the commissaire really wrote everything down, he seems serious.

INSUFFICIENT

A few weeks later, the second summons, on a Thursday morning. The officer with iridescent, stiff hair holds out sheets of paper on which there is *a signature* I recognize. It's *his* version of the story.

'Your case is closed,' he says, 'indefinitely.' Indicating to me, at the very bottom of the page, 'Offence insufficiently clear and lack of material evidence.'

WE ARE
THE BIRDS
OF THE
COMING
STORM

251

THAT CORRECTED VERSION

Begins the same way as my own version.

We arrived at my studio flat as we did every night. I was aware that this relationship was going nowhere. But: nothing special happened, a slightly tense argument.

Rearrange the sheets, smooth them. Reposition the body. Cover the body. Scrub the stains on the sheets. Change the position of the body. And. Don't forget to. Turn off the sound. The sound that doesn't match the picture. *Then*, he says. (Then, after that, to get it over with.)

I took her home, she wanted to sleep at her place. Slightly angry. It's understandable, isn't it. I had just put an end to our relationship. An end.

SHE'S NOTHING

Known prostitute Romania. Homosexual? Obvious manipulation I was so in love but my professional status but I'm not holding it against her my status in the world of music after all   .

'How can you explain that she filed a complaint against you?'

'I think it can be explained by the fact that I'm successful and that she, unfortunately, is nothing. She's even been fired very recently from her dance company.'

nothing

The missing words are scars. The words missing in this story are scars. That evening, I tell both of them, Émile and the Little Girl, that the words missing in *his* deposition are, for me, the shadow of death. Nothing remains of that night. Except what I know. *He* knows too. So there are two of us who know the story. When *he* reorganizes the night by erasing whole pieces of it, *he* knows. Protects his future. *Keep quiet he says*, I think

it's at the beginning, before *he*   . On paper, *he* shuts my
mouth with selected words. The film jumps slightly in the middle, speeds up certain passages.

Very. Agitated. For a long time. Psychological problems.
Ran away, as a child. Uprooted. Agitated. The dance scene. I
tried. But . . .   . When she said no of course I   ! I
would never have   not a monster! *Then took her home.*
Sorry for her. Slandered in my professional milieu! *Nothing.*
She's nothing. It's really sad I wish she   .

THE GEOGRAPHY OF WORDS

Do not, never talk again of madness as a territory, a satellite
of normal life we watch from afar without understanding
its geography. Since that day at the Louis Blanc police head-
quarters, never again will I say, with a knowing air, that girl is
crazy, I think she's going off the rails screaming like that, she's
nuts. After feeling *those words*, slowly heartrending, like
barbed-wire wheels driven into the centre of my flesh, before I
could read them and feel them, those words like harpoons—
one here, another there—inside me, I didn't think losing my
head and the command of my body would ever be possible,
that it was possible to start screaming with fear in front of those
words corrected and rewritten by *him*. Such pain. Before I read
the deposition containing *another version of the night of 14*
September, his. Before realizing that my words had just been
covered over by better words, more reliable, more credible.

CLOSED CASE, CLOSED WORDS

No letters, no cards, no emails, hardly a few neutral SMS.
Émile sometimes made fun of how careful I am never to
answer in writing. She put that down to a typically Romanian
paranoia, what remained of the mistrust from being spied on.
And I didn't dare give the reason for my retention of words,
not even to her. But that night, because of the closeness of the

WE ARE
THE BIRDS
OF THE
COMING
STORM

253

three of us in that little flat, I decide to talk about the evidence the police took out of a drawer, 'closing' my case.

That Thursday in February, in the office of police head-quarters on rue Louis Blanc, the exhibits given to the police by the man they call my *adversary*, which the officer presents to me as if it were a personal victory, are my love letters. One by one, I confirm. I recognize my writing. And it's because of my own words, written before *14 September*, that the case and the night are closed for ever. That tone of a nothing little girl. That tone, dumbstruck at having been chosen by an important man, French, and recognized in his profession.

I love you I kiss you I am. Yours.

To end with, the officer gives me a page from a magazine protected by plastic. And with a sly look, he leans back a little in his seat. I can read:

ARE YOU A SLUT?

In the police station, I ran my finger over that magazine page, which *he* had added to his file.

We must have been sitting at a pavement cafe, the two of us, and I was checking the boxes, in blue, with an ice cube in my throat and a kiss just afterward, a beautiful summer. I'm a slut from Eastern Europe, watch out they're the worst, you saw the results of the test, I have ten triangles, it's mega-slut. My joyful writing protected by plastic, turquoise ink, perhaps even sprinkled with glitter. There was a coffee stain, a little scribble next to the counting of As and Bs, triangles and stars. My *kisses to you* in blue turquoise triangles.

The officer stood up, signifying that my case had expired, my time was up, 'I suppose I don't have to explain why your case . . .' and he articulated scornful quotation marks round that word, your 'case' has been closed. He walked me to the exit.

At the Louis Blanc Métro, Émile was waiting, she was holding out her hands to me that February morning. You might say she picked me up, an incoherent heap that must be gathered and quickly removed from the street and the city too, protected from all those bodies which, out of embarrassment, will avoid that heap of sobs and broken words. Must be guided like an animal blinded by fear, led out of an uneven terrain.

'I will never write letters to anyone again,' I tell Émile and the Little Girl. In the semi-darkness, all three of us lying on the too-short rug, we're listening to Cat Power. Our breathing is syncopated, one-one-two, then one, one-two. Our bellies rise and answer each other gently.

When we go to bed, it is almost daylight, Émile's breathing is more regular than before, with her other heart, it seems to me. In the room next door, the sound of pages turning and when I wake up, this little piece of paper placed on my pillow:

It had been like the Valley of the Shadow of Death, and there are white scars on my soul . . . Besides the battle of my young days all others have been easy, for whatever was without, within my own Will was supreme. It has owed no allegiance, and never shall—it has moved steadily in one direction, the knowledge and assertion of its own liberty, with all the responsibility falling thereon. (Voltairine de Cleyre)

WE ARE
THE BIRDS
OF THE
COMING
STORM

255

The next morning, she wants me to tell her about Dance. Tell me again, asks the Little Girl at the End of the Lane.

Tell her about the taped sprains on which you dance anyway, the hamstring perpetually on the alert in your left thigh—the memory of a strain, you started again too soon—the company doctors who give out anti-inflammatories and the weekly weigh-ins in front of the other students in the dance school.

Tell her about the initiatory passage—you're twelve now—the right to 'mount' on points at last, bleeding to earn the right to rise. Tell how points are broken in by wedging them into the opening of a door to make them supple, some girls hit them with a hammer so they make less noise on stage. Tell how you protect your toes with tape before putting them on. Tell about the evenings, those long hours spent sewing ribbons onto your ballet shoes (cotton ribbons, they stick better to your tights, satin is prettier on stage but slippery). The little rubber band you put round your ankle so your foot doesn't tip over your pumps when you're balancing. And that symbol (clubs, cross, heart) engraved on the sole by the craftsman who makes them to reassure you, the same point shoes should produce the same pirouettes. Those ritual recipes.

Describe your entourage, that little circle of indispensable people. The ballet master who knows everything about you—a mother or a lover. And his counterpart, the physical therapist (or osteopath). One repairs what the other does. The one who holds your hand while you dive in an *arabesque penchée*, who knows your 'best foot' and your fear of overly acrobatic lifts and the other one who hangs up dedicated photos of famous dancers in his waiting room the way other people hang up holy pictures, his pride at having had them, diminished, stretched out and anxious on his table, and he envelopes your thighs in camphor, cold and electricity, will hold out a handkerchief even before you start crying at his suggestion not to 'force' that sprain and to stop for seventy-two hours. And you: 'But I can't stop I can't.'

Tell her about those mornings when as soon as you get up, eyes closed as if for a sleepy prayer, you consult, you test your tendons under the sheet stiffened by the leaps of the previous day. Question: Can I bend this morning (please let me be able to bend). All those attentions, those obsessive habits with which you surround your baby-body so it may obey you—baths, ice packs, ointments (one for muscle pains, another for tendinitis), applied before going to bed, plastic bags cut out and Scotch-taped tightly round the painful knee, heat to speed up healing. That mad routine.

No, you see, honestly, I can't do it all I can tell you about is ballet shoes, ribbons and physical therapists. I don't know how to tell you about the hands of your partner that grab you under the armpits, his thumbs at the edge of your breasts, his body right up against yours, you hear him count—and one, two—to get his exact bearings in the *Rite of Spring*. And when the ballet is over and you freeze at the last note of the orchestra, the two of you clasped together waiting to take your bows, your panting is rough and burning like his salted sweat flowing from his temples to your eyelids, washing the black mascara down your cheek.

'And all over the world, it's always in French, so if you say to a Russian dancer, *sissone assemblé entrechat changement*, he understands it like an alphabet, a universal score if you know what I mean. And so, after the barre, we go to the middle . . .'

'Oh. To the middle of what?'

'It's an expression. It means that you're not at the barre any more, I mean, one hand on the barre. You go to the middle of the room and you do sequences of steps. And there too, there's an order, you never begin by *grands sauts*!'

'Crypto-psycho-rigid fascists of the world, ballet presents itself to you like a ma-a-a-h-r-velous trip!'

Émile has just entered the room. She leans towards the Little Girl and crumples with her intrigued hand the fabric of her navy blue dress with pockets shaped like white and yellow daisies.

'And what Mademoiselle Pseudo-Voltairine—mind you, all female ballet dancers are called mademoiselle, even when they're a hundred and ten—is not telling you is the best part! I remember when we first met, the choreographer had no problem with you dancing the same night you got your sprain. Sure, of course, a couple of aspirins would take care of it. And what's even better is—you did it! With your hu-u-u-ge foot! And without complaining yet! And the only thing that worried you . . .' I try to shut her up and put out a hand to gag her, ''ould it show!'

When they go away, I finish the stretches I do every morning since the Villa. And as she's in the shower, I'm the one who mechanically answers the Little Girl's phone. The pained voice implores an appointment for the end of the afternoon, or tomorrow, but we have to talk, says the fiancé, I can understand she needs time but at least I want to talk to you. We agree to meet the next day at a cafe not far from here. I'm not really interested in what he has to tell me, I'm simply trying to gain time, reassure him, make him disappear from the landscape, keep him far away from us. Unless I've agreed to see him to learn who he is. Or to learn who she is. Is it that which is being organized and settling in, a virus on the path all three of us have been taking.

First he inquires about predictable things. How we met. When. The moment I bring up the Cinémathèque, he comes to life in an exaggerated way. It seems this word confirms the serious suspicions he's had for a long time, that's the kind of girl you meet at cinémathèques. He purses his lips while I overdo it by describing the wonderful programme in detail—a Jodie Foster retrospective next week!—his lips are no more than a small pink oval of tortured flesh.

'Don't you need lots of free time to go to your Cinémathèque every day, are you a student or unemployed, or what?' and his belly begins a laugh that doesn't make it to his face, his pale blue shirt follows the movement of his abdominal contractions. To my 'dancer' (I am a dancer—well, I was), I add very quickly 'classical' in case pictures of fake jewellery, feathers and big stairs to walk down with breasts thrust far out cross his mind.

'And you make a living from it, from dance?' he throws out without really asking me the question, a simple reflex. I think of all the pages I get from the Little Girl at the End of the Lane, pages I put away in that notebook as she gives them to me, the Theory of the Checkout Girl, the theory of the ladder, the abyss of 'after all / really' and her little poem 'Lost'. I really feel like asking him in my turn: How could they have met. Who was she when they made the disastrous decision to love each other.

And I must have bungled the beginning, for now he's explaining at length the problems of his work department, as

WE ARE
THE BIRDS
OF THE
COMING
STORM

259

she would put it so well. I had never heard the English word *consulting* used in French before and each time he pronounces it I have the impression that he's making the crystal of a glass go ting-g-g and he's about to announce his wedding. He smiles at me, a little embarrassed at having talked too much, 'We can't be defined by what we do, I realize that . . . She tells me that often. She is so . . .' I'm afraid he's going to start crying, his 'so' fills up very quickly, it seems I'm going to lose him in this word that rises all round him, like evil waters. For a moment I feel like reassuring him, consoling him. Depicting for him the Little Girl at the End of the Lane the way I see her. Her wonders. A warm violet. Her short sleeves that turn her hands with bitten nails into little acerbic flowers, escaping from them. The Little Girl with her invented words. The Little Girl armed with a fountain pen and a black marker. Who did me JUSTICE. He doesn't know we took a night train ten days ago and that we were part of the occupiers of the Villa mentioned on the front page of *Le Monde*. He knows nothing of our 14 SEPTEMBER NO JUSTICE NO PEACE, he doesn't know we have a file with Europol or that I'm bursting with laughter in the photo. He knows we were in Jumièges.

'Jumièges . . . Oh yes! That painting . . . But really. To leave like that, for such a long time, just to look at a painting? OK, it's true she does read the same books over and over . . .'

'But her fixation on that painting,' he assures me, 'that's nothing compared to the rest!'

And what I do at the moment he brings up that 'rest', that breach is my **first mistake**. I'm no better than he is. It's a good thing we got together—I offer him a little scalpel, I even hold it out to him, so he can cut open that 'compared to the rest'. He immediately and nicely pours out all the details for me. Suddenly takes on the tone of a concerned specialist, that tone he already used when the Little Girl had passed the phone to me on the train for the first time. Uses the words: under medical care, support measures, he lowers his voice as if he were making racist comments in public. Never stops nodding his head, like a nerveless puppet subjected to the movements of a car forward back forward back. He enumerates, eagerly tells stories, a troubled little boy lining up anecdotes like so much evidence. And she did that, and that. And that. And the day she. I can hear and see the Little Girl, comically chanting come on take-them take-them take-them.

'Oh, I think there was a turning point the day we went— we rarely go together—to the cinema, it's been what now? Two weeks? Do *you* know many people in our generation who would make a scene at *Pulp Fiction*?'

Two weeks ago, the Little Girl was coming to see me on the Island for the first time. We had looked at the programme of the Cinémathèque, a Tarantino cycle. I had mentioned to the Little Girl, without daring to dwell on it, that I'd only seen half of that film which so many people our age love. Without specifying that I had left during the rape scene. I hadn't told her about the frightened laughs delighted to be frightened, that vulgar abandon in the enclosed darkness of the theatre, a belly-release, a come-on, just let yourself go—that relief. Watching and laughing at the sight of a black man's arse being penetrated, laughing loudly to turn away from the sensation of your own sex stiffening and then, laughing even louder because you feel embarrassed, laughing together, all together about the animal cries a man makes when he is

I remember walking out of the theatre the way you walk away from an ordinary crowd gathered on a pavement, a pack hoping to catch a good look at the wound, to see how serious it is. And waiting for the little group with whom I'd gone to see that cult film and seeing them come out enchanted, their bodies clean and polished, probably clothed in all-natural cotton, their humid mucous dry now. In the lobby, I was looking them over one by one, all those people to whom the director had just given a roller-coaster ride—finding yourself in the place of the man who penetrates a closed, howling body, a heap of sweating meat braying in rhythm under a wave of laughter in the house, a perfect orchestra under the baton of a director who was selling something but what?

You should get some distance, stop taking yourself so seriously, I was advised nicely that evening. I felt like a clumsy worker, a woman whose hairdo or words had to be constantly rectified. Oh come on, it's only fiction! The music is great. Stay light, that constant concern with lightness, that viscous horror of being caught red-handed in the sin of heaviness. Light and detached, that's how they are here in the West.

I would have liked to become that person equipped with a sense of irony. Here in the West, they have ironic distance. Here in the West, they laugh at everything, talk about everything. Sell pastel sweaters knitted with images of AIDS, film rapes from a 'new' angle, offer up pink vaginas under transparent panties for mineral water, root about in their national identity with one finger until it exults, Karcherized lily-white. Always make sure you back off enough to have a general view of the problem, you understand. Don't get lost in the details.

I cooperate for years. Look conscientiously at images, watch all the films my generation adores, and when it's not a woman being screwed, it's a man being fucked in the arse until he cries like a woman. I watch hours of women's bodies being manipulated, shaken by men thrusting their pelvis violently as they maintain her and penetrate her. That body is a heap of nothing, something half-dead except for the sound, little cat whines. Hours of close-up camera work probing the mouth of a girl who's twisting round, her fear laughable. Limbs spread apart, little begging voices of powerless, weeping mourners with frightened, clumsy gestures. Amber kittens, plasticized petals, kilometres of actresses with useless muscles showing just on the surface of their golden flesh, breasts artificially firmed up, ready for use. Come on, don't get all worked up! they say to me, smiling.

I cooperate for years, listen to those lines—you have no sense of humour—repeated again and again as if we still didn't get it, the story of women who can't run, of women defeated, shackled, enervated, who can't tell their own story, but the story of our cut nerves sells well.

On the Internet, under *Pulp Fiction*, there's an excerpt showing the rape scene, detached from the rest of the story:

ABSOLUTELY NOT TO BE MISSED (hi I'm looking for the music you hear in the background when Marcellus is raped one of the best scenes in the film with fucking great cult dialogue man.)

I watch the fiancé telling me about his *Pulp Fiction* experience. Angry/anxious/compassionate/ashamed/eager to be understood. The little slide show of his expressions. Carefully classified, the emotions of the Little Girl at the End of the Lane are put into the appropriate department. In the middle of the film, the way she turns round for the first time towards that guy who's bursting with laughter right behind her. This is when the fiancé notices she's clasping her hands and sobbing, leaning slightly forward. Noiselessly. Her round, swift tears compose a form of writing, a message in Morse code perhaps, which disturbs the skin of her cheeks, she's sobbing, just opening her mouth from time to time to catch some air. The fiancé then takes her in his arms but she stays very straight, not letting herself be comforted. Then the guy behind explodes again, a laugh in Ah. Then the Little Girl turns round again. Asks, Stop laughing. Not very loud, a tiny tiny entreaty. And maybe he can't hear, because of the sax solo that's giving a certain rhythm to the howls of the penetrated body. And a few seconds later, Ah Ah Ah his laugh staccatos the music and the howls, and the music again, and the thrusts and stop stop she rises on her seat STOP LAUGHING. She's standing now under the protests of the other people in the audience, the fiancé pulls her by the dress to get her to sit down again but the guy's still laughing, what's

WE ARE
THE BIRDS
OF THE
COMING
STORM

263

he laughing about, so what can you do, she leans over a little further and grabs his shirt, STOP. The fiancé can't see what's happening very well. Simply hears that the guy is not laughing any more but struggling, bits of voices, disjointed protestations. The sobs of the Little Girl are like a trampoline for her actions, she draws strength from her gasps, because she is now taking him by the throat with one hand her belly sawed by the back of the seat stop stop stop laughing.

Security has probably been alerted by a furtive silhouette that slipped out of the hall to put an end to that unexpected disturbance, a girl exploding. The fiancé and the Little Girl are then escorted outside in the dark, the guy follows them screaming, he'll press charges, look what she did to me and doesn't talk at all to the girl in a navy blue dress, a funny dress as if it came straight out of an old boarding school that's been closed for years, but he shouts insults at the fiancé, if you can't control her don't take her out. She's sitting next to a cop in the lobby. They bring her a glass of water. She's sitting very straight, very much alone. The guy shakes his head. The fiancé shakes his head. If you can't even laugh any more, after all, it's only fiction, right.

He repeats that phrase to me in the cafe, 'If you can't even laugh any more, come on—freedom of expression, after all,' and then he takes a plastic envelope out of his bag. Inside there are two boxes of pills. 'What can we do?' he asks softly and now that mass of contentment that surrounds his words and his slightly thick thighs spread on the chair is coming undone. I take the bag he gives me like the witness to a race he's giving up for the moment. What will we do with her, with her alert body, a girl watched from afar, a girl almost at the end of a road where no one will ever catch up with her.

I never told anyone this story, not even Émile. I don't want to have to explain, to plead her case. I won't expose the Little Girl to the bites of others.

But I do think about it often, I imagine her ordering that guy to stop and then finally taking his laugh by the throat. Then I feel lifted up, raised, a kind of lift or magic carpet, air, I can almost feel my vertebrae being placed in a different way just under the skin of my back. Stop laughing.

I think it was the day after that STOP LAUGHING screening that the Little Girl came to the Island and offered to go spray-paint *his* street. And all alone, on a little street in the historical centre of Paris, she makes it known in black ink that the silence is beginning to come undone.

When I leave the cafe, I don't know where else to go. I need a little time. Everything the fiancé told me has to fade or fly away. I kneel down next to a large, magnificent door with a tranquilly French knocker. When I arrived in Paris, I thought all bourgeois Parisian buildings were embassies. I thought the world seen from France contained more countries.

I remain sitting for a moment on place Saint-Georges. What I would like to do: succeed in protecting that girl with the sharpened body, oh hug her while giving her room to keep putting together instructions and checkout-girls, birds and skilful nerve-cutters. Her probing mind. And her hands that haven't trembled since the two of us left on a trip, a big holiday, a great vacuum.

And what he confided is of no importance to me if it's not important to her. It's not because he penetrated her that he has the right to talk about her 'mental health'. The fact that she's been fired from her job for having stolen a hefty sum of money, her eighteen-month-old child she hasn't seen for close to six months or that she has what the fiancé, an IT expert on the body of the Little Girl, called a history—'when I met her she used to suck on orange-juice ice cubes and she weighed thirty-nine kilos'—if that's of no importance to her, it's not important to me, that's all.

When I open the door of the flat, she's sitting on the floor with her eyes almost glued to the computer, her eternal cup of tea in her hand.

Ever since I've known too many things, I've been afraid of seeing her only as a tiny girl lost on the road. But she carefully smoothes down her crumpled dress as if she's getting ready for the show at the end of the school year and walks up to me going 'Shhh' before I can make up my mind to tell her I cheated on her.

'Émile's asleep?'

'I don't think so, no . . .' she continues to whisper. 'And that's just what worries me . . . With all that technology, she'll never be able to die and she'll be around for years . . . Listening to her heart . . . It's horrible! Her heart has no need for her any more!'

Émile calls me from her room. The white sheet pulled up to her neck makes her look like an injured woman in an American TV series. With her exquisite complexion, her eyes half-shut, she never really looked sick, even when she was dead.

'No news of the arrests . . .' she whispers, worriedly. The Little Girl suddenly walks in and gives Émile her tea with a peremptory gesture, the way a diva would entrust her shawl to a stage manager before going out on stage. 'But those ridiculous arrests are actually a good thing, Émile! Of course they are! It exposes the real text! The text of the current Instructions, the ones they've been reciting to us since the Election! That's it, the time has come now, yes, absolutely . . . We have to go on, hold up to a flame what's still written in invisible lemon juice in the discourse of the Election! Make it still clearer, can't you see? . . . What do you mean, why in lemon juice? Like in the Famous Five! Come on, Voltairine! Are you illiterate?' Then she develops the parallel between those arrests and the story of the Haymarket Massacre, '. . . they're choosing our martyrs, we've got to be on our guard!' and she frantically traces lines between the dots, 'Give it meaning, Voltairine,' and I know she has remained a Little Girl all the way to the End of the Lane.

Just before curfew, we turn on the radio. Arrests 'to forestall any violation of the law' are taking place all over the country.

'What does forestall any violation mean?'

'It means to prevent—before—to anticipate what you might do . . .' Émile explains.

Can we do something. We should do something. But what can we do? 'No!' says the Little Girl to Émile, who mentions a meeting place for a demonstration of support planned for the next day. 'No, I won't go to a demo. March from point A to point B at a given time with the garbage trucks cleaning up behind me. Then go back home beddy-bye sweet dreams. No way.'

She looks at us, smiling, until the smile becomes a short series of giggles she smothers in the palm of her hand.

'What a strange team we are . . . The Madwoman, the Dead Woman and . . . I'm hesitating, Voltairine, I'm hesitating . . . You're not dead. You're not mad. You defy common sense! You're *The Mute Romanian*—or wait, I know! The Jailbird of the Balkans! And a multi-recidivist to boot!'

The Madwoman. The Dead Woman. The Ex-con. The three bitches. The Girls Worth Nothing at All. The Elf Manqué. The Nut. The Revenant. The Little Girls at the End of the Lane.

WE ARE
THE BIRDS
OF THE
COMING
STORM

267

And all three of us are slowly becoming unhinged. Unbalanced at last. Offside at last, a mechanism is jamming. While no one, absolutely no one, is watching us, our mechanical lives are struck with sudden death and I don't know how, why here and now. Perhaps being together like this for several days has set off chemical reactions, perhaps an interlocking process has slowly developed between the night of the graffiti, getting a police record after the Villa, the atmosphere of the city in lockdown, the curfew, the arrests and Émile's new heart. Everything is speeding up. It's going to happen right away. We are going, says the Little Girl, to strip bare their Instructions, all the Instructions—and make enemies. To get out of peace the way you get out of bed, up from a debilitating rest. Be done with all that innocence, so that we may become real culprits at last. Be done with demands, with those sum-up-what-you-think-in-two-sentences, film-previews for survival. Because what would we do with those answers so generously distributed at any hint of movement. All those phrases we've heard or read, so reasonable and wise (*It's no use*! *It's childish*!) that surround the slightest unexpected gesture, offside, without apparent motives. All they have to offer is conclusions. Since they anticipate our ends, let us seek the beginning, she says.

How can I express that sensation, the opposite of smothering, the body shaken, pierced by little electric shocks, colours like ribbons in the air, and the fatigue that comes in to feed laughter and desire once more, how can I say I'm just beginning to breathe. Three vacuum-packed lives that have been teased with the tip of a scissors until the shell broke. Bang.

Thus we will pose as a principle that in the world of dreams you do not fly because you have wings, you think you have wings because you have flown.

PART THREE

THE SOUND OF FIRES
(A dizzy sensation when moving to the standing position)

THE EVENTS, THE WEEK OF THE EVENTS

To this day, some people still call that spring the Ten Days when, without being able to give any precise reason for it, the whole city fell apart for the first time since the Election.

It has been said that the first fire, the one that broke out in a detention centre for foreigners, gave the starting signal. The centre where an Afghan asylum seeker of nineteen is found hanged. His request has just been rejected, and his expulsion is programmed for the next day. When the others hear this, they refuse to go back to their cells. The fire (set off from a mattress) starts to reach the other floors. Several detainees manage to lock the guards in, they climb up to the roof and with their blankets compose the letters NO JUSTICE, filmed by a TV helicopter. And then other words, questions, until early morning when they're recaptured and brought back to their cells. Very quickly, people assemble in front of the building, the police disperse or arrest them, but others come running and gather in a crowd again after seeing that nocturnal alphabet of cloth. A fire is lit in front of the centre, pieces of wood are set ablaze on the ground, an answer, NO PEACE. All this might have stopped there. But in the next few days, there is an epidemic of arrests in student groups and left-wing organizations. There are more and more police searches at dawn. A hunt for suspicious books in which each text is scrutinized, discussed, the words interpreted.

Then, without the press ever talking about it, little groups without banners begin to walk through the city at night. Then they sit down and don't budge. On place de la République, and at the Rond-Point des Champs Élysées, and at the edges of Paris, increasingly numerous, they stop. Without asking for anything, every night. The police drive them away violently. But when one street is emptied, the adjoining arrondissement refuses to go home to bed. These marches accumulate in a number of cities round the country, opaque and indecipherable. Occasionally, some people read out passages from books that have been declared 'suspicious'. Others dance without music. One evening when I go out to do some errands I run into fifty people or so blocking the Bastille, waltzing clumsily on the pavement with cars up against the back of their legs. Then they go out of the city. Spread out on the Paris beltway. Occupy factories, go into schools, high-school students settle into supermarkets where the female employees sit with them at the centre of the store after removing the anti-theft devices from the merchandise.

All three of us watch from a distance, almost intimidated by this burst of activity in a country weighed down by two years of digestion. True, a few months earlier, there were strikes, with their usual demands, negotiations and washed-out victories, but puzzled sociologists noted that the conflict was not exceptional and the Events were not necessarily linked to all that. No one has succeeded in finding the origin of the Events, why that spring in particular. And in that way.

Those illegible actions—illegible because they are mute—acquire meaning when they accelerate still more, an accumulation of sparks that clarifies and sets the tempo. Fires break out. We don't know what's happening but we understand it. The smell of burning infuses the streets, stocked permanently in the air, the air pierced by the revolving lights of police cars and panicked sirens which are seen as so many clues. So, as the Little Girl says, going over her notebook on the third night of the Events, 'The limits have been transgressed—the fall is imminent—movement does not start only from the centre of the body . . . There was more than one centre!! Forsythe understood everything before we did!'

I don't remember a time organized into day, night, morning, rest. No breaks. Nothing but moments when the memory has to catch its breath to swallow the mass of all that present on the move. Of that first night when we decide to go out and write down a few questions, I've kept the scent of the streets we took, the radio on all the time and the three of us in the flat, arguing over the best words and sentences, trying out markers on pieces of paper, looking all over for an old can of paint Émile was sure was there, mutually forbidding each other to answer the phone for fear of wasting time in conversations, come on, stop, just stop talking, Voltairine.

The curfew was not enough! We're seeing a contamination of fires. No demands. No apparent motive. We have just learnt. Many calls to the vigilance number reported the presence of organized groups. Very young children. We will re-establish order and the public authorities will triumph over terrorism. The choice is yours: you're either French or a thug. The war I have decided to wage against the thugs, that war will take several years, it goes well beyond the situation of an administration or a political party, it's a national war, declared the president. As for the arrests of the past few days. Suspicious documents. Calls for violence. The minister has declared that these groups were intending to

And like that every night. As soon as we heard of a fire, we'd go out, impossible to leave those flaming questions howling in a vacuum, the Little Girl would say. Sometimes we'd think it was all over, we'd go through two or three neighbourhoods, no one there, no smell either, no smoke or sirens. Morning would almost be breaking and no sooner did we get back, sad and dejected, than we'd turn on the radio anyway. Then we had to hurry up and spit the toothpaste into the sink and put our coats on again, it was still going on! Let's take care of After-Sales Service, the Little Girl would shout, and then imitate the sound of a police siren as we ran down the stairs of the building, Émile and I behind her, so sleep-deprived we would keep our eyes open wide all the time to encourage our bodies to skip yet another night of rest. We'd come across a fire in a street, nearly out, and it took several people to revive it, we didn't know anything about fires, we were learning little by little. Gas siphoned out of cars, empty bottles as well as cans of food (we went through all the dustbins to find some), pieces of cloth to make wicks. We'd come upon a small group of people who surely seemed about to start a fire, it was fantastic, we'd say hello and distribute the tasks, the three of us pasted our texts on the opposite walls, which would not get blackened. Our texts grew shorter and shorter as if the time to talk had passed. We kept asking questions: 'WHO?' 'CUT YOUR NERVES?' (Come on, Voltairine, come on, you can't wear out that one! We're not in a fashion show, words don't go stale!) We'd sign Little Girls at the End of the Lane on all the walls, stencilled on the pavements, in the middle of boulevards, squares and small parks.

All three of us were finally having symptoms of oppositional disorder, I pointed out one night to the Little Girl, and without dropping her marker, without answering anything— 'IT IS TIME'—for a moment, I thought I'd hurt her but she smiled, concentrating, '. . . TO MOVE FROM NAUSEA TO VOMITING.'

Sometimes, the situation called for an answer. One evening, in a troubled district just north of Paris, a few high-school girls are arrested for 'not respecting the curfew'. The mother of one of them accuses two policemen of groping them while they were in custody. In the broadcast 'analysing' the case, not one of them is present, the minister in charge of the police and a philosopher specializing in urban violence discuss the incident.

The youngest girl has a blog which is to say the least .
Already sexually active . . . Undermining the credibility of our
police force! We're now witnessing the collective rape of our
republic! So if anyone at all now can because really
those girls are nothing!

Émile and I decide to write a text and supplement it with memories of our Tuesday Evenings. When she reads it, the Little Girl at the End of the Lane proclaims it the Manifesto of the Nothing Girls, she insists on being the first to sign it.

Four nights, five, we probably slept in the afternoon, I don't even know any more. Each of our successes whipped up that desire to go out again. We were (oh what fame!) contacted by mysterious groups that didn't trust the security of the Internet and wrote out personal messages to us by hand at the bottom of a number of our posters, wanting to 'do things together'. In Émile's flat, thrilled to imagine their surprise at finding that we were so completely nothing, we would mimic their disappointment. One night, a girl passing in front of us while we were at work asked if the Little Girl at the End of the Lane group was already very large, if she could join it, I answered that we were only the Eastern section, which made Émile laugh a lot and she accused me of having old Bolshevik leftovers. We decided to make a big thing out of this misunderstanding, a text pasted on the walls of the offices of the Election Party which were burnt every night, in every arrondissement. Words that would partly (maybe?) trigger what was to come.

WE ARE
THE BIRDS
OF THE
COMING
STORM
275

She came by this way. She'll be back that way. As long as she was alone, it was quite all right, but now they ('we') are more than one at night! One Little Girl at the End of the Lane seems like nothing much. The Little Girls at the End of the Lane are never too far off.

Never did we say it won't last, it can't last, why couldn't it last. Every morning, the government would repeat all over the media that order was being restored and thunder away like a sorcerer whose spells were getting all mixed up and losing their effect.

Just as when I talk about Dance, I get lost in details of ballet shoes to be mended and tendinitis, I never did succeed in talking about the Night of the Fires without feeling tremendously frustrated, the details were always missing, those moments I can't manage to relate.

Retrieve what came first. What movement brought on another in the thick air saturated with tear gas, as tangible as an animal. I think again of the faces I met during the Events. All those moments when we were focused on the same problem, confronting things we'd never thought of doing all our lives, our clumsy actions. Thinking together about what seemed most urgent to us, what we should tackle next. Regularly setting dustbins on fire in the middle of streets to attract the police while we moved somewhere else. Thinking of the wind. Which would put out or spread the flames. Thinking of materials, of the best fire accelerants. Of the right quantity of solvent, of the proportions of flour, sugar and chlorate. Of gloves to put on. Of hair to protect so that not one hair should fall on the ground. Of the glasses we never drank in wherever we were, or were careful not to put our lips on. All those nights more opaque than nights, thick with darkness, as the street lamps had been destroyed on the first days to make us less visible to the patrols. All those nights of uneven temperatures, the approach of the fires a burning hole in the motionless cold of the sky. We didn't have to go home any more to learn if the Events really existed, we could see them, those little flashing beacons followed one after the other, a gigantic colour chart of blue and orange carrying the clouds that smoked as they rose, as if they were drawing the fire to them. The curfew took over the silence, ordering it to the streets from 7 p.m. on, a silence interrupted only by the occasional sirens going by at top speed. And the sound of shopping trolleys we pushed over the pavements by the dozen so the piled-up trolleys would reinforce the barricades.

There were dozens of them in Paris at the height of the Events, I think. Big ones on the Grands Boulevards held by hundreds of people, and then others, tiny barricades of hardly four or five that looked like little refreshment stands. Some people spent the night there, talking over coffee. Old people ran up with whole bags full of biscuits and fruit, sometimes apologizing for not staying longer, jumping at the sound of sirens. The children fell asleep under blankets, the Little Girl had bought dozens of markers for the youngest kids, they filled in the inside of the big letters on the posters, sticking out their tongue a little as they breathed. We were equipped with whistles to call one another from street to street and the Little Girl had become very skilful at it—she was able to distinguish a metal whistle from a plastic one, near Émile's place they were mostly metal.

Some neighbourhoods of the city, two rather swanky arrondissements, seemed impregnable. Some of the police who had tried to surround them were wounded. There were reports of several steel workers blocking a boulevard with two-tonne steel ingots transported on fork-lift lorries, who protected themselves thanks to some sort of projectile launcher that shot out scrap iron.

But one story in particular illuminates the way those neighbourhoods held out. The recipe for a Molotov cocktail had been given that morning on an amateur radio station broadcasting in that part of town. That very evening, a little group of cleaning women and nannies arrived at the barricade. Then they sat down and set to work in silence. One of them put in the sugar, the other the flour, then the soap and petrol and, finally, the last one carefully put the bottles in a crate. It was an incredible delivery centre which swarmed out over the whole city.

On the first days, sometimes a face would intrigue me. Not young enough. Not prepared. Too well dressed. Made naive comments. Then I could see myself at a distance with no apparent muscles in my forearms, 'your noodles,' Émile would say, my very long hair and my constant failures (not succeeding in picking up a can of petrol or a gutter grating, panicking when the tear gas burnt my skin). I wasn't really the kind of girl you'd expect to see there. My feet hurt, my back hurt, my throat too, a migraine I fought off from morning to morning, we slept so little—I can't remember one real night of sleep between our return from the Home in Jumièges and the Night of the Fires. Neither the Little Girl nor I were eating anything. Sometimes a mouthful of a chocolate bar, or a piece of bread, I don't know if it was fear or, rather, the desire to remain watchful, to settle down nowhere, remain empty and sharp, the lines of our dead lives finally cut off with a clean break.

During hastily organized meetings, sometimes under doorways, the Little Girl would raise her hand to speak with her shoulders slightly hunched over, her texts in her hand. As if she had done it thousands of times, she would speak of the fire, 'a flower to care for, a child to watch over!' I remember the eyes on her, how proud I was that it was in my ear she would whisper. What were we all doing there protecting the fire and the night. On some evenings, the lack of rest and points of reference in time would wear me out all of a sudden. I would gladly have gone back somewhere in the past but I had no place to go where I could do that and, very soon, the feeling of being ten again and opening my eyes on an unsteady day when anything at all could happen would take hold of me again, our dark blood had stagnated for much too long.

Stunned, both right-wing and left-wing newspapers were waiting for a direction. A demand. A familiar sign. Something

WE ARE
THE BIRDS
OF THE
COMING
STORM
279

to connect the Events to a story already told. And what we could feel in all their attempts to subtitle our mute actions was their fear. What do they want. Who are the leaders.

But no one wanted anything. No improvement. No adjustment. Nothing that could be bought. Nothing that could be negotiated. Reject conciliation, that all-too-lukewarm bed. Nothing but fire, to be together rubbing our bodies like weapons to reload, stones and weed-killers waiting on boxes, just making the hours come alive, running to make time lose its breath, carrying on without a break, just relearning the gestures, retrieving all those lost movements, and spreading the explosive joy of our irreverent, irreconcilable celebrations.

Let them do it. Let them inspect the Events and comment on them. Let them look for clues, for reasons. Let them underline the suspicious words. Written and said. Let them plug up all that with hasty preventive laws applied like acid compresses to our lives, ferocious little animals unleashed between our legs. Times are hard for women who are thieves of fire, Voltairine. Soon they'll probably say that all this never existed. They'll say of us that we did not take place. They'll say of us that we are no more than a rumour. And that is of no importance because they never paid attention to the rustlings of wings.

'PORTRAIT OF THE NEW AMATEUR TERRORIST GROUPS WHO ARE SETTING THE CAPITAL ABLAZE'

Under the headline of this daily newspaper, two photos: an administrative building in flames, the French flag lifted by the wind traversed by flying orange sparks, and the other, a poster pasted on an anonymous wall signed:

THE LITTLE GIRLS AT THE END OF THE LANE

Émile is at her appointment for a check-up at the hospital when she calls me around noon. All I can hear are disturbing little breaths, interrupted by 'it's' and 'me'. So? I ask. My heart's been accelerated, she repeats, laughing, accelerated but not as much as. As. Her computer heart was accelerated with the help of a defibrillating stimulator but not as much as when she saw that unknown poster signed with 'our' name on the front page of the paper.

An hour later, all three of us meet in her kitchen as if for a surprise birthday party, we're smiling to one another, tough old cowboys, almost embarrassed by our emotion. 'That contagion,' and we jump for joy on the tile floor, 'is something we have to find,' the Little Girl insists, 'find out if we agree with the others at the end of the road or if we'll have to eliminate them!'

'I don't think we can call the paper now, right away, to learn the address . . .' Émile points out. The reporter draws the

WE ARE
THE BIRDS
OF THE
COMING
STORM
281

portrait of several groups 'among the most active these past few days'.

The Little Girls: What on earth is that?

This group was certainly born, like many of them, on the night of the Election. Their mode of operation is unpredictable and their equipment is home-made. Their dangerousness resides specifically in their choice of very simple material that anyone can get. Three times, this group left an explanatory note on the premises where the fire broke out, no doubt an explosive 'recipe' for others who might want to do likewise.

There are certainly few girls in the 'Little Girls at the End of the Lane', not to mention little girls. The anti-terrorist brigade that is examining the modus operandi of the group (numerous texts pasted in all neighbourhoods of the city, a call to systematic urban violence papered over by literary references . . .) is inclined to think that this is a gang of athletic, well-trained young people with similar objectives. Although the name they chose for themselves indicates a tendency to humour and even a certain romanticism (unless it's a sign that they're film buffs, since there is a 1976 film by Nicolas Gessner of the same name), the investigators are taking them very seriously. It seems that there is something attractive about these little girls and the attraction is dangerously contagious, as there are now dozens of sites with this name on the Internet. The spokesman for the Socialist Party has declared, in agreement with the president, that their punishment will be exemplary.

Before curfew, the decision is made to go on a random search for the poster, that Little Girl who has invited herself onto our walls, and of whose formidable presence we have just learnt. We go through three arrondissements. We split up to examine more walls. We can't find it but we do find Little Girls at the End of the Lane inscriptions. So we go scrupulously round the letters to make sure that none of us is the author. Hey, do you remember being in the fourteenth arrondissement? Did you ever use red?

The collages we mechanically made for weeks have sometimes seemed pathetic to me. Those rippable, worthless sheets of paper, almost out of date. And our words, repeated, borrowed, written by hand sometimes, also gave rise to poems (sometimes dreadful), drawings of little witches, what's getting into them, all of them, to feel at the end of the lane, the Little Girl asks me at the end of our day of investigations. So we walk along the canal to the Villette, the sun is wavering, gentle and slow, the season's making a mistake. That skateboarder, with his arm in a cast, jumping over upside-down dustbins, Little Girl or not Little Girl? That woman, answering her son's questions in a monotonous tone without ever looking at him, is unanimously voted 'at the End of the Lane'. And that one, the checkout girl from the Monoprix supermarket whom I protect from a thundering 'Little Girl!' as the Little Girl walks towards her, whispering to me, 'You remember the Theory of the Checkout Girls?'

Emily Dickinson—totally Little Girl. Shirley MacLaine in *Some Came Running*! Marilyn Monroe, of course, but Patrick Dewaere too? Oh yes, Patrick Dewaere and James Dean, Little Girls at the End of the Lane, yes of course, and Jeff Buckley too. Arthur Rimbaud—little Little Girl. Glenn Gould, oh yes! The Pelican? suggests Émile timidly. Yes, wonderfully Little Girl, but he was stopped before reaching the End of the Lane. Émile! For you, we'd first have to know what heart we're talking about, were you Little Girl or have you become one because you're electric now, says the Little Girl. As for you, Voltairine, and she knelt down holding her hand out towards the stinking darkness of the canal, her question almost set down on the water, a question hardly breathed, 'We'll have to see . . . You want to stop?' My heart moved in my chest as if before a lie and I didn't have time to answer. She raised her

WE ARE
THE BIRDS
OF THE
COMING
STORM

283

head towards me, 'No! That's just it! Now's when it's getting interesting. Going through emptiness. Actually, we're playing a game. The game of time and empty space. Whoever drops dead first.' Then she stood up and with a little bow specified, 'Alain Tanner, *Messidor*, THE Film at the End of the Lane.'

You taught me that Dance lists the positions from the first to the sixth (even a seventh after Serge Lifar, what a good student I am!) and thus they are understood all over the world. Ever since you introduced me to Mademoiselle Non and her army of shadows covered with the down of swan feathers (it's all about birds, fogs and sudden deaths, but it's strong as a longshoreman!), when I hear 'you have to take a position', I see bodies getting into a fighting pose, stiffly waiting for war to be declared. Motionless, without even daring to breathe. Whereas. In Dance, positions follow one another fluidly until they form a sound, fire that burns without stopping. I found these lines by Nicolas Le Riche for you, that guy Nicolas is intensely Little Girl at the End of the Lane, I think, 'I am ready to sprain my ankle on stage for the pleasure of the moment. What is beautiful in a leap is the momentum, the impulsion, the will to push it to the maximum, to make it dazzling. As for the landing, we'll see what happens . . .'

THE FIREBIRD
Round of the Princesses

(The following enumeration is incomplete and disorganized. It bears the mark of my state of mind at the moment I experienced these events, the urgency, often the fear, the excitement. I have avoided being too precise for obvious reasons.)

I'm not going to dissect the fantasies of the press or list the accusations. To claim we were the ones responsible for this or that action would have no other meaning, today, than to set ourselves up as heroines, models to be followed. Whereas we were nothing, just a trio, a trio of rapid moves and unfurled desires almost at the end of the road, we were done with our tiny rounds, those whirls round ourselves, done with taking those authorized turns round their fenced-in pens.

The day after the 'Night of the Fires', the press counted fifty-nine acts of 'terrorism' round the country, a good twenty or so of them attributed to the 'Little Girls at the End of the Lane'. Among them: Setting fire to the offices of a pharmaceutical company that mainly manufactured neuroleptics. Setting fire (considerable material damage) to the offices of an official daily paper of the State. Also setting fire to the offices of a weekly women's magazine with a circulation of over 100,000 (an article congratulating French women on having the highest birth rate in Europe had been followed by a double page of advertising for a national campaign of sterilization aimed at 'minority women'). The flash distribution on place du

WE ARE
THE BIRDS
OF THE
COMING
STORM
285

Châtelet, very early in the morning of the fifth day, of thousands of fake train and Opera tickets (by a little group of masked people wearing wigs with 'Pippi Longstocking' braids). The explosion of a 'medium-intensity' bomb in the entrance of a building housing an office of psychiatric court experts. A fire at the Saint-Lazare train station that completely destroyed its computer data, including the file of fines, an act signed 'SPRING CLEANING! THE LITTLE GIRLS AT THE END OF THE TRACKS'. Hacking into the security systems of two detention centres for foreigners (the many armoured and double-entrance security doors remained open for nearly an hour). An important director of the branch of a bank taken hostage by twenty-odd people armed with sticks of dynamite, who demand and obtain the cancellation of legal action against customers in debt. Around thirty ATMs made unusable (glue and acid), signed 'THE LITTLE GIRL IS TAKING PART IN THE RECESSION!'

Finally, the evacuation of the psychiatric ward of Sainte-Anne Hospital when a fire broke out in the courtyard. All the rooms on the fifth floor (reserved for serious depressions and anorexics locked up in solitary) are found empty, and the women who occupied them have disappeared, with this sentence on the walls: 'THE LITTLE GIRLS ARE BACK ON THE ROAD.'

ON THE SEVENTH DAY OF THE EVENTS

The Little Girl has turned off her phone and still knows nothing about the meeting with the fiancé, I mean to tell her but don't know how. I did not give her the medication, of course. She lies down on her mattress and starts to write. It's dark outside. Émile and I sit in the kitchen as usual. Émile is half-lying on the little table between the cups, with her head resting between her crossed arms. We didn't turn off the radio and from the living room, we can make out the choppy tones of the premier, an exceptional speech. Ever since I screamed in this kitchen, our friendship has become a little strained. I tell her to go to bed early tonight and anyway we're not going to hang out late either. Just a fancy-looking travel agency that the Little Girl and I promised ourselves to decorate when we went by it in the afternoon.

'Charming holidays in Eastern Europe. Those women radiate such charm and purity! They're not demanding, can be content with a simple life and adjust easily to either the city or the country. Look through many photo albums to complete your selection. How many women you'll meet every day is entirely up to you!'

WE ARE
THE BIRDS
OF THE
COMING
STORM
287

Avenue de l'Opéra, the site of the travel agency specializing in girls from Eastern Europe. The Opera, which I can never manage to write without a capital letter, poses there at the very end of the night, lumbering, with the patina of age on it. The two of us discuss the most appropriate phrase to write.

No one around, hardly a taxi from time to time (a means of transportation authorized during the curfew if you have a pass). For a moment, the Little Girl at the End of the Lane brings up the idea of fire. We don't have what we need here, I reply. But I heard of a bookstore not very far from here that has all the equipment, come on, Voltairine . . . Her red dress is stained with paint, she has put up her hair in a ponytail and the dark circles under her eyes blend with the shadow of fogs. She draws nearer. 'Voltairine,' she says while she's fixing my braids, 'We'll have to get down to it one of these days.' Those are her exact words, that night, in the middle of the avenue, gently scolding, an attentive mother who wants me to start off on the right foot, to leave the oasis. '. . . All right . . . Tomorrow then, OK?' And she's so fast, yes, no, let's do it, good, tomorrow then, that my cowardly caution (we're doing well at spray-painting every night and helping the others with their fires, why change our methods) and my fear of going further hardly have the time to make me ashamed. And I'm not aware of that **second mistake** while she takes aerosol cans of black paint out of her bag and starts writing rapidly on the window.

'. . . YOUR LITTLE GIRL FROM EASTERN EUROPE IS AT THE END OF THE ROAD, THE LITTLE LANE OF THE GIRL AT THE END OF HER ROPE.' She steps back to judge the effect and see how much space is left, perhaps to add, RESTORE JUSTICE BUT KEEP THE FIRE? Talks about a file of customers they'll 'surely' find in the agency the next day before setting fire to it—you haven't forgotten, you little scaredy-cat—and how wonderful, all those addresses, just imagine, Voltairine, just imagine . . . Three times she inquires, 'No patrol?' without stopping her writing, I can't see anyone, the avenue is completely empty. I keep watch humming the adagio from *Giselle*. I do a few steps, dancing on the concrete.

When I launch into a series of little diagonal leaps, my feet boxing the pavement, I'm empty empty, swallowed nothing for the last two days and what's burning, there, what's blowing in the city, delights my back muscles, reconciled at last, eager for *arabesques*. And when I hear that siren, my leaps have sent me three or four street numbers down from the Little Girl who's carefully going over her letters with her aerosol can. She's standing with her back to me, I yell STOP running towards her but maybe I'm too far away for her to hear me, I don't know, or maybe she doesn't understand or absolutely wants to finish her sentence. Emerging from the corner of the street, right next to the travel agency, they surround her and grab her, a blonde woman cop throws the Little Girl flat on her belly on the avenue, sticks a knee in the middle of her back as she holds her wrists, another picks up the can from the gutter. They push me away as if I wasn't part of this whole thing and spit 'Over' into the walkie-talkie. The lady cop goes through the pockets of the Little Girl's red coat on the ground. She's with me, she's with me, I repeat, with me, and from close up, the face of the blonde cop shows no fatigue, no shadow under her eyes, she could keep going for nights and nights. I realize from her black athletic uniform that she belongs to the new Special Brigades, the TNU (Territorial Neighbourhood Units—watchword: 'FIGHTING CRIME NEVER STOPS'). I drop to my knees, the Little Girl at the End of the Lane has hit the pavement, her lip is bleeding onto her chin. I hold out my hand to her, two cops pick me up and push me away. One of them, the older one, seems almost embarrassed by my tears, to him I swear that we're nothing, honestly what's four words written on a window. I insist again, she's with me. Then he asks me the first and last name of the Little Girl at the End of the Lane without looking up from her ID, which he's holding. And I can't answer, I don't know them. A patrol car stops. The old cop pushes me away, staring at me strangely, as if he pictured himself as one of those valiant cops in B-grade films secretly working against his own side.

WE ARE
THE BIRDS
OF THE
COMING
STORM

289

'The description we got on the vigilance number said one girl on the avenue, not two . . .' he recites, while I see her stooping, fragile and handcuffed, to get into the unmarked car, an actress staggering as she leaves a film festival. 'And you, with your accent, it's not a good idea to draw attention to yourself these days.' But where are you taking her, tell me where, I beg, his navy blue trousers making folds at his heavy hips, and without answering he gets into the white blue-and-red car. When I raise my head to the windows of the buildings facing the agency, a few lights go out, hastily.

I have to walk along the whole river to get to the flat, go through the fetid smell of human urine under the bridges. I run, go up streets, zigzag through alleys to gain ground, my hoarse tears cut off the air, nothing in my lungs, the vision of the Little Girl at the End of the Lane on the ground, like a month ago, Émile with her chilled heart. Not going to make it, not going to make it. The vibrations of the concrete arouse the pain in my left ankle, the sirens are threatening through the shouts, those masses of unbreakable glass, this city so prudently knitted, my own prudence and my nerves clipped in this country of solid Islands, secured by anonymous phone calls conscientiously describing—I thought I heard a bird but it was the sound of a spray can, officer—a silhouette in a red coat tracing FIRE on a shop window.

Émile contacts a lawyer who has specialized in the arrests of the past few days and tells me not to think about the worst that could happen—try to sleep a little, she worries.

And it's the Little Girl's cell she's left on a bunch of pages that wakes me up. I can't hear you, get away from the noise, I ask, I make out dull sounds, crates falling, I don't know why I'm sure the person is in a market, maybe a covered food market.

'I'm calling from my place you understand your bullshit's now in my place / and I swear to God I'll / you'll pay for this! I'll find your / real name, you bitch I've got the cops in my flat you happy now, she's fucked, fucked we're / fucked!' A backwash of anger drowned in the hubbub, and the fiancé disappears from the line.

Without talking to each other, Émile and I watch the day extricating itself from the dawn. Later, I tell her about the park, the theory of the ladder at the Villa and the Europol file too, our laughter spattering on their photos and crossing freezing Normandy to go see the Enervated Boys on their raft—do you know Émile what to enervate means—and Dina, when on the last day, she backed out of the lift entreating us not to forget that we boasted of going to the End of the Road. I leave out the blood on the driver's neck that rainy morning in the car taking us to Jumièges and the revelations of the fiancé about the *Pulp Fiction* incident. Then, later in the morning, I change my mind and lay down those stories like aces in a game of cards that you absolutely must not lose. Émile does not declare: that Little Girl really is at the End of the End, after all. She listens to me, hunched up on her chair. I know that all those acts bring back to her, as they do to me, years of questions abandoned in drawers, of sudden deaths.

When the lawyer finally calls back, we're in the middle of breakfast but already the evening is returning. I have good news and bad news, she announces, the good news is, for the moment, she's only being held for questioning, the bad news is your friend is in the anti-terrorist section, but we can be cautiously optimistic, she has attenuating circumstances in her favour, adds the lawyer. Her psychological state. In treatment for the last two years. And the child. All those words form a plausible version of a person's life, but not hers, I say to Émile too loudly, I have never, you hear me, never met one single person as logical as the Little Girl at the End of the Lane. As clairvoyant. I like that word applied to her: who sees clearly, my little witch of truth.

We washed our hair when night fell again. We listened to Cat Power's *The Greatest* and I pretended I was too sleepy instead of crying again because I was thinking of Dolly Parton and of that night at the Home, where the immateriality of my happiness at being with her had taken hold of me like a mean pain that would come someday, the sharp noise of falling rocks.

Before going to bed, I opened her notebook for the first time: Symptoms of the End of the Lane and various antidotes my Little Girl had left on her bed, not far from the biography of Voltairine de Cleyre and I liked this: So we must, in a world where we only exist bulldozed into silence, literally in social reality, figuratively in books, we must, whether we like it or not, constitute ourselves by ourselves alone, surge up as if from nowhere, be our own legends in our very lives . . . Monique Wittig.

I had only known her for a month. One whole month to draw each other over, reshape our contours or even invent them when they were gone.

In the morning, Émile woke me up holding the phone out to me. After bringing up our 'imprudence' in a scolding tone, the lawyer told me my friend would get out the next day. 'The police searched her flat yesterday morning. They found nothing suspicious and that's good. She was referred to a judge who put her on probation with a requirement to get treatment and she's under provisional house arrest in her flat.'

I thought of the yellow Post-it glued in the hallway of her flat, 'WHO?' and her bedroom where the Little Girl hid the definition of 'patient' in a notebook. And of that article too, which she had cut out, about being jailed at home, a new kind of prison. I thought of my lack of imprudence that night on avenue de l'Opéra, that little *pas de fear* she had danced with me out of loyalty.

Before hanging up, the lawyer suggested: 'Since you seem to be very close, if you could think of a list of things that would prove she isn't dangerous, I mean, showing that the inscriptions are an isolated incident. I don't know, think of . . . what you did together these past weeks, anything that comes to mind, I'll sort it out. It would be really good to have positive testimony in her file to get her out of house arrest quickly . . .'

Art. 138 1) Not to leave the following territorial limits without prior authorization: Paris, 75.

Art. 138 2) Not to leave his/her home or residence except under the following conditions or motives: to exercise his/her professional activity, to see his/her lawyer, answer summons of the court and departments specified in the present order.

Art. 138 5) Appear once a week at the Department of Application of the court's decisions.

Art. 138 6) Answer court summons and summons of the person specified below:

Show proof of his/her professional activities or regular attendance at an institution of learning; a trimestral report will be addressed to us.

Art. 128 9) Abstain from receiving, meeting or entering into any relation with or contacting in any way the following individuals:

Forgive me   forgive me

For not having defended you well, not having been a good watcher, oh tell me . . . The first moments of our reunion, on the ninth day of the Events. She rang Émile's doorbell very early in the morning and everything in her is quick, she interrupts me, makes herself a cup of tea, looks through her notebooks without answering. And my **third mistake** is that doubt, oh, hardly for a moment, when the Little Girl at the End of the Lane talks of the requirement to seek medical attention and describes her treatment for 'mental confusion'. That step back, the distance between us when I examine her, evaluating her *transparency.*

She relates her seventy-two hours in custody in a bored voice, as if she had been summoned to the principal's office in high school.

'. . . In full pomp and uniform, mask and gloves . . . If you don't answer, you'll stay here, your flat is being searched, your life is surrounded, you realize we're doing you a favour with this reprieve, oh, the petty tricks of little barbarian kings . . . They showed me pictures of us . . . In the Villa . . . I plead alcohol, strangers we met in a park, a party on the train. And then they throw Ivan at me, an international leader calling on people to commit, wait, no, here, read this, I wrote it down: "Calling on people to commit, in an organized way, violence against persons and property." What is your professional career, we have the list of all the Internet sites you visited, do

you know that girl, this boy and and and they showed me lots
of Little Girls posters . . . I told the truth! Never saw them!
Vaguely heard of an old film with Jodie Foster but aside from
that . . . And then I took out my Cinémathèque card . . . I don't
know. Any Little Girls at the End of the Lane. What lane?'

Her lower lip is still a little swollen, her chin bluish,
scratched. She falls silent. Then she demands some fun, like a
reproach to Émile and me, a little music, put on Mariana
Sadovska is that possible please, this silence, I feel as if I'm
sick, she murmurs, upset.

'Enough of that . . . Let's move on now. Next. I think . . .
We're burying Lautréamont a little too much round here,
talking and talking, analysing the cops, did I tell you, Voltairine,
what Albert Parsons said, no, actually it's August Spies. I have
his portrait in my notebook, that . . . one, here. Look! I can't
imagine—but maybe we shouldn't imagine, everyone in white
the day they were hanged   and the slipknot . . . They sang.
All the boys of the Haymarket. Recited poems to one another,
their faces covered with white sheets in front of the . . . gallows
and Spies, before the reporters who were crying but didn't want
to cry   . And you know that text can't be found anywhere,
in French? What can it possibly mean that we can't find it here,
does that mean something . . .   The time will come. (she
stood up)   When (she held her hand out to me).

'We must recite the words of August Spies!' the Little Girl
was insisting, 'The time will come   when   our
silence   will be more powerful (she glanced at Émile,

who wasn't saying anything, as for me, I was reciting her
words, slightly behind her)   'than   the voicesoices
you stranglerangle today the time will come when our silence

'We're not going to make it.'

I thought (but, no, I didn't think at all) that she was talking
about my bad recitation.

'The words won't be . . . suff-icient they . . . and some words . . . I saw. We're not going to make it.'

She went into the bathroom. Not a sound, then sobs, gasps. But why are you crying too, Émile asked without moving from her chair and I wanted to dispel Émile's embarrassment at that heavy display of emotion, I wanted to dissipate it, lighten the air.

We said nothing more to each other all morning, we performed banal, reassuring tasks. Peeling vegetables, boiling water. Sitting very straight, the Little Girl was keeping her distance from us now, stirring her tea into which she hadn't poured anything, refusing to taste the dish on the table. It's when Émile pointed to the time, maybe she should get back home on time to click on the electronic monitor at least this first day, that the Little Girl spoke at last.

'There's . . . I . . . Something . . . Something else.' And it must be her expression but I stop her with the same gesture my father used when, in our living room in Romania, foreign visitors were about to bring up things considered subversive by the Conducător—he would put one hand on his lips and raise the other towards the ceiling.

'Let's go for a walk,' I said, getting dressed as fast as possible.

All three of us are sitting on the bench whitened with the droppings of obese birds in the little park on the rue Saint-Georges, the Little Girl is rubbing her face with her chalky hands to remain awake. From under her sweater, she takes out a bundle of pages folded in four. Puts them rapidly in order and gives them to us. One by one, we pass each other those pages ripped from a brochure.

WE ARE
THE BIRDS
OF THE
COMING
STORM
297

'They explain to me that I "am not in full possession of my faculties" and the commissaire asks me who she should notify for my release. And then she has to print out a document or whatever. And her printer isn't working any more. She left the room for hardly two minutes and I told myself . . . I was going to bring back a . . . a souvenir. A police seashell. Hold the brochure to your ear and you hear France, Voltairine . . . It was in front of me. I didn't even know what was inside it but it . . . It sure did look like Instructions . . .'

We have one of the Election Instructions in our hands. With its different chapters. Its carefully chosen vocabulary. The 'removed', the 'escorted out', the risks of 'breakdown of the organism' and how to avoid them. The transmission of certain moves, how to teach them. French refinement. We are going through a map of French manners, the way France does things. Told with no doctoring and no missing words.

*Boarding procedure : **extremely delicate** phase. Pre-boarding : **before** the passengers. Out of the passengers' sight.*

How to deal with the escorted foreigner: create and maintain the best psychological conditions for the foreigner who is being escorted back to his/her country so that he/she will accept his/her removal without difficulty. Force and other means should be in proportion to the resistance offered by the foreigner. Physical control over the individual will be carried out in conformity with the professional moves and techniques acquired in the course of initial and continuous training given to escort professionals by the physical and professional instructors of the border police.

We remained silent in the park for a good while, with the brochure tucked under our sweaters, a few pages each. That morning, the air was coming down on us like a mouldy sheet, dirty, humid and slightly sticky.

And then, three days. Maybe more. Remaining locked up, stunned, inside Émile's flat. The Little Girl made quick trips back to her place to punch in, electronically signalling her presence and her allegiance to her requirement to stay in treatment. She didn't say so but I knew Émile was afraid of a police search.

Afraid of the papers lying round, of the Little Girl who kept preparing texts, asking us when but when on earth would we go back to paste them up. As for me, I was afraid for the Little Girl who wasn't complying with her house arrest, afraid for Émile and her mechanical heart, I was afraid of my lack of courage when I felt the rough pages of the Instructions under my sweater. There was talk about contacting other people, groups perhaps, but the curfew made finding them difficult. The Little Girl saw her sides getting covered by little red blotches, maybe she was developing an allergy to ink. When I would go out to buy bread in the morning, it seemed to me that the pages of the Instructions against my body were changing the way I walked, those MOVES were climbing on me, dissolving into my slowed-down blood, I was becoming a clock mechanism, I was continuing, we were continuing to live and do stupid things, wanting a cup of tea, being sleepy and thinking of putting on a sweater in the evening. We were functioning. Surrounded by deadly instructions meant for Others, who were breathing near us, right there, and knew nothing of those Instructions that were waiting for them. I would say 'we' and the Little Girl would interrupt me, beside herself, 'But there is no we for you, Voltairine, stop it! You will NEVER be French enough to be French . . . No more shelter for you, Voltairine. You are the Others!'

Irritated by our tensions, Émile called out one evening, 'Let's just put those pages away. We'll see what we can do later. Or not.'

I thought of her questionnaires lying in their drawer for ever and didn't say anything. During the night, I looked on the Internet for the names of the people who were mentioned as 'technical supervisors' for those Instructions or under 'theory and concept', like in the credits of a film. A good number of them belonged to a social network. Some had even left very easy access to their family photos. Holiday photos. Comments on their favourite films, tips about the best crêpes in their neighbourhood. One would have liked to see some alarming detail to make them stand out, something special that would turn them into incomprehensible constructions, people who could not be apprehended, but there was nothing. They worked. Transmitted moves that had been transmitted to them. Tried to remain as faithful as possible to the instructions for the use of those moves. Had taken training courses. Had taken lunch breaks during their training, no different from all other lunch breaks in all training courses. During which they had talked about their summer vacation and the swimming pool at the hotel, the excursions, problems with recurrent migraine, should they sign up their little girl for violin classes as early as September, I'm the one making dinner tonight, zucchini quiche with parmesan, I have to go home earlier, wait, let me show you this, I was in the delivery room, the greatest moment of my life.

The Little Girl at the End of the Lane had been able to fight one set of Instructions. She had latched on to phrases *don't chew them, the taste is bitter. Panic disorder anxiety disorder social disorder generalized anxiety disorders.*

Had built entire work-sites out of words. Poems. Questions. Swords too. A poetry of little dizzy spells, *dizzy sensation when moving to the standing position.* But these words were polished, with no asperities, mentholated with cleanliness, a hospital lobby of bland words, these words:

LOLA
LAFON

300

*The experience of escort personnel combined with **recurrent difficulties** encountered while carrying out removal measures by air have necessitated the implementation of training actions specifically adapted to this type of mission.*

That simplicity conducive to muffling the sounds and limiting bleeding. Without any 'technical' word. Nothing that might incite us to hidden meanings—an investigation which would have put us back into a fighting mood. But what would we do with that.

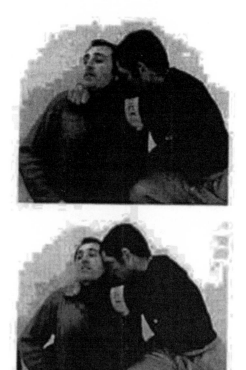

☞ The escorter exercises traction on the clothing, giving it a twisting motion round the neck. He maintains this pressure for three to five seconds to ensure the constraint of phonic regulation and then releases it while maintaining the points of control

☞ Control and dialogue with the escorted individual are maintained throughout the procedure

☞ Important: The times of pressure and release must not exceed three to five seconds. The repetition of these actions of phonic regulation cannot be performed for more than five minutes.

THE RISKS

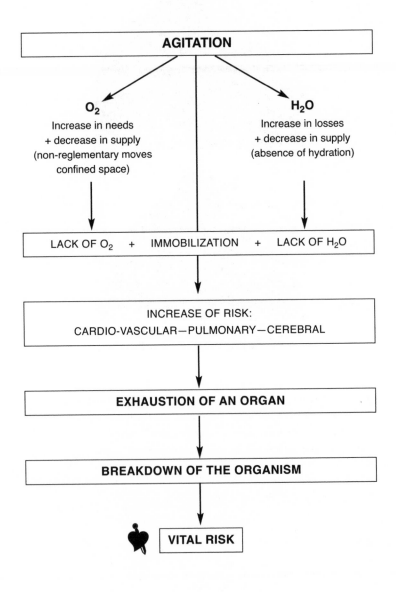

AGITATION

O$_2$
Increase in needs
+ decrease in supply
(non-reglementary moves
confined space)

H$_2$O
Increase in losses
+ decrease in supply
(absence of hydration)

LACK OF O$_2$ +   IMMOBILIZATION   +   LACK OF H$_2$O

INCREASE OF RISK:
CARDIO-VASCULAR — PULMONARY — CEREBRAL

EXHAUSTION OF AN ORGAN

BREAKDOWN OF THE ORGANISM

VITAL RISK

Side effects: Feeling of sickness, nausea, dizzy sensation with weakness, confusion.

Hallucinations.

So, without much conviction, it was decided to photocopy them 'massively'—we had to comb the city, changing shops every twenty copies to avoid suspicion, they informed on you for anything that remotely resembled making leaflets. Early one morning at the exit of a Métro station, we handed them out randomly, despite the fear of giving one to a plainclothes cop. Some people crumpled up our leaflets right away, others slowed down a moment to read them and threw them away afterwards, resuming their rapid pace without even looking at us, uneasy at being alerted, bothered by knowing what they had only supposed. Occasionally, one or two would speak to us. They knew all that already. They knew someone who. Or they suspected as much. Well, almost. Even if, still, those pictures . . . Sometimes someone would remain at our side for a moment after having read it, arms dangling, not knowing what to add. We were producing immobile people. Weighed down and soiled by a deadly prudence, limping, one foot out, one foot in, one foot in house arrest, the other cautiously outside the law, still partying near the fires, we had forgotten the contagious joy of the Little Girls in the city. The newspapers too, which were rejoicing at the 'return to calm', unanimously commented on the end of the fires and every TV channel looped those same images of fires smoking slowly, almost out.

THE RITE, THAT SPRING

No one says to me you dreamt that up, mademoiselle, with a tender, concerned look, no one even doubts what I experienced during those days. I do. And I would like to have made it all up. I wish all that had not existed, both the week of the Events and the Night of the Fires. Because if it hadn't already existed, it could still happen in the future and I would believe in those events, I mean I would believe that they could truly be Events. But all that did happen.

And what is worse, for nights like that, than to be imbued with a sweet nostalgia at the memory of the dates one recalls in a tone full of emotion.

You have to turn the page, they tell me here. Turning the page immediately makes me think of a history book, or a book of stories, and then I know that the **mistake** I made—all of us made it. Go back home. Rest. Take your time. Get some distance. Perhaps we began to celebrate things that had not really happened yet, or not quite. Raising our glasses to our nerves— intact and found again, true but still unsteady. Celebrating the advent of wooden ladders that allowed us to go everywhere, without really going there.

During the days that followed the Night of the Fires, tension slackened instead of going further. And little by little, new faces mingled with us, seeping in like slow water. No one knew when they had first been there, no one was able to say if they were already there on the roof of the Printemps department store or in the corridors of the Sainte-Anne Psychiatric Hospital.

WE ARE
THE BIRDS
OF THE
COMING
STORM

305

There were so many of us, we didn't ask that kind of question, people would pop up, participate, leave, but that's just it, *they* never left. They lay down on the floor with us in occupied gymnasiums, sat in our open assemblies, wore the same torn, dirty T-shirts as ours, often demonstrating concrete knowledge superior to ours, told us how to make the best explosive mixture. Tireless. Never any shadows under their eyes. Then, during a general assembly, there would be a scene, a young guy would point to a girl, signalling her as a police infiltrator. Long discussions would ensue, votes, decisions, the girl would be kept out of things, her friends would go mad, all this was ridiculous, but who were those friends? Everywhere, this was part of how the 'Mediators of the People' operated, agents sent out to the strategic places of the Events. They'd listen to us. Smiling, they would serve something to drink and suggest we take a rest, a break. It's OK to take time off, they'd say. You've gained everything you wanted here, it's not going to vanish just because you go home for one night.

When a mediator who called herself Lou worried about the bags under the Little Girl's eyes, I agreed. The fabric of her clothes was getting detached from her and floated like water round an inert body. Just one night. I even insisted. As for the mediator, she kept quiet and did not interfere. We said goodbye to the people who were trying to get a few hours of sleep right there on the floor of the bookstore. See you tomorrow morning, latest. Probably sooner.

The neighbourhoods of Paris remained so full of bitter smoke that the sky never let go of its night. You'd think a storm was on the way, then you'd see half of a fresh, plump cloud through the chemical fog of the clashes. The lack of sleep and food was transforming everything, smells, taste, my mouth felt as if it were deprived of saliva, painfully dry, ash, and I had the impression of having shampoo in my eyes—a thin, blurry film that fogged everything outside the window of the bus taking me back to Émile's place. At the corner of boulevard du Temple, where we had pasted it a few days before, there it was, not even ripped or covered by another poster. And as the bus was starting up again, I saw that under our signature 'Little Girls of Nothing', the paper was covered with claws, birds' feet carefully laid out next to each other. A disturbing heap, a ball of tight threads, tiny strands pushing one another to be there, below the text, eager to declare their status as Nothing Girls. ValeriePeggyAnnaClaireKadidiaAlineLolaIsaSandrine JykLauretteFoulémataAdelineIsabelleAudeEmmanuelleBintou FloJeanne

We are all Nothing Girls. Or we have been.

We, the Nothing Girls, said no, but apparently not loud enough to be heard.

We have never forgotten what it means to be a doormat, a reversible hole.

We managed to put words on that night only one year, ten years, twenty years later but we never forgot what we have not yet said.

We, the Nothing Girls, were called, or will one day be called, by the courts 'liars', 'mythomaniacs', 'prostitutes'.

We have been or will be accused of 'destroying the life of a family' when we accuse a man above suspicion.

We, the Nothing Girls, have been searched by medical hands, by words and questions, evaluated, interrogated, all that to finally conclude that we were not, perhaps, 'innocent victims'.

We are nothing. But there are many of us who are nothing, or have been. Some of us still walled up alive inside polite silence.

LITTLE GIRLS OF NOTHING
AT THE END OF THE LANE
RESTORE JUSTICE
AND KEEP THE FIRE

WE ARE
THE BIRDS
OF THE
COMING
STORM
307

How long I slept, I don't remember. When I wake up, it's night outside, no message from the Little Girl on my phone. Towards noon, I call her twice, she doesn't answer. Maybe she's still resting, Émile suggests. I know she isn't, I get dressed and go there. I get lost a little, and once I'm in front of the building, I have to wait quite a while for someone to go in, I don't have the entry code.

I've come to see my friend, I say to the brown-haired young woman who opens the door of the flat and immediately, she blocks the way with her foot, the blood rushes up to her made-up cheeks, a dark-red invading tide. She keeps facing me while shouting, Antoine, come quick. The fiancé runs up, pushes her away and takes her place at the door. You don't really think I'm going to let you in, he says. It's a bad telefilm, he seems invested with a mission of protection, to keep me away from her. You can't hold her against her will, she's an adult, I simply want to make sure she's all right. I negotiate but I don't want to plead. Because the moment I begin to cry and beg him, it seems to me—in fact, I know it—our journey will be over. And then, as in a romantic ballet, we will be forced to enter the last act, Act III. The act where the spirits, the fathers and the kings make their triumphal return to the stage.

'The barbarian kings . . . Of the empire. With a capital E on Empire. Or . . .'

I hear that from the end of the hall. Pronounced very clearly, not in a strange voice or one thick from tranquilizers. The Little Girl, as she often does when she constructs her theories, first lays them out aloud, little Lego blocks placed and displaced for hours at a time.

The fiancé doesn't budge and neither does the brown-haired girl, in a low voice, she asks him, 'You want me to go take a look?' And her concern is disgusting, full of what she does not say, of the words missing from that sentence: you want me to go check what the crazy girl talking alone in her room is up to. I walk forward, the hall seems tremendously long to me, the fiancé grabs me by the arm, he doesn't dare to go too far, the brown-haired girl sets herself in front of me, I slap her, I don't mean to, I'm sweeping her presence away, my heart is no longer pumping blood but burning, bitter water, I open the door and there she is.

Her bird-like back hunched over her pages spread out all over, in her sleeveless dress, navy blue and white, the uniform of a school closed since 1975. The tired bird. My bird tired of the sky.

She's writing, sitting at her desk. Turns round, smiles at me, for a moment it seems to me she too is dead and has forgotten everything and is going to ask me who I am, but she's adorable, she whispers, 'I know . . . I'm late but I was going to come back . . . What are *you* doing here?'

I knelt down and huddled up against her, the centre of my body was in the middle of my throat, a suffocating dam of dull fears. Why hadn't she answered me for the last two days, why hadn't she called, we'd said we'd leave again right away.

The fiancé took my wrist, rather gently, 'Come on, you have to leave, just go now, you're not helping her, that's enough . . .'

Then the Little Girl at the End of the Lane gets up. As if she has something important to do that she's forgotten, she walks to the end of the room, that window she's opening, it takes for ever, the time for me to straighten up, I shout WAIT, clumsily, she puts one foot on the sill, and now she's there, standing, impossible to know where we're at, she says, you can't even see the moon in that sky any more, she's holding on to the window frame, you'd think it was Nadia Comaneci, that's the thought that doesn't leave me, Nadia, standing on the lower of the two asymmetrical bars, her hands placed on the higher one. Ready.

They shout. The fiancé and the brown-haired girl whose name I don't know. At that moment, I don't believe she's going to jump. Or, I don't know, it doesn't seem so serious to me. I say WAIT to be with her, my hand is holding hers, in gymnastics it's called being a spotter. Helping the gymnast to perform a dangerous leap. The fiancé grabs her by the wrist and makes her step back down, come on, what are you doing there what are you doing, he repeats as he walks her to her bed. Voltairine, she says, removing his hand, Voltairine, wait wait, I must tell you, I read something about those birds called great tits, yes, great tits and Rosa Luxembourg and her epitaph to the spring . . .

I promise her I'll be there when she wakes up.

The three of us are sitting in the living room; they no longer talk of throwing me out. Valérianne introduces herself as her 'best friend'. They met in high school. '. . . I'm not judging her, besides I never judge anyone!' she proclaims, thrilled to find herself the exemplary limpid friend of a muddy, shackled girl, someone who needs to be rescued constantly. I could tell her I think she hates you. I think you make her throw up, in fact. She loathes you in her texts. I could tell her about the Theory of the Checkout Girl, that loneliness described by the Little Girl as gulps of dizziness. I could ask her what do you want to fill her with, who are you to cut away at her nerves so diligently.

Follows a long, worried conversation between the fiancé and the friend in which I do not intervene, a nurse being kept in the background. They go get the instructions for the neuroleptics and read through it, discretely taking pleasure in finally having physical proof, a leaning body to lay their hands on, those feet hesitating on the windowsill. Do you think it's the rebound-effect dizzy sensation? Mind you, loss of control was anticipated. Maybe a walk at the end of the day, but the curfew limits our movements so much, when I think that didn't even succeed in stopping the Events or the fires, should we call her mother, bring the child, no, especially not in her condition. It's not a suicide attempt, I repeat, not suicide, and I try not to talk loudly, to keep steady, not set anything off. It's one of these things she does sometimes, she unleashes her energy, she expands into every possibility, to the very end of the words she uses, to the very centre of what she feels rising in her, all those times I saw her unfold, a beautiful, tall stork with light eyes, there is nothing that dies in her gestures, no, the air becomes her border. That's all.

I remain in that overheated flat, careful not to let the tide of those practical/pragmatic solutions for the Little Girl at the End of the Lane rise too quickly, everything they consider doing for her, clear away, dig out, arrange for her, more comfortable to hear, plug up the air holes of her sentences again,

WE ARE
THE BIRDS
OF THE
COMING
STORM

311

refine her surroundings, organize her space, put her back to bed at room temperature. They don't dare drive me away and all that late afternoon I go back and forth between their consultation in the living room and her room.

Voltairine.

Voltairine,   you know? When we met, you told me that even long long after your sprain, you kept wearing an ankle brace when you danced. It scared you to dance without it.   You know? And you felt bad about it   as if that showed a . . . I don't know, some kind of cowardice?
You know?   But   it's exactly the opposite!! Wait wait, it's the opposite be-cause . . . the day you put away that ankle brace is the day you stop taking risks, since you're not afraid of hurting yourself any more?   Right?
      . . . Voltairine   Voltairine   I'm thinking about that documentary. Dancing with the memory of ropes, remember. But how can we be sure that what we think—our ideas—aren't surrounded by ropes? Or. Surrounded by the memories of ropes how?

Ha and then. No, I'll be quiet. Because otherwise, see, I talk and and   then there's the diagnosis! I don't know what I'm saying, unmanageable . . . Not inhabitable! Voltairine. I'd like to read you this and   may—   I'm thinking of   outlines, limits you know people say 'there are limits, after all!'

I think of the girls without outlines I was a part of before knowing you, Voltairine, as you were too, perhaps. Our limits got erased because we used them so little. Bodies with no clear border, capable of being silent about everything, of understanding anything.

Outlines redrawn with precision, the eyes in pencil, and the mouth lacquered to indicate that *here* is where it's all happening (those wily, coaxing paintings, a little entreaty of non-aggression in an uncertain territory.) Girls prepared to be the object of a war they never declared.

What is more monstrous than that, Voltairine, what is more monstrous than being the *subject* of a war in progress and not even knowing it any more. No longer knowing any other state than being a battlefield, venerated, then rejected because it's been walked upon too many times, too worn out. Are we condemned to be nothing but ploughed fields, spaces where they play musical scores that are not ours?

What am I going to call this text. War in progress. The progress of the war! What do you think? Voltairine,   are you asleep? No, you never sleep never eat, neither do I! I never eat, besides, you have to digest all that, your life, right? Oh yes, wait, you know the psychological helpers sent to the bedside of waking volcanoes, trains derailing, winds rising, tidal waves? As if everything had to be   calmed down
as if that weren't normal   you know

WE ARE
THE BIRDS
OF THE
COMING
STORM

313

She's writing. The Little Girl seems invaded by thoughts, climbing plants that are accelerating, a dance circling her. She struggles to find a name for those flowerings, she's overwhelmed by everything surging up in her, she needs a pen, quickly, so she can write all that, organize it, night fell a few hours ago and she's still drawing long columns, crossing out everything she already told me. She seems to be afraid of not having enough time. You have to say / cross out what was said / rewrite something else that comes to mind / say / and cross out.

Around eleven, she falls asleep again a little, exhausted. They've taken refuge in the kitchen, they talk about her without daring to go see her or listen to her. The fiancé stuck his head in her room in the course of the afternoon, 'Children's bodies! Charred   in the transformer and and   and eyes pierced in my dream   forcing us not to blink you know? We didn't have the right to blink we had to LOOK at everything   pierced that boy with an eye poked out and   the other too, the Flash-ball. You know all that. I know that you know, photocopies, we didn't make enough of them. You know? Or And what if it were the opposite? We should NOT have. Distributed that, spread it, as if, as if we couldn't cut the putrefied umbilical cord that is still feeding us . . . We didn't think of   Lautréamont we photocopy unhappiness to inspire . . . terror   ,

Every time, the fiancé shrinks back when he hears the Little Girl's words, they attack him, they are corrosive.

Everything she says makes perfect sense, I repeat, yes, I understand what she's saying, it makes sense. It's all mixed up, that's all. It's too fast, she's tired. But everything there is real.

Yellowed and crumpled like an old piece of paper, the fiancé gets up abruptly. 'What the hell have you been doing, you two? She wasn't like that before, there was order, coherence! I could understand . . . OK, let her spend all her days at the Cinémathèque, it's OK with me, it's better than—that.'

'That' is the Little Girl.

We have dinner without talking to one another, the fiancé, the girlfriend and I. Over dessert, he insists on showing us an article 'which is not uninteresting'.

'*European Mental Health Pact.*

'*The Wellness Project.*

'*Today, one out of four people in our country goes through a depressive episode or encounters a mental health problem. What happens if we put a fourth of our human resources in parentheses? We are completely disqualified in terms of economic competition. Our studies show that the costs incurred by psychological disorders are a burden on productivity and place a still greater burden on the reimbursement of medical expenses. Whole workdays lost! Absenteeism or early retirement cost more than the treatments themselves. So beyond big words like humanism, etc., let us tackle what is at stake in mental health with numbers.*

'*Recent progress enables us to identify the cognitive markers of pathologies like bipolar disorder and schizophrenia. The goal is to identify individuals who are not yet ill but who **may** fall ill. Mental health for all, our project for tomorrow!*'

'I could,' I suggest, crushed, 'take her to the cinema tomorrow?'

WE ARE
THE BIRDS
OF THE
COMING
STORM
315

I watch over her all night long, she seems to have equipped herself with an artificial heart, she keeps writing, sitting cross-legged on her bed, surrounded by pages that she fills up with rounds of words, zigzags of sentences, she writes without stopping.

It's still dark out when she calls me in a low voice.

'Voltairine . . . Voltairine . . . Is . . . Isn't madness as simple as grief? Or maybe it's the other way round, I don't know.'

I don't understand her question. She repeats, is madness as simple as grief, or on the contrary, it's grief, you see, that's as simple as madness. I'm thirsty, I'm exhausted and I get up to make us a cup of tea in the silent flat. We're in her kitchen, I have my back to her, and when I turn round, I see her with her eyes closed and her arms squeezed round her chest, she has slipped onto the floor, sobbing noiselessly. Am I crazy, she asks me, like a piece of information, a direction I could give her.

You know all that, the . . . polite bows and bird tiaras and the spindles of Sleeping Beauties, wait that's all I want to write down, wait a second. Pricked by the spindle of conciliation. We're not going to make it. We're not going to make it.

In the morning, there is the first check on her house arrest, a busy woman who doesn't ask me to leave during the conversation with the 'patient'. She sits down clumsily on the bed, her eyes and hair seem to have been treated with the same dye, ultra-shiny and too black. Her dry mouth transforms each of her vowels into little golf balls.

I think, and everyone here thinks, your husband too, right, monsieur, that you're putting yourself in danger if you stop treatment. You're not well at all.

Yes I am.

No you're not well at all.

And . . . The fires?

Sorry? What? The inspector repeats a few times in a suspicious tone: What do you mean, the fires? The fires are over, madame, you don't have to worry about the fires any more.

The Little Girl giggles (and I'd like to regulate, choreograph her body, her gestures, her words, don't giggle like a child, no, don't slump like that, don't speak so softly, raise your head, don't bite your nails).

Why does that make you laugh. Why? That makes you laugh? People DIED, you know. At least, that's what they said, mind you, if it was up to me, I'd take a flame-thrower to all of them, the ones in the street who're never satisfied, they'd throw *us* out if they could! My husband keeps telling me you'll end up with a knife in your back but here we're FREE, we can say anything, so if they're not happy . . . We're fed up with them, those leftists who can't face reality, never tell the TRUTH, right? Who's responsible for the Events in this country? *I* speak without TABOOS.

You're not well at all.

Yes I am.

No you're not well at all. Come to think of it, where were you the Night of the Fires? With mademoiselle? You un-der-stand French e-nough oh-sor-ry-your-accent-made-me   . Where were you, both of you?

Without looking at the Little Girl, I talk of having been stuck in the riots without being able to do anything, you know, not far from the Opera and the department stores. The Little Girl giggles again.

Yes! Shopping and business events! she says behind her hand, her eyes creased with laughter.

That really is a problem. What with your arrest and your house arrest . . . Now, I'm not the police, you understand. Let's be clear about that. But I do have to report the facts. It's a question of transparency. You were under house arrest, here. It's not so terrible to remain at home IS IT. Instead of hanging around outside and all that FOR WHAT?

The inspector's voice swerves up in sudden jumps in volume and the end of her sentences are barks.

Everyone's worried about you . . . Besides, I wanted to talk to you—but you'll surely talk this over with your psychologist tomorrow—about a text. Do you mind that your husband showed it to me? In which you . . . speak of your happiness to feel so light . . . It's pretty. But . . . without 'descendants'? That gives me a strange feeling given your history, it gives all of us a STRANGE FEELING. Can we talk about that?

I know that text. That poem she showed me some time ago. I can't see the slightest allusion to a child in it, I only remember one sentence, something having to do with death, the word 'epitaph' perhaps.

The Little Girl is sitting cross-legged on the bed, a little patient rubbing her nose, embarrassed, she's still smiling at us but not so much any more. Her back perfectly straight, her neck well aligned with her shoulder blades. I didn't say that, she tries in a calm voice, as if not to irritate feverish, incoherent animals. I didn't say that. I write . . . all kinds of things.

Yes. But we need to move forward, MADAME. Start from something REAL. I see this here: 'It's not in the dark that I'm afraid, it's to see our brains shattered.'

'Quietly fractured,' the Little Girl corrects, raising her hand, she glances at me quickly.

'The feeling of standing at twilight on an abandoned shooting range'? That's not very REASSURING at all.

But it's F. Scott Fitzgerald . . .

The inspector continues to lift the corners of her words, rummaging round in search of evidence. Then she moves to the nightmares. We can relieve you of your nightmares. You're not well at all.

Yes, I am.

With images like that in your head? A man with an eye poked out? Bodies 'consumed'? 'Flattening the soul to the size of a coffin'? I must say what's in your head sounds like something out of the Middle Ages, right, monsieur?'

Yes I am well. I don't have nightmares. I never have nightmares.

Yes you do. And you're not well at all. Young women. Of your age. Do not constantly speak of bodies going out the window, madame.

Their voices are lapping round the bed like water, something harmless, but then they begin to interrupt each other, they're getting all worked up, throwing their voices at each other, answering each other on the subject of the Little Girl, but without the subject.

WE ARE
THE BIRDS
OF THE
COMING
STORM
319

I can't let you say that, I mean, write that, really, honey. You're making your life DIFFICULT! What good does it do you? WHERE does that get you? Tell me where, just say it, I know you after all, I'm saying this in your own interest. NO ONE! is more suited for LIFE than you are, really. No one is more fit to be a mother than you are. You're making your life difficult! Don't doubt that for a minute, honey.

Then, in the middle of their words, she raises her finger again. And at that moment, I come to a decision, I was not about to let her shrink up on a mattress, raise a finger to justify her notebooks, I could see her five nights ago explaining her theory of the ladder to a whole group round a barricade, and the way she had of opening her arms like a tall skinny cross murmuring 'it's taking hold of me . . .' with her eyes half-closed in delight when she wanted to express her pleasure.

The conversation was tilting, tilting, a hairpin turn on a mountain road, the kind that makes you nauseous, I cut off the fiancé, 'I . . . would really like to take her to the cinema this afternoon.'

'The cinema? Your friend is under house arrest. We're trying to UNDERSTAND what's wrong with her and you're talking about going to the cinema! It's absolutely unbelievable!' said the inspector before getting up from the bed with difficulty, the corners of her mouth pale and slightly stuck together.

Then there was a cry, a tiny moan, the lapping sound of a stream of blood going from the heart to the throat escaped from her, the Little Girl at the End of the Lane stood up, began to rummage through her things and pull her notebooks out from under her bed. She opened them one after the other, concentrating, keeping her balance, staying calm. She began to read aloud (pausing after each sentence, taking a very small breath):

Forward, you sabotaging queens, and strike!
Exchange your blood for flames (Marina Soudaieva)

Who cut the nerves and broke the bones of those children of the barbarian kings (Jules Michelet)

Let something happen. Something terrible, something bloody (Sylvia Plath)

She closed the notebook, I could hear her breath and her fear, she pulled on the sleeves of her pyjama top.

'. . . Let's look let's look . . . Let's disembowel Voltairine de Cleyre! Look for what she meant, look look, what did she mean: the Valley of the Shadow of Death and the white scars and the hellfire and   Hey Voltairine . . . They're really good at calming me down here, they're Karcherizing me, right from the . . . start of the boarding procedure the . . . escorters will have a . . . positive attitude towards the foreigner . . . Courteous! But also . . . Determined! Leaving no alternative than the certainty he will board a flight for . . . the planned destination   . You remember, Voltairine, the first page of the Instructions?'

Without saying anything, they went out into the hall, closing the door behind them carefully. I joined them, I really wanted to explain, I had to explain, that I wasn't really Voltairine and both of us knew it of course, but the inspector was in the middle of a conversation with the fiancé, 'Very disorganized, opposing everything. I think she feels reassured by being contained by the treatment. And by being protected from her own conflictual aggressiveness.'

He was nodding his head in rhythm to each qualifier, then he said goodbye to the inspector, shut the door and began to weep in the hall.

WE ARE
THE BIRDS
OF THE
COMING
STORM

321

'THE KING COMMANDED THAT SHE BE LEFT TO SLEEP IN PEACE, UNTIL HER HOUR TO BE AWAKENED HAD COME'

He prepared a sort of list of his wife's good sides. Things that could shorten her house arrest. He was writing them down. You could help me, after all, a friend's opinion is important, he was saying, turning his half-filled page to me. I strained my ear to listen and thought she was sleeping too much all of a sudden and no one had given her any medication. I got worried, 'But why is she still sleeping?' And he, calmer since he had regained his place, almost moved, 'She's always been like that. A marmot. Naps in the afternoon and she goes to bed before midnight.'

I thought of her exhausting capacity for staying awake, her way of talking very fast and writing late into the night when we were sleeping in the large salon of the Villa, wrapped like gigantic Christmas sweets.

He was looking at me pensively, 'What could we say that would be positive,' speaking of the beautiful, sombre Little Girl, totally, fiercely high school, for ever.

He would like to help her set *priorities*. Constructive things! You can't, he tells me, only be in opposition, what good does that do and what would come of that.

The thing is to: take the colour out of her ideas. Scratch a little. Strip off the outgrowths from those tubers of mad ideas stretching out like arms. Then cover them with a tight film of better, plasticized, practical thoughts. Thoughts that could be shared, pronounced in public. Because who wants to hear what's pouring out of her brain at top speed, those disjointed cadences, all squeezed together. The Little Girl, a girl so quick, torrential, whose metallic ideas shoot out from all sides, whistling like bullets too.

It's all about *reformulating* her. And at the very moment it comes up, the violence of his desire embarrasses him, and yet, yes, he would like to reformulate her completely (gloved hands plunging into the Little Girl). What comes out of the mouth of the Little Girl at the End of the Lane is frightening and *undesirable*. Start her over again from scratch. You would be so much more beautiful if you were *like this*.

Often, when he hears her speak he thinks she's *not natural*. Most of the girls he meets at work—friends—*are* natural, they really are. Perfumed hair. Jewelled laughter. Little light butterfly eyes. Joyful stammerings and hands in front of their mouths when they laugh at his jokes.

Some mornings, he catches himself scrutinizing her face, her skin, and finding her too transparent, livid, none of that powdered silkiness, that *indispensable base* natural girls put on. And the humidity that darkens the fabric of her dresses under the arms, what an embarrassment. Never seen that on other women. No one sweats any more. Or only old women. Or foreign women. In the street. In the Métro at rush hour.

And also, spending all her time with two girls, as if she were still in high school! And that *mess* she got into. Ending with the police searching the flat (the police were rather courteous, they asked politely before making a copy of the computer's contents). For a moment, he imagined her as a victim surrounded by dark, threatening guys. Then he read the charges against her, but who are they talking about? That train she took illegally with a whole group of people, and she never could stand groups! Not the slightest interest in politics and dinner discussions, never! Do you know that Europol made a file on your wife two weeks ago, we interrogated her about her proximity to the individuals who conspired against the security of the state during the Events. Rebellion and verbal assault. Caught red-handed 'while degrading property' on the avenue de l'Opéra. It seems to him he's observing an agitated big sister (did she *make a spectacle of herself?*), suddenly incomprehensible, except that it's his wife and he's responsible for her, she has to be *contained*, returned to reason. The house arrest is a blessing, an answer at last. It's something solid. There are projects (a new beginning!), treatment, a clear definition of what she's suffering from.

Satisfied to know she's in bed, he would like to have her back the way he always had her.

We can watch a film if you like, baby, he will suggest tonight. Give her books, tomorrow he'll go and pick out a few, biographies perhaps, since she talks so much about that woman whose picture is tacked over their bed, a nineteenth-century feminist (sometimes he's proud of having a wife who cares about feminists in the nineteenth century, the little concentrated look she has when she talks about them). She'll copy sentences from those books in her ragged orange notebook (so many notebooks and not one of them pretty!). She'll read them to him at the end of a Sunday afternoon, shyly, apologizing for having copied that down—but it's poetry, honey . . .

The girls they would wall up there so cruelly, to be rid of them, would die right away, and, by these very prompt deaths, made a horrible accusation against the families' inhumanity. What killed them was not the mortifications but boredom and despair [. . .] the heavy boredom, the melancholy boredom of the afternoons, the tender boredom that causes one to wander off into undefinable languor, would quickly drain their energy. Others were as if furious; their blood, too strong, was smothering them.

He will invite a few friends over next Sunday in a week or so (he'd have to explain to them). Maybe they'll be intimidated at first but then reassured to see that she *hasn't changed at all*. Will enjoy the wonderful story of a bird that nearly fell, was then recovered, saved, patched up. Some who arrived a bit late for dinner, what with that stress—traffic jams—the curfew, what a pain—will talk conspiratorially of 'leaving France soon, it's really getting stifling here', and they'll bring up a whole range of 'nice, open, dynamic' countries where they might 'land', talk of their bodies as if they were aeroplanes they would pilot properly, a methodical itinerary.

He will let the Little Girl walk me back.

So I'm leaving, I'll tell her. Call me. I'll repeat that three times, call me, OK, before she shuts the door, thanking me for having brought her back home after the Night of the Fires, really Voltairine (forgive me for calling you Voltairine!), luckily you brought me back here, maybe all that was going too far.

In the lift, my hand will feel in my pocket a paper all velvety from wear, left there for four and a half weeks, I'll stroke that little piece of paper like a promise, or a future betrayal, mine.

I believe in adding fuel to the flames
In time gained from losing it with you
I believe in what we share
Our ramshackle odysseys
In the face of the clouds that you translate for me.
In our next minutes, Voltairine,
Since we have them.

The days after that, I would like to be sick. Live in the soft boredom of a daily life free of tragedy, perform simple, ordinary gestures, blow my nose, gulp down aspirin, grant myself some useless time. Stay in bed. Let fever dispense me from being coherent and making plans. I don't go back to the Island where summons are certainly waiting for me, the only unknown factor is how many. A new law is passed in four days, doling out a year in prison for foreigners not having 'respected their obligation to report to the police department'. The newspapers no longer talk about Little Girls at the End of Lanes but enumerate the arrests and the special measures being implemented. Triumphant opinion surveys descend on us regularly like big nets, or chloroform.

Émile spends her time saying, hold on, I have another call. She is once again the person who rushes to people's assistance. She's right there for suspects, for people whose homes have been searched. And when the metal detectors in the jails make her heart beep, she's afraid the defibrillator will go wild and shut off suddenly, death like a cautious safeguard. Vassili, the Belarusian boy on the fifth floor, drops by one afternoon for help on his homework, he looks haunted, fearing that Émile will collapse over his maths notebook if he doesn't find the right answers. The American specialist in Greek gymnasia rings her bell every morning, he brings her raw steaks in a plastic bag, talks of the Events, taking down new words in his notebook, riot curfew preventive arrests. One evening, Émile returns from an assembly where some exhausted people accuse others of being infiltrators. Then, one morning, the return to order is announced like the joyful reopening of a department store. 'At last things are becoming clearer,' the main political parties and unions have 'taken things in hand', want 'a return to calm', and spell out their demands. Then the negotiations begin.

WE ARE
THE BIRDS
OF THE
COMING
STORM

327

Have you thought things over. Can you manage to put your thoughts in order. Do you want to talk about it. Here, where I've been for ten weeks now, they're used to seeing me write, since they can't hear me. I sit on the only marble bench in the park—at the dark spot which forms an *S*, the tree whose name I don't know reminds me of a weeping willow with branches stretching out like arms, a star with its points drawn apart without bending. Few patients venture this far, most of them are afraid and stay very close to the main building. They're afraid of shadow and hidden corners, of the sound of bathtubs draining and the bland dishes of the dining hall, afraid they'll be forgotten and afraid their parents' visits will last too long, afraid of getting lost and afraid of being found. Sometimes, a nurse comes to ask me if 'I'm progressing' with the kind of smile nurses have, energetic and horribly combative. Some patients like to tell me what brought them to this convalescent home. I listen to them. Most are not interested in what I'm doing here, and if they are, I answer that I lost someone. At first, I would say, I killed someone, but the psychiatrist was told about it and made it clear that my story was disturbing certain patients. I didn't have access to my record but I know that I am suffering, according to them, from post-traumatic stress (this explains, according to the shrink, your feeling of guilt and your erroneous interpretation of what happened).

'What happened' begins again one Tuesday afternoon, ten days after I did not get sick, with no news of the Little Girl at the End of the Lane.

There is no reason for it. No event. One reason is, I'm not going to let her raise her hand for permission to speak. Putting punctuation back into those shapeless days is another reason, a motive. I go over to her place one more time.

She seems to have melted into the beige walls of the flat, a hologram gliding noiselessly round, look, Voltairine, I'm making an effort at style, she whispers to me, pointing to her hair slightly curled up at the tips. She blinks as she walks by the window, at first I think she's bothered by the light, she brings her hand to her throat as if to check a necklace that she's not wearing. For a few minutes, we don't say anything to each other, like ex-lovers straining to find a sufficiently innocuous topic of conversation. I let her tell me about her past few days, she gets regular visits from friends and family, her treatment— she doesn't always stick to it. She laughs with the tepid lightness of a girl who never sets foot outside the flat. 'I owe you an apology, Voltairine,' she says without looking at me. 'I put you in danger and I left, leaving you all alone to deal with all . . . those things we did. It wasn't right . . . Did people . . . complain?' She's sitting on the edge of the bed, inquiring about my future like the young, affable aunt of an oddly dressed niece.

'I haven't gone back to the Island yet. I don't know . . .'

And, Voltairine, I saw a fantastic story on TV about Marie-Agnès Gillot, the prima ballerina of the Paris Opera, do you like her? I'm sure you love her.

I answer yes, Marie-Agnès Gillot is a deer, an enchanted bird a tidal wave a big girl at the side of the road. Unfurled. She's the new Mademoiselle Non. Then the Little Girl at the End of the Lane stands up. Puts on the hi-fi. Wouldn't you like to dance a little, if I push away the rug, she suggests as she sits down on her bed. I'm short of breath, the tendon to the left of my groin hurts, my ankles are wobbly. '. . . Forgive me, I've been kind of sick, I can't do it, I'm rusty and it's too hot in here,' and I walk towards the high window in her room.

WE ARE
THE BIRDS
OF THE
COMING
STORM

329

Then she, or is it me, I'm not sure any more, we talk about windows. About the last time I saw her, with her feet not very steady on the windowsill. About the fear of windows. About the relief of having windows through which we can lean, lean out far enough to see the pavement as the only ceiling of a possible world. About the fear we have when others seem to be afraid for us. We talk about Dina again backing away in tears to her room at the home, as if it were covered with ultra-powerful magnets. Whereas.

All those Enervated Women on little rafts.

She tells me about her son. 'I'm . . . not really interested in that but you can't . . . say it,' her certainty that having entrusted him to another woman is right (and . . . a beautiful thing to do? she adds, asking me softly.) And she's not sorry about that, nor sad. And since then, it's been over ten months now that she's seen her 'loved ones' watching her closely for signs of a traumatism that does not come. And even her texts—they pounce on them, transform them into a disgusting symptom, oh, what a bad plant she is, with no remorse, not wilting with shame.

I had   done   so well. With you and Émile. At keeping their   world at bay. And now.

It's   over.

You're making yourself sick whereas you have EVERY-THING going for you. Your everything on me, in me, yes. But! How come all of you aren't sick? Get sick! Infected! Stuff their Instructions down their throats till they throw up. Get   sick with   grief so you can. . . . resuscitate at last! Whole. Not in little patched-up pieces, I can see your stitches . . . May   your hands shake at last. The outlines of your world are lined with your re-nunci-ations. STOP! They keep interrupting me with their even voices, they're so . . . Afraid. Of fights, you know? Repeating like a mantra be tolerant be tolerant. Translation: be tolerable! You can't . . .

say   anything! Ah they love their words so much—rest stops on the highway! To get us to leave again as fast as possible—would you like your cervical vertebrae massaged? You're ma-king your-self sick! No I won't surrender! I've hardly begun. I say FIRE! you know. And they shiver, turn their heads away as if I stank. Their faces. When they bring up the . . . Events. But really! What violence are you talking about, they're only objects! That burnt.   Symbols . . . That, you can't say. The outlines of your world all bloody but in permanent self-cleaning mode I tell them. To die without a smell and not one drop of blood flowing, the cops, you know, their Instructions, they use ALL those . . . Words, so clean, no smell of burning   you know?

And in the love department . . . We share everything! Those bodies rubbing each other without ever losing themselves inside one another . . . Exhausted from   the anaesthesia they asked for, themselves! And now they pinch and penetrate one another still a little more just to see if, maybe? But no, nothing. Not the slightest shiver any more. So what can you do . . . You opt for the last possibility in stock! The adored tapeworm, his highness the tapeworm . . . To venture into life at last! That movement inside my belly, the horror of feeling myself . . . snatched away from myself, what, I can't even *say* it? And all those . . . schedules to stick to! Prisons increasingly   smaller, circumscribed, swallowed. You should think of making another one, that would stabilize you, they tell me as if they were plunging two fingers into my vagina to evaluate the freshness of my ovaries. And yet. I proved it, didn't I? I know everything about production but customer service isn't my strong point . . . You don't love life! You are   depress-sive. But me, really, *you* know right, don't you   I reject the *show* you're making of it! Nothing nothing nothing can sustain my body in what you call 'life'. I don't live in life! Remember, Voltairine? Those colours? When we used to mix up . . . The ending of the sun and the beginning

WE ARE
THE BIRDS
OF THE
COMING
STORM

331

of a fire? The sunset would fall like . . . spilt ink! Isn't that right? And we'd wait to see if it took shape and turn into smoke? What's happening to the sky? The sun, don't we sharpen ourselves on it?

I had done so well. With you. At keeping their world at bay, out of my reality. And now. It's over.

Penetration through every hole. That's vulgar they told me. I get up from the table, you know, and I go, leave me alone, after all I can slip away, escape, can't I?

And . . . no what I hear despite myself fills me atrociously, Voltairine, you have to shut your ears and eyes and the windows they open, you know, be a little open, they keep telling me, open up open myself up and dissect everything and stuff myself.

I watched a video yesterday. Mademoiselle Non. The journalist asks her but why don't you sign autographs at intermission like all the other ballerinas, can you imagine, he said all the others, and she says, 'One cannot bow after the mad scene, monsieur. I can't imagine being asked to sign a little programme during intermission. I'll say: let me be dead.'

'. . . Let me be dead. What am I filled with,' she sobs, 'what did you fill me with, you replaced my b-lood. And. I have no more air. I would like to escape like a little wisp of smoke from a cellar window. What is more monstrous, Voltairine, than being this body they're reorganizing for me all the time? They cor-rect me. E-rase me. I am rented out! Rent too high. Learn how to bend over back-wards to fit in- . . . to boots of cars open space offices family dinners and love stories, do not disturb. You remember you remember what I showed you the first time you came to see me here, the inmates in the open prison who maintain the building they're locked into by themselves, the bars replaced by a "social contract", it said it takes around, what is it . . . a month for each inmate not to even try to escape any more. What do I have left, Voltairine, before I

open my mouth myself and ask to be filled? Three . . . weeks?
Three days. Three hours?'

'You told them everything last night? You sure? You don't
have anything in reserve?' I asked, we couldn't wait any longer.

She smiled at me and blew her nose, shaking her head.

WE ARE
THE BIRDS
OF THE
COMING
STORM

333

THE FIREBIRD
Berceuse and Finale

We were holding hands. It felt as if the pavement was gallantly propelling us further on, faster. There were a few minutes left till curfew and the only people hurrying as much as us were the Others.

We must find a place with no windows, I was repeating to myself as we walked, while she kept talking about ballets and birds, 'The Firebird that puts monsters to sleep, you know?' she hadn't been outside for days, the open air was making her reel. We passed the Cinémathèque which closed earlier now that the nights were empty. I stopped in front of the triangular, stubborn face of Jodie Foster at thirteen. In a week, they would be showing *The Little Girl at the End of the Lane*, it was almost an encouragement, in a week maybe, we'd go with Émile to see that film about which I knew nothing except its title.

We made the last train. It was night when we walked the four kilometres that separated the Island from the little station. To come back to the place where I had kept silent, holed up alone for almost two years, and that smell of flowers, lilacs and wisteria at the edge of the paths, a smell of sweating sugar, so sweet it was almost sickening.

I squatted on the riverbank, at the very spot where in the middle of winter Giselle had dived one day pursuing a swan which had then knocked her out with a blow of its beak. The Little Girl sat down next to me.

Are you sad, Voltairine? Because the . . . lights are out?

I said, yes, I'm a little sad (but I don't dare to be sad because I'm the one who backed off who brought you back home, who watched you do things, I'm the one who doesn't know how to go to the end of the road).

You shouldn't be. Those flames play . . . softly, they won't disappear into the void, you know? Those lost flowers are still red . . . Voltairine? I finished my Wooden Ladder notebook. Last page: August Spies. The speech he made in his defence before he was hanged (she read it aloud in English):

'Here you will tread upon a spark, but there, and there, and behind you and in front of you, and everywhere, flames will blaze up. It is a subterranean fire. You cannot put it out. The ground is on fire upon which you stand.'

The ground IS on fire . . . That's what we have to photocopy, not the Instructions, not another set of Instructions, she repeated softly, as she tucked a lock of my hair back under my red barrette.

Sometimes, you know, I'd like to cool off my blood, you know? Mix it with the wind, dilute it with coolness. And calm . . . That furious blood.

Voltairine? Let's not go open your blue envelopes, at the van. Let's just stay here. For a little while?

I nodded yes, we can stay here.

What happened to the three bitches, she asked, testing the water with the tip of her Doc Martens. What was it again, the Madwoman, the Dead Woman, and you, what were you? We weren't bitchy enough. I know you know that.

The moon was shining on her naked arms—she had taken off her red coat with the too-short sleeves—the veins of the night

WE ARE
THE BIRDS
OF THE
COMING
STORM

335

appeared like intermittent lights, a beam of light out there, and then gone. She said, the water, the water's not really cold, it's OK. We kept our clothes on, I simply took off my shoes, both of us were in the water up to our waists, or not even, inside my tights, my toes were sinking into the uncertain bottom, that muddy sand scared me a little. We were holding hands. Then, slowly, without letting go of me, she lay down on her back as if she had to be careful not to fall off an air mattress, her hair remained on the surface of the water for a moment, and then it was submerged by the soft little waves and it disappeared. Haloed with water and moon, her face was like a diamond. So beautiful, a novice nun before her hair is covered with a grey veil and she's pulled out of the world. I drew a little nearer to keep her hand in mine and I thought of the old rotten boat not far from there. It had been tied up in the hollow of a recess in the trees ever since I got to the Island. To reach it, you had to go through part of a rubbish dump, two men lived there—well, maybe. They owned the boat. They would often make fires and burn plastic objects that spread the sad stink of an animal all the way to the van. Round the twisted, dry reeds, from afar, you'd think it was a field of tender poppies, and then when you came closer, it was only pieces of hard plastic eaten away by fire and water, gathered by the wind. Their boat resembled the dump too.

We could have tried to fix up the rotten boat and take off on it, I suggested.

A raft? She asked sarcastically, raising her eyes to the sky. You want us to drift, Voltairine, like two Enervated Girls?

I groped my way forward to the right, where I remembered seeing the boat last time. The water was so much warmer than in my memory and even with the sound of my drowned clothes coming unstuck from my body, that little waltz of lapping water, I wasn't afraid.

I am the child of the air, a sylph, less than a dream.

Dear Sir or Madam:

You have just been admitted to the Health Clinic. Our staff wishes to welcome you. The clinic has four treatment units and is equipped with one hundred and sixty-four beds.

Upon arrival, you signed a treatment contract with the institution and the admitting physician.

You have the right to be informed about your condition. As a hospitalized adult patient, you have the right to designate a proxy (parent, close relative, doctor) who will be consulted if you are unable to express your wishes and to receive all necessary information. This decision can always be rescinded.

Treatment for Pain

A psychiatrist heads the committee. The pharmacist, in collaboration with the Committee on Prescription Drugs and the general practitioners, has developed a plan for setting up a Pain-Control Committee. An 'admissions agreement' will be given to you upon arrival.

WE ARE
THE BIRDS
OF THE
COMING
STORM

337

Dear girl whose heart I know

1) By the end of next week you'll get a call from the lawyer I met, pretty good, I think.

2) I spoke to your 'referring psychiatrist' about an early release. You have to make the request yourself.

3) OK for the subscription to your dance magazine but the minimum is one year and you'll be out before, of course.

4) They're telling me you keep mute, my exiled little kiddo. I answer yes, that's normal, she thinks with her feet. You can't possibly imagine the silence at the other end of the line, an abyss . . .

5) My news: I'm getting rid of the monitors (no more appointments every Thursday at the hospital). I haven't started working again yet, officially. But there are so many people in jail or on trial that I run around all day (in slow motion, let me reassure you).

PS. I wrote to her parents as you asked; I'll go see next week if they did engrave the whole quotation (her mother wasn't sure there'd be enough space . . .). 'From time to time had her soul torn apart and hung it up on a line as if it could be dried in the sun.'

PS2. Sorry to bury you under all this chatter, but: just had a long conversation with 'your' shrink. For the request to get out, you have to present a 'plan' to the floor nurse, a letter stating that you think you'd do better outside, you have a job offer and sponsors. I found a few possible translations you could do. If they agree with this plan, it will be brought up to the team (the shrink said *team* in English, you would have loved it). Given what they call your 'history', you'll certainly be required to convince them at the 'oral exam' and go before a sort of medical tribunal, three psychiatrists, a psychologist, the nurse and one or two officials who are usually close to the drafters of the Wellness Plan (not good news, I know . . .). Your shrink also brought up your 'history', which might hurt you (you would then be under house arrest indefinitely). Their new mental health programme . . .

I heard you're giving lessons? Write to me or I'll write to you again.

Émil-(lienne)

WE ARE
THE BIRDS
OF THE
COMING
STORM

339

Émile,

Getting out of here, you say. But even my room seems too big for me, I would need a hole, a recess under a landslide of rubble, dust, roots twisted together, concrete. Just be buried. Wanting to sleep, hoping to sleep and never sleeping enough, longing for disappearance, for shadow and dark corners.

The lawyer called me yesterday. Thanks for that. Dictated the first sentence of the letter I should write, 'I admit to being responsible for Mademoiselle X having violated the terms of her probation on April 23.' The first sentence of a letter I won't continue.

Because what. Tell a clever story? Vindicate myself? Say as well as possible that it's not my fault. Tell the right story. To say what. That on that day, she was panic-stricken at the idea of staying in her flat and had already attempted to throw herself out of the window in front of witnesses. That I took her to the Island where I reside. That it seemed like a good idea, because I live in a little van low to the ground. That she went into the water fully dressed and I followed her. That I thought of the boat, I pulled it towards the riverbank, four minutes went by.

'You want us to drift, Voltairine, like two Enervated Girls?'

I will never write that letter because it would be too short. I would have to make a long line of Post-its or postscripts written horizontally not in the order of their importance, without a beginning or an end. All the PS's in a line, a clothesline of little added words fluttering in the wind, I can see butterflies.

PS.

I constantly hear her calling me.

Voltairine. That tone. You know, as if she were pleading for whole fields of Voltairines to be born and pop up, poisons in the middle of meringue flowers. She called me Voltairine. But she was the one who was Voltairine. And me, I was the girl who talked about the end of the road and never went there.

WE ARE
THE BIRDS
OF THE
COMING
STORM

341

My Dear Little *jetée battue assemblée* (my favourite girl),

I don't want to patch you up at all costs. But I'll ask you again tomorrow and next week if you wrote that request to be released.

(The shrink told me you didn't have 'access to your familiar objects for two weeks'?)

Émile

Émile,

Yes . . . Two weeks, deprived of the contents of my handbag, my notebooks, my pencils. Can you commit suicide
with words, I would ask, when they came into my room
with the meal tray, babbling, 'I am not allowed to talk to
you, you will get your belongings back when you're less
oppositional.' My notebooks in exchange for my actions,
for the two times I threw my hands forward, the crash of
the plate, the spoon and the metal bouncing on the tile
floor, the nurse running back in with a doctor, the prompt
mopping up around the bed and the door shutting again.

What do they want to fill me with. These letters are
my 'reward', I suppose, for good conduct . . .

And now, in the 'context of my therapy', they've
entrusted me with a dance workshop. I give classes to ten
people of all ages. They come in wearing jogging pants
and oversized T-shirts. Clumsy . . . They try to round their
ugly arms (flabby or bony) in a crown over their head and
they puff and suffer, pinch their mouths when they throw
themselves into a pirouette that looks like a Lego Tower
of Pisa made of flesh.

You're too human, I yell at them, think whisper-
breath (dance is wings, it's birds and departures into the
forever, and returns vibrant like arrows, let's thank Mallarmé,
I think, Voltairine).

Dance is a bow bent between two deaths, but that, I
do not tell them.

WE ARE
THE BIRDS
OF THE
COMING
STORM

343

A young man (who, to the question how are you, answers me every day that he's being taken for someone else, I am not me, he adds politely) comes regularly. At the start of the week, he inhales and exhales conscientiously then throws himself into a simple pirouette, which, to his great surprise (and mine too!) ends in a double. He hardly staggers when he comes to a standstill. He is loudly applauded but he picks up his things and leaves the room, the others see him crying.

I run after him in the grounds. His thin back in a white shirt gives me the feeling of pursuing a little anxious pirate looking for a path that would take him back to the road.

Then yesterday, he comes back to class and shows me this without saying anything, written in a small notebook in which he has written lots of illegible things, like bird scratches.

'Teach me what does not die.'

PS.

What did your friend die from, the little anxious pirate asked me last night in the grounds, as if he were waiting for the end of a fairy tale. I say, the Little Girl dies from her dream-birds swallowed the wrong way.

Dear girl,

I went to the van the day before yesterday to get your post.
Then I walked to the lake. The cranes you see behind the
orange lights of the detention centre look like parallel bars
and I thought of you.

And also of last summer, when Giselle had disappeared and you kept looking for her every morning, going
round the Island as if she had simply fallen asleep somewhere. When the grocer said to you, casually, that she had
certainly drowned, you insulted him, you ran, I found you
sitting at the end of the Island, I never saw you cry like
that, not even on Tuesdays (especially not on Tuesdays).

I'm still waiting for your butterflies.

PS. And maybe we should finally let her be 'unmanageable'—even in her absence? Grant her even that, the freedom to be no more. She saw in you *a* Voltairine, so please,
do not bury the Little Girl at the End of the Lane under
final Instructions logically explained . . .

WE ARE
THE BIRDS
OF THE
COMING
STORM

345

Émile,

Some butterflies:

PS. NEVER DO

There's a writing workshop every Thursday. Yesterday we had to write 'never dos'. I say:

— 'Never perform your movements half way when you dance (you might get injured).'

The psychologist says, very good, keep going.

—'Never underestimate the danger of not going all the way to the end of the road.'

—'Never confuse (I confused) refuges, oases, islands and prisons.'

—'Never take little girls tired of the road back to their house.'

She stops me (a tense little smile), 'Your proposals are not transparent. Could you reformulate in a way that makes them clearer?'

PS. GISELLE

'But, Accursed Child, you will kill yourself and when you are dead, you will become a Willi; you will go to the midnight ball in a moonlight dress with bracelets of dewdrops on your cold, white arms; you will pull travellers into the fatal round and throw them into the icy water of the lake,

all panting and dripping with sweat. You will be a vampire of dance!'
—Théophile Gautier, author of the book of *Giselle*, 1841.

It's the first ballet in which Willis appear, those *'fiancés who died before their wedding, poor girls who cannot remain silent in the grave. In those dead hearts, in those dead feet, the desire to dance, which they could not satisfy during their lives, still remains; they get up at midnight, go through the streets in groups and attack the young men they find there . . .'*

I made three more steps towards the boat. I had just let go of her hand. 'I'm thinking of something Voltairine all of a sudden,' she said. 'It's . . . Giselle. That story is a microbe . . . Another bird falling. A girl who died from having danced too much . . .'

I stopped moving forward, the noise of the fabric against the weight of the water and my breath—pounding—I couldn't hear what she said after that, just this: you won't die from having danced too much. I kept moving away towards the boat.

PS. IN THE KINGDOM OF THE MRI

I can bear the word death. But not autopsy. Not digging all the way to the gaping, transparent obscenity of the void. Wanting to 'manage' her to infinity. The bythinella.

WE ARE
THE BIRDS
OF THE
COMING
STORM

347

My Little (Little) Girl (this is not a questionnaire)

Last week I read the biography of Lucy Parsons. Who was not just a 'wife of' (Albert Parsons, one of the Haymarket martyrs).

Born a slave in Texas (of Mexican and Native American origin), she was a famous orator, her speeches attracted tens of thousands of people. And for over thirty years, the police tried to arrest her before she reached the podium (this was found in their archives: 'Lucy Parsons is more dangerous than a thousand rioters.').

This probably explains why when she died, in the fire that burnt her house down in 1942, the authorities carefully destroyed the only texts that had not burnt, judging that even after her death, her words might well inspire generations of readers. (In 1884, she ends her leaflet 'To the Vagabonds, to the Homeless' with this practical little piece of advice: 'Learn to use explosives!')

Lucy Parsons and Voltairine de Cleyre. Those Little Girls walked tirelessly (your Voltairine paid homage to the Haymarket in dozens of different cities every 11 November until her death . . .). Little Girls with burnt words, with bodies drowned in Instructions and condemnations, Girls who are sometimes, you're right, anxious pirates at the end of the road.

So I insist on sending you back your butterfly, which seems to me a bit too sure of itself (for a butterfly). You say, never bring Little Girls with rustling, tenacious wings and white scars back to their house. You point out your (our?) mistake: we didn't go 'to the end' (and like in Dance, you say, when you only go halfway through with your movement, you hurt yourself, yes).

When we met, remember, I asked you if you didn't get tired of going through the same movements in the same order every day, *plié*, *dégagé*, and you answered no, that each time you repeated the same gesture you learnt a little more about the way to initiate that movement.

To start over. You see, I think there's something wrong with that expression. As if you were starting the same thing twice. Whereas what you restart is filled with what has not (yet) happened. What has already been danced fuses with what has not yet been danced.

I'm enclosing this press clipping dated the day before yesterday.

POSITIVE IDENTIFICATION

There is every reason to believe that despite arrests, some individuals responsible for the Events may have left the country. Indeed, very similar texts have been seized in a university in Tunis and found in Greece at the spot where a court was destroyed by fire.

'Every year we hear yet more plainly the whizzing of the wings of those birds of the coming storm, and sometimes we would like to hear, we wish we could already hear the sound of the storm itself . . .

'They say of us that we never existed. Or hardly. See, everything is back to normal. So, now that we no longer have to fear that all this will end, we have all the time in the world . . .

'We will disrupt your morbid, immutable ceremonies again. We will not share only indignations.

'The little friends at the end of the road.'

WE ARE
THE BIRDS
OF THE
COMING
STORM

349

The first sentences are by Voltairine de Cleyre, I'm (almost) sure of it. The rest? I seem to recognize the style of the Little Girl at the End of the Lane. But soon, we'll hesitate—we'll come upon a poster, we'll decipher a few words on a wall and wonder if by any chance that one could be hers or perhaps inspired by her or inspired by all the people who inspired her? I still have dozens of her texts at home. I also recovered all her notebooks that her boyfriend gave me, he doesn't want them, sees the cause of everything in them . . . I won't put them away in a drawer.

I open her Wooden Ladder notebook, which she begins like this:

Let us keep conspiring, Voltairine! Let us become the feverish bandits we once were, children determined not to stay where they put us. Times are hard for girls who are thieves of fire . . . We may have to be pitiless again and without giving up anything of our lives or bodies, saturate every atom with wandering pleasures without ever paying for it . . .

You ask me, you ask yourself, should we tell the story of the falling birds. You don't want to write the story of a falling bird, you promised her never to tell the story of the falling birds. But these words are not the words of a falling bird.

This is not the story of a falling bird.

ACKNOWLEDGEMENTS

To Luis P., resuscitated and alive.

Thanks to Jérémy L., 'little girl . . .' who gave me a future.

Thanks to Patrick Verscheren (Olivier, Julie, Caroline and the whole team . . .) for welcoming me (autumn and winter 2009–10) as a resident at the Fabrique Ephéméride, on the island.

Thanks to Claudine (and her compass). And to the workshops of the Espage home (Maguy, Yvette, Evelyne, Monique, Micheline, Yolande . . .).

Thanks to Berlin, summer and autumn 2010 (and to the people I met there . . .).

For reading and rereading, for who she is and all the rest, thanks to Jeanne Lafon-Galili.

Henri Lafon for the storms and the eighteenth century.

To Isabelle Lafon for   .

Ama for her (setter's) uninquisitive presence.

Sandrine and the Tuesday girls.

The documentaries *Un monde sans fous* (A World without Mad People) by Philippe Borrel and *Sainte-Anne: Hôpital psychiatrique* by Ilan Klipper.

Thanks to the Little Girls at the End of the Lane and other anxious pirates, all authors of the texts of *The Little Girl at the End of the Lane*:

Bernard Aspe, Voltairine de Cleyre, Emily Dickinson, F. Scott Fitzgerald, William Forsythe, Marie-Agnès Gillot, Sylvie Guillem,

WE ARE
THE BIRDS
OF THE
COMING
STORM

351

Gelsey Kirkland, Laird Koenig, Lautréamont, Violette Leduc, Nicolas Le Riche, Arthur Rimbaud, Clarice Lispector, Rosa Luxembourg, Jules Michelet, Las Mujeres Creando, Albert Parsons, Lucy Parsons, Sylvia Plath, Rote Zora, Maria Soudaieva, August Spies, Alain Tanner, Tarjei Vesaas, Simone Weil, Evariste Vital-Luminais, Monique Wittig.

(To riots past and future.)

Olivier L for everything.

Without forgetting Haymarket Square: August Spies, Albert Parsons, Lucy Parsons, Adolph Fischer, Louis Lingg, George Engel, Samuel Fielden, Michael Schwab.